Every Tear

Pirates & Faith – Book Two

Molly Evangeline

Every Tear

www.mollyevangeline.com

ISBN 13: 9781442162471
ISBN 10: 1442162473

Dedication

To my Creator, Father, and Savior, for how greatly He has blessed me with the gift of creativity. I had such unforgettable experiences while writing this book. Thank You, Lord, for answering all the prayers I raise to You and for guiding me to a place I never imagined I'd be a year ago. I thank You for the trials I've been through that have increased my faith and drawn me close to You.

Mom, without you, I couldn't do this. Thank you so much for the days and hours you spent reading and re-reading my manuscript and for what you continue to do to help me accomplish my dream.

Thank you, Dad, for all the books you sold for me out of your work truck. You got my first book out to more people than I ever could have on my own.

Jake and Sam, life really would be rather dull without you. I love you both. And, Jake, the night we were up way too late and you spent over an hour trying to figure out the clues in this book is one of the funniest memories I have of writing it.

To my whole family, I will never forget the time we trudged through the swamp all those years ago, hopping from one dry area to another, a little lost and not sure if we'd reach our destination without getting soaked. It's one of my favorite childhood memories. I never could have imagined then that it would inspire me to write one of the scenes in this book.

Jordyn, you've meant so much to me all these years I've been writing. I can't tell you how much I love you and your input in all of my books.

Kara, I've never heard your voice, but you're one of the best friends I've ever had. I don't think I've met anyone else I share more in common with.

To my wonderful cousins, family, and friends, and all the people who have read and loved *The Pirate Daughter's Promise*. I am so excited to finally be sharing this new adventure with you.

You have taken account of my wanderings;
Put my tears in Your bottle.
Are they not in Your book? – Psalms 56:8

Prologue

Light flickered bleakly against the walls of the small, dusky room from a candle stub sitting on the dresser where a woman, small and frail, leaned with her head buried in her hands. The never ending hum of voices and drunken laughter drifted up through the floorboards from the main room of the tavern below. The sound, however, was quickly drowned out by the distressed and helpless cries coming from an old cradle in the corner. Slumped over the dresser, the woman held her head as the terrible, alcohol-induced headache intensified with every cry. Finally, she could stand it no longer and slammed her hand down on the dresser causing the baby's cries to intensify.

Turning, the woman stared with remorse at her child, knowing he was hungry. She scanned the room with little hope. There was no food to give him and no money to buy it with for what little she made working as a bargirl she'd spent on her drinks. She could barely recollect the last time she had eaten herself.

The baby's cries did not subside, and the woman squeezed her eyes shut tight. With great reluctance her thoughts turned to the man she had been married to, the baby's father. She had promised him she would take good

1

care of his son, but, even then, she'd known it was a promise she would never be able to keep.

As the cries increased, the woman realized she had to do something soon or her son would eventually die. Having neglected him steadily for longer and longer periods of time, she had contemplated her options over the last couple of months, though they were precious few. She knew now that she could no longer put off making a decision.

With a deep, defeated sigh, she crossed the room to the cradle and lifted her son from his bed, thankful that he finally quieted at his mother's attention. She slid something off the top of the dresser and slipped it into her pocket before making her way out of the room, down the stairs and through the noisy main room of the tavern. She cringed when the baby started crying again and walked quickly up to the bar where the barkeeper, her employer, stood frowning at the stares of annoyance she was receiving.

"I need to go out for a little while," she told him. "I'll be back soon."

"Well, you'd better hurry or ya won't have a job when ya come back," the barkeeper warned gruffly.

She hurried from the tavern knowing she must not lose her job. It was all that kept her alive. Heading quickly through the dark city streets, thankful only that it was warm because she had no coat for herself and no blanket for her child, she came to the large, brick building which had beckoned to her every time she passed by. Once again, her eyes were drawn to the sign next to the two big doors. *St. Thomas Orphanage.* Taking a deep, resolute breath, she glanced at her son and knocked. The doors opened only a moment later by the old orphanage governess.

"What can I do for you?" the governess asked kindly.

There was hesitation in the woman's voice. "This child...his mother left him with me," she lied, ashamed of what she was doing. "I cannot care for him."

2

The governess looked at the teary-eyed baby and nodded. "Bring him in."

Timidly, the woman stepped into the orphanage. Just beyond the doors stood one of the orphanage's young nursemaids. Spotting the baby, she stepped closer and immediately her heart swelled at the sight of the small, dark haired child.

"What is his name?" the nursemaid was first to ask.

"William," the woman answered quietly.

"And his surname?" the governess wanted to know.

The woman opened her mouth to give her maiden name, but her thoughts went again to her husband. How he had adored his son. Guilt struck her. She shouldn't have taken William from him.

"James," she said, giving her son his father's name. "His name is William Jonathan James."

"And his age?" the governess asked.

"Eighteen months. Two years on the twenty-eighth of October." As she finished speaking, William began crying loudly again. "He has not eaten in some time," the woman explained guiltily.

The governess nodded and turned to the nursemaid. "Mary, take him and feed him."

"Yes ma'am," Mary replied, happy to care for the child.

Gently, she took William from his mother's arms. He quieted a little as he looked at Mary with helpless brown eyes. She smiled at him while she turned and left the room.

William's mother watched until they had disappeared from sight and wondered if she would ever see him again. Finally, she turned back to the governess.

"Please take good care of him," she pleaded.

The governess smiled gently and nodded. "We will. I can see already that Mary has taken quite a liking to him, and you can know he'll be very safe in her hands."

"Thank you," the woman murmured. She turned to leave but then remembered the trinket. Turning back, she pulled from her pocket a necklace with an engraved locket. "This belonged to his father. He wanted William to have it. Please be sure he gets it when he's old enough."

Taking it, the governess smiled again. "We will give it to him," she promised.

The woman lingered hesitantly a moment longer, tears beginning to pool in her eyes.

"Also . . . tell him . . . tell him that his father loved him more than anything . . ."

Mary smiled as she knelt in front of the bright-eyed four-year-old. He was quieter and kinder than all of the other children and a bit shy with anyone but her. Brushing a stray piece of dark hair out of the boy's eyes, Mary said, "I have something for you, Will."

"You do?" Will asked.

Mary nodded. "Yes, it's something we've been saving for you since you were only a baby. But, seeing as it's your birthday today and you're so big now I thought it was the perfect time to give it to you."

She held out the necklace they had been instructed to give him, and Will reached out for it with his small hand. He looked at it curiously.

"What is it?" he wanted to know.

Mary smiled. "It's a necklace with a locket. One half is missing, but if you look closely you will see that your name is engraved on it." Her heart turned over as she watched him bend his head close to peer intently. "It was your father's, and he wanted you to have it. He loved you more than anything you know."

"He did?" Will's eyes brightened even more.

4

"Yes," Mary told him, still smiling.

Will smiled in return, but a frown replaced it. "How do you know?"

"Well," Mary began. "We were told he did the day you came to live with us."

"Mary, what happened to my mother and father?" Will asked, becoming sad. "Didn't they want me?"

Mary's face grew sad as well. Most of the children who had been there since they were babies didn't ask much about their parents, but Will was different.

"Of course they did," Mary told him. "They just wanted you to have a better life than they could give you themselves." She hoped it would satisfy the young boy because she hated to see him unhappy.

Still, Will kept frowning. Mary forced a smile to her face.

"Cheer up, Will. It's your birthday," she reminded gently. "Let's go have some fun."

Finally, Will's sparkling smile surfaced again, and he turned to join in some of his birthday activities with the other children. Mary followed behind, thinking of their discussion. It saddened her that he was having to grow up without a family. He was such a wonderful, special little boy. It had shown, even as baby. How could anyone have just left him?

Tears trickled down Will's five year old face.

"Mary, are you all right?" he cried as flames leapt up around them.

Mary lay on the floor, pinned by the debris that had fallen while she tried to guide the children out of the burning orphanage. The rest of the children had fled when she fell, but Will stayed by her side.

Mary tried to answer, but started coughing. She knew something was very wrong because she could barely breathe and the taste of blood was in her mouth.

"Will, you must get out of here," Mary gasped.

Will quickly shook his head. "No, I can't leave you."

"Will, you must! Go . . ." Mary's words trailed off as her eyes closed.

"No Mary, please wake up," he pleaded, shaking her arm gently. She did not respond. "Mary!"

Chapter One

When my anxious thoughts
multiply within me, Your consolations
delight my soul. – Psalms 94:19

William James' eyes flashed open suddenly. In the dark of predawn, he found himself staring up at the beams of the ship's cabin. Breathing heavily, he sat up, putting his legs over the side of his hammock which swayed gently with the rhythmic motion of the ship. Sweat glistened on his chest and back, and his heart hammered against his ribs. Seventeen years had passed since that fateful night in the orphanage yet nightmares of it still sometimes troubled his sleep.

Will breathed deeply, resting his elbows on his knees and his head in his hands. Trying to calm his body, his mind wandered over memories of the fire. It had claimed the life of one of the few people he'd ever held dear. The pain of losing Mary had dulled over the years, but he still found himself missing her. She felt like the mother he'd never known. He also had a small, stinging pang of regret that he'd been too young to do anything that might have helped or even saved her.

A sharp sound broke into Will's thoughts. He looked up to peer down the line of hammocks hanging in the crew's quarters easily finding the source of the loud snores which had quite suddenly invaded the peaceful silence. Corey, the cook. Despite his sadness over Mary, a smile grew on Will's face as he glanced at the rest of the sleeping crew and saw that not a man stirred at the sound. All had grown used to it after all the years of sailing together. Though Will had been sailing with them for only a tiny fraction of that time, he had grown used to it as well, but he knew he would not be able to return to sleep.

With a sigh, Will stood up and reached down to pull on his leather boots. Despite the hot, stagnate air of the cabin, he knew the early spring breeze outside which propelled the ship would be quite cool. He grabbed the shirt that hung next to his hammock and slipped it on.

As quietly as possible, Will made his way out of the cabin. Along the way, he noticed one of a few empty hammocks. *Caleb.* If Caleb was on watch that meant it was close to dawn. Climbing one of the stairs, Will emerged onto the open, moonlit deck of the *Grace.* The sky was deep blue and the eastern horizon was just beginning to show the faintest sign of sunlight.

"Corey keeping you awake?"

Will turned to the voice and saw Caleb near the railing. The man's sea-blue eyes sparkled in amusement, and the wind tugged at his darker, sandy brown hair. Will smiled and shook his head, the wind ruffling his own dark hair.

"No, I just felt like I needed some air."

"Well, if you intend to stay up, I think there's someone who would enjoy the company." Caleb inclined his head toward the direction of the ship's stern. "She's been up there for two hours now."

Will's eyes shifted to the quarterdeck. He was unable to hide his tender smile from Caleb's teasing, but good-natured grin. Standing behind the wheel, steering the ship with as much expertise as sailors who'd been at sea their entire lives, was Skylar McHenry. She was nearly twenty now and the most amazing, beautiful person Will had ever known.

8

Will turned briefly back to Caleb. "I think I will."

He walked across the deck and ascended the stairs leading up to the raised quarterdeck. Skye had a smile waiting for him when he reached the top. For a moment, Will was silent as he studied her face, all thoughts of his dream vanishing. Skye's eyes glittered like perfect sapphires in the moonlight and her nearly black hair seemed to shimmer as the breeze whipped it around her face and shoulders.

"Good morning, Will," her soft voice greeted him.

Never taking his eyes off her, Will echoed, "Good morning, Skye."

"Couldn't you sleep?" she asked thoughtfully.

Will shrugged and his dream returned to him again. "I woke up and felt like some air."

Skye's face knit into a frown. Having known him for most of her life, it was easy to pick things up in Will's voice. She heard sadness and a slight vulnerability that was not often present. Peering closer at his deep brown eyes, Skye could also see that his mind was full.

Are you all right, Will? Is something wrong?"

Will smiled, not wishing for her to be upset. "No, I'm fine. I just had a dream about the fire again."

Skye looked at him sympathetically knowing well how much his dreams bothered him sometimes.

"I'm sorry," she said. "I wish there was something I could do to take them away, but only God can do that."

"It's all right," Will replied, shaking his head. "God had a reason for allowing that to happen." He paused. "If I had never been taken to the Kingston orphanage I would never have met you."

Skye smiled. "God blessed us so greatly with each other even though we were both placed there under tragic circumstances."

9

Will nodded slowly with a smile of his own. Silence followed their words for a few moments and only the sound of the ocean against the hull and the strain of the rigging could be heard. Finally, Skye spoke up again.

"In a few hours we'll reach Kingston," she observed. "It will be good to be back home even though I know I'm going to miss the sea in a couple of days."

"So will I," Will agreed.

They had been out to sea for a few weeks now, but all of them were returning to regular life. Though Skye's father, the famous former pirate Daniel McHenry, had given up sailing as his main occupation and settled down to ship building, another job he was equally skilled at, neither he, nor Skye, nor their crew could completely give up the sea. Because of this, when Daniel was not busy building, he would use his own ship, the *Grace*, one of the most prized ships in the area, to deliver goods for Skye's merchant grandfather. Will also had a job of his own working as a blacksmith for Skye's uncle, Matthew McHenry, but he was given time off to sail with Skye and her father since he enjoyed sailing nearly as much as they did.

Dawn's light crept over the ship as the crew awakened and left their quarters to go about their work. Skye was relieved from her position at the wheel by Jesse, one of the crew's oldest and most experienced members. As she stepped away from the wheel, Skye looked at Will. He had been very quiet during the last half hour, and she could see that he still had not fully shed thoughts of his dream. Wishing to cheer him up, Skye stepped up beside him as he descended the stairs of the quarterdeck.

"Will, why don't you join me and my father today while we read?" she invited, speaking of the daily Bible reading she always had with her father.

Knowing how special those mornings were to Skye, Will hated to intrude. Smiling, he shook his head and kindly declined the offer.

"Please Will," Skye persuaded gently. "I'd really like you to."

Will paused and looked at her for a moment. "All right," he decided finally.

Skye was glad. Though she enjoyed the times alone with her father, she wished Will would join them more often. Still, she was touched by how careful he was about her feelings.

The two of them went below deck to get their Bibles. After retrieving hers from her cozy little cabin, Skye went to her father's cabin.

"Good morning, Skye," Daniel greeted his daughter lovingly with a kiss on the forehead.

"Good morning, Father," Skye returned the greeting with a smile. As they moved towards the table, she told Daniel, "Will is going to read with us. He had another dream this morning about the fire, and I'm hoping this will help him." Concern was evident in her voice since she was just as mindful of Will's feelings as he was of hers.

"I'm sure it will," Daniel said, understanding her concern.

A moment later, a gentle knock was heard at the cabin door, and Daniel turned to answer it. He opened the door wide with a welcoming smile. "Good morning, Will. I'm very glad you've decided to join us this morning."

"Thank you for sharing your time with me," Will said gratefully as he stepped into the large captain's cabin holding his Bible.

"We are more than happy to," Daniel assured him.

Skye smiled at Will and motioned for him to sit. He took a seat at the table next to her, and Daniel sat down on the other side. With his eyes still on Will, Daniel said, "Skye told me you dreamt about the fire again."

Will nodded solemnly. "Yes."

"I know what that is like. I remember after Skye's mother died, I had dreams about it. They can leave you feeling very downcast, but I once found a verse that has always given me comfort. It's Psalms 94:19. Do you know it?"

Will nodded again. "Skye has shown it to me before. It is comforting, and I will be sure to remember it next time."

Daniel smiled. "I'm sure it will help."

He then turned his eyes to his Bible and opened it to the passages he had chosen to read that morning. Skye and Will opened theirs as well and the three of them studied God's Word. The peace and happiness of reading together lasted for nearly an hour until they closed their Bibles knowing that Corey would soon have breakfast ready. Before leaving the cabin, Daniel prayed for God's protection over all of them and for wisdom and guidance in always following Him. He also prayed for God's ever present comfort for Will.

Following Skye and Daniel out of the cabin a few moments later, Will felt considerably better than he had earlier. The time with Skye and her father had been just what he'd needed.

As Will entered the large cabin off the ship's galley, he smiled at the sound of cheerful conversation and laughter as most everyone gathered for their breakfast. The crew had become like one big family to him as they were to Daniel and Skye.

Shortly, Corey brought enough food for them all to the tables and they quieted for Daniel to offer a prayer of thanks before they ate. It would be the last they'd have together until the next time they sailed which wouldn't be for at least another couple of months.

When the meal came to an end, the crew returned to their work and began preparing to reach land. The *Grace* continued to glide swiftly and effortlessly through the warm Caribbean Sea towards her destination. The sun had just reached its peak in the sky when the port of Kingston came into view.

For a few moments, Will stood at the bow as Daniel steered the ship into the bay. As he stared at the city, he remembered seeing it for the first time all those years ago when he and all the other children from St. Thomas had been brought over to be placed in the Kingston orphanage. He had felt so horribly alone. But Will smiled fondly as he remembered meeting Skye. His life had changed that day. He'd found someone to be close to again, and he'd come to know God, something he'd be forever thankful for.

Turning away from the sight of the busy port, Will walked across the deck to go below and gather his belongings. A few other crewmen were also in the cabin preparing to go ashore as well. As he packed up his clothes, Will listened to them talk contentedly to each other about what they were going to do now that they were home and what they'd do with their share of the payment they were to receive for the cargo they had sold. Will knew that he'd save his for when he had a family of his own which he prayed God would bless him with soon. With that thought still in mind, he glanced at the small portrait that sat on a shelf near his hammock. It was a portrait of Skye that she'd had made not too long ago. Will too had had one done of himself for her so that whenever they were apart they still felt linked to each other.

Will reached for the portrait to pack it away safely. As he pulled it from the shelf, the edge of it caught on another object which dropped to the floor. Bending to retrieve it, Will found the necklace that Mary had given him on his fourth birthday. On the front of the metal, oval-shaped locket were etched many tiny designs. Turning it over in his hand, Will looked at the inside on which was engraved his name, William Jonathan James. He ran his finger along the edge of the locket where once had been hinged another half. Will knew the orphanage had received the necklace as it was now, and he wondered whose it had been and what had been on the missing half.

Will continued to stare at the locket. It was the only link to his past, yet it could never answer the questions he had always lived with. Who was he, really? Who had his parents been, what were their names, and why had they abandoned him to live the life of an orphan? Still, whatever had happened when he was a baby was what God had planned for his life, and Will trusted Him. He had told himself that maybe it was a good thing he didn't know the answers to his questions. Perhaps he had come from a background that he wouldn't want to know about. Without the answers, the name James was only what he made it to be, and he took great care to make sure it was a name people could respect.

Will was slightly startled when his thoughts were interrupted by someone saying his name. He turned to find Caleb approaching.

"You ready to go ashore?" Caleb asked. "I'm sure Daniel's about ready to drop anchor."

Will nodded and slipped the locket into his duffel. "Yes, I'm ready."

He picked the duffel up and followed Caleb out of the cabin. They had just reached the deck when they heard the splash of the anchor hitting the water. The *Grace* had reached her dock with another successful voyage behind her. The gangplank was quickly lowered, and the crew secured the ship to the dock. Everyone went ashore with their belongings in tow. As they neared the beach, Will smiled when he saw two familiar faces, Matthew and Skye's grandfather. His smile grew as he watched Skye hurry over to them and first give Matthew a hug and then her grandfather, something that only two short years ago, Will could never have imagined her doing.

"Hello, dear, how are you?" Skye's grandfather asked her with a smile. "You didn't enjoy yourself too much I hope."

Skye laughed, her eyes sparkling mischievously. "No, I missed you far too much to *truly* enjoy myself."

It was her grandfather's turn to laugh this time. He then asked more seriously, "Was it a good voyage?"

Skye nodded with a beaming smile. "It was wonderful. We couldn't have had better weather, and the ports we visited were just beautiful."

"Yes, and we got very good prices on the cargo," Daniel added.

"Good." Skye's grandfather was very pleased.

As Daniel went into a little more detail, Will worked his way over to Matthew who greeted him warmly, having missed the young man very much.

"It's good to have you back, Will."

Will smiled in return having missed Matthew's friendship and mentoring. "It is good to be back although as Skye said on the way here this morning I think I may find myself missing the sea in a few days."

Matthew nodded. "I'm sure you will. I miss sailing too. I think next time I'll have to find someone who can take over our work for us for a while and go along with you."

"I hope you do," Will encouraged. "I know everyone would enjoy that."

Will's attention was brought again to Skye's grandfather who addressed everyone.

" . . . now I insist that you all join me for dinner and continue telling me of the voyage."

The invitation was one Skye's grandfather made every time they returned home from a voyage. Something Will and even Skye had just recently discovered was that hidden behind her grandfather's proper, businesslike demeanor he actually had a sense of adventure. He had once been a merchant sailor but had retired when Skye's mother was born, and Will suspected that he had a longing for the sea every bit as strong as the rest of them. Therefore, whenever they returned he loved to hear of the places they had visited.

Everyone, except those who had families they were anxious to go home to, followed Skye's grandfather to his huge merchant's house near the center of Kingston. His spacious dining room was soon filled with the sound of not only cutlery clinking on fine glass dishes as servants placed food before them, but also Daniel's voice as he recounted the last couple of weeks.

The meal was spent leisurely, and it was not until more than an hour later that they finally rose from their seats to follow Skye's grandfather back to the foyer where they had left their belongings. The haphazardly stacked pile of duffel bags looked very out of place in the spotless, richly furnished room. Saying good day to Skye's grandfather and thanking him for the meal, Daniel's crew left the house with their belongings and headed home. Will and Skye, along with Daniel, Caleb, and Matthew were the last to go. As the five of them began to leave, Skye's grandfather stopped Will and Skye at the door.

"Are the two of you planning to resume your lessons again now that you're back?" he questioned.

Skye looked at Will to see what he was thinking. The lessons her grandfather referred to were lessons in social etiquette that he had been teaching them since neither Skye nor Will had been able to learn them as children while growing up in the orphanage.

When Will nodded, Skye told her grandfather, "Yes. We will resume them."

16

Although, learning how to be a perfectly proper woman in the strict social world she lived in was not one of Skye's favorite pastimes considering how different her life was at sea. Still, her grandfather believed it was important, and she wished to please him. Skye knew Will didn't like it any better than she did, but learning together made the experience much more enjoyable.

"Shall we start again tomorrow?" Skye's grandfather asked.

Skye looked again to Will. "That would be fine," he answered for both of them.

"Good," Grandfather said briskly. "I'll expect you tomorrow afternoon for tea."

Bidding him farewell, they wandered out through the beautifully gardened courtyard. The others were waiting for them on the busy city street. It was time for Will and Matthew to go to the blacksmith shop, and Skye would go home with her father and Caleb. Turning to Will, Skye smiled, happy to be home, happy to have him in her life.

"Goodbye, Will."

Will responded to her infectious smile. "I'll see you tomorrow."

After saying their goodbyes, they all parted ways. Skye followed her father and Caleb away from the busy part of the city to a more wooded, less populated area where their house stood. Skye found herself smiling again as they ascended the hill upon which it sat. A fresh breeze blew the smell of salt air towards them making it feel like they were closer to the sea than they really were.

Reaching the front door of the medium-sized house the three of them shared, Daniel pulled out a key and unlocked it. They stepped into the small, sunny foyer, and Skye scanned the room.

"Well, I see that I have a bit of work ahead of me," she commented, scrutinizing the cobwebs and dust that had collected in their absence.

Skye climbed the staircase which led to the second floor where her bedroom was located. Stepping through the door, she entered her peaceful haven-like room. It was dark inside, but Skye quickly pulled back the drapes that hid four big windows which all faced south towards the ocean. Pushing the windows open to let the breeze into the room, Skye stood for a moment gazing at the brilliantly blue sea water that she could see shimmering just above the treetops. She sighed happily as she was filled with contentment, thanking God for another safe voyage and this wonderful home to return to.

Chapter Two

The city was noisy with people and carriages hurrying about as Will and Matthew made their way down the cobblestone street towards the blacksmith shop where they lived and worked. Will looked around comparing city life to life onboard a ship. The two couldn't be more different from each other. Life on a ship was orderly and everyone was working together towards one goal, a good safe voyage. It was the one aspect Will missed the most about sailing. That and the fellowship with the men he knew so well who also shared his faith. Sometimes it was a near perfect world at sea with only the weather and the ship to be concerned with.

Will's attention was quickly directed back to Matthew who was telling him how business had been and of different news from around the city. As they were nearing the shop Matthew said, "By the way, I had a visit from Ryan Collins the other day."

Will turned to him with a keen look. "You did?"

The eagerness in Will's voice was not lost on Matthew. "Yes. Actually, he came to ask me when you would be returning. He wanted you to go over and see him when you got back." Matthew watched Will's reaction curiously. He was fairly certain he knew what Will's business with Ryan Collins was, but he wondered if Will would tell him anything.

"I think I'll go over there as soon as I unpack," Will said, preoccupied.

Matthew only nodded not wanting to press Will for answers, knowing they'd come in time.

When they reached the large barn-like blacksmith shed, Matthew unlocked and opened the door. Inside, sunlight filtered through the soot-smudged windows, and there was an orange glow of crackling embers in the forge. Besides the blacksmith tools and metal there was also a supply of lumber and carpentry tools. Matthew was a blacksmith, but his first love was carpentry. Most of the time, Will took on all of the metal work while Matthew worked to satisfy the never-ending demand for furniture. His work was the best to be found anywhere in the city and everyone knew it.

"Go ahead and unpack," Matthew urged Will. "I'm going to get back to a table I've been working on."

Will crossed the shed to a door which led into the small house that he and Matthew lived in. He carried his duffel down a short hall which, oddly enough, resembled a passageway on a ship. His bedroom was at the end of it, a small room, only large enough for a bed, a dresser, and a nightstand, all of which Matthew had constructed. The walls themselves were bare. Will didn't spend his money on decorations or other luxuries. Light blue curtains that Skye had made hung beside the room's one window which overlooked the street.

Will walked over to his bed, the old wooden floor-boards creaking beneath his feet, and set his duffel down on the mattress. Untying the drawstrings, he opened the heavy canvas bag and began taking out his belongings. First, his Bible and the portrait of Skye which he set carefully on the nightstand, and then the locket. He stared at it again for only a moment before dropping it into the small nightstand drawer. Turning back to his duffel, he started to pull out his clothes.

During this time, Will's mind turned to Mr. Collins and what he would learn on his visit to the man's house. Mr. Collins, a young man in his thirties, lived with his wife on the edge of Kingston in a gorgeous little house that sat looking right out over the ocean. Many times on their walks along the beach, Will had heard Skye's wishful comments stating that if there was any place in all the city that she would love to live it would be that house. Since then, Will had heard Mr. Collins mention the possibility of selling the house one day, and Will had made certain that Mr. Collins knew if he ever did sell it, Will would be interested. Now, it seemed from Matthew's words that the possibility of the house being for sale might have become a reality.

As soon as Will's duffel was emptied, he placed it under his bed and changed into a more formal pair of clothes which he kept for church and for appointments. Walking back into the shed, he paused to inform Matthew he'd be back in a little while.

Will felt his anticipation grow as he hurried through the city. It did not take long for the lovely house to come into view. The little, sunny white porch where the front door stood was a very welcoming sight. Two chairs and a small table stood on it matching the house wonderfully. It was the perfect place for someone to relax or enjoy afternoon tea.

Climbing the porch steps, Will came to the door and knocked gently. As he awaited an answer, he could hear the rhythmic sloshing of waves on the shore not too far away. He could not see the water, however, because it was hidden by the thick stand of trees that surrounded the house.

Only moments later, Will heard movement inside the house. As the door swung open, he was greeted by Mr. Collins' wife, Abigail, a lovely, kind woman.

"Good afternoon, William," she said with a welcoming smile.

"Good afternoon, Mrs. Collins. I hope I'm not intruding."

"Oh no, not at all. We've been expecting you," she said with an understanding twinkle in her eye. "Please come in."

Will followed her into the foyer where they paused.

"I'll go and get Ryan. He's upstairs in his study," Mrs. Collins said. "You may wait in the sitting room if you'd like."

Will smiled. "Thank you."

Mrs. Collins turned for the carpeted staircase which led upstairs. Will waited for a brief moment before walking towards an open doorway at the opposite side of the foyer. It beckoned him into the most splendid room of the house. Directly across from him, huge windows which stretched almost from floor to ceiling took up the entire wall giving the room a breathtaking view of the sea. Sunlight flooded the room, warming the salty breeze which blew in through an open door leading out onto the back porch. Will walked along the windows over to the door to get an even better look at the water. If not for the white sand beach, one would almost feel as though the house were at sea. It was for that reason Will knew Skye loved the house so much.

A minute or two passed as Will stood in admiration of all the beautiful sights before he turned to the sound of Mrs. Collins entering the room with her husband, a tall, dark haired and kind looking gentleman.

"Will, I'm so glad you visited today," Mr. Collins said with a smile. "How was your trip?"

"It went very well."

"Good," Mr. Collins responded happily. He motioned to a sofa which sat on one side of a small table. "Please, sit down."

Will thanked him and took a seat. Mr. and Mrs. Collins each sat down just across from him.

"I'm sure you've guessed that it's the house I wanted to see you about," Mr. Collins began.

"Yes."

"You're still interested, I'm sure?"

"Yes, very much so."

"Good, because Abby and I have finally decided to sell it and move back to England, closer to our families," he explained. "Knowing that we already had someone interested in the house has made the decision easier."

"Thank you for keeping me in mind. It means a great deal."

Mr. Collins smiled. "You are the only one we've spoken to about it and we're very glad to sell to someone who will really appreciate the house's beauty and location. Now, since you've been such a good friend to us over 'the years, we've decided to sell it to you for five hundred fifty pounds. I do hope that is satisfactory to you."

Will smiled expressively and nodded. "Yes, it is. Thank you."

"So, it is settled then? You will purchase the house?"

"Yes, I will."

"All right, then perhaps tomorrow we can go over to the bank and take care of the payment. Would you be free around one o'clock?"

"That will be perfect," Will decided. He knew he would not have to be at Skye's grandfather's until two and the transaction at the bank wouldn't take more than an hour to accomplish.

Having completed their business, Will stood with Mr. and Mrs. Collins.

"Oh, one more thing," Mr. Collins mentioned on their way out of the sitting room. "I hope it is all right that Abby and I are going to have to stay here until everything is taken care of in England. We will have to arrange to have our things transported."

"Of course," Will replied. "That won't be a problem."

By now, they were standing near the door.

"One other thing I was going to mention. There is no way we can take everything with us so we're also leaving some of the furnishings with the house. They will be yours as well," Mr. Collins told Will.

"But that is very generous of you, Mr. Collins," Will said hesitantly. "Are you sure you do not want to sell them?"

"No, the sale of the house will be enough. Abby and I are very happy to do this."

Will shook his head, overwhelmed by their generosity. "I don't know how to thank you for everything."

Mr. Collins smiled. "There is no need. Besides, by agreeing to buy the house so quickly, you're helping us. Now we can get right on with our plans and not worry about finding a buyer."

"I'm glad it worked out so well for both of us."

Mr. Collins agreed and then paused for a moment. "Pardon me for prying into you personal life, but are you intending to live here alone?" There was a sparkle of curiosity in his eyes.

Will grinned. "No, I certainly hope I won't be."

Mr. and Mrs. Collins shared a smile.

"Does that mean we could be expecting an announcement from you in the near future?" Mrs. Collins asked him.

"I am hoping so," Will told her.

"Well, allow us to give you an early congratulations," Mr. Collins said.

"Thank you," Will said to both of them. "Also, if you would please keep it a secret that I am the one who bought the house I would very much appreciate it. This is meant to be a surprise."

"Of course," Mr. Collins assured him.

"Thank you," Will said again, grateful for their generosity to him. He then said good day and made his way out the door.

On the way back to the shed, Will was filled with anticipation as he imagined what Skye's reaction would be when he told her the house was hers because, of course, she is the one he had bought it for. It was one of the most special gifts he could give her.

When Will entered the shed, his happiness was evident, and Matthew looked at him expectantly. Will smiled at him knowing he couldn't keep his plans a secret any longer, especially now that they had all worked out.

"Mr. Collins and his wife are selling their house and moving back to England," he began. "I'm going to meet Mr. Collins at the bank tomorrow and buy it."

A smile lit Matthew's face as well. "I thought you might come back with news like that. Am I wrong to assume that you are not the only one who is going to be living in that house?"

Will laughed a little and shook his head. "Mr. Collins wondered the same thing. No, you're not wrong."

"When are you going to ask her?" Matthew was curious.

"Well, I have to talk to your brother first," Will told him.

"I'm sure he'll say yes."

"Hopefully Skye's answer will be the same."

Matthew smiled reassuringly. "You two have loved each other since childhood. It will be."

Will knew this to be true, but a little apprehension would still remain until he proposed and Skye accepted. "My next task will be finding the time to talk to your brother. He always has a lot to do when we get back."

"If he knows there's something important you want to speak to him about, he'll make time," Matthew assured him.

And that being true, Will was encouraged.

"So, is the house a surprise?" Matthew wanted to know.

"Yes. I won't tell her until afterwards."

Matthew smiled at the joyful thought that created. "She's going to be very surprised. I know she will love it."

Will agreed. "Now, I suppose I should change and help you finish up for today."

"You don't need to unless you want to."

But Will decided he would. "I think it would be nice to get back to work again."

The beautiful spring weather which had graced their days of late greeted Will as he and Mr. Collins walked out of the Kingston bank the next afternoon having just finished the transferring of money inside. The house was now officially Will's, and he could scarcely believe it. Not only was it the largest purchase he had ever made, but it was his first house. How he longed to tell Skye!

Coming to a stop at the edge of the street, Mr. Collins turned to Will and extended his hand. "It has been a pleasure doing business with you, Will," he said sincerely.

Will shook his hand with a smile. "It's been a pleasure doing business with you as well, Mr. Collins. I hope that the rest of your plans for moving go well."

"I'm sure they will. Now, let me wish you luck on whatever plans you may have."

"Thank you," Will replied.

Mr. Collins nodded smartly. "Well, I'd best be getting back. I'm sure I'll be seeing you again soon. Perhaps you and Skye can come for a visit sometime before we leave."

"Yes, I'm sure Skye would love that."

Before leaving Mr. Collins stressed, "You are both welcome any time. Good day, Will."

"Good day, Mr. Collins."

As Mr. Collins headed for home, instead of returning to the shed, Will started in the opposite direction towards Skye's house. It was only a little after one thirty. He had just enough time to meet Skye and walk with her to her grandfather's.

He had gone only a short distance from the bank when someone bumped into him quite abruptly. Surprised, Will looked down to find a woman of questionable age, perhaps forties or fifties. It was hard to tell for she looked as if she'd lived a very hard life. Her clothes, while obviously meant to impress, were tattered and too big for she was disturbingly thin.

Looking up at Will, she begged, "Please excuse me, sir. I didn't mean to run into you."

Will quickly shook his head to relieve her. "That's quite all right." Then, seeing how pale and sickly she looked, he worried that maybe she had hurt herself by running into him. "You're not hurt are you?"

At first, the woman seemed hardly to have heard him. She stared into his face so long Will began to wonder the reason why. Finally she spoke, mumbling, "No, I'm fine." She turned then without another word and hurried away.

Will watched her go with a frown still wondering over the strange encounter, but soon his thoughts returned to the house and Skye as he too continued on his way.

"Thank you for always coming over to help me, Mrs. Henley." Skye turned to the older woman who had just helped her to button up her dress. She was one of their closest neighbors and friends. Whenever Skye had some sort of social meeting like the lessons with her grandfather, Mrs. Henley would always come over and help her dress properly which was no easy feat alone. "I'm not sure how I'd manage without you."

"It's always a pleasure, dear," Mrs. Henley replied with a smile. "I can only imagine how difficult it is not having a mother around to help you with these things. I rather enjoy it myself. Ever since my Sarah moved away, I've been kind of lonely without a daughter to care for. Besides, you're such a lovely young woman. Anyone would love to help you look your best. Oh, your mother would be so proud to see you," she breathed melodically.

"Thank you, Mrs. Henley, for your kind words," Skye replied with all sincerity. "It means a lot to me."

"You are very welcome, dear. Now, is there anything else you need me to assist you with?"

"No, I think I can manage the rest, thank you very much," Skye told her, smiling sweetly.

"All right, I will go down and see your father while you're finishing up."

Skye nodded. "I'll be down in a few moments."

Mrs. Henley turned and let herself out of the room. As the door closed, Skye walked over to her dressing table and sat down to make sure her hair was still arranged nicely after dressing. Most of it was pinned up elegantly at the back of her head and a few perfect, dark ringlets framed her face. All of it had taken Mrs. Henley over an hour to do. Seeing that everything was in place, Skye picked up a small, delicately decorated straw hat, set it on her head, and tied the silky ribbons at the back of her neck to keep it on.

Finally, Skye stood and walked over to the full length mirror, a gift from her grandfather, which stood in one corner of her room. She almost chuckled upon seeing herself all dressed up in her ice blue satin gown and three white satin petticoats. The laughter was constricted however by the stays she was wearing underneath. Sighing a bit wistfully, she recalled the days when she hadn't needed to wear one and couldn't have afforded one even if she had wanted to. Now that her social standing had gone up because her grandfather had acknowledged her as his granddaughter, the stays was required for any type of social event no matter how small.

Finished with her inspection, Skye walked to open her door, momentarily taking note of how unsteady she felt in her high heeled shoes. Over the last couple of weeks, she had grown used to wearing only her sturdy leather boots. She descended the stairs to the foyer very carefully, praying that she would not trip on her way to her grandfather's or while there and embarrass herself.

Skye followed the voices of her father and Mrs. Henley into the sunny sitting room where the two stood talking. Both turned to her as she entered.

"You look positively lovely today, Skye," Daniel told his daughter with fatherly pride and then he couldn't help a grin. "I think your grandfather will be impressed with how easily you've gone from shirt and breeches to gown and petticoats."

Skye laughed. "Yes, I do believe he will be. I'm a bit surprised myself."

A knock at the door came before anyone could speak again. Daniel stepped out of the room to answer it, and Skye and Mrs. Henley followed. A smile broke over Skye's face the instant her father pulled the door open, and she saw Will standing on the other side.

"Hello, Will. Come in," Daniel invited.

"Thank you, Captain McHenry," Will said, stepping into the foyer. "I thought I'd walk Skye over to her grandfather's." His eyes shifted to Skye who was walking toward him.

"Thank you, Will," she said, smiling sweetly. "You didn't have to go to the trouble of walking all the way out here."

"It was no trouble," Will told her.

"What a fine gentleman," Mrs. Henley praised as she stepped up beside them.

Will greeted her warmly, "Hello, Mrs. Henley."

"Hello, William," she replied. "It is good to see you. Now, I'm sure you two are eager to be on your way, and I'd best be getting along myself." She looked at Skye. "I'm sure I'll see you tomorrow to help you prepare for church."

"If you would, Mrs. Henley, I would really appreciate it," Skye said eagerly.

"I'll be here," Mrs. Henley assured her.

She said good day to each of them and left the house.

"Well, she seems to think very highly of you both," Daniel remarked after she was gone.

Skye smiled. "She's very sweet."

Daniel glanced at the clock hanging near the door. "I should get back to Caleb at the docks. We'll probably still be gone when you get back, Skye."

Skye nodded. "I'll just finish some of the work I was doing earlier."

"I'll see you later then," Daniel told her. "Try to enjoy yourself if you can today. I know that neither of you are overly fond of this."

A slightly sheepish smile came to Skye's face. "Is it really that obvious?"

Daniel grinned. "Only to me."

"Good, because I know how important it is to Grandfather, and I'd hate for him to think we don't appreciate his help."

"Don't worry, even if he knew, I think he'd understand," Daniel said, and then he was on his way.

Will and Skye turned for the door, and Skye slipped her arm in through Will's as they started away from the house. After a brief moment, Will looked at her with a smile.

"You look beautiful."

His smile was easily returned.

"Thank you," Skye replied, feeling wonderfully cherished. She paused. "I must admit though, that these clothes are going to take me forever to get used to again." She chuckled lightly. "Do not be surprised if I fall sometime during the day because of these shoes."

Will laughed a little too before saying, "I'll try not to let that happen."

"You're a fine gentleman, William James, just as Mrs. Henley said."

They smiled at each other lovingly and continued on a few yards in a companionable silence. When Skye looked up at Will again, she found that he was still smiling happily. It made her smile too. She loved to see him like this instead of how he had been on the ship the morning before.

"You are very happy today," Skye commented. "Is there any particular reason?"

Will looked at her soft, beautifully tanned face. How badly he wished to tell her about the house and even more, to ask her the question he'd wanted to ask for so long. However, he knew he couldn't without first talking to her father so he only shrugged.

"I'm happy to see you. It was kind of strange having breakfast this morning without you and everyone else."

Skye quickly agreed. "Father and Caleb were talking about how quiet it was this morning. I always miss everyone's laughter."

"So do I."

Skye and Will's conversation continued as they made their way into the heart of the city. It took but another few minutes to reach the front door of the house. Will knocked and they were let in a moment later by one of the maids. Skye's grandfather entered the foyer from another room at about the same time they did.

"You are right on time." He was pleased. "And may I commend you on how splendid you both look. Your transformation, Skye, is amazing. You look stunning."

"Thank you, Grandfather," Skye replied. "I'm glad you're pleased."

"Oh, indeed I am." He smiled.

Skye returned it and then her attention was drawn to the maid who asked, "May I take your hat, miss?"

"Yes, thank you."

Skye quickly untied the ribbons and gave the hat to the maid who turned to put it away. Skye found her eyes lingering on the maid as she did so. It wasn't long ago that she was no more than a servant herself, and she always felt uncomfortable now being waited upon by others.

"Shall we go to the parlor?" Skye's attention was brought back to her grandfather with his words. "I'm sure the tea is ready."

Skye quickly nodded, hoping her grandfather hadn't noticed her sudden distraction. It was one of the few things the two of them didn't quite see eye to eye on—her sympathy for servants and the lower class people. Although her grandfather wasn't as arrogant and uncaring as some might have made him out to be, he still wasn't as sympathetic as Skye. She concluded that it was because he had been raised that way while she had grown up the exact opposite, having experienced lower class living.

Skye's grandfather turned to lead them to the parlor showing no awareness of what Skye was feeling. As Skye moved to follow him, she felt Will's gentle hand on her shoulder. She looked at him, and he smiled. He was aware of how she felt, and Skye found that comforting.

Tea progressed with all formality. The subjects they discussed were the most boring that Skye could imagine. Although her grandfather only meant it as more or less a training exercise, Skye knew they were the kind of conversations most people had all the time, and she dreaded the thought of having to engage in a conversation like that with someone for real. She wondered where peoples' imagination and sense of adventure was, and she credited their absence to upbringings that were far too strict.

As they finally neared the end, Skye felt like congratulating both herself and Will. Both had done everything to near perfection as though they had been doing it their entire lives. However, one thing Skye would later admit to Will was that at one point she had nearly started laughing for no other reason than that she almost couldn't bear the whole thing any longer. Luckily, she had been able to compose herself before anyone noticed.

Skye had just emptied her tea cup and set it down when a maid entered the room and addressed her grandfather.

"Excuse me, sir. Mrs. Whitman has arrived."

"Good, please show her in."

Skye's grandfather turned back to them.

"I thought today I'd see how well your dancing is since it is what you've been best at, and if I find it satisfactory, we won't have to continue with these particular lessons," he said. "Were you able to practice at all during your trip?"

"A little," Skye told him. "Unlike tea, we were able to find some time for it although it's a little more difficult on a swaying ship."

He smiled. "Well, perhaps that has made you better."

At that moment, Mrs. Whitman entered the room. She was an amazing piano player and always provided the music for the dance lessons. Skye, her grandfather, and Will each offered her their greetings before the four of them walked into the huge ballroom. Mrs. Whitman seated herself at the piano, and Skye and Will stepped into the middle of them room while Skye's grandfather stood off to the side to observe them. This was by far Skye and Will's favorite of all their lessons, and Skye would be disappointed to see them come to an end.

They spent nearly an hour in practice of several popular dances. With only a minimal number of critiques Skye's grandfather had encouraging words for them when they had finished.

"You both did marvelously. I don't think there is a need to continue lessons, however, and because this is the last, allow me remind of a few things. As much as I'm sure you'd like to spend the evening of a dance dancing only with each other, dances are meant as a way for you to become acquainted with others. Your responsibility, Will, is to always watch for women who are available to dance, noticing those who might be passed over by others less chivalrous than yourself. And Skye, in addition to dancing with Will, it is your responsibility to accept invitations which are extended to you by a variety of partners. Be sure that you never turn down one man and then accept another. That would be very rude unless he has displayed some sort of bad behavior that would of necessity keep you from dancing with him."

Skye and Will nodded in understanding though it was something both had a bit of trouble with for neither of them were particularly outgoing.

"We'll remember, Grandfather," Skye told him.

"Very good," her grandfather replied. "Now, I think that shall conclude our lessons for today. Soon we should have another dining lesson since it is something you both seem to be struggling with . . ."

Skye glanced at Will who half smiled at her. The dining lessons were certainly their least favorite. How anyone could ever learn the differences between the countless pieces of silverware and when to use them she didn't know.

Before Skye could dwell any further on those thoughts, her grandfather continued, ". . . still you two have done very well. Your dancing especially has come along beautifully."

"It is something we both really enjoy." Skye hoped it didn't sound like she was actually saying they didn't enjoy anything else they were learning. Hoping to avoid that, she continued with a smile, "Ever since I was younger, I've always had this dream of dancing on a beach under the stars with no worries of how good I am or if it's being done properly."

Her grandfather smiled gently, but Skye knew he probably thought it was a bit silly. "Unfortunately, there are very few times like that when we don't have those kinds of worries. It just comes with who we are."

Skye knew he meant that it was because of their higher class where appearance meant everything. With that knowledge, Skye felt very thankful that her grandfather wasn't as strict as he could be. If he had been, she likely would never have been permitted to be courted by Will whose status hadn't changed just because hers had. She was very glad that her grandfather had always held Will in high regard.

The large clock standing against the wall began to chime the four o'clock hour before Skye could begin to formulate a reply to her grandfather.

"My, it's gotten late," he remarked.

"Yes, it has," Skye agreed. "I should probably be getting home so that I can finish some of my work and get ready to prepare supper before Father and Caleb return from the docks."

"I'm sure there's some work to be done at the shed," Will added.

"Very well then, I'll see you to the door."

Skye and Will said their farewells to Mrs. Whitman and followed him to the foyer.

"I will see you both at church tomorrow," he said at the door. "Being Sunday, we won't have any lessons."

Skye nodded. She was handed her hat by a maid and put it on. Saying their goodbyes, she and Will left the house. Out on the street, Will turned to Skye.

"I'll walk you home."

"Are you sure? You don't have to."

"Yes, I'm sure."

Skye was glad for the company and the escort. After a few moments of walking quietly, Will spoke.

"What you said about dancing on the beach . . ." he began.

Skye looked at him. "Yes?"

A smile came to Will's face. "We'll do that sometime. We won't have to worry about anyone or anything else."

Skye grinned happily. "Is that a promise?"

"Yes, that's a promise."

Chapter Three

Whom Will walked into the shed, his lingering smile caught Matthew's attention.

"It went well then?" Matthew asked.

"Very well. Except she nearly started laughing during tea."

They both knew very well who Will referred to, and the bit of information set them both to laughing.

"Did her grandfather know?"

"No," Will shook his head, "I don't think so. I didn't notice anything so I doubt he did either. She told me about it as I walked her home."

"She must have hidden it well then."

"Yes, very well," Will realized, another laugh escaping as he thought of her sitting there so demurely. How he loved her.

The late afternoon passed quickly into evening as Will busied himself with his work. There was much to do since it had piled up some while he was gone so he hoped to work hard over the next couple of days and catch up with it. Matthew too was quite busy working with different pieces of furniture.

Later that evening as the sun went down and the city was beginning to grow dim, Will stood at the forge with his back to the open door of the shed. Despite the steady ringing of his hammer upon the glowing metal he was working with, he could hear people passing on the street outside, most heading for their homes. He didn't notice any of them particularly until he started getting the very distinct feeling that someone was watching him. At first, he ignored it, but the feeling escalated until finally he turned to look. Standing in the street just outside the shed he saw the woman who had run into him earlier in the day. Strangely, she just stood watching him, and Will had the feeling she'd been doing that for quite a while. Why she would be watching him, he hadn't the slightest guess, but he wished he knew. It wasn't until Will heard Matthew walk up beside him that the woman finally turned away and disappeared.

"Do you know her, Will?" Matthew asked.

Will shook his head slowly, feeling a strange foreboding.

"No, I don't." But he hesitated, thinking. Something about the woman seemed so familiar. "What about you, Matthew?"

"No. She's been a stranger in town for about a week now. I see her go past here just about every night on her way to the tavern. I think that's where she's been staying."

"I wonder why she has been acting so strangely around me," Will murmured, disconcerted.

"What do you mean?" Matthew asked with a frown.

"I saw her at the bank today. She ran into me by accident, and before she turned away, stared at me like she was doing now."

Matthew shook his head again, wondering at the strangeness as well. "I don't know, Will. It does seem very odd."

"What makes it even more so is that for some reason she seems familiar to me," Will shared, clearly troubled by the thought. "Yet, I don't know why that would be. I have no recollection of where I might have seen her before today."

"Could it have been somewhere you've visited on a voyage?"

"I suppose it could, but we see hundreds of people. Why would I remember her? And why would she be here in Kingston and acting like this?"

Matthew's frown deepened. All that Will had said left him feeling disturbed.

"I don't know, but I think it would be wise if you were a bit cautious until we figure it out, or until she leaves," Matthew cautioned.

"Do you think she's dangerous?"

Matthew shrugged. "It's possible. All I know is that the whole idea of you feeling like you've seen her somewhere before and then running into her here and having her show a strange interest in you doesn't leave me with a good feeling."

"Me either," Will admitted.

"Just keep an eye out for her and anyone she might have with her. If this continues perhaps you and I, and maybe Daniel and Caleb, will make a point to talk to her and find out what she wants."

Will nodded, knowing until that time he would simply have to trust that there was nothing wrong.

By this time, the street had grown quite dark and there were no longer as many people using it or milling about.

"I think we should call it a night," Matthew decided.

He and Will turned back to their respective tasks. Will set aside what he had been working on so it would be ready the next time he worked on it and then returned his tools to their places. Matthew took care of his tools as well before closing the doors, paying particular attention to making sure they were all locked.

Once inside the house, which Matthew made sure was locked securely as well, he started supper, and he and Will soon sat down, hungry to eat it. The meal was unusually quiet as both their thoughts lingered on the woman. Will tried to figure out when and if he'd ever seen her before, but he came up with nothing.

Later that night, after he'd read his Bible, Will prayed. He prayed for Skye, all the people he cared about, and for himself. Lastly, he prayed concerning the woman, that whatever her purpose in the city, it wouldn't affect him or anyone else negatively.

Musical chiming of bells echoed through Kingston as people made their way to church early the next morning. The church the McHenrys and their friends attended stood at one edge of the city and had been dramatically improved and enlarged over the last two years. Upon Skye's request, her father had paid for the building process with a portion of the treasure they had not split up among friends. The orphanage too had seen wonderful improvements, not only structurally, but in supplies and staff as well.

Will and Matthew were among the crowd gathering in the churchyard, their cheerful voices mingling with those of everyone else. Will was very glad to see the members of Daniel's crew along with their families. He and Matthew greatly enjoyed visiting with them as they waited for the service to start.

Will kept his eye out for Skye's arrival which came a short time later. She was escorted by her father and Caleb, and Mr. and Mrs. Henley were with them. There was just enough time for Will and Matthew to greet them all before people started entering the church. Daniel led the way inside and coming to one of the middle pews, they all seated themselves, Caleb first, then Matthew and Daniel, and finally Skye and Will.

The service began shortly with a beautiful collection of hymns which everyone took great pleasure in singing. The hour and a half sermon that followed was also thoroughly enjoyed, especially by Skye and Will who had always looked forward to Sunday mornings. Both had such wonderful memories of church, having attended together since they were children in the orphanage, and it was there also that they had met Matthew.

Before long, the sermon came to an end. Everyone rose from their seats, and they spoke briefly with several friends and neighbors, including Skye's grandfather. He told them that he had a business meeting in the afternoon the next day so they would postpone their lesson until Tuesday, perhaps. He would send a messenger to let them know when he decided.

They left the building, stepping out into bright, warm sunshine. At the bottom of the church's front steps, Daniel turned to everyone and looked particularly at Skye.

"I'd say it's a beautiful day for a picnic on the beach, wouldn't you?" He knew how much his daughter loved to do that.

"Yes, let's," she said smiling. "It is a perfect day."

Daniel turned to Will and Matthew. "What do you two think? Would you like to join us?"

Will and Matthew nodded without hesitation. Because it was Sunday they had no work to do and a picnic sounded very enjoyable. Besides, Matthew was anxious to spend some time with Daniel since he'd just gotten back.

"Well, let's all go back home and change then," Daniel said. "I'll help Skye get food packed and Matthew, you and Will can meet us at our house. We'll all go down to the beach together."

"All right, we'll see you shortly," Matthew said.

As soon as Skye reached home, she went up to her room to change. First, she took off her pale yellow gown and lace trimmed petticoats. Laying them over a chair to be washed separately, Skye next removed the pannier hoops Mrs. Henley had been insistent that she wear to make the skirt of her dress more full.

Going to her wardrobe, Skye picked out a gown of her mother's which was one of her favorites. Before putting on one of her older, but still nice petticoats, she slightly loosened her stays though it wasn't severely tight to begin with. Finally, she dressed in her mother's gown, and wishing to let her hair be blown by the breeze, Skye went to her dressing table and pulled out the pins that held it up. Her silky dark hair fell free to the middle of her back when once it had reached all the way to her waist. That was before it had been viciously cut off by the cruel pirate, Francis Kelley.

Picking up her brush, Skye brushed her hair smooth before putting on a wide brimmed straw hat. Lastly, she slipped on a flatter, more comfortable pair of shoes and returned downstairs to the kitchen where she began putting together a meal. Her father and Caleb joined her within a couple of minutes and helped her pack the food into a basket. They had just finished when there was a knock at the door. Caleb went to answer it, and Will and Matthew followed him back into the kitchen.

"Now all we need are some blankets and we can be on our way," Daniel said.

"I'll get them," Skye volunteered.

She walked out of the kitchen to one of the hall closets. Though Skye was tall, she found herself not quite able to reach the old blankets that her father had stowed at the back of the top shelf. Thinking she'd have to get help, Skye was about to turn when someone reached up behind her and pulled the blankets down. She turned around to face Will who had followed her unnoticed.

"Your father said you probably wouldn't be able to reach them," he told her, as her eyes climbed to his.

"Thank you, Will," she said blushing lightly. "I think he forgets sometimes when he puts things away that I'm not nearly as tall as he is."

Offering to carry the blankets, Will followed Skye to the foyer where the rest of the men were waiting. The five of them left the house, locking it behind them, and headed for the beach. It took a few minutes of walking through the soft, warm sand before they came to their favorite picnic spot, a small sheltered cove that was far enough away from the busyness of the docks. It was a gorgeous place that many people usually enjoyed, but today they were the only ones there. They spread out the blankets near the water's edge and started their picnic. The area soon echoed with their voices and laughter.

Not too long into the picnic, Skye looked to be sure there was no one around that could overhear her.

"I wonder where John and Kate are right now. It's been a while since we've heard any news of them." The subject of the two pirates was one they only spoke of when they were alone. If anyone were to find out they willingly let John and Kate go and even supplied John with a ship, things would not go well for them. Aiding pirates was considered a very serious crime—one that you could even be hanged for, hence their extreme caution.

"That it has been," Daniel agreed, eyes settling on his daughter. Only a few days ago, she had expressed some worry for their two friends, and he knew she was feeling it now. "They probably decided to settle somewhere for a while and let the interest in them die down. We did that once, remember?"

Skye nodded, but still she didn't seem to be very comforted.

"We would have heard if they'd been caught," Daniel said to encourage her.

This time Skye looked at him and smiled. She knew he was right. Looking out to sea, her smile grew. "I wonder if we'll ever see them again."

Everyone else smiled as well. Each of them would have loved to see the two people they owed so much and who had become two of their closest friends.

When everyone had eaten their fill, they put everything back into the basket. As Skye folded one of the blankets with help from Will, she heard her father say, "We should go for a walk after we take the basket and blankets back to the house."

"I can take them back," Caleb offered.

"I'll help you," Skye said wanting to give her father and Matthew some time to talk alone for a little while. Will volunteered to help as well.

"Thank you" Daniel said, pleased. "We'll wait for you here then."

Skye, and Will and Caleb, started on their way, each carrying something.

"It's nice to give your father and Matthew a chance to talk," Caleb said after they'd gone a ways.

Skye smiled. "Yes it is."

Though they walked slow to give Daniel and Matthew a little extra time, they soon came to the docks and entered into the city. Glancing to his left, Will stopped abruptly.

"What is it, Will?" Skye asked as she and Caleb came to a stop as well.

"That woman, this is the third time I've seen her in two days." And this time she was watching him again.

Skye and Caleb had only enough time to see the woman's form retreating down a street.

"Twice now I've caught her watching me," Will continued. "Matthew said she's a stranger in town, but I feel

44

as though I've seen her before. We can't figure out why she has shown an interest in me, but neither of us has a good feeling about it."

Skye frowned, getting the same bad feeling. "What could she possibly want?"

Will shook his head. "I don't know."

"Does Matthew know where she's staying?" Caleb asked.

"Not positively, but he thinks the tavern. He sees her go there every night. Last night we found her standing outside the shed watching me."

"Have you spoken with her?"

Will shook his head. "Yesterday afternoon when I first saw her she accidentally ran into me and apologized. But other than that, no."

"Perhaps it was not an accident." Caleb wore a frown that showed he didn't like it any more than the rest of them. "If she is staying at the tavern, maybe we should go and talk to her."

Will nodded. "Matthew said the same thing last night, although we hoped she would leave before that became necessary."

Caleb thought this over for a moment before speaking. "Let's get these things to the house. We need to talk about this with Daniel and Matthew."

Back at the beach, they found Matthew and Daniel standing in the cove. Will approached Matthew directly. "I saw her again."

The smile Matthew wore disappeared. "Where?"

"Near the docks. I have a feeling she was following us."

Watching this exchange, Daniel frowned. "What's all this about?"

Will and Matthew quickly explained.

"I think we should talk to her," Caleb said when they'd finished.

Daniel nodded, his face somber. "I agree. We should find out what she wants."

"We'll have to wait until tonight," Matthew said. "She doesn't return to the tavern until then, and I don't know where she is during the day."

"What time does she come by?" Daniel asked.

"Around dusk."

"Caleb and I will come before then," Daniel said to which Matthew nodded, and then he glanced at each one of them. "I suggest that since there's nothing more we can do now, we proceed with our walk."

The carefree brightness of the afternoon was gone and though they tried a few times to change the subject, Daniel and Matthew and Caleb, who were walking a few feet ahead of Skye and Will, continued to discuss the woman and her business. Skye and Will, however, were both unusually quiet. Finally, Will looked at Skye and asked, "Are you all right?"

Skye shrugged. "I'm just a little concerned, like everyone else. This is just really strange."

"I know, but I'm sure everything will be fine," Will said comfortingly. "We'll find out what is going on tonight."

Skye nodded.

A restless feeling followed them through the remainder of the day. After their walk, Will and Matthew ended up staying at Daniel's. When evening arrived and the sun had slipped behind the trees, the men left the house and started for the tavern. Though she had been reluctant, Skye had agreed to stay at the house knowing it wouldn't be best for her to go along.

Several minutes later the men were greeted by the lantern-lit front door of the tavern. It was the first time Will had ever stepped foot in the Kingston tavern, and he hoped it would be the only time. The inside was much the same as the Tortuga and Puerto Seguro taverns, full of men talking

46

loudly amidst milling bargirls and the smell of alcohol. Having unpleasant memories from last time, Will couldn't wait until they could leave, but first they needed to find out about the woman.

Daniel led the way to the bar. The barkeeper, a heavyset but tall man named Barlow, looked at the four of them in surprise because they were the last people he would have expected to see.

"What can I do for ya?" he asked with a puzzled frown.

"We're looking for someone," Daniel told him.

Barlow nodded, understanding now why they were there. "Who are ya lookin' for?" he asked.

"A woman. Matthew sees her coming here every night. She's new to the city."

Barlow nodded again, knowing instantly who Daniel was talking about.

"Yup, I know the one, but she hasn't come in yet tonight."

Daniel glanced at the others. "We'll wait until she does. In the mean time, can you tell us anything about her?"

"What's your reason for wantin' to know?" Barlow asked.

"She's been showing a strange interest in Will, and we want to know why."

"I see. Well, I'm afraid I can't really tell you anything. She first came here a week ago Friday. She leaves at dawn and doesn't come back 'til, well, around now."

"So you know nothing about her?"

"Nope, not really."

"Does anyone ever come here with her? Do you see her with anyone particular?" Daniel asked.

Barlow scoffed. "She talks to just about every man in here tryin' to get 'em to buy her drinks. Don't think I've ever seen a woman drink like she does. Other than that I haven't noticed her with anyone in particular."

Daniel nodded. "We'll wait for her then."

"You could wait over there." Barlow pointed to a table that sat in one corner away from all the rest. "I don't suppose there's anything I could getcha while you're waitin'."

"No, thank you," Daniel told him.

Turning away from the bar, they walked to the table across the room, each taking a seat so they'd have a good view of the front door. The minutes ticked by, punctuated by loud guffaws and rowdy snatches of song. Several times the door opened and they'd expect to see the woman, but it was never her. Minutes turned to hours. Every so often, Will glanced at the clock and watched it getting later and later. Finally, Daniel sighed heavily. It was now ten o'clock, and there was no sign of the woman.

"I don't think she's going to come." His voice sounded weary.

Matthew sighed as well. "She may have seen us come in here and stayed away."

Daniel nodded. "She probably did and if so, there's no reason to stay here any longer. We'll have to try again another time."

He stood up, and they followed his lead. Walking back to the bar, they stopped to talk with Barlow.

"I don't know what to make of it, Daniel," Barlow said. "This is the first night she hasn't come back."

Daniel shook his head ruefully, baffled as well. "We'll have to try again if we don't see her sometime during the day. But if she does come in yet tonight, don't tell her we were here looking for her."

"I won't say a word," Barlow assured them.

"Thank you."

Disappointed and fatigued, the four men left the tavern, scanning the dark corners and alleys suspiciously as they made their way down the street. Reaching Matthew's house, they all went inside to discuss their next move.

"When do you think we should go again?" Daniel asked. "If we go back tomorrow night she might expect that and not show up then either."

Matthew agreed. "We should probably wait a day or two."

Daniel nodded. He glanced at the clock seeing that it was now quarter after ten. "Caleb and I should get home. I'm sure Skye is concerned."

"Tell her goodnight," Will said as they turned for the door. "And not to worry."

Daniel smiled over his shoulder. "I will."

Back at Daniel's house, Skye had had a very long evening waiting for them to return. At first, she had tried to read a book, but she couldn't keep her mind on that so she took out her Bible instead. That she found much easier to stay focused on. It was ten thirty when she finally heard a knock at the door and her father's voice.

Quickly she opened it to them, and they walked in from the darkness. "What did you find out?"

"Nothing, I'm afraid," Daniel answered. "She never showed up. We waited as long as we could."

Skye sighed with disappointment. "What are we going to do now?"

"We'll try again in a day or two, but all we can do at the moment is pray."

Skye nodded. She had already been praying a great deal and would most certainly continue.

Daniel slipped off his coat. "I don't know about you two, but I'm going to get some rest."

"Yes. As long as you're home I guess I can go up to my room," Skye said.

She gave her father a hug, and saying goodnight to both men, Skye turned for the stairs. On her way up, she heard her father say, "Will said goodnight."

Skye paused and looked back at her father with a smile.

"And he said not to worry."

The smile stayed with Skye as she continued up the staircase to her room.

Chapter Four

Heavy dark clouds blanketed the early morning sky hiding the sun's warmth from the Caribbean island. The spring rains which had been surprisingly absent over the last several days had returned. Will awoke to the ticking of raindrops pelting the windowpane. Outside it was gray, and the muddy street was empty. Will, however, did not so much mind the weather. With no lessons and no other business to attend to, it would be a good day to get a lot of work done.

Wishing to get an early start, Will got out of bed and dressed. Rarely ever going a day without it, he next took out his Bible and read several passages before praying. The previous night, he had made up his mind not to think about the woman or worry about it, and he prayed that God would help him continue to do so.

Shortly after that, Will left his room and came to the small kitchen where Matthew, who had the same thoughts about the weather as Will did, already had breakfast started. Matthew too seemed to be trying to forget about the woman. Neither mentioned her during the meal and instead had their normal conversations about work and such. As soon as the table was cleared after they were done eating, they went to the shed. Will slipped on his leather blacksmith apron and got to work firing up the forge.

Even before she looked at the clock on the wall, Skye knew she had overslept. Not that it surprised her for she was usually in bed earlier than she had been the night before, but she never liked to oversleep. Quickly she got up and put a robe on over her nightgown deciding to dress later. She always tried to be up before or at the same time as her father and Caleb to make breakfast for them, and she hoped that perhaps today, they had overslept too.

But the house was quiet as she descended the stairs, and when she entered the kitchen it was obvious someone had worked in there that morning. Skye could smell the aroma of food, and at one end of the table was a plate with a covering over it. There was a piece of paper on top of the cover. Picking it up, Skye began to read the note written on it.

Skye,

I'm sorry that Caleb and I cannot be here this morning to have breakfast with you, but we got a message from the docks. One of the new ships has a leakage problem, and we have gone down there to help. We may not make it home for dinner, but I'll make up for missing breakfast tonight. I'm guessing that it won't be too long before you are up so I set a plate of food out for you. Also, here are several references to passages I thought you would enjoy. I will see you later this afternoon.

Your Loving Father

Skye smiled and scanned the verse references he'd written at the bottom. She would read them as soon as she was finished with her breakfast. Sitting down, she lifted the cover from the plate and found the food still steaming with warmth. She picked up a fork and began to eat. As she did so, her thoughts turned to Will. For a long time before falling asleep, she had asked God to help her not to worry and to trust that He would watch over Will. Here, alone at the table, she silently prayed the same prayer again.

Work continued at the shed with the ringing of metal and the sound of hammering and sawing of wood. Will was very pleased with the amount of work he was getting done, and Matthew seemed to be too. Their talk was cheery inside the warm shed despite the dreariness outside. Every so often, while letting some metal heat, Will would pause and watch Matthew expertly carve wonderfully intricate designs in different pieces of furniture. His skill was amazing.

"I don't know how you do that, Matthew," Will commented shortly after dinner as he watched him work on a dresser for a very rich merchant.

Matthew smiled. "Through many years of practice. I've been doing it since before I left England."

"You have an incredible talent," Will told him.

"Thank you very much, Will. I appreciate that."

Will turned to go back to work when a man came into the shed.

Matthew looked up and smiled. "Jeremy, it's good to see you."

Jeremy worked at the Kingston mill and had been a friend of Matthew's for a long time. Will greeted him as well before Matthew spoke again.

"What can we do for you?" he asked.

"Well, this shaft broke at the mill, and we don't have a spare. There's not much we can do without it, so I was wondering if there was any chance you could fix it and the sooner the better," Jeremy said hopefully.

Will stepped over to examine the broken metal rod.

"I can fix it for you this afternoon. I don't have anything pressing to get done, and it wouldn't take that long," he told Jeremy.

"We'd be very thankful if you did," Jeremy said. "I'll come back then and get it. How long do you expect it to take?"

"It shouldn't be more than about an hour, but I can bring it over to the mill when I'm finished with it," Will offered.

"Thank you, Will. That's very kind of you."

Will could tell how appreciative Jeremy was. "You're welcome," Will replied with a smile, happy to help.

He took the shaft from Jeremy who said good day to both of them, and as Jeremy left the shed, Will turned to the forge to work on the shaft. It was an easy fix, one that would take only the time to heat the metal and then hammer it back together. Steadily he worked on it and true to his word, it was repaired and ready to be used again in just under an hour. Satisfied with his work, Will began taking off his apron.

"I'll take this over to the mill then," he told Matthew, slipping on his long leather coat. He picked up the shaft and walked into the street. Outside the rain had ceased, but the dark clouds threatened to open up with more.

Several minutes after Will left, Matthew was startled by a voice, a woman's voice. He turned quickly and was even more surprised to find that it was the stranger.

"William is not here is he?" she asked, her eyes darting nervously around the shed.

At first, Matthew was too shocked to answer anything but, "No."

"When will he be back?" The woman's eyes finally came to rest on Matthew's face.

This time, Matthew asked a question of his own, "What is your reason for wanting to know?"

"I have a letter for him." She pulled it out of her pocket. "I want to know when he will get it."

Matthew wondered if this was good news or bad. "What is in the letter?"

"It's a personal matter. Please, when will he be back?"

Feeling uneasy, Matthew sighed and answered cautiously, "Soon, he only went to deliver something."

The woman nodded in relief. "Good, please see that he gets this when he returns."

She held the letter out to him, her bony arm encased in damp and frayed clothing. Matthew took it slowly, suspicious of the heavy odd shape inside the letter. He lifted his eyes back to the woman.

"Excuse me if this seems rude, but I would like to know who you are and why you've shown such a mysterious interest in Will."

"I can tell you little. What's in that letter should at least partially answer your question. As for who I am, that's something William must be the first to know. Now if you'll excuse me, I must be going."

She didn't give Matthew a chance to respond before she turned and hurried out of the shed. He stared after her for a long moment still just as confused about this strange woman as before, if not more so. Finally, he looked at the letter in his hand. As to what was inside, he hadn't the slightest guess, but it filled him with foreboding.

⸎

Will smiled to himself as he walked through the streets on the way back to the shed. Jeremy and the others at the mill had been very grateful to him for repairing the shaft, and it made him happy to have been able to help them. When he reached the shed, he walked inside expecting to see

Matthew still busy at work, but instead he found him waiting near the door.

"She was here, Will."

This stunned Will. "What?"

Matthew nodded. "She came in shortly after you left."

"What did she want?"

"She wanted me to give you this." Matthew handed him the folded letter.

Will turned it over in his hands, shocked and confused. Resting his eyes on the front of the crinkled and stained paper, he saw his name, William, written clearly in black ink. He found himself first wondering how the woman had known his name and then thinking that it was strange she had not included his surname.

"Do you know what it is?" Will asked continuing to inspect the dingy packet.

Matthew shook his head. "All she said was that it's a letter. What else is in there, I don't know."

Will looked up at him. "Did you find out who she is?"

"No." At his young friend's hopeful look, Matthew was regretful. "She said it was something you must be the first to know. She also said that what was in the letter would partially answer the question of why she has been following you."

Looking back to the letter, Will turned it over again. There was no reason to hesitate. If it would answer even some of their questions, he would be grateful for that after the unrest her presence had caused. Carefully he broke the wax seal and began unfolding the letter. Tipping it, the object inside slipped out causing Will to have a sharp intake of breath. He could barely believe what he saw. The missing half of his locket lay in the palm of his hand.

Made out of the same oval shaped metal, the rounded outside was intricately designed just like the other half, his half. On the inside it was flat and smooth, and words were engraved there in the same way his name was engraved on the half he had possessed all these years. Will was barely able to breathe as he read the words.

Will's eyes climbed slowly to Matthew's. "It looks like the other half to the locket I was given as a child."

They stared at each other for a long moment, and then Will walked quickly to the door leading into the house. Going to his room, he pulled open his nightstand drawer and took out the locket. Though there really was no doubt, Will had to be sure the piece was indeed the one that matched his. Putting them together, their two hinged sides fit together perfectly. Slowly Will opened the halves and read the engraved words together. *William Jonathan James, Beloved Son of Edward and Marie.* Tears stung at his eyes as he read the words. To finally know his parents' names was a feeling he could not describe.

Will heard the floorboards creak behind him and knew Matthew was there. He turned to him.

"It's the other half," Will said, his voice thick with emotion. "It has my parents' names engraved in it." He handed the locket to Matthew so he could read it for himself.

"How would that woman have gotten this?" Matthew wondered incredulously.

Will remembered the letter in his hand. He finished unfolding it and began to read aloud.

I know this has been a big mystery to you, but I can explain now. Please come to the table at the tavern where you sat with your friends, and I will answer all of your questions.

Will and Matthew looked at each other.

"Do you think she means right away?" Will asked.

Matthew shrugged. "Since she doesn't say when I would expect she wanted you to come as soon as you received this," he reasoned. "She asked me twice when you'd get back."

Will stood for a moment in an uncertain silence. "Do you think I should go?" A part inside was desperate to find out what he could from the woman, but another part wasn't as sure.

Matthew was hesitant to encourage Will but it seemed the only way Will would learn anything. "This woman obviously knows something about you and where you came from. If you want to find out then I think you should go."

Will was silent again before finally nodding. "I do. I will go."

He was still unsure, but he knew if he didn't go, he would forever question the decision.

Will's mind raced as he walked towards the tavern. What would he learn from this woman? The good he hoped for or bad things as he feared? Whatever it would be, he was still in shock over just the little he had already learned.

The tavern came quickly into view, and Will's heart pounded. Reaching the door, he paused briefly to pray quietly.

"God, please help me with whatever I might learn."

Will pushed open the door and walked into the tavern which was very full due to the weather. Looking to his right, in the corner where he'd been the night before, he saw the woman sitting alone at the table. Her gaze stayed fixed on him as he walked slowly to the table and sat down across from her. Both could tell that the other was nervous.

Will spoke first. "Who are you and . . . how did you get this?" He held up the completed locket, his eyes almost pained in their intensity.

The woman's first words to him were not in answer to his question. "I'm glad they gave it to you." She smiled slightly, apparently in relief. "I was afraid they might not have."

Will remained silent, waiting for her to answer his question. All trace of the woman's smile vanished, and she gazed at Will with serious eyes.

"William . . . " she began slowly. "I am your mother, Marie."

With those words, Will experienced the shock of his life. As obvious as the news now seemed, it was the very last thing he had ever expected her to say.

"You're . . . my mother?" he stammered in a low voice.

Marie nodded.

As the shocking news slowly started to sink in, Will's thoughts were overrun with all the things he'd heard and thought about this woman who had turned out to be his very own mother. Her frail, sickly appearance, the things Barlow had told them about her drinking, and the noticeably immodest clothes she wore. He could barely believe that she was his mother or maybe it was more that he didn't want to believe it.

Somehow, Marie could sense his thoughts.

"Whatever you think about me," she said awkwardly, "I want you to know that your father was a very good man, and from what I've seen and heard, you are just like him."

Though Will found this news comforting, he was disheartened by her use of past tense when speaking of his father.

"Was?"

Marie lowered her gaze. "I'm afraid he is dead."

Will's heart sank. Though he had lived all his life believing his parents were likely dead, it still hurt to be told as much. It hurt especially because, though Marie had barely told him anything, he felt that his father was someone he would have loved to know.

"I'm sorry to have to tell you that, William," Marie said apologetically.

Her words pulled Will's attention back to the present. Looking at this woman now reminded him of the question which had haunted him his whole life. Why had he been abandoned? Now, seeing the kind of woman his mother was, he could understand how it had happened, but it still hurt him deeply.

"I was told you left me with a woman and that she put me in the orphanage because she couldn't care for me. Why?" His voice plainly expressed the hurt and confusion of years.

"I lied to the women at the orphanage," Marie confessed. "I was the one who left you there."

The confession only made Will feel worse since it meant that his mother had completely abandoned him instead of leaving him with someone she trusted could care for him better. It is what he'd always believed and hoped was true.

Man or not, no one could know the enduring pain of the abandoned child. "Why did you just leave me?"

Marie lowered her eyes in shame. She hated talking about her past.

"It's a fortunate thing that I did," she said, her voice hardening. "You've grown up better than even your father could have hoped."

"I need to know why you left me." Will couldn't settle for anything less than the truth.

Marie sighed and knew she had to tell him everything. "I had no money. I worked as a bargirl in St. Thomas and what little I made I spent buying drinks for myself. I couldn't feed or take care of you so one night I took you to the orphanage."

Will swallowed hard. "My father was dead then?"

Marie shifted uncomfortably. "No, he wasn't."

"Why wasn't I with him?"

Marie didn't answer for a moment, stalling. "Because. . . I took you from him."

Will could barely comprehend these words. "What do you mean?"

Sighing in defeat, Marie decided to tell him the whole story. He would learn it anyway by asking questions.

"We lived in England. You were our first and only child and your father couldn't have been more proud. He adored you. But . . . I had fallen in love with someone else. . ." Marie watched the look of disbelief come to Will's face, but she continued. "At that time we lived in a small house and didn't have much money. I wanted to do more than just stay at home. Yes, I know it was my job as a mother to do that, but I just wasn't meant for it.

"There was a businessman named Brandon. Your father and I grew up with him. At one time, they were friends, but Brandon became jealous of your father, especially after he married me. You see, Brandon had wanted to marry me as well, but your father asked first." She shrugged. "After we were married, Brandon tried to convince me that I'd made a mistake. He kept offering me things secretly and making promises. Shortly after you were born, I gave in and believed him.

"One night he came to the house and told your father that he and I were going to leave and that we were taking you with us. Your father wanted to stop us, he tried, but Brandon had a gun. Before we left your father gave me some things he wanted you to have. That locket is one of them.

"Brandon and I left England then, but things were not as I had imagined they would be. Brandon hated you. I think it was because you were a reminder of your father. It wasn't long before he said that either I had to get rid of you or he'd leave. As terrible as you think I am, I would never have chosen him over you. Brandon left me in St. Thomas with no money, no extra clothes, and no means of survival. The job at the tavern was the only one I could find. After a couple of months, I realized I couldn't take care of you and that's why

61

I put you in the orphanage. I was honestly afraid that you would die."

"But why didn't you take me back to my father?" Will questioned, horrified by all that she had told him.

"I had no means of doing that and . . . to be honest, I didn't want him to know what happened," Marie answered.

Overwhelmed, Will tried to digest everything he'd been told. He found it very difficult to imagine how anyone could do all that his mother had done and then simply abandon her child knowing his father clearly longed to see him again. It was beyond his understanding.

An uncomfortable silence followed and lengthened. Finally, Will asked, "Why did you keep one half of the locket?"

"I wanted a way to prove my identity if we ever met."

Will sighed heavily. It was all so very depressing.

But Marie had one more bit of information. "The locket isn't the only thing your father wanted you to have. There is more."

"More?" Will wondered if there would yet be any good to this story.

"He gave me a letter for you when we left and then . . . about two years afterward, a letter from him somehow miraculously found its way to me. Inside was another letter he wanted me to give to you when you were older. It seems he has a friend in Lucea. Your father left something with this man, something that he wanted you to have."

Will felt a wealth of emotion well up inside at the prospect of even this small contact with his father. "Do you know what it is?"

Marie shook her head slowly. "It must be something of value though . . ." Her words trailed off into silence.

"Where are the letters?" Will asked.

"I didn't feel comfortable bringing them here so I hid them safely in the forest, not far from here." Marie got up from the table and said, "Come, I'll get them for you."

Will stood and followed her out of the tavern. It was darker outside than when he'd arrived, but still no rain fell. Marie led him away from the tavern and into the forest which bordered the city. They had not gone far when Marie stopped and turned to Will. She had an odd look on her face, as though uncertain.

"William . . . I . . . I'm sorry . . ."

Will frowned, wondering the reason for her apology, and then he heard the snap of a stick behind him. He spun around, but saw nothing before something hard smashed into his head, and he fell.

Chapter Five

Slowly, Will's mind began to clear as consciousness returned. His head throbbed painfully, and he felt a wetness trickling down the side of his face. Whether or not it was blood, he did not know because it had begun to rain.

When he tried to move his arms, he found them bound tightly to the tree behind him. After blinking several times, he slowly raised his head and focused on the broken down side wall and roof of an old building directly in front of him. Standing beneath it, sheltered from the rain, was his mother and six rough-looking men.

When Marie saw that Will was conscious, she hurried to his side. Kneeling down, she reached out to inspect a large cut on his forehead from which blood was indeed seeping and asked, "Are you all right?"

Will did not answer and instead turned his head away from her hand. He didn't want her sympathy or help. She, his own mother, had betrayed him, and the pain he felt because of it was beyond description. Marie let her hand fall away with a look of remorse. Yet, Will could not stop himself from turning back to her.

"How can you be my mother?" The pain he was feeling caught in his voice and contorted his face.

Tears pooled in Marie's eyes. "I'm so sorry, Will. You must believe that I had no choice."

Will shook his head. He could not, would not, believe it. His attention was drawn to the sound of one man. The authority in his voice and his stance identified him as the leader.

"Bring 'im over here," he said in a hard voice.

A smaller, wiry man pulled out a knife and strode over to Will. He sliced through the rope that bound Will to the tree, but Will's hands remained tied. The man took hold of his arm and jerked him to his feet. Will was shoved toward the others and then yanked to an abrupt stop in front of the leader. He was a dark-haired sailor, quite big and muscular, a little bigger even than Skye's father. His cold, hard stare was very intimidating.

"What do you want with me?" Will demanded, holding his gaze firmly.

The man was amused. "Ah, the young Mr. James. My name is Dreger. I'm sure yer wonderful and caring mother has told you about the letters yer father left you, particularly the one informing you to retrieve somethin' from one of yer father's friends. The fact is, I need that item, and I need you to help me get it."

"I won't help you do anything," Will told him defiantly.

"You'd best let me finish before you make any decisions like that," Dreger warned. "Not only do I need you to get me the item, I need your help securin' a ship to Lucea. Seein' as how yer such good friends with Daniel McHenry that should not be a problem."

"No," Will declared firmly, shaking his head. "I will not let you involve them in thi—."

Dreger cut his words short by backhanding him. Marie quickly stepped between them.

"Stop it!" she cried, but Dreger roughly shoved her away.

"Watch it, Marie," he hissed. "I warned you about interferin'."

"You said he wouldn't get hurt!"

Dreger paid no heed to her words for he had already turned his attention back to Will. Spitting out some blood from his bottom lip, Will glared at Dreger.

"I *will not* endanger my friends."

Dreger narrowed his eyes. "Let me be more specific. If you do not cooperate, shall we say somethin' may just happen to a certain young woman . . ."

The threat and the thought of Skye and all she had gone through so short a time ago shot instant fear through Will. Dreger could see it in his expression. It pleased him.

"Good, now that we're both on the same page, let me explain again what it is I need you to do. As soon as it is dark, which won't be long, we are goin' over to the McHenry house and you are gonna explain to them what we need. For their sake, you'd better hope they comply. Then, in the morning, providin' we have the ship, we are goin' to Lucea and you are gonna get me what I want. Now, if everyone cooperates, no one will get hurt."

"How do I know that?" Will asked. "You obviously told the same lie to my mother."

"Well, you're just gonna hafta believe it because it ain't gonna change anything one way or another," Dreger told him. He looked at one of the other men. "Tie him back to the tree."

Will was pushed back out into the rain which was now falling steadily. He could hear Marie protest.

"Why can't he stay in here?" she demanded.

"Because I say 'e goes out," Dreger shot back. "If you want to go out there too and share in his hardships then be my guest. You are his mother, after all."

Marie tried again, but then fell silent. The men forced Will to sit on the muddy ground and his arms were again tied to the tree. Because it was a palm tree it offered little shelter from the downpour and it wasn't long before his clothes were soaked through. Hanging his head, Will immediately began to pray. It was all that could be done in his situation. He had no answer for why God would allow this to happen, but he knew God was the only hope for rescue that he had.

Will heard footsteps as he prayed and looked up to find his mother standing beside him.

"You don't have to stand out here," Will murmured, looking away. Her presence made him uncomfortable, and he preferred sitting alone in the rain rather than wondering what he should say to her.

"I feel that I do," Marie told him softly. "I know you probably don't believe me and have every reason not to, but I *am* sorry. I didn't think they would treat you like this."

"That makes little difference. You betrayed me."

For this, Marie had no excuse and silence fell between them once more.

After a bit she could not help saying, "You looked like you were praying before."

Her observation surprised Will, and he looked up at last.

"I was."

"Your father prayed a lot too," Marie remembered. "He spoke about God like He was a good friend or even family."

"He is. He is our Father."

"I'm afraid I never knew Him like that."

"You still can," Will said simply.

Marie laughed a hard, cynical laugh. "After all the things I've done . . ." She shook her head.

As Will watched her and heard her words, his feelings of hurt, though not assuaged, were pushed aside a little by pity, and he began to regret his coldness towards her.

"God shares His love with anyone who will accept it," he told his mother, "no matter what you've done."

Marie's face was emotionless. "Perhaps."

She reached up and pulled her shawl tighter around her shoulders, but, by now, it was soaking wet and could offer her little warmth. With his eyes still on her, Will said, "You should get out of the rain."

Marie opened her mouth to speak, but no words came. She turned her head away from the son she had failed and walked silently back to the shelter. Will watched her, his feelings torn. She had betrayed him, but Will also knew she'd had a horrible life and though it was hard to believe, he could see that her remorse was genuine.

The air cooled drastically as darkness approached. It was Will's only indicator of time which was passing with agonizing slowness. His body began to shake as the cold rain continued to pelt down and drench his clothes. He tried not to show it, but he longed for some bit of warmth though not only physically.

Rain hammered against the glass, and the wind could be heard picking up outside. Night had fallen and all that could be seen through the windows was ink-like darkness, but inside, the warm sitting room glowed with light from oil lamps and the crackling logs in the fireplace. Skye, once again in her nightgown and robe, sat next to her father on the sofa, her head resting comfortably on his shoulder. His voice filled the room as he read to her from one of her favorite books. Caleb sat in a chair across from them, next to the fireplace, staring at the flames as he listened as well. For Skye, it was more than enough to make up for the missed breakfast together.

A loud knock on the front door suddenly shattered the wonderful peacefulness. Skye started and lifted her head. Her father and Caleb glanced at each other with puzzled frowns.

"Who could that be at this time of night?" Daniel wondered, concerned that someone might be in need.

Caleb could only shrug as he stood. Daniel rose as well and hurried towards the foyer as the knock came again. Whoever it was seemed desperate. Skye and Caleb were right behind him as Daniel quickly unlocked the door and opened it to the unpleasant elements outside. In stepped Matthew, water streaming from his hair and cloak.

"Is Will here?" he asked before any other words could be spoken.

The question as well as the way he asked it, his voice full of worry, sent a sharp pang of fear through Skye, and her heart began to pound.

"No, he isn't," Daniel answered, immediately concerned for Will's well-being.

"Has he been here at all?"

"No. I've not seen him since last night."

Matthew's shoulders sagged as the last of his hopefulness vanished. "This afternoon, while he was out briefly, that woman came in with a letter for him. When he returned we opened it to find the missing piece to a locket he's had since he was a child. We knew then that she must know something about where he came from so he went to meet her at the tavern. That was about three o'clock this afternoon. When it started to get dark I was worried so I went over there and Barlow said that Will and the woman had left not too long after Will got there. That means that Will has been out somewhere for the past six hours, and I know he would have come and told me if he planned to be gone that long."

Skye's heart pounded furiously. "We have to find him," she said desperately.

Daniel quickly snapped out of the shock Matthew's words had caused and stepped immediately over to a wardrobe along the wall. He pulled out a coat and tossed it to Caleb before pulling out his own. He looked at Skye.

"I know you will not like this, but you need to stay here."

"But—"

"Skye. Someone needs to be here if Will comes looking for us."

Skye swallowed. "Yes, Father."

Daniel and Caleb hurriedly put on their coats, and Skye murmured quietly, "Please, God, let Will be all right and please show them where he is."

Her desperate prayer came as tears welled up in her eyes, but she quickly blinked them away knowing she needed to stay strong.

"I think you should get your swords," Matthew suggested ominously. The anxiety in his voice, the dread in their hearts, was not comforting to any of them.

Daniel nodded. He and Caleb had just turned for the weapon cabinet when another knock surprised them. They looked at each other with hope, and Daniel reached for the door. But as soon as he had turned the doorknob and begun to open the door, it was pushed open forcefully. Skye gasped as Will was shoved into the room by a group of men and her hand went to her mouth. Bright red blood ran down one side of his face and neck, and his chin too was stained with blood. His clothes were soaked and muddy. By the defeated look in his eyes, she could see just how miserable he was, and it made her heart ache. Skye then felt her father's protective hands on her shoulders as he pulled her closer to him. Matthew was about to reach for his sword, but stopped when he noticed that the one of the men had a pistol pressed against Will.

"That's right," Dreger said with a cruel grin. "Don't try anything foolish. Take off the sword and toss it over here."

Matthew gingerly slipped off the sword belt and tossed it to Dreger's waiting men.

"What is this?" Daniel demanded.

Dreger looked at Will. "Tell 'im."

He pushed his pistol harder into Will's ribs. Will grimaced slightly, looking first at Skye and then tearing his eyes away to address Daniel.

"I've learned my father left something for me with a friend of his in Lucea. They want me to get it for them," he explained, inclining his head toward the men. "They want you to take us there with the *Grace*."

"What do you say, Captain McHenry?" Dreger asked. "All you need to do is take us there and no one will get hurt."

"It seems that's already an untrue statement," Daniel said, referring to Will's condition.

"I'm talkin' about the rest of you," Dreger replied with a glare. "It would be a pity for somethin' to happen to that lovely daughter of yers, would it not?"

Skye's heart skipped nervously, and she felt her father grow tense.

"And what will happen once we reach Lucea?" Daniel wanted to know.

"As soon as I get what I want, you'll be free to return home."

Daniel capitulated. "When do you want to sail?"

"First thing in the morning," Dreger answered.

"I don't know if my crew can be ready that quickly." Under an emergency, Daniel knew they could, but he hoped to buy some time.

Dreger shook his head. "I don't want a full crew. Five at the most should be sufficient, and they will have to be ready. Do we have an understanding?"

Daniel stared at him for a long moment. "Yes," he answered finally.

Dreger smiled. "Good, now if you would be so kind as to offer us some hospitality, we are all rather cold and wet."

"There is a fire in the sitting room," Daniel said with reluctance.

Dreger nodded in satisfaction. Turning his attention to Will he said, "I don't have to worry about you, do I?"

Will didn't answer, but it wasn't necessary for Dreger had already warned him quite explicitly what would happen if he caused trouble. Knowing he would not attempt anything, Dreger slipped his pistol into his belt and pulled out his knife to cut the bindings from Will's hands. Once he was free, Will stepped away from Dreger and towards Skye knowing how hard this was for her. Skye reached out and took his ice cold hands in hers.

"Are you all right?" Her voice, barely more than a whisper, was full of ragged emotion.

Will nodded, his loving eyes sinking gratefully into hers.

Skye wanted to ask him what had happened, but her attention was drawn back to Dreger as he and his men took off their coats and tossed them thoughtlessly into a sopping heap in a nearby chair. Daniel, Caleb, and Matthew took theirs off knowing they wouldn't be going anywhere. Thankful to finally be able to rid himself of some of his wet clothes, Will removed his coat as well, and Daniel took it from him to hang it up. Meanwhile, Dreger gave orders to his men.

"I want someone guardin' this door and a coupla men to search the house for weapons."

Two men left the group to start the search and one took his place at the door. Satisfied, Dreger looked at Daniel.

"Now. Would you care to show us to the sittin' room?" he said haughtily.

I'd far rather show you the door, Daniel thought, but he gestured and turned towards the sitting room doorway.

He led Skye along with him, keeping himself between her and Dreger. Will and Caleb and Matthew followed with Dreger and his men close behind. It was not until then that Skye first noticed Marie. Because Skye did not yet know who Marie was, she was confused to see how sullen and remorseful the woman looked even though she seemed to be working with Dreger.

In the sitting room, Dreger and his men quickly claimed the couches and comfortable chairs leaving the others to carry in chairs from the adjacent dining room. Skye put one close to the fire and told Will to sit down after which she carefully examined the wound on his forehead.

"How did this happen?" she asked.

Will began to speak, but Dreger cut him off.

"My sword hilt." There was a tone of pride in his voice.

Skye shot a glare in his direction. "You could have killed him." Just speaking those words sent a chill through her body.

"Well, it's a good thing I didn't, ain't it?" he jeered.

Skye would never understand the extent of some people's cruelty. She knew it would be best to try to ignore Dreger, but it would be hard.

"I'll get some water and something to put on that cut," she told Will gently.

As Skye turned to go to the kitchen, one of Dreger's men stood to follow her. They were keeping a close watch on anyone leaving the room. Seeing him, Daniel walked over to Skye.

"I'll go with you," he told her while at the same time giving the other man a warning look.

Skye led the way into the kitchen where she took a kettle of warm water from the stove which she had earlier intended to use for tea. She poured it into a large bowl and grabbed several clean cloths. Going to the medicine cabinet, she took out a bottle of ointment, and they returned to the

73

sitting room. Her father pulled a small table and a chair up beside Will to make it easier for her. Skye set the medical supplies down on the table, but before sitting down, she went to get a quilt out of the cupboard.

"Here," she said quietly as she laid it around Will's shoulders for she had noticed that he was still shivering.

"Thank you," he said, giving her a hint of a smile, something he hadn't yet done since arriving.

Skye picked up one of the cloths and soaked it in the water. As she began gently cleaning the blood from Will's face and cut, the men that had been searching the house came into the room carrying several weapons. They set them down on a table near Dreger.

"We found all of these in a cabinet and this one was under the girl's bed." One of the men held up a wooden case containing Skye's sword.

Dreger opened the case and inspected the weapon. He looked at Skye. "An odd item to be found under a young woman's bed."

"Not if she knows how to use it," Skye replied flatly.

"Indeed."

Dreger seemed amused by her, and Skye found it very discomforting. She quickly busied herself once again tending to Will and prayed fervently for God to protect them, to help them out of this distressing situation.

There was a short lull during which Skye calmed somewhat, but she cringed at hearing Dreger's voice again. This time he addressed Will.

"It seems, William James, that you have been remiss. There is someone here you have forgotten to introduce." He gave Will no chance to speak. "This," he said gesturing towards Marie, "is Marie James. Oh, excuse me," he said dramatically, "Marie Clark, as she prefers to be called. She is. . ." He let a suspenseful second develop. ". . . his mother."

Stunned, Skye and her father, and Caleb and Matthew, all wore the same expressions of shock. Skye looked at Will, unable to believe it. He met her eyes and nodded, proving that it was true. They all turned their eyes to Marie who was looking very uncomfortable. Enjoying her discomfort, Dreger grinned cruelly.

"Why don't you tell 'em how much you've been helpin' us, Marie," he urged.

Marie could take no more of it.

"Stop it, Dreger!" she cried. "I was never willing to help you. You forced me to!"

"It seems, if I remember correctly, that you were just as interested in gettin' that item of yer son's as we were," Dreger countered.

"That was before I found out how you would do it."

"The fact still remains that you did intend to steal from 'im."

For this, Marie had no defense. Dreger had trapped her.

"But I never intended for him or anyone else to be hurt," she murmured miserably, hoping that Will and the others would somehow believe her, but their blank stares were unreadable.

Marie retreated to a corner, as silence settled over them once again. Skye finished helping Will, feeling better once all the blood was gone from his face, but it still bothered her to see it staining the collar of his shirt. Daniel had wanted Caleb to take Will upstairs to get a change of clothes, but Dreger refused to allow it.

Hardly a word was spoken for the next quarter hour. Finally, Will looked over at Marie and caught her gaze.

"Do you have my father's letters?" he asked.

Marie nodded.

"May I at least read them?"

"Yes, of course." As if afraid Dreger might stop her, Marie stood quickly and went over to him. She reached into her pocket and pulled out two crinkled letters which she placed in Will's hands. "The first letter is the one your father gave me the night we left. The second is the one that explains what he has left you."

Slowly, Will turned the first letter over. The seal was obviously already broken so he unfolded it with the utmost care, laying eyes for the first time on the words his father had written. Immediately, his throat closed and emotion began building up inside him.

My Dearest Son, William,

If you are reading this, you probably don't even know me, but I want you to know that I love you and will always love you even if it comes to pass that I will never have the joy of seeing you again. You are one of God's greatest gifts to me and even if He only allowed me to enjoy you for a very short period of time, I will be forever thankful. Still, everyday I will pray to Him for your return. I will also pray daily for His protection over you and that somehow He will find a way into your life...

It was here that Will had to pause for a moment as he brought his hand to his eyes to wipe away the tears blurring his vision. He was overwhelmed by the realization that Skye was a direct answer to his father's prayers. She was the one who had led him to God. Feeling Skye rest her hand on his arm, Will fought to regain control and brought his hand away from his eyes to lay it on hers as he continued to read.

...I pray that God blesses you in your life and fills it with goodness and with people to cherish. I will always watch for your return, and you will always be welcome.
Your Father, Edward James

Will took a deep breath as he finished. All but one of his father's prayers had been answered and he thanked God with all of his heart that they had been. Especially now that he knew what his life could have turned out like if he had been left in the care of his mother. Still his heart was heavy with an intense longing to know his father, one which could never be fulfilled until he reached Heaven.

Will turned his eyes to Skye and gave her the letter, wishing to share his father's wonderful words.

"Are you sure?" Skye asked.

"Yes," Will answered. "The others can read it too."

As Skye began to read, Will opened the second letter.

Dear William,

At this time, I know you are three years old, although I don't expect you to get this letter until you are much older. It seems doubtful that you may ever receive it, but however doubtful it may be, I trust that God will somehow get it into your hands if that is what He wishes. The purpose of this letter is to tell you of something I would like you to do, though it is your choice to be made. I have a friend named Jacob Tucker, and I pray that he will still be living when you receive this. He lives in Lucea, Jamaica, and I have left in his possession something I wish for you to have. My hope is that it will provide you with joy and help you in your life.

Forever Your Loving Father, Edward

When he had finished, Will pondered the question of what his father could have left him, but even though he wanted that link, it paled in comparison to reading the words of his father's heart. He looked at Skye who was just finishing the first letter and saw her wiping at streaks of tears falling down her soft cheeks. He took her hand as he handed her the second letter and continued to hold it as she read.

He looked at Marie. "You said he gave you the first letter the night we left?"

"Yes," Marie answered quietly.

"How did he know to write it?"

Marie shook her head with shame. "He must have suspected I was going to leave. Looking back, I think it was obvious."

Filled with compassion for a man he had never met, Will thought about how hard it must have been for his father to write a letter, knowing that he would be losing someone he loved so much.

Chapter Six

As dawn crept in the next morning, the sky was gray, but the wind and rain had ceased sometime during the night. Skye sighed wearily. Her body felt stiff and achy. Though she had been able to sleep on and off, sitting in the hard wooden chair had taken its toll. She looked around at the faces of her friends and her father, finding them tired and gloomy at best. There was little contrast but some small measure of gladness in her heart that Dreger and his men were looking bored and ill tempered from having to stay up all night to guard them.

Needing to be active and wanting to be useful, Skye stood, stretching her tired muscles. She knew everyone would be hungry, especially Will because he hadn't had supper.

"I'm going to make breakfast," she murmured, touching Will's arm and glancing toward her father.

Daniel rose to go with her, as did one of Dreger's men. In the kitchen, she set about making a meal as quickly as she could. She knew she had to make a great deal more than usual because Dreger and his men were bound to eat a lot. Skye was very glad for her father's help otherwise it would have taken her much longer to accomplish. Half an hour later the food and dishes were set out on the large dining room table. Everyone came in from the sitting room, and the chairs at the table were quickly filled by Dreger and his men, leaving everyone else to stand.

As the meal progressed, Dreger looked at Skye. "Yer a very fine cook, Miss McHenry," he said with a grin.

Skye was tempted to tell him that she would have poisoned the food if not for her father and friends, but she kept silent and picked at her food unable to find her appetite.

Dreger and his men ate quickly wanting to be on their way so it was not long before they were finished. Skye carried the dishes back into the kitchen, knowing that she couldn't take time to wash them so she threw away the uneaten food and stacked the dishes neatly next to the wash tub. She barely had time to finish before Dreger ordered everyone into the sitting room.

"All right, now," he boomed, "we're gonna decide once and for all who's goin' and who's stayin'."

"My daughter is staying here," Daniel declared.

Before Skye could protest, not wanting to be separated from Will, Dreger shook his head.

"No, she ain't," he stated. "She is what's makin' sure you continue to cooperate, and I intend to keep it that way."

In a way, Skye was relieved to be going, but she could see how worried her father was.

Dreger pointed to Caleb. "Is he part of yer crew?"

"He's my first mate," Daniel confirmed.

"All right then, you only need four more of yer crewmen to join us." Dreger looked next to Matthew. "Seein' as how you are not part of the crew and have a job here, you are gonna stay. I don't want people gettin' suspicious at yer departure." Matthew looked like he was going to protest, but Dreger quickly made sure he didn't by warning, "And there better not be any trouble about it."

This maddened Matthew, but he didn't argue. "Then let me at least return home to get Will some of his clothes. I think if people saw him walking around in a bloodstained shirt it surely would arouse suspicion."

Dreger pondered that for a moment and realized Matthew was right. "Fine, but one of my men will go with you, and if he has any trouble along the way, I promise you someone will get hurt. And be warned, you have fifteen minutes to get back here, so you'd better hurry."

Matthew wasted no time in leaving with one of Dreger's men trailing behind. Once the door had closed and they were gone, Dreger turned back to Daniel.

"Now Captain McHenry, we need the rest of yer men. I want you to send yer first mate out to secure four men of yer choice to meet us at the ship, and they'd better be quick about it. As with yer brother, one of my men will go with him, and alertin' anyone to yer plight will be done at yer own peril, understand?"

Daniel nodded solemnly and looked at Caleb. "Why don't you get Corey, Nick, Pete, and Jess."

Caleb knew that Daniel had chosen those four men because they were the only ones who didn't have families they'd have to leave. He sent Daniel an earnest look. "I'll see you at the ship. We'll start loading the supplies we need."

Skye turned to her father when Caleb had left and said, "I need to go upstairs to dress and get some of my clothes."

Daniel looked at Dreger. "May I take my daughter up to her room so she can pack some clothes for the trip?"

Dreger allowed it with a silent nod. Skye and Daniel started towards the doorway to the foyer but stopped as he spoke.

"Go with 'er, Marie, and get some clothes for yerself."

Marie frowned. "But they belong to Miss McHenry."

"So? I'm tired of seein' you dressed like some beggar from the street," Dreger spat harshly.

81

Marie looked back and forth between Dreger and Skye not knowing what to do. Finally, Skye nodded and said quietly, "Come with me."

Uncomfortable, Marie followed Skye and Daniel upstairs. Skye led Will's mother into her bedroom and closed the door while her father stood just outside to guard it from Dreger's men. Neither woman spoke for a long and awkward moment as Skye went to her wardrobe to look at her dresses.

"You don't have to give me any of your best ones," Marie murmured, mortified by her circumstances.

Skye glanced back over her shoulder but didn't know what to say to this woman. She knew that Marie had hurt Will deeply, and was finding it difficult to want to be kind, but she kept reminding herself of what God would want her to do. She also remembered what little Will had been able to tell her privately during the night. Marie didn't have a personal relationship with God, and Will pitied her despite what she had done. For a moment, Skye paused briefly, closing her eyes and praying silently. *God, help me show her kindness and let her see You in that kindness.* Opening her eyes again, she focused on the contents of her wardrobe.

"Here." Skye pulled out a couple of gowns and petticoats that her grandfather had bought her. "You can have these." She laid the dresses down on the bed near Marie and retrieved two duffels from beneath it. One was smaller than the other and Skye handed Marie the larger one knowing the dresses would take up more room than what she was planning to pack. "You can put the extra clothing in this one."

"Thank you," Marie whispered, overcome.

Skye nodded and walked over to her dresser. Pulling open two of the drawers, she took out some white shirts, a couple of waistcoats, and three pairs of breeches and stockings. She set the pile of clothing down next to her duffel and took off her nightgown. She was soon dressed in one of the pairs of clothing she had laid out. Marie too had changed into a new dress. For a brief moment, the two studied each other, both looking quite different with a change of clothing.

Undeniably, Marie looked much better in the clean, better fitting dress. Skye tried to imagine her not so pale and skinny and could see a faint resemblance between Marie and Will. Marie's hair was not nearly so dark as Will's and her eyes were green, not brown. Skye guessed that Will looked far more like his father.

Marie's impression of Skye was a little bit of a surprise because she had never really seen a woman wear men's clothing, at least never one as nice and beautiful as Skye. Still, the clothes suited the Skylar McHenry that Marie had heard about, and she knew she was going to see the tougher, less ladylike side of Skye that hadn't been present during the night.

Skye snapped quickly out of her thoughts when she heard a voice from downstairs and then her father's.

"Dreger is calling us," Daniel urged through the door.

Skye and Marie hurriedly stuffed their clothes into their duffels. Before pulling the drawstrings closed, Skye grabbed three items from her dresser; her Bible, a portrait of her mother, and the portrait of Will. She put them inside the duffel, tied the strings, and went to open the door. She and Marie followed Daniel downstairs to the foyer.

Matthew had returned, and Will entered the foyer about the same time they did having changed clothes as well. Skye felt relief at seeing how much better he looked with clean clothes and his hair freshly pulled back though the dark cut was a constant reminder of their situation.

Dreger nodded in approval when he saw Marie. "That's better." He shifted his gaze then to Skye and grinned in an unsettling way. "Well, Miss McHenry, I'm not sure what I like more. You dressed as a woman or as a man."

Skye narrowed her eyes in displeasure before making a pointed move to ignore him.

Unaffected by her rebuff and anxious to be on their way, Dreger asked if everyone was ready to leave.

"We just need our coats," Daniel told him, knowing the weather was still rather cool out.

Walking over to the wardrobe, Daniel pulled Skye's coat out first, a long, dark leather coat that had once been Will's. He'd given it to her when he'd grown out of it, and it was the favorite of all Skye's coats. Will was handed his coat next, which had dried over night, and then Daniel took out his own. After Skye had put hers on, she walked up beside her father and pulled out one of her warm shawls. Turning, she gave it to Marie.

"It will be cool once we begin to sail," she said.

Marie was becoming ever more surprised by Skye's kindness. "Thank you."

"You are very welcome," Skye said softly. She heard Dreger snickering at them and glanced disdainfully at him as he turned and grabbed his coat from among the pile on the chair. Dreger then pulled his pistol from his belt and draped his coat over it and his arm, concealing the weapon. With a nod of satisfaction, he looked up and fixed his gaze on Skye. She shifted nervously.

"Come here," Dreger ordered.

There was a tense silence in the room. Finally, Skye took a few reluctant steps towards him and stopped. She flinched when he reached out, clamping a vice-like grip on her arm and yanking her closer. Daniel and Will both took an involuntary step towards them, but stopped at the warning whip-like glare Dreger shot them. Skye stood stiffly, wanting nothing more than to pull herself away from his grasp, but she knew it would only make things worse.

Dreger transferred his gaze to Daniel. "All right, Captain McHenry, you an' the boy lead the way. If there's no trouble, yer daughter gets there just fine, if there is . . ."

Skye heard the clicking of his pistol hammer and swallowed knowing how easily it could go off by accident.

"Fine, Dreger, but if that pistol goes off you won't be seeing Lucea, but rather a jail cell and the gallows," Daniel warned.

Dreger smirked and eased the hammer back into place.

"And now what of the people who will wonder where we've gone?" Daniel continued. "Like the rest of my crew?"

"He will take care of that." Dreger nodded at Matthew. "But I don't want to find anyone followin' us." His voice left no question as to the folly of that, nor what the outcome would be. "Now, let's go."

Dreger motioned towards the door. With a sigh of resignation, Daniel reached down to pick up Skye's duffel and he, Will, and Matthew stepped out the door. Dreger released Skye and pushed her forward. Outside, Dreger told Matthew to go back to the shed. Matthew traded solemn looks with Will and Skye and murmured quietly to Daniel, "I'll be praying for you all."

Daniel nodded gratefully. "Thank you."

Matthew turned reluctantly and walked away. With a sense that this could not be done until it had begun, Daniel guided everyone towards the docks. A pall of silence hung over them as they made their way along, and it seemed to Skye, Will, and Daniel to be the longest walk they'd ever taken to the beach. All were relieved they met no one on the way to which they'd have had to make an explanation to.

As the *Grace* came into view, they saw Caleb and four crewmen loading a few barrels and crates of supplies onto the ship. The man Dreger had sent with Caleb stood on the dock watching them. Caleb was obviously relieved to see that they had made it without incident.

"Is everything aboard?" Daniel asked when they had reached the dock.

Caleb nodded. "Corey and Jess just loaded the last of it."

Daniel nodded. "Good."

He led the way up the gangplank, and the crew followed as soon as they had untied the mooring lines. On deck, Pete, a middle aged man whom they had saved from a shipwreck when Skye was a child, walked over to Daniel. He glanced warily at Dreger and his men.

"What's going on, Captain?" he asked cautiously.

"I'll explain once we're on our way," Daniel told him loud enough that the rest of the crew could hear as well.

Pete nodded without further questioning. He and the others were already aware that something was not right, but they trusted Daniel completely and not one of them considered staying behind.

Making a quick visual inspection of the ship, Daniel proceeded to give the orders to weigh anchor and set course for Lucea. Because they were shorthanded, Skye and Will quickly stepped up to help do the extra work that needed to be done. Both, however, were quite happy to do it since keeping busy meant staying away from Dreger who stood at the quarterdeck watching them like a hawk. Meanwhile, his men conducted a search of the ship, likely checking for any weapons.

It was not long before Kingston was behind them and they were out at sea, sailing west along Jamaica's coastline. Once all the chores had been accomplished and no one was needed elsewhere, Daniel called the crew to the quarterdeck where he stood with Dreger and Caleb who was at the wheel. When everyone was present, Daniel looked at each one of the men.

"Yesterday, Will learned some things about his parents, one of which is that many years ago his father left him something with a friend in Lucea. I wish I could tell you that we are just taking him there to get it, but I can't. Mr. Dreger here, a stranger to all of us, wants the item as well. He can't get it without Will's cooperation, and ours. However, I'm sure you understand, our lack of cooperation will have dire consequences," he said pointedly.

The crew looked astonished by what Will had learned. There wasn't a one of them who hadn't grown to care genuinely for Will in the short time they'd known him. They were deeply shocked and offended by what Dreger was doing.

Dreger glared menacingly at them. "And let me inform every man here that if he causes me any bit of trouble it's Miss McHenry who's gonna suffer for it."

Everyone cast a concerned glance at Skye who stood unmoved by the threat. Each one of them looked on Skye as they would their own daughter or, in Nick's case, sister for he was only a couple of years older than she was. None of them would ever do anything that would jeopardize her safety.

"Now, as long as we're getting' things straight, let's discuss lodging," Dreger said looking at Daniel. "My men will stay in the forecastle with yers and you too will stay there as I will be takin' the liberty of usin' yer cabin." Daniel and the crew looked very displeased by this, but Dreger didn't give them a chance to say so. "Marie will stay with yer daughter in her cabin."

As much as they all wanted to oppose Dreger they knew they couldn't so they kept silent. They were glad at least that the trip from Kingston to Lucea was only a three day voyage, however those three days were likely to be a quite a challenge.

Chapter Seven

As nightfall set in, clouds which had blanketed the sky throughout the day began to break up. The sun shone from its position just above the horizon, and the sky was brilliantly painted with a pink sunset signaling clear weather the next day.

From the mainsail, the first sail of the mainmast, Will's gaze followed Skye as she crossed the deck below him and made her way to the very front of the ship. That was where she could be found at this time of evening whenever they sailed. Will glanced over his shoulder to the quarterdeck where Daniel was at the wheel as he had been for most of the day. Whether it was just to make things difficult or that he actually believed it, Dreger had insisted that Daniel and Caleb were the only ones skilled enough to get them to Lucea as fast as was possible and would not allow anyone else to man the wheel. Daniel had tried to tell him otherwise, but Dreger would not listen to reason.

"It's too bad the captain probably won't be joining her tonight." Jesse's voice quickly reminded Will that he was in the middle of a job helping the old crewman fix some loose rigging.

Will looked at him and sighed. "Yes, it is."

Daniel and Skye had watched the sunsets together since Skye was a child, but having just relieved Caleb at the helm, there didn't seem to be much chance that Daniel would be leaving any time soon.

A moment of silence followed until the rigging had been tightened.

"That oughta do it," Jesse said.

Will let go of the rope he had been holding and the two of them descended the ratlines. Once on deck, Will's eyes strayed to Skye again. He wanted to go to her, but not if Daniel still intended to join her somehow. Yet, when he caught sight of Daniel who seemed to know exactly what he was thinking, Daniel nodded to him, and Will took it to mean that he was telling him to go be with Skye.

Will crossed the half of the deck that lay before him to reach the forecastle deck at the front of the ship. Skye stood at the railing alongside where the bowsprit was attached and stretched out before the bow. As Will drew near, she looked at him over her shoulder and smiled.

"I'm glad you came up here," Skye said. "I don't enjoy it as much alone."

Will stopped beside her. "I'm sorry your father can't join you tonight."

Skye nodded and turned to look at her father manning the wheel. "I know. It's sad because I know he really enjoys it though I guess it isn't the best day to enjoy it anyway."

She turned back again to the sea and both were silent. Will unconsciously focused on the wooden figure just below the bowsprit. It was a woman with long flowing hair and a dress that ran down the stem of the ship. She had been carved specifically to look like Skye's mother, and as Will's eyes climbed up to look at Skye he realized again just how alike they would have looked. Not for the first time, Will wished he could have met Grace and found himself wondering how Daniel had been able to bear her death. He had loved her like Will loved Skye, and Will couldn't imagine the heartbreak Daniel had born. These thoughts set him once again to praying desperately for Skye's safety.

When Skye looked at Will a moment later, she found his expression hard to read. He was obviously deep in thought.

"What are you thinking about?" she asked.

Her words brought him out of his reverie and he smiled. "Your mother and how much you must look like her."

Skye gave him a funny little smile. "Really? Because I was just thinking about your mother. Though, I cannot say the same thing about you looking like her."

They shared a laugh over her words and both were very happy to see the other in a lighter mood even if it was only for a moment.

"No, I don't look very much like her, do I?" Will murmured.

Skye's smile lingered for only a fleeting moment before it disappeared as she stared down into the churning water rushing past the ship. The brief few moments of happiness were gone and reality had set in once again. Will continued to study her wishing there had been a way she would not have had to be affected by what was happening.

"Don't worry," he said gently, bringing her eyes back to him. "In another two days, we'll be sailing back home and everything will be all right."

Nonetheless, Skye's face showed sadness. "I will still feel bad for you though. To have found out who your parents are, to now know about your mother, and yet to not be able to have whatever it is your father left you . . ."

Will put his hand on hers. "As long as you are all right, and everyone else is all right, it does not matter. Finding out who my father was and reading the letter he wrote to me has given me something I never thought I would ever have. It is hard for me to know what my mother did, but it has only made me more thankful that God put you in my life and made it what it is despite all of the odds that were against me."

His words filled her with a quiet, thankful joy. Turning toward him fully, she wrapped her arms around him to give him a long hug. Will returned it readily, and Skye heard his whispered words in her ear.

"I love you, Skye."

"I love you too, Will."

Darkness fell around nine o'clock. Having decided the night's watch, Daniel again called everyone to the quarterdeck.

"There will be two four hour shifts. Caleb, Jess, Corey, and Nick have the first one. Skye, Will, Pete, and I will relieve you at one o'clock."

"Aye, Captain," the crew replied.

Caleb took over at the wheel when Daniel left the quarterdeck with Skye and Will and Pete. Marie followed silently from several yards behind.

Once below, Daniel stepped into his cabin to gather up a few of his things before they came to the small passage where Skye's cabin was located. When they stopped at the door, Daniel turned to Skye.

"I am going to sleep here outside your door," he told her.

Will was very much relieved to hear this having been worried that Skye would be sleeping away from the rest of them.

"Are you sure?" Skye asked, feeling bad for her father to have to sleep on the floor, but relieved just the same.

"Yes," he assured her before addressing Will and Pete. "You two go on and get some rest."

They nodded, but as Pete moved past Daniel, Will paused next to Skye.

"Good night," he said. "Try to sleep well, all right?"

"I will," she promised. "Good night, Will."

Will bid Daniel good night as well and followed after Pete to the forecastle. Skye's gaze stayed on him as he went, but was quickly drawn back to her father.

"Do you still have that dagger hidden in your mattress?" he asked her in a whisper.

Skye nodded grimly. "If Dreger's men didn't find it, yes."

"Good, keep it there," Daniel instructed.

A creaking caught their attention and proved to be Marie walking towards them shyly. She glanced briefly at Daniel before turning to Skye.

"I can sleep elsewhere if you wish," she offered.

Skye shook her head. "No, you are welcome to share my cabin."

She realized that the thought of having someone in her cabin made her feel better than being alone, even with her father outside.

"I will get some extra blankets for a bed," Daniel told Skye.

As her father walked away, Skye motioned for Marie to follow as she opened her door, and the two of the walked into the small cabin. The bunk that was built against one wall took up close to half of the space and a small nightstand and dresser stood next to it. There would be just enough room on the floor for one of them to sleep.

Skye lit a candle on the nightstand which cast a soft glow on the wooden walls and ceiling. Glancing at her bunk, she turned again to Marie.

"You can sleep in my bunk," Skye told her.

Marie looked surprised, her eyes meeting Skye's sparkling blue ones, and shook her head. "Thank you, but no, I won't do that. It is your bed. I want you to sleep there."

Skye did not insist. Her father returned a couple of minutes later with several blankets that Skye used to help Marie construct a bed. After it had been made, Skye closed her door and they began to prepare for sleep. Marie removed her gown and petticoats so that she was wearing only the chemise underneath. Skye only pulled off her boots and took off her waistcoat knowing that in four hours she'd need to get up. Getting into bed, she looked at her Bible which she'd set beside her and then at Marie.

"Do you mind if I read for a little while?" Skye asked.

"No, I don't," Marie answered.

Skye propped her pillow against the wall behind her and sat back. As she opened her Bible she prayed that God would comfort and encourage her through what she read. After several passages, He had done just that. Skye felt better than she had all day. Closing the book, she began to pray silently, thanking God for keeping everyone safe so far and asking Him to continue. When Skye had finished, she turned to set her Bible back on the nightstand and lay her pillow down. She had assumed that Marie was sleeping, but upon hearing her voice, Skye knew she was wrong.

"How long have you known Will?"

Skye was surprised by the sudden question and looked at her. Marie was staring up at the ceiling.

"Almost thirteen years."

"That is a long time. You must know him well."

"Yes."

Marie finally turned her head to look at Skye. "Despite what you might think, I do care what happens to him, and I never wanted this to happen."

Skye sighed. "Then why do you keep helping Dreger, and why do you never try to stop him?"

Skye didn't want to sound harsh, but she hoped to gain some small understanding of Marie's actions.

"Dreger threatened to kill me if I didn't help him. I was scared," Marie tried to explain. "What could I have done?"

Skye averted her gaze and didn't speak, thinking of the great difference between them. She would have done anything outside of disobedience to God before endangering Will. However, she kept these thoughts to herself having no reason or desire to make Marie feel worse than she obviously did already.

Turning, Skye blew out the candle and lay down. In the still darkness she slowly reached into a hidden pocket on the underside of her mattress. The cold polished handle of a small dagger met her fingertips. She pulled her hand out again with a quiet sigh and closed her eyes.

In the forecastle, Will lay in his hammock, eyes scanning the worn pages of his Bible in the light of the lantern hanging from the post above him. Lantern light also emanated across from him where Pete was reading. A low grumble was heard from one of Dreger's men a few hammocks down. Will glanced at him only briefly before continuing to read. Several seconds ticked by before the stillness was suddenly broken again when the man sat up angrily and glared at Will.

"Put out them lanterns or I'll do it for ya!" he barked.

Will looked over at Pete and, with a sigh, closed his Bible and slipped it onto the shelf beside him. Sitting up, he blew out the lantern. Pete did the same and the cabin was swallowed up by darkness. Will slid back down in his hammock and made himself comfortable. He heard a little rustling from the other man and then there was quietness again except for the rise and fall of breathing.

The dawn sky was clear as the sunset had predicted, but a fierce wind was picking up as the hours progressed. From where he stood with Skye and Pete, Will saw the others come up from below. Breakfast could not be eaten together as usual because every available person was needed on deck to keep the ship from drifting into the dangerous shallow water near the shoreline. The tension which had existed the day before had heightened with the weather. With such a small crew, one mistake could be disastrous.

That one mistake nearly came to fruition later that morning.

Skye had just finished tying down a line that had worked itself loose when she heard a loud snap just above her. She looked up immediately to see a main line on the mainsail had broken. The canvas was whipping around wildly, and it would only be minutes before the other lines snapped too from the strain. Pete, who was higher up on the mast, started quickly down to try to fix it. Everyone else was occupied up in other masts except for Jesse who hurried up to help Pete. Skye continued to watch them for a breathless moment but knew almost instantly that they were having trouble. It was not long before Pete called out.

"We need help up here!"

Skye would have gone up without hesitation, but knew that she would never be strong enough to help them. A quick look around proved there was no one besides her who could leave their position. Except for her father who was at the wheel. She ran up to the quarterdeck.

"I can take the wheel," she said.

Daniel didn't hesitate, knowing his daughter was fully capable of handling the ship, and he knew that Pete and Jesse needed help quickly. He made sure Skye had a good grip on the wheel before letting go and hurried towards the mainmast. On his way he heard Dreger begin to complain, but Daniel quickly cut him off.

"She's as good at the wheel as I am," Daniel told him brusquely, "and if I don't get up there to help my men, we'll lose the sail. That would be more of a delay than getting off course."

He started up the ratlines leaving Dreger standing effectively silenced behind him.

Skye glanced a few times at her father and the other men working valiantly to secure the mainsail, but otherwise kept her eyes glued to the choppy water in front of them. The wind and waves both were trying to force the ship towards land and it took a great deal of Skye's strength to keep the wheel straight.

A slice of apprehension cut through Skye as she saw, out of the corner of her eye, two of Dreger's men beginning to make their way up to the quarterdeck. She realized that they had found the *Grace's* small store of rum reserved only for sickness and injury. Both had an almost empty bottle in their hands, and it was obvious even with the swaying of the ship that they were already very intoxicated. Halfway up the stairs, one stopped and said something quietly which made the other laugh drunkenly. As they continued up, Skye gripped the wheel firmly and focused straight ahead, trying to ignore them when they reached the top. She tensed as one stepped closer.

"Wanna drink?" he asked.

Skye moved as far away as she could. "No."

"Ah, come on, have a drink."

Skye saw him holding out the bottle and shook her head. "I'm trying to do a job here, leave me alone."

"Come on," the man insisted. He put the bottle in front of her face and the smell of alcohol turned her stomach.

"Stop it." Skye gritted her teeth and turned her head away, but the man persisted and became more insistent. Finally Skye had no choice but to take one of her hands off the wheel to try to fend him off.

"Stop it!" she said again.

As she had feared, the wheel suddenly slipped in her hand, and the ship began to pitch. Seeming not to notice, the man continued his intention to force the drink on her, but Skye was able to grab the wheel with both hands again to set it straight. Becoming irritated with her stubbornness, the man grabbed her arm. Skye tried to shrug him off, but her effort would have done little if he had not been suddenly yanked away from her and pushed into the railing near his friend.

"Leave her alone!" Will glared at them angrily.

The two men glared back at him before looking at each other. They rushed forward suddenly and grabbed Will who tried to pull away from them, but could not despite his strength. Knowing she could not leave the wheel, Skye could only watch and try to dissuade them with her voice. To her horror, the man who had wrestled with her raised his bottle to hit Will.

"No!" She reached with one hand and grabbed his arm. Enraged, the man spun around. He grabbed her waistcoat and yanked her back. Her hand slipped from the wheel and she fell backwards, head hitting the deck. Through her daze, Skye was aware of the wheel spinning. She started to get up, but the ship turned sharply and she fell again. Even if she had been able to get up, Skye knew she probably couldn't have stopped the wheel from spinning without injuring herself quite badly.

In an instant, both her father and Caleb were on the quarterdeck. Caleb grabbed the wheel and quickly spun it back the other way, turning the ship away from land. Both Daniel and Will, who had been released, went immediately to Skye and helped her up. Once on her feet, Skye reflexively put her hand to the back of her throbbing head.

"Are you all right?" Daniel asked anxiously.

Skye could see how worried he and Will were. Caleb too looked over his shoulder to hear her answer.

"Yes, I'm fine," Skye assured them.

She heard them each breathe a sigh of relief. At that moment, Dreger climbed the quarterdeck and, having seen their fight with Will, glared furiously at his men.

"You stupid fools!" he bellowed. "You wanna kill 'im? How are we gonna get that map if he's dead?"

Neither man said anything and Daniel spoke, sounding angry himself.

"Not only could they have killed him, but they could have killed my daughter or the rest of us. Do you know how close we came to running aground?" he demanded.

Dreger glanced at him and for once his anger was centered only on his men as he continued to glare at them.

"Stay away from the boy and the girl, got it?" he warned. "Either that or I'll throw you both off this ship, land or no."

Dreger turned then and stormed away. His men followed slowly, glowering and muttering under their breath. Daniel watched them for a moment before turning back to Skye. He put his hands on her shoulders and looked at her closely, checking her eyes for any sign of concussion.

"Are you sure you are all right?"

Skye nodded. "Yes, I just have a bit of a headache."

"Why don't you sit down for a few minutes," Daniel decided, his eyes ranging around the ship. "I should make sure no one else got hurt." Turning to Will, he said, "Help her find a place to sit down."

Will nodded as Daniel walked away.

"Come with me," Will said softly as he put his hand on her arm and gently guided her to the stairs.

Down on the main deck, Skye took a seat on a barrel.

Looking up at Will, she said, "What about you? Are you all right?"

Will nodded. "Yes, don't worry. I'm fine."

Skye sighed. "I knew something like that was bound to happen."

Will agreed and saw Skye frown.

"Is something wrong?"

"No," she said tentatively, "but did you notice what Dreger said to his men?"

"Yes, I did," Will told her, knowing immediately was she was talking about. "This thing my father left me is a map."

"A map to what?" Skye wondered.

Will shook his head. "It could be anything."

The two of them pondered it silently for a moment, but before they could share their thoughts, they heard Marie's voice and turned towards her.

"Are you both all right?" she asked looking and sounding genuinely concerned.

When they assured her they were she nodded, visibly relieved. "Good."

She said no more after that and walked away.

"She is the one who told me you were having trouble," Will said, still watching Marie. He turned back to Skye. "I was climbing down from the foremast and didn't see that Dreger's men had approached you . . . I'm thankful she did."

"So am I," Skye replied. "If I had lost control of the wheel sooner, we may have gone aground."

Moonlight shone on the water like thousands of glittering gems as Will walked slowly along the side of the ship late that night. The rest of the day had thankfully passed with no more incidents, and the wind had died down to a gentle breeze. Will paused at the bow, deep in thought when he heard his name said quietly behind him. He turned to find that it was Marie. She crossed the short distance that lay between them and came to a stop beside him.

"I don't want Dreger to know, but I want you to keep these." Marie handed Will both of his father's letters. "I have no reason to keep them and at least you will have something from your father since Dreger is taking what else there is."

Will slipped the letters safely inside his waistcoat.

"Do you know what it is?" he wanted to know.

Marie shook her head. "No, I don't. Dreger never told me."

"I heard him say today that it is a map."

Marie frowned. "A map? To what?"

"I was hoping you would know," Will said.

"I don't. It must lead to something that's worth Dreger going through all this trouble, but I can't imagine what it could be. When your father and I were together we were poor. Perhaps things changed for him after I left, but I don't know."

"How did Dreger find out about the map?"

"I think he knew your father. Dreger is the one who told me that he . . . is dead."

Will's reply came slowly. "Did he tell you how he died?"

"No."

"Maybe he killed him," Will murmured quietly.

Marie lowered her head and did not respond knowing it was a likely possibility. Will sighed sadly wishing even more to know his father. When he said no more, Marie turned to walk away, but Will stopped her for one more word. She looked at him wondering what more he had to say.

"Thank you for telling me earlier that Skye was in trouble. I am grateful to you."

Marie was surprised to see that he had a small smile on his face, the first he had ever given her. How wonderful it was to see.

"You are welcome." A smile flashed across her face as well. Continuing to stare at Will, whatever motherly instincts Marie had deep inside were beginning to make her curious about Will's life and his future. "She told me last night that you two have known each other for almost thirteen years."

"Yes."

"I can see you care a great deal about each other." Marie paused. "You do not have to answer this, but I am curious, are you only friends or more than that?"

"We've been courting for two years . . ." Will glanced around to be sure no one was near. ". . . I love her and plan to marry her." Will waited for Marie to say something, but she only nodded and didn't speak. Finally, he spoke again. "You haven't anything to say?"

"I didn't really think my thoughts would be worth much," Marie replied.

Will held her gaze steadily. "You are still my mother. I would like to know what you think."

Marie looked into his dark eyes and saw no hate and no anger, as she might have expected, only complete honesty and it touched her.

"I can't tell you how wonderful it is to hear that." Her voice wavered a little with emotion. "Both you and Miss McHenry are two of the most remarkable people I've ever met, and I know you will be so happy together." There was a pause. "I wish your father could see you and know of all this. He would have been so proud and so happy. Maybe it could have taken away some of the pain I caused him."

Marie's emotions had overwhelmed her, and Will saw tears glisten as they slid down her face. Seeing her in this state gave Will a deep feeling of compassion for her. He reached out gently and drew her into a hug, an action which greatly surprised Marie, but she found it wonderfully comforting and wished with all her heart that things could have been different.

"I'm sorry, Will," she murmured. "I really am."

"I know you are."

Marie stepped back. "I will make this up to you somehow. I promise."

Will shook his head. "No . . . after tomorrow, we start over. Whatever has happened doesn't matter."

Marie found that a wonderful thought and could not imagine how Will could be so forgiving after everything she had done.

Chapter Eight

Will inhaled deeply as the fresh wind propelled the ship into the port of Lucea. His mind was anxious at the thought of meeting a friend of his father's. It was his hope that after Dreger and his men left he could get to speak further with Jacob Tucker and learn more about his father, things that Marie was not able to tell him.

Daniel maneuvered the *Grace* alongside one of the docks. Everyone helped to furl the sails and the anchor was dropped. Before them stretched Lucea, a prosperous city though not quite the size of Kingston. It was the first time any of them had been there; however, no one was able to show much interest in it because Dreger quickly called all to the main deck. He and his men were obviously not taking any chances for they were armed quite heavily.

"All right, William James. It's time for you to do what I've brought you here for. Go into the city and find Jacob Tucker." Then Dreger pointed at Daniel. "And you are goin' with him because everyone's heard of Daniel McHenry, and it will make Tucker even more sure to believe that Mr. James is who he says he is. Now once you find his house you will get what I want and bring it straight back here. I don't want Tucker or anyone else to know what's goin' on so you'd better be convincing," he advised, "and I'm only givin' you a short period of time to do this so you'd better just get it and leave. My men and I will stay here with the crew and Miss

McHenry. Nothing will happen to them if you do just what I've said. Is that understood?"

Will and Daniel traded glances and answered resignedly, "Yes."

"Good, now go and get it. Remember, you don't have much time," Dreger warned.

Will rested his gaze on Skye, their eyes locking for a poignant moment before he turned reluctantly and led the way off the ship.

Will and Daniel walked down the long wooden dock to the beach and made their way into the city streets. Before too long they stopped to look around.

"We need to ask someone where Mr. Tucker lives," Will said, ". . . . if he is still alive."

Daniel agreed and presently stopped a gentleman walking by.

"Excuse me, sir, but does a Jacob Tucker still live here?"

The gentleman nodded. "Yes. He lives on the northeast edge of the city near the shore. He's got a small house just inside the forest. It's one of the only homes built there so it should be easy to find."

"Thank you for your help," Daniel said.

"You're welcome," the gentleman replied with a nod as he walked away.

Will and Daniel followed his directions and very shortly came to a small wooden house built just inside the trees of the forest that surrounded the city. Stopping at the door, Will took another deep breath and knocked. Anxiously, he waited, many questions coming to mind, the most prominent of these being whether or not Jacob Tucker would believe him when he told him who he was.

In only a short moment, Will heard a creak and the door opened wide to reveal a man of about sixty-five though he looked younger. His short hair and beard were gray, and he was tall, much like Daniel, with the same kind blue eyes.

"Mr. Tucker?" Will inquired.

"Yes?"

"Mr. Tucker, my name is . . . William James."

Jacob's eyes widened in utter shock, and a look of unspeakable joy came to his face.

"I never thought this day would come!" he exclaimed. "Thank the Lord for answering our prayers! Please, come in!"

Jacob ushered them inside the neat little house. In the small foyer, he looked Will up and down and shook his head.

"I should have known who you were the instant I saw you. There's no doubt you are a James!" It was then he fully noticed Daniel. "Excuse me, sir, for the absence of my welcome. I am just so stunned."

Daniel smiled. "I understand completely." He extended his hand. "I'm Daniel McHenry."

Jacob became even more surprised. "*Captain* Daniel McHenry?"

Daniel nodded and Jacob shook his hand firmly.

"It's a pleasure to meet you, Captain. I've been a long time admirer of yours."

"Thank you," Daniel said humbly.

Another voice was heard from deeper inside the house. "Who is it, Jacob?"

Jacob turned and called, "Naomi, come in here."

A moment later, a woman about Jacob's age walked into the room. In her hands was a dishcloth, and she looked at Jacob questioningly.

"He's here, Naomi," Jacob told her, smiling brightly.

"Who?" Naomi asked with a frown.

"William." Jacob nodded at Will and Naomi gasped, her hand going to her mouth.

"It's a miracle," she said, finally taking it away. Tears glistened in her eyes.

Jacob next introduced her to Daniel before then introducing her as his wife. Their greetings were full of joy, and it touched Will deeply how happy they were to meet him.

"I have so much I would like to ask," Jacob told Will. "I can barely believe you are really here."

Will smiled. "Yes, I have many things I would like to ask too . . ." His smile disappeared remembering Dreger's warning. ". . . but I'm afraid that Captain McHenry and I are. . . on a very tight schedule. I will come back very soon, but I am here now because of this letter." Will brought out the letter from his father.

Jacob nodded. "Of course, come with me. I've got the item safely in a trunk in my study."

Will and Daniel followed him out of the foyer and into a small room rimmed with filled bookcases and an old writing desk cluttered with various paper articles. In one corner was an old trunk. Jacob removed what was stacked on top of it, unlocked it, and lifted the top. He rummaged through all that was inside until he had nearly reached the bottom where there lay a small wooden box. Opening it, he flipped through several important letters that were stored there before pulling out one which had browned over time.

"I honestly never expected to be taking this out," Jacob told Will as he stood again.

Will took the letter which Jacob held out to him. He looked at the back of it and was glad to see no seal so that he could look at the contents before giving it to Dreger. Will unfolded it revealing a perfectly hand-drawn map. Upon further inspection, Will found the map led to a tiny island somewhere north of Jamaica. Daniel, who was standing behind Will, made sure to memorize exactly where the island was so they'd still know its location once Dreger had possession of the map.

Having seen what he wanted to see, Will slowly began to refold the letter. Meanwhile, Jacob spoke hesitantly in a careful manner that Will noticed with some curiosity.

"Do you want me to let your father know you were here?"

Will's heart stopped as his eyes went instantly to Jacob's face. He opened his mouth to speak but nothing came out until he cleared his throat of the emotion Jacob's question had caused. "He's . . . alive?"

Jacob nodded, perplexed. "Yes."

"You're sure?" Will could barely allow himself to believe it was true fearing the disappointment of finding that it wasn't.

"I just received a letter from him two days ago," Jacob told him.

"I was told he was dead." Will's astonishment and his joy were obvious in his voice.

Jacob smiled. "Well, I don't know who told you that or why, but no, he's very much alive. He owns a large estate in Virginia as well a trading company." He paused and continued slowly. "He remarried too. Has four daughters."

Will sighed with relief, to know that it was real and true, and a smile broke free as he looked at Daniel incredulously and then back to Jacob. "That is the best news I've received since I got his letter." He thanked God with all his heart that his father's death had been a lie.

Jacob's smile grew. "I'm very glad you feel that way. I must admit it is not what I would have expected considering certain circumstances."

Smiling, Will replied, "Most things about my life are not as I think you would expect thanks to God and the wonderful people He has put in my life."

Jacob was overjoyed by those words realizing Will must have a relationship with Christ, one he and Edward had never ceased praying for.

Daniel was the next to speak. "You asked Will if he wanted you to tell his father that he came?"

Jacob looked at him and nodded. A smile came to Daniel's face. "You don't have to. I'll see to it that he can tell him in person."

Will turned to Daniel with immense gratitude. "Thank you."

"I would do nothing less for you, Will. This is a wonderful turn of events."

Turning back to Jacob, Will knew that they had to get back to the ship, but there were a few more things he needed to know. "The island on this map, why does my father want me to go there?"

"Because of what he left there for you."

"And what is that?"

"Letters," Jacob answered simply. "Over the last nearly twenty years he's put letters there for you to read."

"Only letters?" Will wanted to know.

"Perhaps a little money, but as far as I know it's only letters."

Will couldn't understand why Dreger would be after the letters. Maybe he thought it was more than that. There was one thing more that Will did not understand.

"Why did my father want me to go to you and not to him?"

"Well, there are three reasons. First, at the time he was moving so often he wanted it to be someone who would always be in the same place so that you could find them. I once told him I'd never leave Lucea so you see why he directed you to me. Secondly, he was afraid that something might happen to him and then you'd never get the letters. And lastly, he wanted you to make the decision to find him on your own. He thought he'd let you get to know him through the letters and then decide whether or not you wanted to contact him."

Will nodded now with perfect understanding. "Thank you, Mr. Tucker. I can't tell you how much this all means to me."

"You are quite welcome. Naomi and I have been waiting years for you to come. I'm sure we are nearly as happy as you are," Jacob replied.

"Yes, and I'm so sorry we cannot stay longer, but right now, I think Captain McHenry and I should be going." Will's thoughts had gone back to Skye and the crew, and he worried that they may have stayed too long already. "I will come back as soon as I am able."

"Please do," Jacob said. "You are both quite welcome here, and I would very much like for you to tell me how this all came about and of your life these years."

Will nodded. "I will be happy to tell you."

He and Daniel then said goodbye to Jacob and Naomi, and Jacob showed them to the door. Outside, they made their way quickly back to the *Grace*. Will felt incredible joy from the news of his father, and it relieved him immensely when they reached the ship to see everyone still gathered on the main deck which meant that no one was harmed. Everyone turned expectantly towards Will and Daniel as they approached.

"Did you get it?" Dreger demanded.

Will nodded reluctantly. "Yes."

He held out the letter, and Dreger snatched it from him. Unfolding it, he studied the map. While he was occupied, Will walked over to Skye and Marie who were standing next to each other.

"Is it a map?" Skye asked.

"Yes," Will answered.

"Do you know what it leads to?"

"An island north of here. My father left letters there for me over the years."

"What would Dreger want with the letters?" Marie asked.

"I don't know, but I learned more." Will lowered his voice and glanced at Dreger to be sure he wasn't listening. "Dreger lied to you. My father is alive."

Marie and Skye were stunned.

"Will, that's wonderful," Skye whispered joyfully.

"Yes it is," Will agreed, smiling.

A moment later, Daniel addressed Dreger and everyone turned to them.

"All right, Dreger, you have what you wanted. Now you and your men can leave my ship," he said with authority.

Dreger slowly began refolding the map as he looked at Daniel. "As you wish, Captain McHenry. However, so that none of you attempt to follow us, my men will escort you, yer daughter, Marie, and yer crew below to one of the cells. I'm sure that someone will come along eventually and hear yer calls for help."

"There is no need for that," Daniel told him solemnly.

"Oh, I think there is," Dreger insisted.

He nodded to his men. Amidst everyone's useless protesting, the men began to guide all but one person to the hatch leading below. It was like reliving a nightmare when Skye saw Will being pulled away from them instead, and taken towards Dreger.

"Will!" she cried.

Everyone else noticed the situation as well.

"What are you doing?" Daniel demanded. "You said we could all return home after you got what you wanted."

"I said that you, yer daughter, and yer crew would return home. I never referred to Mr. James."

"What further need do you have of him?" Daniel protested, a bit of desperation sounding in his words.

"It's all part of a plan. I'm gonna make sure he can't go stickin' his nose into it, and the less you know about it the better," Dreger told him. Looking once again to his men he ordered, "Take 'em below."

The men began to push them again, but Marie slipped past them and hurried over to Dreger.

"You can't do this!" she cried. "I've just stood by all this time and watched you, but I will not let you take my son."

"Get back, Marie!" Dreger growled.

"Let my son go!"

What happened next happened so quickly that no one could have tried to stop it. Marie gasped loudly and everyone froze. She stumbled back, a crimson stain seeping through the front of her dress. Dreger stood there with a blood-covered dagger in his hand. Everyone watched in stunned horror until Will pulled away from Dreger's men and caught Marie just as she collapsed. Carefully, Will dropped to his knees holding her gently in his arms.

"Mother." His voice echoed with sorrow and the desperate hope that she would somehow be all right.

A weak smile came to Marie's face despite her pain.

"That's the first time I've heard you call me that," she said with a gasping breath.

"You shouldn't have tried to stop them," Will told her sadly.

"I did what I should have done a long time ago. I only regret that I couldn't stop this." The look on Marie's face and in her eyes no longer showed the frail, uncertain woman she had been, but someone very different. She was the mother Will had lost as an infant. "Thank you, Will," she continued, "for forgiving me."

Blood was beginning to show on her lips, and Will could only nod and force a quick smile as tears stung at his eyes. Marie raised her hand, and Will took it, squeezing it gently.

111

"I'm truly proud of you," Marie told him. "And I love you. I know God will continue to watch over you as He always has. I'm sure He will rescue you from this." There was a pause, her words becoming more and more labored. "Goodbye, Will."

Will swallowed hard, his words breaking. "Goodbye, Mother."

Marie said no more as her eyes slid closed. She was dead. Staring at her lifeless face, Will could not believe he had just lost his mother whom he'd known for so short a time.

"Get up." Dreger's cold voice pierced Will's thoughts, and he knew he had no time to grieve despite his intense sorrow. Gently, he lay Marie's body on the deck and slowly rose, looking at Dreger who now held a pistol. The man had just murdered his mother; there was no telling what else he would do. Dreger fixed everyone with an icy glare.

"I won't hesitate to do the same to anyone else who resists me," he warned angrily. "That I can assure you." He ordered his men to continue and said, "If any one of 'em resists, kill 'em."

The group was pushed forward, and Will was shoved nearer to Dreger. All were silent except for Skye who pled with Dreger desperately. Tears stained her face, and as he heard her anguished cries, it was all Will could manage to keep himself from trying to do something to stop this. Daniel gently but firmly guided her along with him not wanting her to be hurt or killed by Dreger's men.

As they disappeared below deck, Will turned to Dreger with a request.

"Please, let me say goodbye to them."

Will tried again when Dreger paid him no heed. Finally, Dreger spun around furiously, but Will was not about to back down.

"I want to say goodbye to them," Will repeated once again.

"Forget it," Dreger spat.

"I may never see them again, the least you could do is let me say goodbye."

Dreger glared at him and clenched his teeth. "Fine," he spat.

He took Will by the arm and shoved him roughly to the hatchway. Below, Dreger's men were just locking everyone inside one of the cells. Skye came to the bars the instant she saw Will hoping that Dreger had changed his mind, but his words showed her he had not.

"Make this quick," Dreger ordered, releasing Will.

Will went quickly to the bars and took Skye's hands.

"I had to say goodbye," he told her.

Skye's tears started afresh. "How can this be happening?" she wept.

"God's plans are not always easy to understand," Will murmured sadly, Skye's question echoing in his own heart.

In the background they heard Dreger telling him to hurry. Skye knew there was something she had to tell Will before he was gone.

"Will, last night your mother asked me some questions about God. We talked a little about salvation. I don't know if she believed or not, but there is a chance she could have before she died. She did seem different to me this morning."

"Thank you, Skye," Will said, unable to tell her just how relieved he was.

Dreger cut off, Skye's reply. "All right, time's up."

He started towards Will who looked Skye deeply in the eyes. "I love you."

"I love you too." Skye's words were choked off by a sob.

Their eyes stayed locked on each other as Dreger and another man grabbed Will. His hands slipped out of Skye's as he was yanked away from the cell.

Right before they left, Dreger turned to everyone in the cell. "After you get free I suggest you return home and forget about this if you know what's good for you."

"And just forget about him?" Skye demanded incredulously.

"If you want to live," Dreger sneered.

Skye had no choice but to watch as Will was led away and to wonder with sorrow and uncertainty if she would ever see him again.

Chapter Nine

Nothing happening around Will was capable of attracting his attention, neither the people nor the buildings they passed. His mind was still on what had taken place, and he was more or less in a slight state of shock. More had happened in this recent short period of time than he had ever dreamed would happen, ever. Following so quickly on the heels of the wonderful news that his father was still alive, his mother had been murdered right before his eyes, he'd been taken from the woman he loved and the people he cared most about, and his life was in the hands of his mother's murderer. He expected with certainty that Dreger was going to kill him because that was how it seemed, but a conversation between Dreger and his men had given him hope.

After leaving the *Grace*, they had traveled into and through Lucea. Once reaching the far edge of the city, they had gone into the forest where they paused only long enough for Dreger to bind Will's hands tightly behind him so they would not have to guard him so closely. It had not been done earlier for fear of drawing attention, but Dreger's threat to kill Will and then burn the *Grace* with everyone still locked onboard kept Will from attempting an escape.

Venturing deeper into the dense forest, Dreger's men continued their conversation.

"Why can't we just kill 'im?" It was the same man who had snapped at Will and Pete to put out the lanterns the first night they sailed. "It woulda saved us all a lotta trouble."

Dreger's eyebrows crunched down. "Because you-know-who was too much of a coward to let us do what shoulda been done and the captain decided this was the next best thing to keep him out of sight and from causin' trouble."

"What if he gets away?" another man asked.

"He won't," Dreger stated. "Hale's had experience with this before, and the captain wouldn't 'ave picked 'im if he didn't trust 'im to do the job."

"You sure he's gonna be there?"

"The captain told 'im to be there so he'll be there."

That ended the conversation and silence took over once again. Will thought about their conversation along with all of the other information he had gleaned over the last days, but he couldn't make sense of any of it. There were no answers as to why Dreger was interested in the letters from Will's father nor enlightenment regarding the plan he had mentioned. Why Dreger thought he would, or even could, cause trouble when he barely knew anything seemed ridiculous to Will. He couldn't believe he'd gotten himself involved in this dangerously tangled mystery when only days ago he hadn't even known his parents' names.

The trek through the forest was long and difficult with the undergrowth so thick. Will had to work hard to keep himself from tripping and falling and could only imagine where they were headed. He estimated that they had been traveling for over an hour when the forest suddenly opened up before them to reveal a rocky beach and a small bay. Two ships lay anchored in the water. One was a smaller merchant vessel while the other was a larger square-rigged ship.

Milling about the beach were several men, obviously pirates. They were keeping to two separate groups, but all turned to look as Dreger came out of the trees. His men pushed Will forward to follow Dreger to one group, which consisted of five men. One man, older with a bushy gray beard and thick gray hair, stepped forward to meet them. He wore a dark blue, navy jacket and light colored breeches. Whether or not he was former navy was impossible to say. His eyes were steely blue and cheerless, and Will realized uncomfortably that the man was staring specifically at him all the while he came towards them.

Will shifted his gaze to a second man coming along just behind the first. This man was much younger, close to thirty, with dark hair and dark eyes, much like Will himself. There was something Will found more pleasant about him than the first man, but he knew looks could be deceiving. It didn't seem that any of them meant him well. *God, please help me,* Will prayed silently as he had been doing steadily since Dreger had taken him. *Only You can watch over me and provide me rescue from this.*

Shortly, the two groups came to a stop in front of each other.

"Captain Hale," Dreger addressed the older man. "You are right on time."

"Of course," Hale replied stiffly. "Captain Hendricks doesn't put such high trust in me for no reason."

"Indeed he doesn't," Dreger agreed.

Hale's eyes turned once again to Will. "So this is the boy?"

"That's him," Dreger answered.

Hale nodded slowly, still peering closely at Will. His expression showed that he was either unimpressed or unconcerned. Will couldn't tell which.

"Sailing experience?" Hale wanted to know.

Dreger nodded. "Quite a bit. He's strong too. Was the blacksmith back in Kingston when 'e wasn't at sea."

117

Hale looked Will up and down as Will became ever more uncomfortable, feeling like some farm animal being inspected for sale.

"I oughta warn you though," Dreger began. "He can be a bit stubborn if you don't got somethin' to threaten 'im with, like someone he cares about. I'm afraid I couldn't accommodate you there seein' as how the captain told us to let the others be."

"I've dealt with it before," Hale replied, clearly unconcerned with Dreger's words. "It matters little as I've already agreed to take 'im, so as long as yer here we will be on our way before a ship comes along and sees us. I risked my neck plenty comin' here in the first place."

"Well, I know the captain's grateful and will see that you get yer pay," Dreger said.

Hale merely nodded and turned to the younger man behind him.

"Get the boy and bring 'im to the boat." He had barely finished speaking before striding off towards the water's edge where a long boat waited.

Will was handed over to the younger man who took him by the arm and led him after the captain. One of the other men took Will's duffel which Dreger's men had carried along from the *Grace*.

At the boat, Will was reluctant to get in for he knew that once on the ship his chance of escape was not good at all. Calling upon God once again, he stepped in and was forced to sit near the back of the boat with the younger man. Two of the men picked up the oars and began rowing out into the bay. It took only a short time for them to come to the square-rigged ship. Looking up at the stern of the ship rising above them, Will read the name *Seabird* painted in faded white letters. He tried to remember if he'd heard the name before but couldn't recall that he ever had.

The men brought the boat to a stop alongside the ship. Captain Hale and the three other men climbed aboard. The man beside Will took out a knife and cut the ropes around Will's wrists.

"Climb aboard," he said. His voice was quiet and not harsh like the captain's.

Without a word, Will got up and began to climb the side of the ship. On deck, the captain was waiting for them. He looked at the man behind Will and ordered gruffly, "Mr. Worthy, take 'im below until we're underway."

Once again Worthy took Will by the arm and guided him towards a hatchway. Along the way, Will's eyes scanned the faces of the crew as they watched him pass by. Most stared blankly, but Will noticed one man in particular glowering at him menacingly. Will couldn't guess the reason for his animosity, but he knew the man was not someone he wanted for an enemy. The man was big, heavily built, and had black hair and cruel eyes nearly as dark as his hair. Knowing instinctively this man meant him ill, Will shifted his gaze away towards the hatchway they were heading to.

Below deck in the cargo hold alongside one of the ship's sides was a dank, musty cell. Its flat iron bars were rusted over. Worthy grabbed a key that hung on a post nearby and pulled on the cell door. The rusty hinges shrieked loudly as it opened. He motioned for Will to go inside. Feeling defeated, Will said nothing in protest. He walked in quietly, and the rusty lock clanked dully as the door closed behind him.

"Don't worry, you won't be down here that long." Will looked back over his shoulder as the man spoke. "The captain will want to see you again. I'll leave the lantern here." Worthy hung the lantern he had lit on a hook which was attached to one of the cell bars.

It appeared to Will that Worthy was trying to be kind to him so he murmured a quiet, "Thank you."

Worthy nodded slowly, not having expected Will to be in any mood to say anything to anyone on the ship, especially not in thankfulness. "You're welcome."

Turning, Worthy made his way out of the hold, and Will was left alone. Darkness engulfed the cavernous space except for the small ring of light around the cell. Will hung his head with a deep and heartfelt sigh. His situation was very bleak and being separated from those he loved was weighing on him heavily. Right when all had been good in his life everything had been thrown into turmoil. He had been so close to finally asking Skye to marry him, to telling her about the house. How would she now hear of what he had done? From Mr. and Mrs. Collins when she returned to Kingston? Will shook his head. No, Skye would not return home. He knew that much for certain because he never would go back without searching for her. That thought should have been comforting, but it wasn't. Dreger's warning to Skye and the others was burned into in Will's mind.

"Please, God, protect them," he prayed.

Turning to take stock of his surroundings, Will noticed a small bench at the back of the cell. There was no denying that he felt weary so he picked up the bench and set it against the bars near the lantern. Sitting, his hand went to the pocket of his waistcoat and he pulled out his small, oval-framed portrait of Skye. He was so thankful that Matthew had packed it for him. With a wistful smile, Will stared at the likeness of Skye and ran his fingertips over the inscription along the silver metal frame. *Always together in heart.* The words soothed his heart and played over and over again in his mind. Their comfort was great in light of all the sorrows he was facing. He could not help but wonder why God was allowing all of this to happen.

"I wish I could understand," Will murmured, leaning his head back to rest on the bars of the cell. "Please, show me Your reason for this, Lord."

He quickly lost all track of time for it seemed to stand still down in the darkness of the ship. The only sounds were the rushing and splashing of sea water and the creaking of timbers. Nothing could be seen except what was touched by the small circle of lantern light and that was only the soggy, mildewed floor planks and a couple of sealed crates standing near the cell. Occasionally, the black streak of a rat would cross the very edges of light, but nothing else. The stale, fowl-smelling air made breathing unpleasant. Will could hardly imagine a worse place to be held prisoner, though he had yet to find out if he would indeed be kept here. It made him thankful that when Skye had been held prisoner by Kelley, the condition of her cell had been far better than this.

Just when Will began to wonder if anyone would come for him, lantern light shone through the hatchway several yards away, and he saw Worthy descending the ladder. Walking towards the cell, Worthy grabbed the key and unlocked the door.

"The captain wants to see you now," he told Will, swinging the door open.

Will stepped out of the cell and followed Worthy to the ladder. Once on deck, Will had to shield his eyes from the bright sunlight. Captain Hale stood waiting at the ship's stern. When they reached him, both came to a stop. Hale studied Will with a hard gaze.

"Yer name is William James, is that right?" Hale asked, his voice never losing its harsh edge.

"Yes," Will answered quietly.

"All right, Mr. James, there is something we need to get straight right now. When addressin' or answerin' me you will either use *Captain* or *sir*, is that clear?"

Will nodded reluctantly. "Yes, sir."

"Do you know why you are here?"

"No, sir, but I would very much like to know."

"You are here now as part of my crew."

"As a slave?" Will questioned despondently.

"As a crewmember," Hale corrected him. "You will replace a man we've recently lost."

Will felt a bit of relief at the prospect of not being a slave, but it was only fleeting.

"If I may, Captain . . . why was I brought here?" Will questioned, speaking more boldly. "I know it was not solely to replace one of your crew."

Hale crossed his arms. "You were brought here to keep you from askin' questions." His voice was smug, and Will knew he would answer no more. Instead, Hale began speaking again of Will's position on the ship. "Yer duties will be that of every other shipmate and you will follow the ship's articles the same as well. The rules are simple. If you do not work you do not eat, and if you cause trouble or don't follow the articles there will be consequences, make no mistake about that. Now, come with me to my cabin."

Will had no choice but to follow Hale. Worthy too came with them. Inside the captain's cabin, Hale picked up a large book, the ship's log, and laid it on his cluttered desk. He opened it to a page near the beginning. Looking at Will, he said, "I'm assumin' you can read."

"Yes," Will replied, quickly adding *sir* to the end, having nearly forgotten.

"Good. These here are the ship's articles you are to follow. Read 'em."

Will stepped closer to the desk and began to read from the book. The hand written words were sloppy and poorly spelled, but he could understand most of it. The articles were rules that all pirates on the ship must follow. They dealt with stealing from one another, striking one another, and arguments between crew members to name a few. Punishments were very harsh and consisted, as far as Will could tell, of being shot, marooned, severely beaten or whatever the rest of the crew saw fit to mete out, all of which he prayed earnestly to avoid.

"Do you understand everything?" Hale asked when Will had finished.

"Yes, sir."

"Good," Hale said brusquely. He reached and flipped a few pages in the book to one with a long list of names. Most were very poorly written and could barely be read while others weren't even names at all but strange marks made by those who could not write. Will also noticed that several of the names were crossed out. He looked again to Hale as the captain held out a quill. "Put your name down."

Taking it, Will looked down at the page, very reluctant to sign. Seeing his hesitation, Hale told him, "You either sign or you go back down in the hold until you do."

With a quiet sigh, Will signed his name, the neatness of it highly contrasted with all others but one. Several names above his, most of which were crossed off, was one also neatly written. The name was Michael Worthington, and Will surmised that it was Mr. Worthy since the name Worthy was not on the list.

Will handed the quill back to Captain Hale. He was now an official member of the *Seabird's* crew. Being a member of a pirate crew worried him, and he would have to be careful because he knew that at any time he could be given an order that would go against what he knew was right. He'd have to refuse to do it. Unfortunately, sympathy and mercy were not things he was going to find on a pirate ship.

Hale returned the book to its spot on a shelf before turning back to Will. "Mr. Worthy here is the quartermaster. You will report to him, and he will give you yer daily duties. Right now he will find someone to take you to the forecastle and show you where you'll sleep. Afterwards he will give you yer work. Yer belongings are there." Hale pointed to Will's duffel sitting next to the door. "Mr. Worthy has gone through it so yer free to take it." He turned his eyes to Worthy. "Find someone to take 'im below."

"Aye, Captain," Worthy replied and looked at Will, waiting for him to follow.

Will walked to pick up his duffel, and followed Worthy out of the cabin. On deck, Worthy looked around.

"Mr. Fowley," he called.

An older, heavier set man came forward. His face was unshaven and his thin, wispy gray hair blew in the wind.

"Aye?"

"Mr. Fowley, take Mr. James to the forecastle and show him where he is to sleep," Worthy commanded.

"Aye, sir," Fowley replied.

Fowley gestured for Will to follow and led him below deck again. Both men were silent along the way. When they reached the large cabin, Will immediately noticed four men, one of which was the man who had been glowering at him earlier. He was reclining in his hammock peering at Will with eyes like some evil animal. The other three men also wore cruel expressions. All was quiet as they watched Will and Fowley.

"You can have this here hammock," Fowley said, motioning to the first empty one hanging alongside them.

Will began to nod, but a voice from farther down caught their attention.

"No 'e can't."

Fowley turned to the man in the hammock. "Why not?"

"'Cause I may feel like switchin'," the man answered, smirking.

Fowley rolled his eyes. "Then 'e can have yers."

The man got up and lumbered over to them. "He can't have either."

124

"Don't make a problem outta this, Slade," Fowley entreated.

"Or what?" Slade jeered. "You'll go to Worthy?"

"Let's not do this," Fowley tried. "He's parta the crew. He's gotta have a place to sleep."

"And I say the floor's as good a place as any," Slade insisted.

To prove his point, he pulled out a large, sharp dagger and plunged it into the hammock, slicing it right down the middle.

"What did ya do that for?" Fowley demanded, his voice a little high-pitched.

"He sleeps on the floor," Slade uttered menacingly.

Fowley didn't respond, not wanting to challenge Slade. He turned back to Will and mumbled, "I'll getcha some blankets later to sleep on."

Will nodded and Fowley moved past him to leave the cabin. As he was walking out, Slade spoke again and Fowley paused.

"If Worthy comes to me about this, I'll know it was one of you that told 'im." The words were an obvious threat.

Fowley continued on without a reply, but by the way he had already backed down, Will was willing to bet that he wouldn't be saying anything to Worthy. A long, uncomfortable silence followed during which Will wasn't sure what to do. He knew Captain Hale expected him back on deck to work, but he wasn't sure where to leave his duffel. Slade answered the question for him.

"If yer gonna be in here, stick to this corner, got it?" he growled. "And keep outta my way or you'll just have more trouble to worry about."

Slade began to turn away, but he stopped mid-step when Will dared to speak.

"And just what is your position in the crew?" Will didn't want Slade to think he was some weakling who

125

couldn't fend for himself. He got the feeling that showing a little resistance to the man might be better than not.

Slade looked at him with narrowed eyes. "What's the difference?"

"Well, you're not the captain or the quartermaster so unless you're something I'm not aware of I thought all were equal and had equal share in the sleeping area."

Slade showed surprise and there was anger in his eyes, but Will had no desire to be bullied, at least not without putting up some bit of a fight.

"Watch it, boy," Slade warned.

This time, Will opted to keep silent but held Slade's icy glare until the man turned away. Watching him for only a moment, Will set his duffel in the corner and walked out of the cabin. Normally he would not have wanted to leave his things where Slade could go through them, however, he knew the only thing of importance he'd had inside was his Bible which he fully expected had been taken out when Worthy had gone through his duffel.

Everything else that was dear to him, Will had on him. Skye's portrait, the locket, and his cross necklace which meant a great deal to him since God had used it to save his life when Kelley had tried to shoot him. Will knew he'd have to be careful to keep all things well hidden, but the question was, for how long? Would he find a way off the ship? He knew from experience how nearly impossible that was. All depended on God and His reason for putting Will where he was.

Chapter Ten

Still locked up on the *Grace*, Skye collapsed on a long bench at the back of the cell and wept. Her throat was raw from calling for help, and her hope of rescuing Will before he and Dreger got very far was gone. Over an hour had passed and there was no sign that anyone could hear their desperate calls.

Leaving the bars where the others all stood, Daniel took a seat beside his daughter. Putting his arm around her trembling shoulders, he hugged her gently.

"What do you think Dreger is going to do with him?" Skye asked, large hot tears rolling down her face.

"I don't know," Daniel told her quietly, inwardly very troubled.

"Do you think . . . he killed him?"

"He could just as easily have killed him here so I don't think killing him is Dreger's intent."

Skye felt some small measure of relief from her father's words, but her tears continued.

"I don't care what Dreger said, we must find him," Skye declared with determination.

Daniel nodded. "We'll do everything we can to find him, Skye. Dreger's warning will not stop us."

Caleb and the others continued to call for help, praying that someone would come near enough to hear them. Daniel stayed with Skye offering the comfort she needed, however, it was easy to see that everyone's hope was beginning to fade.

Finally, they heard what they had prayed for all afternoon. Someone was calling on deck.

"Is anyone here?"

"We're down here! We need help!" Caleb called as Skye and Daniel pushed anxiously to their feet and came to the bars.

They waited breathlessly for what seemed the longest moment and then Jacob appeared.

"Mr. Tucker," Daniel said both surprised and relieved.

"Captain McHenry!" Jacob was equally surprised.

Daniel wasted no time. "The cell key is hanging on that hook." He pointed to a small hook on the ship's bulkhead across from them. Jacob quickly retrieved it and freed them.

"What happened?" He looked around. "Where is Will?"

"He's been abducted," Daniel informed him regrettably. "Four days ago, Will met his mother for the first time. Through trickery she brought him into contact with a man named Dreger who forced Will to get his father's map from you. That is why we were in such a hurry at your house, he had my daughter and crew held hostage. When we returned to the ship Dreger took the map and left, taking Will with him"

"But why would he take him?" Jacob queried, puzzled.

"We're not sure. He said something about keeping Will from interfering with a plan," Daniel explained. "Whatever it is, we need to find him."

Jacob nodded, visibly troubled, as they followed Daniel.

"How long ago did Dreger leave?" he asked.

"A couple of hours," Daniel told him. "Mr. Tucker, Dreger never said anything about what he was doing or where he was going. Do you know of anywhere he could be hiding or would have gone if he left Lucea?" Daniel knew that without any prior knowledge of where to search for Will finding him would be literally impossible.

"In a city this size there's any number of places he could hide, and I'm sure I don't know the half of them. But if I were trying to get out of Lucea without anyone knowing, there is one place I'd go," Jacob answered.

"Where's that?"

"A bay about an hour's hike northeast of the city. It's small and secluded, but big enough for a ship or two."

"We need to start for that bay right away," Daniel urged. "If that's where they went that means they have at least a two hour head start."

"We're going to need weapons to go after them," Caleb cautioned.

Daniel nodded and strode into his cabin with everyone following. "Hopefully Dreger left the key to the weapon cabinet."

Daniel immediately began pulling out and rummaging through drawers to his desk. When he came to the third one, he found what he was looking for, a small key.

"Here it is," he said.

Turning, he went to a tall, metal cabinet at one side of the cabin. Hurriedly, he unlocked its two locks and opened the door which revealed many spare weapons as well as all the ones Dreger's men had found around the ship. Quickly, he began distributing them. Skye was a bit surprised when he handed her a sword and a pistol since she had half expected him to ask her to stay on the ship. Catching his gaze, she knew that he understood how badly she needed to go. She couldn't stand by and wait to find out what happened to Will.

After all of the crew had been armed, Daniel looked at Jacob.

"Will you come with us or stay?" he asked.

"I'm coming with you," Jacob declared. "There's no chance of me turning my back if Will's in trouble."

Daniel nodded and gave Jacob a sword and pistol as well after which they all left the ship and followed Jacob as he led the way into and out of the city towards the forest. Along the way they asked anyone they came to if they had seen Will, but all had the same answer, no. They had just about given up when one man said he might have. This gave everyone hope and they hurried on. At the forest edge, they stopped briefly.

"Someone's been here just recently," Jacob said, pointing out where the ground was trampled. "They had to have come this way."

As quickly as possible they made their way through the trees. In many spots it was easy to see where Dreger and his men had been. Having traveled faster than Dreger, Skye and the others came to the beach in just under forty-five minutes. Hoping against hope to find Will in time, they spilled out into the open and looked quickly around. Skye's heart sank. The beach and the bay were empty. She could see the smoking remains of a fire and footprints were everywhere, but not a living person remained. Looking down she studied the footprints before them. Having walked with Will on the beach countless times, she had no trouble distinguishing which were his. Tears pooled in her eyes as she looked out into the empty horizon which was beginning to fill with dark clouds.

"We're too late," she murmured tragically.

Skye felt her father's gentle hand and turned towards him. She could not hold back her tears and buried her face in Daniel's chest. He held her tightly and begged God to ease her sorrow.

After a long moment, Skye raised her head and looked at Daniel. "Do you think they're taking Will to the island on his father's map?"

"It's possible," Daniel shrugged, heartsick as well. "My instincts tell me yes."

"Then we should go there. I fear we're losing time."

Daniel didn't reply right away. His eyes were on the clouds. He knew it would be dark by the time they got back to Lucea, and he could feel that a storm was coming. There was no way they could leave yet that day.

Looking to the others, Daniel said, "We need to get back to the city."

Turning silently back to the forest, they found the return trip much slower because everyone was weary and discouraged. Skye wished they'd hurry, but she began to realize her father did not intend to leave yet that day. She listened silently along with everyone else as Daniel told Jacob along the way what had taken place over the last few days.

"That was Marie on deck, wasn't it?" Jacob asked.

"Yes," Daniel confirmed. "She tried to stop Dreger from taking Will."

As Jacob shook his head in dismay, darkness crept in quickly, and it was not long before the clouds began to pour down rain causing travel to slow even more. Though she couldn't tell the true time, it seemed like hours to Skye before they emerged from the forest, wet and exhausted. Trudging slowly though the dim, lantern lit streets, Jacob spoke.

"You all are welcome to spend the night with Naomi and I. We'll make room," he invited.

"We don't want to trouble you," Daniel replied.

Jacob shook his head. "You wouldn't be troubling us at all. Actually, after Naomi finds out what happened, I think she'd be upset if I didn't bring you home with me."

Skye looked at her father. If he accepted the invitation that would confirm to her that they would not be leaving. Daniel looked down at her with compassion.

"We are even more shorthanded now that we've lost Will, and we are all tired, Skye," he reasoned gently. "In the dark with this weather, we cannot leave port tonight. I hope you will understand."

Swallowing hard, Skye nodded slowly. All her sailing senses were telling her the same thing. "I know."

Daniel was proud that Skye was being so reasonable even with how hard this all had been. He put his arm around her and held her close as they walked.

"We won't give up," he whispered to her.

Daniel turned back to Jacob and said, "We would be very grateful to accept your hospitality."

"Good," Jacob said, pleased.

"You go on, Captain," Jesse spoke for the rest of the crew. "You know we prefer to stay with the ship when we're at port."

Daniel acknowledged Jesse's words with a nod.

"Daniel, you and Skye go ahead with Mr. Tucker," Caleb said. "I'll get someone to . . . take care of the body, and I'll join you later"

Again Daniel was overwhelmingly grateful for crew and friends. "Thank you, Caleb."

After Jacob gave Caleb instructions to his house and the coroner's, the group split, Caleb and the crew going one way and Skye and Daniel following Jacob another. Very soon, they came to Jacob's house. He opened the door and led Skye and Daniel into the warm, lamp lit foyer. The moment they walked in, Naomi was there to meet them.

"Jacob, where have you been?" she wanted to know. "I've been worried sick!"

Putting his hands on his wife's shoulders, Jacob explained to her what had happened. Tears came to Naomi's eyes, and she prayed right there for God to watch over Will and bring him back to safety. She turned to Daniel.

"What are you going to do?"

132

"Find him, God willing," Daniel answered simply.

There was a short moment of silence before Jacob spoke to his wife. "I asked them to stay with us tonight."

"Good, I would have been disappointed if you hadn't," Naomi replied, her eyes settling on the young woman she had never met.

"Forgive me, Mrs. Tucker," Daniel uttered, realizing that Skye had been on the *Grace* when he and Will had visited earlier. "This is my daughter, Skye."

Naomi held out her hands to clasp Skye's warmly, seeing the young woman was trying valiantly to hide the fact she was distressed. "It is wonderful to meet you, my dear. We must have a good talk later. But, what about the rest of you?" she said to Daniel. "Surely there are more?"

"My first mate will be coming later, but the rest of my crew preferred to stay with the ship," he answered. "We thank you for your hospitality, Mrs. Tucker."

"You are most welcome, Captain McHenry," Naomi said with a smile. "Now, you three come in by the fire to warm up and dry. I will heat up supper."

She led them into the sitting and dining area of the house where there was a nice fire going in the fireplace. Once they were seated with blankets near the warm flames, Naomi went to the kitchen.

Skye stared at the fire with a far-off look in her eyes as she remembered the couple of days before Dreger had showed up. Life had seemed so wonderful, and it amazed Skye how long ago it all seemed though it was only days. Unshed tears glittered in her eyes as she recalled the promise Will had made to her after their dance lessons. She pleaded with God to return Will safely and to be able to keep his promise.

A short time later, Naomi returned and put supper on the table. The four of them took seats and put food on their plates.

"When do you expect your first mate to come, Captain McHenry?" Naomi asked. "I can keep everything warm for him."

"I'm not sure exactly how long he will be." Daniel glanced meaningfully at Jacob.

Jacob looked at his wife wishing he didn't have to say what he had to say. "Naomi, there's something more I should tell you."

"What is it?" Naomi asked worriedly.

"Marie was with them."

Naomi looked surprised. "She was?"

"Yes, and she tried to stop Dreger from taking Will." Jacob paused. "I'm sorry to say, he killed her."

Naomi looked horrified. "How terrible," she murmured. Shaking her head, she asked, "How many people are we going to lose from this?"

"No more, I pray," Jacob replied.

Everyone else agreed with a nod. Silence came to the table with only the clinking and scraping of forks. Skye took a couple bites of the food, and though it was very good, it didn't settle well in her stomach. The rest she picked at with her fork, her mind feeling numb as fatigue set in.

Several minutes later, Jacob broke the silence.

"I understand if it is too painful to talk about, but I was wondering if you could tell Naomi and me about Will," he said. "We were so looking forward to getting to know him, especially since it appears that God has done such amazing things in his life."

"He has." Skye's voice was quiet and all eyes turned to her. She put her fork down knowing she could eat no more. Slowly she began telling Jacob and Naomi about Will. She started with all he had told her about his life in the St. Thomas orphanage. Skye found it very difficult talking about Will, almost as if he were dead, but she kept telling herself that he wasn't, that he was alive and that they were going to find him. Tears were shed by both Skye and Naomi, and Skye had to pause several times.

Caleb arrived a short time later, and Daniel introduced him to Jacob and Naomi. As Naomi got him supper, he told Daniel and Jacob that everything had gone fine on the ship, but said no more so that Skye could continue speaking. It was getting late by the time she finished, and by then they had all taken seats by the fireplace.

"Thank you, dear, for telling us all about Will," Naomi said, putting her hand gently on Skye's arm, knowing how hard it had been for her.

Skye nodded slowly. "You're welcome."

Daniel put his arm around her comfortingly. He looked at Jacob then.

"Mr. Tucker, could you tell us about Will's father?" he asked. "I think we were all as surprised as Will to find that he is alive."

"I'd be glad to." Jacob took a deep breath and began. "I've known Edward since he was a boy. We were neighbors before I moved here from England. He was always as happy as he could be no matter what life brought. Will's birth was one of the happiest times in his life, but after Marie left him nothing seemed to go right for a long time. His father died about a year later, and he was always on the move to find a good job, but he never seemed to be able to keep one.

"A couple of years afterward, his younger brother, Chris, who sailed for a merchant in America, was captured by a cruel pirate named Hendricks. Of the crew, Chris was the only one spared. All others were killed mercilessly. That's when Edward left England and used what little his father had been able to leave him to try to find Chris. He was finally able to raise the money Hendricks was demanding for ransom, but Chris nearly died from the treatment he received on board Hendricks' ship.

"Finally, things started getting better for Edward. The merchant Chris worked for had no children to leave his company to so he offered Edward half ownership. A couple of years later the man retired and left the whole company to Edward. He built up a large estate and married a widow with two daughters eleven years ago. They had a daughter a year later and then another almost two years ago. All are lovely girls and you'd hardly know the two eldest are not truly Edward's daughters. They're all very happy. God has definitely blessed them."

Skye wiped away a few tears as he finished for it was a touching story, and it saddened her very much to hear it before Will was able to. Looking at her, Daniel could see that aside from the sadness she was exhausted. Knowing that only made everything worse he said, "I think you should get some rest."

Skye nodded. "Yeah," she murmured though she wasn't sure how she could sleep.

Daniel looked at Naomi. "Mrs. Tucker, do you have a place for my daughter to sleep?"

"Yes, of course," Naomi answered. She looked at Skye with a smile. "Come with me, dear."

As the two women rose from their seats, Caleb told Skye, "I brought your duffel from the ship."

"Thank you, Caleb."

Naomi led Skye to a hallway just off the sitting room, opened the first door, and lit the lamp inside.

"This was my daughter Rosalie's room before she was married. You can sleep here. Your father will be in my sons' room just down the hall."

"Thank you, Mrs. Tucker."

Skye set her duffel on the pink quilt of the bed and looked around. The walls were pale pink as well and it was very much a girl's room.

"Do you have a nightgown in your bag?" Naomi asked from behind Skye.

Skye turned to her. "No, actually I don't. I was in a hurry when I packed and planned on sleeping in my clothes. I thought we'd be going home after today."

Naomi smiled. "I thought that might be the case. I will get you one of Rosalie's."

She turned to the white painted wardrobe that still held a few of her daughter's things. Meanwhile, Skye opened her duffel. Carefully she pulled out her Bible and laid it on the bed next to her. Next were the portraits of Will and her mother. She stared at both of their faces wishing so badly for both to be there with her. After a moment, Skye noticed Naomi standing behind her. She turned.

"Your mother?" Naomi asked, nodding to the portrait.

Skye smiled sadly. "Yes . . . she died when I was five."

Naomi felt a great sympathy for her. "You've had your share of sorrow, haven't you?"

Skye nodded slowly, beginning to get choked up. "But I know God has a reason for it even when I don't know what it is, and I trust Him. He's done so much good for me that I can't complain about the bad and someday I'll understand what I don't now . . . like this."

"You have an amazing attitude," Naomi told her. "He will reward you for that."

Skye nodded again. Naomi smiled kindly at her and then held out the nightgown.

"Here," she said. "This should fit you. Rosalie was tall like you. I suspect you both got it from your fathers."

Skye nodded with a quick smile and took the proffered nightgown. "Yes. Thank you, Mrs. Tucker. For everything."

"You're welcome," Naomi replied, returning the smile. She turned to go, but paused wishing to say more to Skye, to try to help her, sensing the deep sorrow she had inside. "I'm sorry, Skye, that you have to endure this. I know how hard it must be."

Two glittering tears slid down Skye's face. "It is. Will isn't only a friend. I love him very much, and I just can't imagine life without him."

Naomi touched Skye gently on the shoulder. "And God knows that, my dear. Do you know Psalms 37:4?"

Skye nodded. *"Delight yourself in the Lord; And He will give you the desires of your heart."*

"Yes. I'm sure right now that one of your heart's greatest desires is to be reunited with Will, and I'm sure his is to be reunited with you. God knows this and if you continue to trust and serve Him I'm sure He will honor that. Don't forget that He has protected and brought you back together in the past."

Wiping away a few more tears, Skye nodded again, feeling encouraged. "Thank you, Mrs. Tucker. I won't forget anything you've said."

Chapter Eleven

And we know that God causes all
things to work together for good to those
who love God, to those who are called
according to His purpose. – Ro. 8:28

Rainy darkness engulfed the ship as Will retreated below deck. He was wet, cold, and tired having finally been released from his work above. Several other crewmen in the same shift followed. In the forecastle, Will saw that Fowley had put a pile of blankets in the corner where Slade had told Will to stay. It relieved him to see that his duffel had not been touched and that because Slade's shift was just beginning instead of ending, he was not in the cabin.

Will laid out the blankets for sleeping and then reached into his pocket to pull out Skye's portrait. He was relieved to see that no water had leaked in between the frame and the glass. Remembering that he still had his father's letters in his waistcoat he retrieved them from the inside pocket. They were damp, but none of the words were smudged.

Hiding the portrait and letters under the blankets, Will reached for his duffel to take out a dry pair of clothing. He was very pleasantly surprised to pull out a shirt and find his Bible tucked safely between his other clothes. It was not where he had put it so he knew it had to have been put there by Worthy. Will wondered what had made him take such care with it and not confiscate it in the first place.

After changing, Will sat back against the cabin bulkhead. He pulled out his Bible and glanced at the other men who were preparing to sleep as well. He would not try to hide what he was doing from them, but he was worried that someone would take his Bible. Praying that wouldn't happen, he opened the book. He needed to read. It was his only comfort.

One by one the lanterns were put out, but Will was glad to get in about a half an hour of reading before the light became too dim to see. Carefully, he returned his Bible to his duffel and lay down, pulling one of the blankets over himself.

Despite his weariness, sleep did not come easily. The sounds of the men rustling around in their hammocks seemed especially loud and the blankets did little to cushion him from the hard floor. When sleep did come, it was restless and every noise would wake him, but the worst was sleeping amongst people who were strangers and unfriendly.

Groggily, Skye pushed back the quilt and sat upright at the edge of the bed. Through an east facing window she could see sunlight just starting to sparkle through the trees, rain water still dripping from their leaves. All was quiet, and Skye wondered if she was the only one awake, though she knew her father would be shortly if he wasn't already. With a sigh, she ran her fingers through her hair, smoothing away the matted tangles.

The fear and worry she'd placed before God the night before and asked Him to calm still lingered, but she'd awakened with a fresh sense of trust and determination.

140

Sometimes during terrible sorrow, it was easy to ask why and forget that there was a plan behind it, but reading Romans 8:28 with her father the night before had encouraged Skye.

Like Will, Skye's sleep had been fitful, but instead of letting her mind dwell on the bad that was happening she remembered all the times God had rescued her and Will from impossible odds and His care throughout their lives. Psalms 121:7-8 said, *The Lord will protect you from all evil; He will keep your soul. The Lord will guard your going out and your coming in from this time forth and forever.* She knew His care and protection of them would never cease.

Skye pushed herself to her feet and made the bed before lifting her duffel from the floor and setting it on top. A bit subconsciously, she pulled out what she needed, her mind not on the clothes, but on what the new day would bring. She slipped out of the nightgown, laying it neatly on the bed and dressing quickly.

Fixing the white collar of her shirt, Skye stepped to the window, staring into the forest trees. Her hand slid down from the collar to her cross necklace. She squeezed it tightly and murmured in a soft voice, "Thank you, God, for Your love and care. Thank You for giving me strength during hard times. Without You I couldn't face them. Please, let the same love, care, and strength be with Will because I know what he is facing is much worse than what I am. Comfort and encourage him and keep him from being harmed. Please, help us find him. Bring him back safely . . ."

Warm tears left glistening streaks down Skye's face by the time she had finished praying. Slowly wiping them away, she turned towards the door as she heard a gentle knock. No doubt it was her father, and Skye hoped to draw even more comfort and strength from their reading together.

As dawn arrived, Will began to work again. The atmosphere around ship was very discouraging. He was ignored by everyone, or worse, avoided, except when he was being told what to do and that was usually by Worthy. Slade was the only other person who paid any attention to him, but Will would rather he didn't. Slade would glare at him hatefully whenever he passed by, and Will couldn't figure out why the man had taken such an instant dislike to him. In time he would come to find out he was not the only one.

When dinner was called, all who were not on their watch started below deck. Will lingered behind until the rest had gone before moving to the hatchway himself. He hoped and prayed to avoid trouble, especially since Slade would be down there. Reaching the hatchway, Will was about to descend into the noisy cabin below when someone called to him. He turned to see that it was Worthy.

"Yes, sir?" Will asked respectfully.

"Why don't you join me in my cabin for dinner," Worthy said.

Will was unsure of Worthy's reason for the invitation, but the man had shown him kindness so far and eating with him sounded a lot better than with Slade and the rest of the crew.

Will nodded. "All right."

"Good, come with me."

Worthy led Will to another hatchway where they went below. A few steps down a passageway stood a door that Worthy opened into his cabin. Though it was smaller than the captain's, it would be considered quite large and it was well furnished. Hale's cabin had been cluttered and disorganized; however, Worthy's was quite the opposite.

Everything was stacked and put away to an impressive degree of neatness.

Worthy motioned to a small table with a couple of chairs. "Sit down. I'll go tell Les to bring food for both of us," he said, speaking of the ship's cook.

Will took a seat, and Worthy walked out the door. While he waited for him to return, Will's eyes scanned the cabin. It didn't seem like part of a pirate ship at all. One thing that really stood out were the many books Worthy had filling several shelves. Most pirates couldn't read and even if they could the books were mainly for navigational purposes, but Worthy's were of many subjects. Almost immediately, Will noticed that one of the books was a Bible. It was becoming increasingly strange that a man like Worthy would be a pirate, but then Will found it a bit difficult to imagine Skye's father as having been one too.

Worthy returned shortly, helping Les carry trays of food. Les was a very large man with a bad limp in his right leg, which Will guessed was the reason he'd been made a cook. Unlike Corey who got his job because he was good at cooking, most pirates were made cooks if they had some injury that kept them from doing other ship work.

The food was set on the table, and Worthy took a seat across from Will. Les turned and made his way, limping out of the cabin.

"Thank you, Les," Worthy said to him.

"Yeah," Les replied in a low, almost inaudible grumble.

Will watched him go, wondering if everyone but Worthy was always going to be that standoffish around him. Once the door was closed and they no longer heard him shuffling down the hallway, Worthy looked at Will.

"He's usually not that ill-tempered," he said.

"Is it because of me?" Will asked.

"No, not at all," Worthy told him, which surprised Will. "It's not his leg either," Worthy said, causing Will to wonder. "It's his name."

Confused, Will said nothing, waiting for an explanation. Worthy grinned. "It's short for Lesley."

Now Will understood. The name would suit some men, but Les was not one of them, and Will understood how it would bother him.

"I'm not sure how that bit of information ever came to light," Worthy continued, "but it's been a joke on the ship for quite a few years, and one of the men just brought it up again. I wouldn't let on to Les that you're aware of it though."

Will shook his head. "I won't."

A few moments of silence followed as both turned to their food though Will found himself lacking much of an appetite. When Worthy didn't say anything, Will spoke again.

"Mr. Worthy—"

Worthy stopped him. "Just Worthy is fine right now," he said. "Around the captain is about the only time any of us use titles. Now, what name do you prefer to go by?"

"Just Will."

Worthy nodded. "All right, Will, what did you want to say?"

"Well, I was wondering if I may ask a few questions," Will answered cautiously.

Worthy nodded. "Yes."

"This may seem like an odd question, but I keep wondering why you left my Bible in my duffel."

Worthy shrugged. "I didn't see any reason you shouldn't be allowed to keep it."

"I see you have one." Will wasn't sure if it was a good thing to say or not.

Worthy glanced at the old, worn Bible tucked in between the other books, many memories flashing through his mind. He nodded, but said nothing.

"Do you ever read it?" Will asked slowly.

"I did, some . . . a long time ago." Worthy's voice was quiet, and Will knew better than to press him for more information despite his curiosity.

"I don't want to sound ungrateful," Will began after a moment. "But why have you treated me kindly when everyone, including the captain, acts as though they would rather either harm me or have nothing to do with me."

"Ask anyone and they'll tell you that I've never been one to behave like the rest of the crew," Worthy told him. "I have no desire to harm or show cruelty to anyone unnecessarily."

"That is not what I would have expected from someone on a pirate ship," Will admitted for though he had met some good people like John and Kate who were pirates, it was extremely rare.

Worthy nodded in understanding. "Well, many of the men here have lived this way for most of their lives and don't really know anything different, and then some just enjoy being cruel to others. I, on the other hand, have only been a pirate for a few years, and it's not really that I chose it, in a way I was forced into it."

"How?" Will asked.

Worthy sighed. "It's a long story, but I joined the navy when I was fifteen. I guess you could say that I did very well because I worked my way up in rank quite quickly. Then when I was about twenty-three, something happened, and I was accused of murder, which I hadn't done, but all evidence said I did. It was either face the gallows or run. The sea is really all I know as far as work, but I couldn't get an honest seafaring job without getting caught so . . . I turned to piracy. Hale offered me the position of quartermaster here on the *Seabird* because I knew so much about how the navy worked. I admit though, that most times I wish I hadn't come this far, yet with a record of piracy, redeeming myself is now impossible."

Will only nodded, not sure how to reply. Eventually he asked, "Is your name Worthington? I didn't see Worthy in the captain's log."

Worthy nodded. "Yes, it is."

"How did you end up being called Worthy?"

"That was Mr. Krahn's doing."

Will frowned, not having heard the name before. "Mr. Krahn?"

"Slade," Worthy told him and Will nodded. "He meant it in disrespect, but I didn't mind it so pretty soon everyone, even the captain, started using the name Worthy. I think they got tired of a long name like Worthington. I now actually prefer Worthy myself."

"I know I am asking a lot, but I have one more thing I would like to ask," Will said.

"You're free to ask whatever you want," Worthy replied. "But know that I really don't know much about why you're here and even if I did, I probably couldn't answer you."

Will understood and asked his question. "I noticed that a lot of the names between yours and mine were crossed off. What happened to them?"

Worthy's mood suddenly changed, and he became more somber. "They all died."

There was something in his voice that told Will there was a lot more to it than he had said.

"How?"

Worthy sighed and looked at him seriously. "This is actually the main reason I asked you to join me . . . I feel I need to warn you."

146

"Of what?" Will asked uneasily. For the first time since arriving on the ship he'd felt relatively comfortable while talking to Worthy, but that had all disappeared in an instant.

"The men who died were all young and here against their will, like you. They were forced here by people who wanted them out of the way for whatever reasons." Worthy paused briefly.

"What happened to them?" Will needed to know.

"None of them died by accident," Worthy said, meaningfully. "Though it's always meant to look that way, everyone knows it's Slade who killed them. For some reason whenever the captain decides to take on someone like you, Slade immediately takes a disliking to them and sets out to get rid of them. I don't see it being any different with you."

Will took a deep breath, wondering what he'd do with a man wanting to kill him. There was no place to escape to on a ship.

"If everyone knows it's Slade, why doesn't the captain do something?" Will asked, feeling frustrated.

Worthy shook his head. "By hearing him speak on land, no one would doubt that Hale is the captain, but here, on the ship, though he pretends to, he doesn't have much control. He lets Slade get away with anything because he's afraid Slade will lead a mutiny. I'm the only one who ever stands against Slade, but I can't stop everything."

Will didn't know what to think. Worthy made it sound like he had no hope.

"What can I do?" he asked.

Worthy sighed. He truly wanted to help Will all he could. "Stay alert. He may try to make it seem as though you've broken one of the articles."

Will nodded and Worthy continued. "Other than that, watch your back. Something that you have working in your favor is that you seem to be observant and one who can handle himself. The others were young and inexperienced. That's what Slade is used to. I can see you are not like that."

~~~~~~~

The *Grace's* sails billowed like white clouds and her sleek black hull sliced swiftly through the water, the bow pointed north, leaving her home waters of the Caribbean. They were a few hours now from Lucea having left shortly after breakfast with Jacob and Naomi. Supplies had been replenished quickly, and Jacob had told Daniel of some friends of his, retired sailors, who would be happy to join the crew temporarily and make up for those who were missing. In all they'd obtained seven new men, older in age, but just as capable of doing the work as the rest of them.

Through much discussion, the plan was made to sail to the island on Will's map, hoping to catch Dreger. If they couldn't and Dreger had left by the time they arrived, they'd sail on to Port Henry, Virginia where Will's father lived. All hoped he would know better how to find Will because if they missed Dreger, they wouldn't know where to look for Will next.

Having worked nearly nonstop all morning, Skye sat down to rest on the top stair of the quarterdeck where her father stood at the helm. Her mind was full, going from one thought to another, but now it stopped on a conversation she'd had with her father earlier. It was just after she had heard him talking to Caleb about how dangerous going after Dreger could be. She had wondered if Daniel would decide to have her go back to Kingston where she'd be safe while they searched for Will.

"Are you thinking of having me return home? Because if you are, I'll do whatever you ask of me, but I don't know how I could bear waiting to hear word from you."

148

Daniel shook his head. "No, Skye, I'm not. The decision is yours. You are an adult now and have long been old enough to make your own decisions."

Skye looked into his eyes. "But I'll always be your child."

She could still remember the feeling of his hug afterwards as she turned to look at him now standing straight and tall at the wheel. She loved her father so much and didn't want to think about what it would be like to not have him now to help her through this. Right there she thanked God again that He had kept Daniel alive all the years she had thought he was dead.

Finally, Skye stood and made her way down to her cabin. Blankets still lay on the floor from Marie's bed. Skye felt sadness thinking about her. She hoped with all her heart that Marie had thought seriously about the discussion they'd had about God, and that she had trusted Him as her Savior before she died. Skye wished they could have attended her funeral which Jacob had kindly offered to take care of, but Skye knew that Marie would have wanted them to do everything possible to rescue Will.

Skye folded the blankets in a thoughtful silence and set them in a pile on her bunk. Just as she finished, she heard a soft knock on her cabin door. Turning, she found Nick in the doorway and felt some of her sadness lifted by the presence of one of her close friends. Nick took a step into the cabin. He was about the same height as Skye and had the same sandy brown hair as Caleb. His light blue eyes always seemed to show great caring for everyone. He was quiet, not saying much at times, but when he did he always seemed able to say the right thing at the right time.

"What is it, Nick?" she asked.

"Dreger took all of Will's things," Nick said, "but this was still hanging on the post by Will's hammock. I thought you'd like to keep it until we can give it back to him."

Nick held out a shirt of Will's. Skye took it and ran her hand tenderly down one of the sleeves.

"Thank you, Nick," she said tremulously, her voice quiet and emotional.

"You're welcome," Nick replied. After a pause he said, "Don't worry, Skye, we'll find him. You weren't here last night, but I was talking to the others. None of us are going to give up until he's safe."

"I don't know how to thank all of you," she told him gratefully.

Nick smiled. "What are friends for, right? Besides, we have been looking out for each other since we were kids. Wasn't it you who talked your father into letting me be the cabin boy? It changed my life. I owe you something for that."

Skye shook her head with a little smile. "You don't owe me anything."

Nick shrugged. "Still, I want to help you like you helped me."

"Thank you," Skye told him again as she thanked God in her heart for giving her such wonderful friends.

Chapter Twelve

It was surprising how quickly the days passed for Will aboard the *Seabird* as work kept him busy for most of the day and sometimes into the night. He was worked hard which Worthy apologized for in private, but it was Captain Hale who ordered it believing if Will was busy he'd be less likely to cause any trouble. Different members of the crew began warming up to him some, though most still kept their distance. Worthy told Will that it was because they knew Slade was going to try to kill him, and they had no interest in making friends with someone they didn't think would be around very long.

So far, Slade had not yet attempted anything to get Will in trouble or to harm him. He'd taken to calling Will *Mr. Religious* because of his Bible reading, but words and dark looks were as far as he'd gone. However, Will expected him to make a move at any time though he kept praying he'd be proven wrong.

During the third afternoon on the *Seabird*, the weather became noticeably cooler as the ship continued on the northerly course it had been traveling from Jamaica. Will knew they were no longer in the Caribbean and were now in waters he had never seen before. That knowledge made him feel even farther from home than he was though there was comfort in knowing that he was closer to his father.

Will bent down and tightened a line to one of the belaying pins, being sure to knot it securely so it wouldn't come undone. As he straightened he grimaced, his back protesting painfully. Not used to his sleeping conditions, most of his body ached. Reaching up, he rubbed one of his shoulders as he turned to go about his work.

"Mr. James."

The call came from Worthy who made his way over to Will. He had advised Will against acting as friends in front of the rest of the crew fearing Will's situation with Slade may be made worse as a result. Worthy stopped beside Will and made it look as though he was merely giving him orders.

"How are you doing?" Worthy asked quietly. He had noticed Will's lack of energy.

"As well as I can in my situation."

"Are you sleeping all right? You seem to be especially tired these last two days."

Will sighed. "No."

"Why not? Is there a reason?"

Will glanced at Slade, which Worthy noticed easily. "I'd rather not borrow trouble."

"I see," Worthy said thoughtfully.

~~~

The island was quite small—only about a mile across. From where she stood on the rocky hill jutting up from the island's center, Skye was able to see the ocean on all sides. They had found the small, tunnel-like cave which was barely big enough for two people to fit inside, but apart from dark emptiness, they had found nothing within. Dreger had beaten them to the island and left with the letters and whatever else was meant for Will.

Skye looked to her father as he took a step out of the cave entrance. Their eyes locked for a long moment, both praying that God would lead them to Will because they felt a feeling of horrible helplessness. Skye turned her eyes once again to the ocean, praying for some sign of Dreger's ship, but the water held no sign of anything. They were too late, again.

Glancing at the others, Daniel said, "We're still three days from Virginia. I say we go back to the ship and set course for Port Henry."

The men nodded in agreement and turned towards the beach. Along the way, Daniel walked beside Skye and tried to give her hope.

"When Kelley held you prisoner, Will and Matthew didn't know where you were either, but God led them to that small island that you and Kate were stranded on. Remember that."

Skye nodded and spoke quietly. "I will."

~ ~ ~

When late evening descended on the *Seabird*, Will sat down in the forecastle with many of the other crewmen getting what rest he could before his watch was called again. He sat silently, propped up against the cabin's side, reading his Bible. The cabin was noisy because Slade and his boisterous friends were there, but Will kept focused on the words of comfort he was reading.

Suddenly, Worthy appeared and everyone quieted.

"Inspection," he said loudly.

Will lowered his Bible, and the other men looked at Worthy in surprise. Slade, however, looked angry.

"You never told us you were doing no inspection," he growled. "And this ain't no navy ship. Why don't you go inspect your own cabin?"

153

"No, this isn't a navy ship, but I do inspections anyway. And I didn't give you prior notice because I wanted anything you might have hidden beforehand to be out in the open, which leads me to the question of why he is on the floor?" Worthy gestured towards Will.

Instead of answering the question, Slade glared murderously at Will before looking back to Worthy. "He told ya didn't 'e?"

"No one told me anything," Worthy snapped sternly. "I already knew before he arrived on this ship that you were going to make his life miserable, and I came to see in what way you have." Without taking his gaze from Slade, Worthy said, "Mr. Fowley."

"Aye, sir," the man replied.

"Get me another hammock."

Fowley glanced briefly at Slade before moving grudgingly past Worthy. Meanwhile, Worthy continued his so called inspection, checking the condition of the cabin and telling some of the men to straighten up their belongings. Only a short minute passed before Fowley returned carrying a new canvas hammock. He handed it to Worthy who looked at Will.

"Mr. James, will you help me with this?"

Will got to his feet to help Worthy string up the hammock. Once it was hanging from the posts, Worthy peered at each of the men, particularly at Slade.

"If anyone touches this hammock, I'll see to it that they regret it."

Slade scowled and Worthy glared at him warningly. He glanced once more at the others before exiting the cabin. Slowly, Will turned back to his bed on the floor to move his things over to the hammock. He was careful to keep Skye's portrait hidden in the folds of one of the blankets. Though Will kept his eyes on what he was doing he could feel Slade's burning gaze. All was uncomfortably quiet.

154

Once settled, Will read for a short time more, finally in the comfort of a hammock, but his mind and body were tense. Though everyone else had gone back to conversation, he heard no more from Slade. His silence would have been a relief since his language was foul, but if he was not speaking that could only mean that he was plotting silently.

With a desperate plea for protection and guidance, Will turned to put his Bible back in his duffel. When he was sure no one was watching, he also slipped Skye's portrait into the pocket of one of his waistcoats.

Sighing deeply, Will put out his lantern and lay down. One by one, the other lanterns were extinguished as well and there was darkness. Will closed his eyes and tried to sleep knowing how much he needed the rest, but it would not come. Everything he didn't want to think about came to his mind. His mother's death, the heartbreaking look on Skye's face as he'd been taken away from her, the thought of not seeing her again, and now the prospect of Slade planning to kill him. It was all nearing the point of unbearable, but Will laid out all that he was feeling before God knowing that Satan was trying to overwhelm him with his thoughts. With some effort and God's help, Will was finally able to calm himself and fall into sleep.

Daybreak arrived several hours later with the sound of the bell on deck. Will felt that some of his energy had returned because his sleep had been comfortable. He began to dress, thinking regretfully of how he was never able to read in the mornings since he could have no light in the cabin while the rest of the men were sleeping. Putting on the waistcoat he'd slipped Skye's portrait into during the night, he reached into the pocket and his breath caught. It was empty. Will got down next to his duffel and searched through it, praying that the portrait had somehow fallen out of the pocket. Dread settled in his stomach when he heard footsteps come to a stop behind him.

"Lookin' for somethin'?" Slade taunted cruelly.

Sighing heavily, Will got up and faced Slade. The portrait was gripped in the man's hand. Slade grinned viciously.

"A real fine lookin' young woman ya got there." He held up the portrait. "What's 'er name?"

Will refused to answer and looked from the portrait to Slade.

"I want it back," he said firmly, having nothing to lose by trying though he knew it was pretty much hopeless.

Slade raised his eyebrows. "Oh ya do, do ya?" he asked mockingly. "Well, that's too bad because there ain't much to look at around here so I think I'll keep it."

The thought of a man like Slade looking at a portrait of Skye made anger rise up within Will, but he knew there was nothing that could be done without quite possibly getting himself killed as a result. Asking God to help him with his anger, Will forced himself to turn away from Slade and leave the cabin. He heard Slade's snickering echo evilly from behind.

The day was very difficult. Will was sick over what had happened though he had expected it sooner or later. Slade used every opportunity to taunt Will with the portrait, and Will spent a good portion of the day praying just to get through it.

Finally, evening arrived and Will went to the forecastle while everyone else ate supper, hoping to be granted some relief from the day's hardships. He sat down in his hammock trying to take his mind from all his troubles. Looking around the gloomy cabin, his eyes came to rest near Slade's hammock, and he was stunned to see Skye's portrait sitting in plain sight on top of Slade's pile of belongings.

156

Will stood up instantly, but stopped himself after he had taken a step. Finding it sitting right there was too easy. Slade never would have done it if not purposely. Will was reminded of one of the ship's articles. It dealt with stealing from another crewmember and the punishment was either to be marooned or shot. From what Worthy had told him, Will knew the articles wouldn't be applied to Slade in this instance, but to himself. Even if he was only taking back what belonged to him, the captain would never stand up to Slade no matter if Will pointed out Slade had stolen the portrait from him. His only recourse was to find some way to get the portrait back from Slade without getting himself into any more trouble.

All night, Will was restless as he expected Slade to pounce on him at any moment like a cat on a mouse. Throughout breakfast and the morning hours of the next day, Will watched Slade carefully, but it was not until he had let his guard down for only an instant that Slade acted. Nearing the noon meal, a shadow loomed over Will, and he was grabbed roughly from behind. Before he could react, he was shoved with great force and slammed into the side railing. The impact nearly took his breath away as his chest hit the hard wood. He turned quickly and was grabbed again as Slade pushed him up against one of the masts and pointed a pistol in his face.

"Where is it!" he demanded furiously.

Will had no chance to answer before the crew gathered around, and Hale worked his way quickly through them.

"What is this?" he asked.

"He stole from me," Slade said angrily, his grip on Will never loosening.

Hale looked at Will accusingly.

"No, I didn't," Will said.

"Liar!" Slade shouted. Will feared he would pull the trigger of his pistol, but Slade looked back to Hale. "He stole from me, Captain, and the articles say the punishment for it is being shot."

"Yes, they do, Mr. Krahn, but Captain Hendricks may want 'im alive," Hale replied.

"Well, there are other punishments that don't involve killin' 'im," Slade said nastily, though the prospect frustrated his thirst for Will's demise.

"I didn't steal anything," Will said again, but Hale didn't look convinced.

Turning from Will back to Slade, Hale asked, "Since you are the one 'e stole from, what do you suggest?"

A purely evil grin crossed Slade's face, and Will prayed for deliverance. Just as Slade opened his mouth to speak, they heard Worthy's voice, and Will was filled with relief.

"What is going on here?" Worthy demanded.

"Mr. Krahn says that Mr. James stole somethin' from 'im," Hale declared.

Worthy looked first at Slade. "Mr. Krahn, I want you to put away that pistol now and release him for if there is to be any punishment, I, as the quartermaster, am the only one who can administer it." His voice held great authority, and Slade really had no choice but to comply though it infuriated him. Worthy turned next to Will. "Have you stolen anything from Mr. Krahn?"

Will shook his head. "No."

"He's a liar," Slade growled.

"Is he?" Worthy looked completely unconvinced. "What did he steal from you?"

"That's none of yer business," Slade countered.

"Seeing that I'm the quartermaster I beg to differ," Worthy responded. "And if the item you are accusing him of stealing is this portrait that I have here it would make a big difference." He held in his hand the portrait of Skye.

"Where did you get that?" Slade demanded with narrowed eyes.

"I was looking for Mr. Fowley last night and found it sitting on top of your belongings. I remember this belonging to Mr. James so the question is how did you get it? It would seem, Mr. Krahn, you are the only one who has done any stealing and therefore whatever punishment you intended for Mr. James should rightfully be your own."

Slade didn't seem to be intimidated by this, only more angered.

All looked to Captain Hale for his response. Will found it no surprise that he looked uncertain. He glanced uncomfortably at Slade before finally speaking.

"Enough with this! We've wasted too much time already," he groused. "Everyone back to work."

Looking at each other with expressions that were hard to read, the crew departed wordlessly. With a smug look, Slade moved past Worthy who watched him angrily, but Will could see the defeated look in his eyes. Finally, he looked back to Will.

"Are you all right?" Worthy asked.

Will rubbed his hand over his bruised ribs and nodded. "Yes."

"Do you want the portrait back or would you like me to keep it?"

Will sighed. "I think you should keep it."

Worthy nodded feeling that was best. "Whenever you want it, you can come and get it."

"Thank you." Will lowered his voice. "And thank you for helping me with this."

Worthy smiled. "You're welcome."

Will returned to his work with great relief knowing that the portrait was out of Slade's hands and safely in Worthy's.

He thanked God that Worthy was able to help him, even if nothing had been done about Slade. This small victory gave Will hope, something he sorely needed.

The remainder of the day passed better for Will than the last couple. Slade kept his distance and a few of the men seemed to be even more open to Will. All of the men were shocked he had survived his first encounter with Slade and many hoped it wouldn't be the only time he prevailed. They were tired of Slade always being the victor.

As night approached, Will was asked to get a lantern for them. Wanting to better establish himself among the men, he hurried below. He came to the end of one of the passageways and was suddenly grabbed by the front of his waistcoat and pulled into a dark corner. A razor sharp blade was held against his throat. Slade stood before him, eyes full of an intense loathing which would have sent chills of fear through anyone. He spoke in a low, sinister voice.

"I know Worthy told you about me and don't think that just because you two succeeded today that this will end. I *will* get you and after that, Worthy is next. You can tell him that."

He held onto Will for another few seconds, adding dangerous pressure to his dagger before storming off. For a long moment, Will did not move from the spot. He let out a long, deep breath, his heart racing. Closing his eyes in relief, Will prayed, "Thank You, God, for not allowing him to kill me."

Slade could have cut his throat so easily.

Chapter Thirteen

Port Henry, Virginia bustled with ships and fishing boats coming and going, filling a good portion of the city's harbor. Good as he was, it took Daniel some time to find a place to dock.

From the railing, Skye's eyes scanned with fascination all the buildings lining the edge of the beach. Something seemed different about American cities from those of the Caribbean. The land was not tropical or mountainous like Jamaica and other Caribbean islands. Still, it wasn't only the land that made it different though Skye couldn't tell what it was, but she was very anxious to go ashore.

Once they finally found an empty space at one of the docks, they moored the ship and Skye followed Daniel and Caleb down the gangplank. Everyone else opted to stay near the *Grace*. The city streets were as busy with people as the water was with ships. Though Port Henry was smaller than Kingston it seemed to be a center of business. Skye had never been to England, but she imagined its smaller cities would look much like this.

Walking along the shoreline they checked the buildings for the name of *Westin & James Trading*. Though Mr. Westin had passed away since handing his company over to Edward, Jacob told them that he had still kept the name. It did not take them long to find the building, a very expansive, well established place that Skye guessed had been started at the city's founding.

The three of them looked at each other, all feeling the significance of this moment. Taking the lead, Daniel started for the front door. Skye felt a mix of feelings she wasn't sure how to interpret as she followed him. Again she was struck with sadness that Will wasn't here with them. She also felt what could only be described as nervousness, wondering what Will's father would be like.

Inside the building, Daniel walked up to a large desk where a clerk stood.

"Can I help you?" the man asked.

"Yes, is Mr. James in?"

"I'm sorry, but Mr. James is away on business," the clerk informed them regrettably. "But he should return in a day or two. Do you want to leave him a message?"

"No, thank you. It's of a rather important matter that pertains to a family member, and I'd rather speak with him in person," Daniel replied. "However, I would like to know if his family is still at home."

"Yes," the clerk answered. "They should be."

"Can you please direct us to his estate?"

"It's about five miles north of here along the shore. Would you like me to have someone get you a carriage?"

Daniel thought about it for a moment, knowing it would be quite late by the time they arrived at the estate if they walked.

"Yes, we'd appreciate that."

"All right. You can have a seat while you wait." The clerk motioned towards some benches lining the wall and walked off to get someone to go for a carriage.

The three of them sat down, and Daniel sighed. "I wasn't sure if we should go talk to Mrs. James or not. What do you think?"

"Well, she probably knows exactly when Mr. James is going to be back and the sooner we see him the better," Caleb reasoned. "She may even know something that would help us."

Daniel agreed and they continued to wait until the clerk returned to say their carriage was waiting outside. They thanked him and walked outside. The inside of the carriage was very luxurious with cushioned bench seats at both ends. Skye and her father took a seat on one, and Caleb sat across from them. It was one of the first times Skye had ever ridden in a carriage. At home she always walked wherever she was going.

During the ride, Skye stared out the window at the strange, yet beautiful countryside they passed. Everything here fascinated her, and she wished deeply they were here for different reasons and that Will was with them. She would have loved to explore with him and take in the different scenery together. However, her thoughts remained on their mission, and she began wondering again what the James family would be like. Would they be like Will or completely different?

Twenty minutes after leaving the city, the forest trees opened up around them, and the carriage rolled onto a gravel path. They had reached the James' estate. Skye saw beautiful green lawn, flower gardens blooming with early spring flowers, sparkling ponds, and decorative shrubs and trees. Outbuildings stood around the edges, but Skye could not see the house until the carriage came to a stop in front of it and they climbed out.

Skye was in awe of the place. The house was about the same size as her grandfather's, but unlike her grandfather's estate, everything seemed bigger because of the huge area of land surrounding. Though she couldn't see it, Skye knew that the ocean was near because she could smell the sea air and hear the splashing of waves.

Daniel paid the carriage driver, and they walked up to the huge porch of the house whose roof was supported by large white pillars. He knocked and as they waited for an answer, Skye gazed around her taking in every detail of the magnificent house. A moment later, she heard the door open, and they were greeted by a younger black woman.

"Can I help you?" she asked. Her face was kindly and her voice pleasant.

"We were told that Mr. James is away, but we were hoping to speak with Mrs. James if she is available," Daniel said. "It's very important."

"Of course," the woman replied. "Please, come in."

She let them inside the large, hall-like foyer. Dark mahogany furnishings sat against walls painted a soft golden yellow. It had a cathedral ceiling and a long rug extended from the front door to a massive winding staircase that led to the second floor. From the foyer she led them into the beautiful little parlor off to their right.

"Please, make yourselves comfortable. I will tell Mrs. James that you are here," the woman said to them.

"Thank you," Daniel said politely.

Only a minute or two passed before she returned in the presence of another slightly older woman who had dark chestnut colored hair and soft brown eyes. Smiling sweetly, she said, "I am Mrs. Edward James. What can I do for you?"

"Mrs. James, I am Captain Daniel McHenry, and this is my daughter Skylar and my first mate Caleb Jordan. We came to Port Henry to speak with your husband but have found that he is away. In his absence, we have a need to speak with you."

"I'm very pleased to meet you, Captain. My husband has expressed great interest and admiration for you on many occasions. I'm sorry that he isn't here. What is it you need to speak with him about?"

"Well, Mrs. James . . ." Daniel paused. There was not really any gradual way to put it so he continued, ". . . we know his son, William."

A look of astonishment came to Mrs. James' face. "You know William?"

Daniel nodded.

"Is he here?" Mrs. James asked in shock.

"No, and that is why we've come. I'm afraid the reason he is not with us is because he was taken captive a week ago in Jamaica. We had hoped your husband would know how to help us find him."

"Captive?" Mrs. James looked very upset. "Why?"

"We don't know, but it has something to do with a map your husband left for Will with his friend, Jacob Tucker, in Lucea. Your husband is the only one who might know what is going on. Without his input we don't know where to search for Will or how to find him. How soon will he be back?"

"I expect him home tomorrow afternoon. I'd send a message to him, but it would barely get there before he was already on his way back," Mrs. James answered. "In the meantime please stay here for the night so that you'll be here when he arrives."

"Are you sure, Mrs. James?" Daniel asked. "We'd be perfectly content to stay on our ship."

"Yes, I'm quite sure and please, call me Rebecca."

It was at that moment they heard a plaintive voice.

"Mama, Molly said I ask too many questions and to leave her alone."

Rebecca turned as ten-year-old Emma walked into the room. She had long, dark brown hair and dark eyes. Skye was instantly reminded of Will.

"Emma, dear, we have company," Rebecca admonished lightly.

Emma looked at the three newcomers, and blushed a little in embarrassment. Skye smiled at how cute she was.

"Sorry, Mama."

"That's all right," Rebecca told her with a gentle smile. She motioned for Emma to come closer. "Emma, this is Captain Daniel McHenry, his daughter Skylar, and his first mate Caleb Jordan."

Emma's eyes widened as she looked at each of them. She seemed nearly speechless. "Really?" she asked in little more than a whisper.

Rebecca nodded and Emma continued to stare wide-eyed.

"Aren't you going to greet them?" Rebecca prompted after a moment.

"It's nice to meet you," Emma said, becoming a bit shy.

They each greeted her with kind smiles.

"Emma, why don't you get your sisters," Rebecca suggested.

"All right, Mama."

Emma turned and dashed out of the room. Before she was completely out of hearing distance, they heard her shouting, "Lydie! Molly! You'll never ever guess who's here!"

Everyone chuckled.

"Her father tells her about you all the time," Rebecca told them. "You're certainly some of her greatest heroes. I think this was the only time you'll ever see her speechless or shy."

Daniel smiled. "We're honored to be so highly thought of."

Rebecca smiled as well before turning to the maid. "Rose, will you please tell Samuel that we'll have three extra for supper?"

"Yes ma'am," Rose replied, turning for the kitchen.

"Why don't we go into the drawing room," Rebecca told Daniel. "If it is not asking too much, I would like to hear more about Will. His father still speaks of him often and despite the fact that I've never seen him I've almost come to feel as though he were one of my own children so your news saddens me deeply. Edward will be very dismayed to hear it."

By this time they reached the beautiful, spacious drawing room that was decorated much like the foyer. It held many areas for sitting, and a stone fireplace which was nearly as tall as Skye stood at one end. They all took seats on two of the sofas.

"There are so many questions in my mind that I'm not sure where to begin," Rebecca said. "I guess all I can really ask first is what is William like? Edward could only describe him to me as an infant."

"Will is an extraordinary young man," Daniel told her. "Very devoted to God and those he cares about. But I think Skye should be the one to tell you. She's known him far longer than I have, ever since they were children."

Rebecca looked to Skye.

"My father described him well," Skye said. "He is a very hard worker and is always caring of others." Remembering Will's portrait, she reached into her pocket and handed it to Rebecca. "This is a portrait of him."

A loving smile came to Rebecca's face. "Ah, he looks like his father," she commented, touched. "He has the same kind look that seems to run in the James family."

Skye nodded and added in a quiet, sad voice, "There's no one I've ever met who has been more kind or caring than him."

A bit of commotion from outside the room stole their attention. Presently, two girls entered the room. One was about seventeen and the other fourteen. Both had brown hair and eyes like Rebecca. Emma walked behind them, pushing them along.

". . . he really is here. Mama will tell you that I'm serious." They caught the end of what Emma was saying as she entered.

The two older girls looked first at their guests and then turned questioning eyes toward their mother.

"Mother," the older began, "Emma keeps insisting that Captain McHenry is here. Is she telling the truth?"

Rebecca nodded, smiling. "Yes, she is."

The two girls looked at each other in astonishment, and Rebecca promptly introduced them.

"These are my daughters. Lydie," Rebecca spoke first of the older one, "and Molly." Lastly, she introduced her guests to her daughters.

Both Lydie and Molly exchanged greetings with the same shocked, but polite reactions as Emma had.

"I told you I was telling the truth," Emma reminded her sisters excitedly.

They glanced at her in a bit of disbelief. Finally, Lydie looked at her mother.

"May I ask what this is about?"

Rebecca nodded. "They are here because they know your brother, William."

"They do?" All three girls asked the question at the same time.

"Is he here too?" Emma asked, her voice full of excitement.

"I'm afraid not," Rebecca told her with regret.

"Why not?" Emma was heartily disappointed.

"Well," Rebecca began slowly, "something bad has happened, and Will was captured by some men."

"Oh," Emma said, her face falling. "Are we going to rescue him?"

"When your father gets home, yes. He will help Captain McHenry find him."

"I will pray for him and maybe God will rescue him and get him here sooner," Emma said hopefully.

"You do that, Emma," Rebecca encouraged. "We should all pray for him."

Emma looked down at her mother's hands. "Is that Will?" she asked, pointing to the portrait.

"Yes, it is." Rebecca held it up for her to see. Lydie and Molly crowded around it as well.

"He looks like Papa, doesn't he?" Emma said brightly.

Rebecca nodded with a smile. "Yes, he does."

"I hope Papa and Captain McHenry find him and bring him home. I want to meet him, and it would make Papa really happy."

"We all do."

A moment later, Rose entered the room. "Excuse me, ma'am, but Samuel will have supper ready in a half an hour."

"Thank you, Rose."

"Mama, are they staying for supper?" Emma questioned hopefully.

"Yes, dear. They're going to stay until your father gets home."

Emma grinned. "Really?"

Rebecca nodded. She then turned her attention to Daniel. "Why don't I show you to your rooms, and you can freshen up before supper."

"Thank you, Rebecca."

They stood up, and Rebecca looked at Rose. "Could you please bring water and towels to the guest rooms?"

"Yes, ma'am."

The girls all tagged along behind as Rebecca led everyone upstairs. As they made their way up, Rebecca said, "At supper you will get to meet my youngest daughter, Ashley.

169

She's almost two now and should be waking up from a late nap shortly."

On the second floor, Rebecca stopped and pointed to two of many doors dotting the length of the hall. "Captain McHenry, you and Mr. Jordan may have these two rooms. Your daughter will be just down there." She pointed to a door not far away.

Daniel thanked her, and he and Caleb entered their rooms. Rebecca led Skye down to hers. They stepped inside it, the three girls still following.

The room was amazing. It was at least twice as large as Skye's room at home.

"Is there anything I can get you?" Rebecca asked.

Skye shook her head. "No, but you'll have to excuse the fact that I'm not really dressed for a meal." She was feeling a bit out of place in her soiled sailing clothes, ones she'd worn for the last two days.

"You could wear one of my dresses if you'd like," Lydie spoke up. "You're a little taller than me, but we seem about the same size."

Skye smiled. "Thank you. That would be very kind of you."

"Come with me to my room," Lydie invited.

She led the way farther down the hall. Emma and Molly were only a couple of steps behind. Inside her room, Lydie went to a massive wardrobe and pulled the doors open.

"What is your favorite color?" she asked Skye.

"Blue."

Lydie smiled. "Mine too."

She pulled out a blue gown and petticoats before going to a dresser where she took out a chemise, stays, and stockings. Meanwhile, Emma looked up at Skye curiously.

"Miss McHenry, do you always dress like a boy?" she asked.

Skye heard Lydie sigh and Molly looked embarrassed, but Skye smiled at Emma, not minding her bluntness at all.

"When I'm sailing, yes. I couldn't climb the rigging in a dress."

"Do you climb all the way to the top?"

"Sometimes."

"My uncle, Chris, helped me climb up once on one of Papa's ships, but I didn't get to go very high," Emma said. "You're lucky. I wish I didn't have to wear a dress and could sail to all the neat places you do. Is it fun sailing with your papa?"

"Yes, it is."

"Does Will sail with you too?"

This question seemed to interest Lydie and Molly too.

Skye nodded. "Yes, he does."

"How did you meet him?"

"In an orphanage when he was just about your age."

"Why were you in an orphanage if you have your papa?"

Lydie walked up to her. "Okay, Emma, I think that's enough questions for now."

"But—" Emma began.

Lydie stopped her, saying it was time to get ready for supper, not time to be asking questions.

The four of them returned to Skye's bedroom, and Lydie laid everything out on the bed. Rose came in just after them with a pitcher of warm water and some towels which she set on a small table at one side of the room. After she left, Lydie looked at Skye with a grin that looked much like Emma's and asked, "Would you like me help you with the nasty stays?"

Skye smiled and almost laughed, seeing that though she was older and more mature, Lydie seemed as fun loving as Emma. "Yes, that would be very helpful."

Lydie then turned to Molly who Skye noticed was the quieter one of her sisters.

"Molly, could you go ask Mother for a pair of shoes. Mine would probably be too small."

"All right." Molly was happy to help.

"Emma, you should get ready for supper too," Lydie told her other sister.

"I want to stay here," Emma informed her.

Lydie gave her a bit of a warning look, but let her stay.

Once the door had closed after Molly, Skye began to undress. When she pulled off her shirt, she heard Emma gasp and remembered the long scar she had along her shoulder and down part of her back from Kelley's whip.

"Lydie, do you see that scar?" Emma asked not so quietly.

"Emma!" Lydie whispered sharply, frowning at her little sister.

Skye turned to a horrified and embarrassed looking Lydie and smiled understandingly.

"It's all right, Lydie," she said. "Really."

"You'll have to excuse my sister," Lydie told her apologetically. "She can be a bit too inquisitive sometimes."

Emma screwed up her face. "I'm not inquisitive, I'm curious."

Lydie looked at her with a bit of exasperation. "It's the same thing."

"Oh," Emma said. She looked at Skye. "Miss McHenry, how did you get that scar?" Lydie frowned at her again and Emma added, "If you don't want to tell me you don't have to."

Skye smiled. "It's quite a long story. How about if I tell you later?"

"Okay," Emma replied happily though hardly able to wait.

"And, I'd like for you all to call me Skye."

172

"Okay, Skye." Emma smiled. "That's a pretty name."

"Thank you," Skye replied. "You and your sisters have pretty names too."

Emma looked pleased.

Once Skye had washed up and was dressed and Lydie, Molly, and Emma were ready as well, the four of them met Daniel and Caleb in the hall and they all went back down to the drawing room. Rebecca was waiting for them holding Ashley. The little girl's thumb was in her mouth, and her big dark eyes still showed sleepiness. With her free hand she toyed with some of her wispy dark brown hair. She definitely looked like a James.

Everyone walked closer and smiled for the girl was adorable. It made Skye think about how Will must have looked as a baby.

"This is Ashley," Rebecca said. She looked down at her daughter. "Ashley, can you say hello?"

Ashley looked at the three strangers and buried her head shyly in Rebecca's shoulder. Her mother smiled.

"She'll warm up to you after a couple of hours," she told them.

Interested only in the precious little girl, no one had noticed that someone else had entered the room until he spoke up.

"Rebecca."

Everyone turned.

"Stephan," Rebecca said in surprise. "I didn't know you were coming this evening."

The man before them was about the same age as Will, perhaps a year or two older. His eyes and hair were lighter in color, and he looked very much the business type, elegant in dress and manner.

"I thought I'd stop and see how you were doing with Edward away," Stephan replied.

"We're doing just fine," Rebecca told him. Right away she turned to make introductions and introduced the man as Stephan Daley, Edward's nephew, the son of his older sister.

"So you actually know my cousin William?" Stephan said after Rebecca had explained everything to him. "That is very shocking. My uncle was always optimistic that some-day this would happen, but I honestly never believed it would."

"It's been a shock to both sides," Daniel replied. "I wish it would have come about under happier circumstances."

Stephan agreed. "Do you have any guess as to why he is being held captive?"

"No, but there is some sort of plan afoot that they didn't want any of us looking into."

"Aren't you concerned about what may happen when you go after him?" Stephan wondered.

Daniel shook his head. "They can make whatever threats they want, but we won't return home without Will."

"You're very brave," Stephan commended them.

But Daniel replied, "It's not bravery. We care deeply about Will and won't simply abandon him."

Stephan raised and lowered his brows in a nod of understanding.

Rose then came in once again to announce that supper was ready.

"Stephan, would you care to join us?" Rebecca asked. "Samuel always makes enough for someone extra."

"If it is no trouble I'd be delighted to," Stephan answered eagerly. "I'll admit that I'm rather curious to hear more about William."

They turned for the dining room. Stephan looked at Skye, surprising her a little.

"May I?" He extended his arm with a charming smile.

At first, Skye was slightly hesitant, not used to being escorted by young men other than Will, but she knew that feeling of reluctance was going against what her grandfather was trying to teach her. Remembering her manners, she returned the smile and nodded, taking hold of his arm. He guided her along to the dining room, and Skye could tell that every one of his gentlemanly manners were perfect likely having been practiced since childhood.

"If I may, Miss McHenry," Stephan said along the way, "I would like to compliment you on your beauty. Stories travel far, but until now I didn't realize you are as lovely as people say."

Skye smiled politely. "Thank you, Mr. Daley. I am flattered."

"Someday you shall make someone a very lucky man," Stephan added.

Skye only nodded quietly, not speaking as her thoughts took her elsewhere.

"I'm sorry, have I upset you?" she heard him ask a moment later.

Skye quickly shook her head. "No, I was only thinking."

"Of someone?"

Skye nodded. "Yes."

"Would that by any chance be William?"

Again, Skye nodded.

"I understand," Stephan said. "I'm sorry about your loss."

"We'll find him," Skye replied with a surety that surprised even her a little. "I believe God will help us."

By this time they had reached the dining room, and Stephan didn't have a chance to reply. The room was finely decorated like that of Skye's grandfather's, and the dark stained table was long enough to accommodate many guests. Stephan pulled out a chair for Skye, and she sat down. Daniel did the same for Rebecca before taking a seat beside Skye.

There seemed to be more talking than eating during the meal. Questions were asked by both Rebecca and Stephan and Skye, Daniel, and Caleb told them all about Will and what had happened back in Jamaica. Lydie, Molly, and Emma were transfixed by what was being said, and Emma had to be reminded several times to eat her food before it got cold. They remained at the table even after the dishes were cleared. Finally, late in the evening, Stephan rose.

"I really should be getting home," he said. "Perhaps I will stop by tomorrow to see Edward."

They bid him farewell, and he left the room. Caleb looked at Daniel.

"I should go back to the *Grace* and get our things before it gets late."

Daniel agreed.

"I can have, Isaac, our stableman take you with one of the carriages," Rebecca offered.

"Thank you very much," Caleb replied gratefully.

Everyone rose from their seats.

"Rose, will you please tell your brother to hitch up one of the carriages," Rebecca instructed.

Rose nodded and hurried out of the room. Fifteen minutes later she returned with news that the carriage was ready. Caleb started for the door.

"I think I'll go with him," Daniel told Skye.

Skye nodded. "All right."

After they had both left, Skye followed Rebecca and her daughters into the drawing room. By now, Ashley was becoming a little more interested in all that was going on. Rebecca set her down on the floor, and she walked around near Skye looking at her with curious eyes. Skye spoke to her softly and before long was rewarded with a smile. It took some coaxing from Rebecca, but Ashley finally let Skye pick her up and after that, Ashley didn't want to leave her. Skye enjoyed it all immensely. She loved children and wasn't around as many as she had been in the orphanage. It was one of the only things she missed about working there.

After a while, Skye noticed Emma starting to get restless and remembered that she had told her she'd tell her how she got her scar.

"I promised you a story didn't I, Emma?" she asked with a smile.

"Yes, you did," Emma answered eagerly. "Let's go upstairs and you can tell it to me."

"All right," Skye said.

She got up to give Ashley back to Rebecca, but Ashley held on tightly to Skye.

"Can she come with us?" Skye asked.

Rebecca smiled. "Of course." She looked at Ashley. "Ashley, do you want to go with Skye?"

Ashley took her thumb out of her mouth for a moment. "Kye," she said making everyone smile.

Skye, Ashley, and Emma turned to go upstairs. Lydie and Molly quickly got up to follow. All five of them went to Skye's room where they gathered on the bed. When everyone was comfortable, Skye began telling them the story of her life. Each one was very quickly captivated and hung onto her every word. All lost track of time and were quite surprised when there was a knock on the door. They looked up to see Rebecca and Daniel in the doorway.

"Sorry to bother you," Rebecca said. "But Molly and Emma, I think it's about time you got to bed."

"What time is it?" Molly asked.

"Almost ten."

Molly started to get up.

"Ah, Mama. We were just about to find out how they got off the island to go save Will," Emma tried to explain.

Rebecca smiled. "You can finish tomorrow. You don't want to be tired when your father gets home, do you? If you are you'll have to go to bed early, and I don't think you want that."

"Okay," Emma sighed.

She and Molly walked out of the room. They could hear Emma talking about what Skye had told them as they made their way down the hall. With a smile, Rebecca came over to the bed to get Ashley who had fallen asleep against Skye. Lydie got up as well.

"I guess I should get some sleep too," she said. "Good night, Skye."

Skye smiled. "Good night, Lydie."

"Thank you for spending time with them," Rebecca told Skye after Lydie was gone. "I know Emma enjoys it immensely. This is a dream come true for her."

"I very much enjoy it myself," Skye said.

With a goodnight to each of them, Rebecca left Skye and her father alone. They smiled warmly at each other.

"Here's your duffel." Daniel set it on the bed before turning back to his daughter. "How are you feeling?"

"It's amazing to be here," Skye answered. "It almost doesn't seem real. I can hardly believe yet that this is Will's family. I wish so much that he was here."

Daniel nodded. "He will be very happy when he gets to meet them. They are a wonderful family that will obviously welcome him with open arms."

Skye agreed. "Yes. They make you feel very comfortable." She sighed. "I just want so badly to be enjoying it *with* him."

Daniel put his hands on her shoulders. "Tomorrow we can start searching for him again, and we *will* find him."

Chapter Fourteen

Whatever you do, do your work heartily,
as for the Lord rather than for men, knowing
that from the Lord you will receive the reward
of the inheritance. It is the Lord Christ
whom you serve. — Col. 3: 23-24

Sunlight poured into the room through the light colored curtains of the room's large windows as Skye woke the next morning. For a while, she lay still, thinking and talking to God. It felt so good to tell Him all that was in her heart.

Just as Skye was planning to get up, she heard her doorknob turning slowly. There was some muffled movement, and she heard Ashley's quiet voice.

"Kye."

"Shh!" It was Emma.

Skye smiled to herself, her back to the door. She waited and heard their quiet footsteps nearing her bed. They finally stopped right near the edge. Skye waited a few moments more before rolling over quickly to face the two nightgown clad girls with a grin. Ashley shrieked with delight and giggled. Emma lifted her onto the bed and crawled onto it herself.

"Can you finish the story?" Emma asked with a grin of excitement.

Skye smiled as Ashley quickly made herself comfortable, crawling under the blankets next to her.

"What about Lydie and Molly?" Skye wanted to know. "They'll want to hear it too."

Emma thought about it for a moment. "Well . . ." She tried to come up with a solution, but sighed. "I guess we'll have to wait for them to wake up."

"You won't have to wait long." Lydie's voice drew their attention to the door where she and Molly were standing, both still in their nightgowns as well. "You didn't wake her up, did you, Emma?"

"No," Emma answered quickly. But then she looked at Skye in uncertainty. "Did I?"

Skye shook her head. "No, I was already awake."

Emma smiled in relief. "Good. Can you finish the story now?"

"If Lydie and Molly want to stay and listen," Skye told her.

Those two smiled and quickly took seats on the bed next to Emma. Skye propped her pillow up and made herself more comfortable, putting her arm around Ashley who cuddled into her and reached up to fiddle with Skye's dark hair as she sucked her thumb. Skye then continued the story from where she had left off the night before. The three older girls were amazed by the trials Skye and Will had faced and were thrilled by the outcome. Skye ended the story with that one wonderful day a month after they'd returned home, and Will had come for a visit.

". . . He came in as I was putting up the curtains in the sitting room and asked my father if he could court me. My father said yes, and we've been courting for two years now."

"Ah, that is so sweet," Molly murmured.

Both she and Lydie were thoroughly enjoying the thought; however, Emma wasn't quite the age nor the type

180

yet to truly enjoy the romantic part of a story. She loved the adventure.

Skye smiled and nodded to Molly just before Emma had a question for her.

"Did you ever see John and Kate again?"

"No," Skye answered, shaking her head. "It's been quite some time since we've heard anything about them." She looked at all three girls. "One thing I'd like to ask you three is to please not tell anyone about them. If people knew we were friends with pirates we would get in trouble."

"What kind of trouble?" Emma wanted to know.

"Serious trouble," Lydie told her. "Don't you remember you can be hanged for helping pirates?"

Emma gulped. "I won't tell anyone, Skye, I promise."

Lydie and Molly both promised that they wouldn't either. A few moments later, there was a gentle knock and Rose peeked into the room.

"Excuse me, misses, breakfast will be ready in a bit," she told them with a smile.

They thanked her and started getting up.

"Do you need another dress?" Lydie asked.

"I have a couple my father brought me from our ship," Skye said, referring to the ones she had originally given to Marie. "But, if I may, I could still use the stays."

"Of course," Lydie told her. "You can keep it as long as you need it."

Molly left the room followed by Emma, upon Lydie's insistence. Lydie stayed with Skye to help her with the stays again. As Lydie was tightening the laces, Skye hesitated for a moment before asking her a question.

"Lydie, I hope you don't mind my asking, but are Rose and the others . . . slaves?"

Lydie shook her head. "No, they're not, and I understand your asking. Father has never kept slaves. They used to be slaves, but Father bought them and freed them. He

181

said they didn't have to stay here, but they like working for us and Father pays them very well."

Skye nodded, feeling relieved. Once she could easily finish dressing on her own, Lydie left. Skye finished putting on her gown and sat down at the dressing table to fix her hair. Finally ready, she got up and walked to the windows. She pulled aside the full length curtains and was stunned by the breathtaking view before her. Her gaze was met by the bright blue ocean. Waves splashed against the beach a few hundred yards away from the house. It was beautiful.

Another knock at the door drew Skye's attention, and she called for the person to enter. The door opened and Daniel walked into the room with a smile.

"Good morning," he said.

Skye returned the greeting, and her father asked, "Did you sleep well?"

"Yes. Wonderfully."

"Since you're dressed, we should have just enough time to read before breakfast is ready. I talked to Rebecca, and she said we have about twenty minutes."

Skye smiled. "Good. We can read here." She gestured to the window seat beneath the windows.

Sitting down, Daniel looked over his shoulder. "Beautiful view, isn't it?"

"It sure is," Skye answered. "It reminds me of home." There was wistfulness in her voice as she thought of how peaceful life had been. Her attention then turned back to her father as they opened their Bibles.

When breakfast was called, everyone gathered together in the dining room and took seats around the table. Emma chattered the whole time, telling Rebecca things that Skye had told her although they were in no particular order. When the meal eventually started coming to an end, Emma looked at Lydie.

"Let's show Skye the horses and go for a ride," she suggested eagerly.

"Perhaps she doesn't know how to ride," Lydie was careful to say.

Emma turned to Skye. "Do you know how to ride? If you don't, we can teach you."

Skye smiled as she was reminded of when she'd been fourteen and a friend in Kingston had let her and Will ride one of his horses along the beach. It was a wonderful memory—one that she always cherished. "Yes, I know how to ride a little."

"Do you want to ride with us?" Emma's face expressed how much she wanted Skye to say yes.

Skye smiled again. "I would love to."

Emma grinned, standing up. "Let's go put on our riding habits. Lydie will let you borrow one of hers, won't you, Lydie?"

Lydie nodded. "Of course."

"Good, let's go!"

"Hold on, Emma," Rebecca stopped her. "Aren't you forgetting something?"

Emma paused. "Oh, may I be excused?"

Rebecca smiled. "Yes, you may."

"Thank you," Emma said, already on her way out of the room. She called for Skye and her sisters to follow.

Lydie and Molly asked to be excused and led Skye after Emma. The four of them quickly changed into outfits better suited for riding. Skye followed them outside to the stable which was very large and beautiful. The strong, musty but pleasant smell of horses met them as they walked in. Both sides of the long building were lined with stalls. Some of the horses poked their heads over the doors to look at them. Out of another room to their right walked Rose's younger brother Isaac.

"Are you ladies planning on doing some riding?" he asked with a friendly smile.

"Yes," Lydie answered. "We thought we'd show Skye around."

"Should I bring Charlie out for Miss McHenry?" Isaac wanted to know.

"Yes, please," Lydie told him. She looked at Skye. "Charlie's a sweetheart. He'll do whatever you ask him to."

Isaac walked down the middle of the aisle to one of the stalls. Lydie, Molly, and Emma followed to go to their horses' stalls. Skye was amazed when Isaac led Charlie out. He was a tall horse, his muscles rippling under a sleek, jet black coat. His black mane and tail were very long and smooth. Skye had never seen a more beautiful horse. After Isaac tied him up, Skye walked over to Charlie and ran her hand gently down his soft face. His long lashed, dark eyes watched her with curiosity. Isaac brought a saddle and bridle and showed Skye how both were put on. Skye watched closely and thought she could probably do it on her own next time. Finishing, Isaac went to assist Emma with her red chestnut pony, Poppy.

Once Lydie's dapple gray mare, Duchess, and Molly's dun gelding, Admiral, were saddled as well, all four horses were led outside. Skye had no difficulty mounting Charlie because he stood perfectly still. Skye found the feeling of being on a horse again very satisfying and regretted not having done it more.

Emma took the lead from the stable and rode past the house to the beach. As they plodded along in the sand, they talked over the sound of the waves.

"You have such a beautiful home," Skye told the girls. "I didn't realize how close your house was to the ocean until I looked out the window this morning." She smiled. "It reminded me of a house in Kingston that I would love to live in."

"Really, what's it like?" Lydie asked.

"It's a smaller house, but beautiful. It nearly sits right on the beach and the sitting room has huge windows that look out at the water. It almost feels as if the house is at sea, and I love that because I love sailing. I begin to miss it when we've been at port for a while."

"Who owns the house?"

"A very nice younger couple. They've lived there since they were married."

"Would they ever think of selling?" Molly wanted to know.

"Once they were considering it, but then decided not to. I don't know if they ever have again."

"If they did, you could buy it with your treasure, right?" Emma asked.

"Actually, Emma, I couldn't," Skye answered. "My father, Caleb, and I spent our share on the church and the orphanage."

"That was really nice of you," Emma decided.

Skye gave her a smile.

<hr />

"Thank you, Will," Worthy said.

Will had been more than happy to help the man move one of the desks in his cabin. As Will turned to leave, Worthy stopped him.

"I wanted to ask you, has Slade made any more threats?"

"No," Will answered. "But, by the way he's always watching me, I know he's merely waiting for the opportunity to try something."

Worthy sighed. "Just keep doing whatever you can to avoid him and possibly . . ."

"What?" Will asked when he didn't continue.

Worthy hesitated a little and spoke quietly. "Well, it's a long shot and likely impossible, but I've been thinking of ways to get you off this ship."

"Do you mean having Hale put me on another ship or... escape?"

"Escape."

Will was surprised, but all ears.

"Like I said, it's likely impossible," Worthy said, "and it wouldn't be until the next time we make port, which may not be for quite a while because we'll have to either run out of supplies or come across some merchant ship and fill the hold, but I will do what I can when the time comes. Just make sure no one suspects it."

"I will," Will promised quickly. He paused. "You're sure you want to? Hale would probably have you killed, especially if Slade has anything to say about it."

"As sure as I've been about anything," Worthy replied. "You've got a wonderful life back home and the love of a gorgeous young woman. It's everything I had before coming here, and I don't want to see you lose it like I did. Besides, I think maybe it's time I got off this ship too."

"I don't know how to thank you," Will said.

Worthy smiled. "You don't have to. You're a good man, Will, a good friend. I've seen quite a few young men die at the hands of Slade and when you came along I was determined to at least try to keep it from happening again. Although I must confess that I had little hope. Also, I carry some of the same guilt as the crew because though I was kind to you, I was hesitant to befriend you, afraid like them, of making a friend I'd lose. Not becoming friends, however, was impossible, and I certainly wouldn't trade your friendship now that I have it."

"Thank you, Worthy. I'm honored that you feel that way. I have been very thankful for your friendship. It has been a great comfort to me here."

"I'm glad," Worthy said. "I can only imagine what it must be like to be in your position."

Will thanked him once more, and as he went topside, his spirits were lifted considerably. Even the smallest possibility of escape from the ship filled him with hope. The six days that had passed had gone quickly but felt like an eternity at the same time. He missed home deeply and prayed for the strength and patience, as well as protection, to endure the days until they could make port.

Sometime later that afternoon, Will heard Slade shouting and braced himself, automatically expecting it to have been caused by something he'd done, but he quickly realized that someone else was at the receiving end of Slade's anger. It was quite common for him to be angry with the rest of the crew as well. Will didn't even have to try to hear what was being said.

"You'd better get that repaired right this time!" Slade spat furiously. "It coulda killed me when them stitches of yers came out. The whole thing nearly knocked me off the mast!"

The poor crewman before him, a younger man, barely twenty-five, named Robbie, sat on a barrel with a torn sail in his lap and a needle in his hand. Slade didn't even give him a chance to defend himself.

"If it happens again I swear I'll make ya pay for it," Slade threatened.

"I can't help it if I can't fix this thing as well as Russ used to," Robbie complained, getting angry too. "And for all I know, yer probably the cause of what happened to him just as you were the cause of the last few deaths on this ship."

Everyone near enough to hear them held their breath and watched Slade closely. He narrowed his eyes.

"Would ya like to repeat that?" There was a low, murderous tone to his voice.

Robbie stared at him for a brief moment before looking away.

"I didn't think so," Slade said.

He turned away from Robbie and everyone sighed with relief as they returned to their work. Will, however, continued to watch Robbie as he clearly struggled with the sail. Making up his mind, Will walked over to him.

"Why don't you let me do that for you?"

Robbie looked at him in surprise. "Yer crazy for wantin' to, and I'd be crazy to let ya. As soon as it ripped, Slade would kill ya right then and there."

"It won't rip," Will told him. "Besides, Slade's out to kill me already."

Robbie shook his head. "I don't think it's a good idea."

"I know I can repair it so it won't rip and that way Slade will have nothing to get angry at either of us for," Will told him.

Robbie sighed and shook his head again. "All right, but know that I ain't comfortable with it. Yer takin' yer life in yer own hands."

Will nodded and switched places with him. Robbie handed him the sail and needle and was about to walk away, but Will asked him to stay.

"I can show you how to do it," Will offered.

He turned his eyes to the sail. After pulling out Robbie's stitches, he began stitching his own. Robbie's had been loose, uneven, and unequally spaced, but Will's were the opposite, perfect in just about every way. Robbie was amazed and very quickly, other men were gathering around to admire his work as well. The commotion soon caught Slade's attention.

"What's goin' on here?" he demanded, pushing his way through the men.

Will looked up at him confidently. "I offered to repair the sail after I heard you threaten him."

Slade was clearly confused. "Why would ya do somethin' stupid like that, because when it rips the threat's gonna apply to you."

"It ain't gonna rip, Slade," Robbie told him. "He's doin' a better job than Russ ever did."

Slade was taken by surprise to see that it was true, but no one gave him time to speak.

"Where'd ya learn how ta repair a sail like that?" Fowley wanted to know.

At first, Will was hesitant to speak, but he told the truth. "I worked as a tailor once."

He knew before it happened that Slade was going to laugh.

"A tailor?" he said, laughing loudly.

"Yes," Will replied calmly. "I was not good at it, but obviously what I did learn is useful now."

To a pirate, tailoring sounded like a woman's job.

"What's wrong, James? A man's job too hard for ya?"

"No, I was a blacksmith before that, but I couldn't earn enough money so I got a different job. Tailoring was all I could find because I was an orphan and no one would hire me." Despite another outburst of tormenting laughter from Slade, Will continued, "And I am not ashamed of it because no matter what anyone says, it was an honest job, and it kept a roof over my head and food in my stomach."

"It don't matter what ya want to call it, it's still a woman's job," Slade laughed. However, he noticed that he was the only one doing any laughing. The other men simply stared at him, unamused, and seemed to be siding with Will.

"That is only your opinion," Will responded. He'd heard it all before and was not going to let it get to him.

He turned back to the sail and said no more. Slade stared at him in loathing. Finally, he stormed off with nothing further to say, furious that what he had said only seemed to bolster Will's qualities. *I'll get him yet.*

189

The other men slowly left as well, knowing they had work to finish. Soon Will and Robbie were alone again. There was a long moment of silence in which Will noticed that Robbie looked like he was going to speak, but didn't.

"Did you want to say something?" Will asked him finally.

"Well, there's a coupla things I just don't get about you," Robbie answered slowly.

"Like what?"

"For one thing, you really work hard. Now, if it were me and I was stuck on some ship against my will, I don't think I'd want to do much of anythin'. Only what I had to so I'd keep outta trouble."

Will looked at him. "I don't want to be working on this ship, but since I have no choice I do it well because the Bible says to do your work as if you're doing it for God and not for men. I want to at least know every day that He is pleased with me."

"I used to be religious too . . . when I was a kid," Robbie mumbled.

"What happened?"

"My parents died and me and my sister were stuck in an orphanage. My sister got sick there and died. What kind of God would let all that happen?"

Will considered how to reply and asked, "Do you mind if I tell you my story?"

Robbie shrugged. "Go ahead."

"I didn't even know my parents' names until just two weeks ago. You heard me tell Slade I grew up in orphanages too. The first one I lived in burned down when I was five, and the woman who had always felt like a mother to me died in that fire. When I was placed in the second orphanage, I met a girl whose mother was dead and her father had just been killed or so everyone thought. She's the one who first told me about God. At first, I was like you and wondered why God would allow everything that has happened to both of us, but I quickly realized that even though not everything can be understood there is a reason for it nonetheless. I put my trust in God, and it has given me great peace and contentment despite all I've been through. Two weeks ago, I was forced from my home and then taken from the people I dearly love. I saw my mother who I'd only known for a few days get murdered by the man who brought me here. I could never deal with all of that and what I'm going through here if God wasn't giving me the strength, love, and protection I need."

Robbie was silent for a long moment, and Will hoped his words might reach him.

"Yeah, well," Robbie said finally, "I just hope that the protection you say He's givin' ya lasts."

"I believe it will, but if I die then I can still be happy because I'll go to Heaven and live with Him forever."

"Ya really believe that?"

"I know it, and anyone else can as well." Will hoped that Robbie would want to know more, but he wasn't surprised when the man didn't speak again. Remembering that Robbie had said there were a couple things he didn't get, Will asked, "Is there something else you were wondering about me?"

"Well, I don't really know why you'd wanna help me at risk to yer own life when I haven't even tried to get to know ya."

Will smiled. "I want to show the same love and kindness that God shows me. I know, if Slade had done something to you, I would have felt terrible if I hadn't helped you with this."

Robbie shook his head. "I still can't imagine havin' that kind of attitude, but I can't say I'm not grateful for ya helpin' me out."

Chapter Fifteen

Laughter erupted from the beach and seagulls flew
screeching into the air.

"Emma, you're not going to catch one," Lydie called.

"You always say that. How do you know I won't?"
Emma asked.

She ran back to the blanket they had laid out on the
sand and grabbed a few more morsels of food left over from
their dinner.

Beckoning to her little sister, she asked, "Do you want
to help me, Ashley?"

Ashley looked up from the sandcastle that Skye was
helping her build and shook her head, pointing at Skye.

"Kye," she said, clearly meaning she wanted to stay.

"Okay," Emma decided, running happily off again,
farther down the beach.

Lydie looked at Skye with a smile. "Ashley seems to
have a new favorite person, don't you Ashley?"

Ashley nodded slowly without looking up from what
she was doing. Skye smiled as well as Ashley handed her a
shell to put on their castle. Between talking to Lydie and
Molly, watching Emma try to catch seagulls that always
outsmarted her, and playing with Ashley, Skye was kept
very happily entertained. Though they had been on the
beach for hours, it didn't feel like it, and they didn't even

192

realize that mid afternoon was upon them until Molly looked off towards the house.

"Do you hear that?" she asked. "It sounds like a carriage."

They looked at each other and jumped to their feet. Lydie scooped Ashley up and said with a grin, "Papa's home."

"Papa!" Ashley repeated with a happy giggle.

"Emma, I think Father is home!" Lydie called.

Emma ran back to them, and they hurried away from the beach. Very shortly, a carriage came into view, stopping in front of the house.

"It *is* Papa," Emma said excitedly, rushing ahead.

Near the carriage, the four sisters all gathered around to greet their father. Skye stayed a couple of yards behind them. She was filled with the same anxiousness as when they'd first arrived in Port Henry. It was the moment she'd waited for all day.

Her breath caught when the carriage door finally swung open and Edward stepped out. Skye saw instantly where Will had gotten his appearance. Edward had dark hair that was tied back and neatly trimmed facial hair. His eyes were deep brown, and he was quite handsome. When he smiled it was very kind and sincere, like Will. Skye felt tears pooling in her eyes. Without a doubt, this man was Will's father.

"How are my girls?" Edward asked in a loving voice. He held his arms open wide and they all went to hug him at once. Skye could see how much they loved their father, just as she did hers.

Edward took Ashley from Lydie and kissed her on the cheek. He grinned as he brushed some sand out of her hair. "It looks like you've been down at the beach."

Ashley giggled and twisted around in his arms to point at Skye. "Kye!"

Edward followed her gesture. "I see we have company," he said with a smile.

"Yes, Papa, and you'll never guess who she is!" Emma exclaimed. "She's Skylar McHenry, Captain McHenry's daughter! And he's here too, Papa!"

Edward was obviously quite shocked and perplexed by his daughter's news.

"Emma, why don't you let Skye talk," Lydie suggested before Emma would try to tell him everything at once.

Skye stepped closer with a smile. "How do you do, Mr. James? I've been looking forward to meeting you."

"It's a pleasure to meet you as well, Miss McHenry." Edward paused. "Forgive me for my surprise, this is just the very last thing I expected on my return home, and I admit that I am quite perplexed over this, though pleasantly."

"I fully understand," Skye said, putting him at ease. "You see, my father and I arrived in Port Henry yesterday to see you. Your family was kind enough to let us stay here until you returned."

"I see," Edward said with a nod. "Are you here on business? I certainly never expected to be honored by a visit from you and your father."

Skye hesitated wondering the best way to break the news to him about Will. She was saved from having to decide when the door to the house opened, and Rebecca came out followed closely by Daniel and Caleb. The three joined the group, and Rebecca walked up to her husband. Edward gave her a kiss and asked her how she was.

"I'm well," Rebecca told him with a smile. She turned and introduced him to Daniel and Caleb.

Edward greeted them with the utmost respect and enthusiasm. Skye could see how much he enjoyed meeting them, and she hated that they had to spoil it by giving him such bad news. After their greetings, Edward asked of Daniel, "To what do I owe your visit, Captain?"

"Well . . ." Daniel hesitated too. "We are here in regard to Will."

A mixed look of disbelief and hopefulness came to Edward's face. "My son, Will?"

Daniel nodded. "Yes."

"You know him?"

Daniel nodded again.

"He is not here?" Edward asked after a stunned moment, his eyes hurriedly scanning the group in case he had missed the face of the one he longed to see. "Is he alive?" Heart pounding, the raw question burst up from Edward's chest.

"He *is* alive," Daniel assured him, "but I'm sorry to tell you that he is not here."

"Does he know about me? I mean, did he choose not to come?" It would be painful to bear, but Edward had to know.

"He would have done almost anything to come, but something has happened," Daniel explained regretfully. "Very recently Will learned, not only that you are alive, but that you had left something for him. He was forced by a man named Dreger to get the map you left for him with Jacob Tucker. After he secured the map, Dreger took both the map and Will and now we don't know where they are. All we could do was come here and hope that maybe you would know better than we did why Dreger would take him and where they might be."

Edward looked almost like his whole world was about to fall apart at the news. He shook his head. "I wish I did know, but I don't. I've never heard of a man named Dreger, and I can't even guess why he'd want that map or even how he would know that I left it for Will. I have told very few people."

Skye's heart sank, and she looked forlornly between him and her father. What would they do now? Both Edward and Daniel shared the same helpless expression.

"Maybe if you told me more about what happened, there might be something I could figure out, but I just . . . I don't know," Edward murmured in despair. It made Skye very sad to see how hard the news was for him.

Daniel nodded. "We'll tell you everything."

Amid much commotion, everyone entered the house and gathered in the drawing room where Skye and Daniel told Edward all that had taken place in the last two weeks. There was nothing that could have shocked him more. When they finished, Edward sighed in discouragement.

"I don't know what kind of plan these men have, and I can't think of anything that has happened here recently that could be part of it. It just makes no sense to me. All I left for Will was letters. They must think it's more than that, but if that's all they wanted, why wouldn't they just have let Will go?" Edward thought for a moment. "There is one person who might be able to help us figure it out. My brother, Chris. He's very good at finding just about any kind of information. If there is anyone who can find out where Will is, it's him." Edward called Rose into the room. "Rose, please have someone take a message to my brother as quickly as possible. He needs to know that it's urgent he comes here as soon as he can."

"Yes, sir," Rose replied.

Edward turned back to their guests.

"Chris lives a little less than an hour from here. If he leaves as soon as he gets the message he should get here in about an hour and a half."

They nodded, each praying that Chris could help them. Emma then looked up at her father from where she was sitting beside him.

"Skye has a portrait of Will, Papa, and he looks just like you."

Edward looked from her to Skye. "You do?"

Skye nodded and gave him the portrait. As Edward looked at it, tears began to fill his eyes. He was overwhelmed to be able to see what his son looked like.

"Are you all right, Papa?" Emma asked after a moment.

Edward rubbed his eyes. "Yes, sweetheart, I'm fine." He looked at Skye again. "I can't tell you what it means to be able to see this."

Skye nodded, tears in her own eyes. "I can't imagine it."

"Will you tell me about him?"

"Of course, I'll tell you everything about him."

Rebecca looked at her daughters. "Girls, why don't you go and do something else for now. You haven't done your studies yet today."

Emma was especially reluctant to leave, but the three of them did as their mother told them. Rebecca wanted to be sure there would be no interruptions for she knew it would be a very emotional time.

⌒⌒⌒

Once the crew realized how expertly Will had mended the sail, he was quickly put to work on other sails that needed mending. He was quite happy to do it because it gave him a chance to take a break from the hard labor he'd been assigned to. It also seemed less likely for him to land himself in trouble with Slade by just sitting and working on a sail.

Some time after he'd begun, one of the men came to Will.

"Captain wants ta see ya in 'is cabin," he said.

"All right," Will replied wondering what the captain might want to say to him. Whether it was good or bad was

197

anyone's guess. Quickly, Will went down to the door of Hale's cabin and knocked.

"Come in." There were no clues as to his mood in his voice.

Will opened the door and stepped in a bit cautiously.

"You wanted to see me, sir?" he asked.

Hale looked at him. "Yes. I heard whatcha did for Robbie, and how you've been repairin' all the sails."

Will nodded, not quite sure what Hale thought of it.

"It's a good job yer doin'." Hale seemed unsure of how to act. "I'd offer ya an extra share of rum, but I was told ya don't drink."

"No, sir," Will replied.

"Well, I don't s'pose there's anythin' else I could offer ya."

Will wished he could say something about Slade, but he knew it would be pointless. Worthy had tried to get Hale to do something for years. It also wasn't a subject he liked to discuss, so instead, Will replied, "Sir, my greatest desire is to return home, but I know that is something you can't give me."

"No, I can't."

"Then there is nothing else you could offer."

Hale nodded and said quietly. "All right then, you can go back to yer work."

~⚓~

By the time Skye had finished, tears were shed by most everyone. For a few moments, Edward could not speak. Finally, he looked up at Skye.

"Thank you," he said, his voice thick with emotion. "Thank you for telling me about Will and thank you for leading him to Christ. You are an answer to many years of prayer."

198

"You are very welcome, Mr. James," Skye replied, struggling to hold back tears. "And I know how hard it must be for you not to have known him all these years, but I have to say that I don't know what I would have done without him during so many times in my life. He's such a good person."

"I'm so glad you both had each other," Edward told her. "Knowing that he has done so well and has such good friends like you makes me very happy. I can see now God's divine plan for allowing Will to be taken from me."

Skye smiled and then there was a gentle knock at the door. Everyone looked up.

"Yes, Rose?" Edward asked.

"I'm very sorry for interrupting," Rose apologized sincerely, "but your nephew is here."

"You can bring him in," Edward told her.

Rebecca looked at her husband. "He stopped here last night to see how we were doing. He said he'd probably stop in to see you this afternoon."

"Does he know about Will?"

Rebecca nodded.

Very shortly, Stephan entered the room.

"I'm sorry if this is not a good time. I could come back later or tomorrow if you'd like," he offered.

"No, Stephan, that's fine," Edward told him. "Won't you sit down with us?"

"Thank you." Stephan came to sit in an empty chair and greeted everyone. Looking at Edward, he said, "I hope I haven't interrupted you."

"No. Miss McHenry has just finished telling me about Will."

"Amazing isn't it?"

"Yes. God answered my prayers so fully. I only wish now that Will was here safely with us."

"Do you know yet what you're going to do to find him?"

Edward shook his head. "No, but I did have a message sent to Chris. He is the only one I can think of who could help us figure this out. None of us know why anyone would take Will captive, but Chris might. He should be here any time now."

"Well, I hope he proves to be as helpful as you are hoping, both for your sake and for Will's."

Something in Stephan's voice, perhaps a bit of sarcasm, confused Skye. She sensed it instantly, and it made her wonder what Chris was like since all she knew about him was what little Jacob had mentioned. Why had Stephan spoken like he had, especially when speaking of his own uncle?

"I'm sure he will be." Edward either didn't notice Stephan's tone or purposely overlooked it.

Stephan only nodded.

Another several minutes went by as they all conversed until Rose finally returned to the room again.

"Mr. James, I believe your brother has arrived."

Edward went quickly to the foyer, reaching the door just as the knock sounded. He opened the door to his brother and brought him directly back to the drawing room.

"I got here as quickly as I could, Edward," Chris said, following along at his brother's side. "Isaac told me this has something to do with Will." He sounded as though he could hardly believe it.

"It does."

"What did you find out?" Chris asked eagerly.

"It would take far more than a quick explanation to tell you everything, but first," Edward said, as they arrived back, "I think I should introduce you to a few people."

When Skye first laid eyes on Chris James she saw that he had the same dark hair and brown eyes characteristic of the James men, yet there was something different about him. It was not in his appearance but his eyes. Though Skye could not pinpoint it exactly, they seemed less trusting, devoid of the sparkle of happiness in Edward's eyes and Will's. Skye was reminded again of what Jacob had told them briefly. Chris had been treated horribly as a prisoner, and she believed this was why he seemed different.

Edward proceeded to introduce Skye and then Daniel and Caleb. Chris was bewildered by their presence, though Skye could tell he was very pleased to meet them. As Chris shook hands with her father, Skye couldn't help but notice terrible scars around his wrists. Inwardly Skye shuddered at the thought of what this man had endured, and her heart was troubled for him.

"They've come with information about Will," Edward told Chris after the introductions. "Miss McHenry has known him for thirteen years. They grew up in an orphanage together."

Chris looked at Skye. "You did?"

Skye nodded. "Yes."

"Where is he now?" Chris wanted to know.

"That is why I wanted you to come," Edward said. "We don't know where he is, and I am hoping you can help us figure out where to look for him."

"I don't fully understand," Chris said.

"Something has happened," Edward explained. "Will found out about the map I left for him, but some men have taken Will by force, presumably followed the map, and have gone searching for something, we know not what or where. Captain McHenry has already gone to the island where I left the letters, but they were gone and there was no sign of the men. He has no idea where they've gone now. You are the only one I could think of who might be able to find them."

Chris sighed deeply and nodded. "Of course, Edward. I will do whatever I can."

Edward had no chance to give him more detail, before Lydie, Molly, and Emma suddenly appeared in the doorway to see who had come.

"Uncle Chris!" Emma exclaimed with excitement.

They gathered around him and each gave him a hug. It was then that Skye saw Chris smile for the first time. She could tell he enjoyed his nieces very much.

"Uncle Chris, are you going to help rescue Will?" Emma asked, her face sad. "I want him to come home."

"Yes, Emma, I am," Chris promised. He finally looked to Daniel. "The men who took Will, you don't know their reason?"

"Not specifically, but their leader said something about keeping him from interfering in some plan they have," Daniel answered. "They warned us to stay out of it as well and to go home, but they should have known we wouldn't just abandon Will."

"Do you know any of their names?"

"Only the leader. His name was Dreger."

Chris immediately paled at the mention of the name. "Dreger?" he repeated.

Skye's heart skipped a beat, fearing what he knew that they did not.

"Yes," Daniel answered him slowly.

Chris shook his head in obvious distress.

"What is it, Chris?" Edward asked, as worried as Skye.

Chris looked at him. "Dreger is first mate to the pirate, Hendricks . . . he is the man mostly responsible for what happened to me on Hendricks' ship."

Everyone reacted instantly, feeling sick. Skye could barely hold back the tears that sprang to her eyes.

"And he has Will." Edward's voice was full of helplessness and despair. "Please, Lord, protect my son."

Skye and each of the others prayed their own desperate pleas for Will's safety.

"Chris, do you think you can find out where Hendricks is?" Edward asked. "We can only assume that Dreger took Will to him."

"It's possible. It may take a few days, but I could probably find someone who knows his whereabouts. Before that though, I think you should tell me everything else so that maybe we can figure out what Dreger and Hendricks are up to."

Edward agreed and, this time, the girls were permitted to stay. Again, Skye and Daniel recounted the last two weeks, trying to remember every detail that might help Chris find a reason for it all. By the time they had finished, he didn't look much less confused than they were.

"One of the biggest questions I have is what did Dreger and Hendricks want with the letters? And what about their plan would require taking Will with them?"

"The thing I'd like to know is how they found out about my map in the first place." Edward didn't sound pleased. "Either someone overheard me talking about it or someone I have trusted gave away the information."

Chris pondered it all for a long moment.

"Hendricks can't be after the letters unless he thinks you wrote something in them that he hopes to find. To have gone through all of this, he had to have thought you left Will something very valuable." He was silent again until a sudden look of realization came to his face. "Maybe that's it... "

"What?" Everyone seemed to ask at once.

Chris looked at Edward. "Hendricks thinks that Ben told you where the Monarrez Treasure is. He'll have figured it was either on the island in your map or that you wrote the location of it in one of your letters to Will so that Will could find it."

Edward nodded slowly as he thought about it. "I think you might be right. It seems like the only explanation."

Skye, her father, and Caleb could only stare at them in confusion. Edward noticed this and quickly began to explain. "I don't know if you've ever heard of the Monarrez Treasure, but it was a pretty popular subject around here years ago."

"I might have," Daniel replied. "Did it have something to do with a Spanish explorer who was going to die? One who hid his treasure somewhere leaving behind only difficult clues as to how to find it?"

"Yes," Edward responded, "and many years ago, just before Will was born, a friend of ours, Ben, was searching for it. He always wanted Chris and me to help him. Finally, we did, about twelve years ago after I first came to America. We searched for several months, but Chris and I gave up because Hendricks was also searching for it and tried to attack us twice. We weren't going to risk everything on a treasure that I wasn't all that convinced even existed.

"Ben, however, had devoted so much time to it and thought he was getting close so he kept on. We got a letter from him a few weeks later saying that he'd found something and that he was going to return and show us. Sadly, his ship never did arrive here. No one is sure what happened. Either the ship sank in a storm or was attacked by Hendricks. Whatever happened, we never did find out what it was that he found or if he knew where the treasure was. It now seems to make sense that Hendricks thinks I know where it is, and that I left that information for Will."

"Yes, it does," Daniel agreed.

"There's still one question," Chris said. "I still don't understand why he'd keep Will if all he wants is the treasure, unless he's planning on holding him for ransom."

"Yes, he probably is."

"Well, in any case, we still have to find him," Chris said. In a lower voice he added, "We must get him off that ship."

"When will you start looking?" Edward asked.

"I'll check out a few of the taverns tonight to see if I can pick up on anything. Whatever I do, Hendricks will probably know we're looking for him before we find out anything, but that may bring him out."

Edward nodded and then Stephan spoke.

"If you'll all excuse me, I should be getting home." He stood and Edward started to rise as well to see him to the door. "That's all right, I can show myself out," Stephan told him. "Also, if there is anything I can do to help, please let me know. I'd be glad to do whatever I can."

"Thank you," Edward replied. "I will."

Stephan looked around the room, saying goodbye to everyone. Chris was the final person he addressed, and his voice was a bit cold.

"Uncle."

"Stephan." Chris' tone was the same.

Obviously their relationship was strained. Stephan stared at him for a second longer before turning away to leave the room. It was a moment or two before Chris turned back to Edward and began asking questions about Will. Before long, they were informed that Samuel had begun the evening meal and everyone went off to prepare for supper. Skye went to her room to wash her face from the crying she had done earlier. At her door, she pulled Lydie aside for a moment as she and her sisters were off to their own rooms.

"Lydie, I don't mean to pry into your family's business, but may I ask why Stephan and your uncle don't seem to get along?"

"Oh, don't worry about asking. It's been going on for as long as I can remember and everyone is aware of it," Lydie told her. "Chris thinks that Stephan takes advantage of Father's generosity and wealth, which is true in some ways. Stephan, of course, doesn't like to be accused of that, so they've always been unfriendly towards each other. What I find sad about it is not so much that they don't get along, but Stephan is pretty popular around here and most people side with him. They don't seem to like Chris because he seems so reserved and quiet to anyone who doesn't really know him. Though I wouldn't admit this to Stephan, I agree with Chris, and I wish more people would try harder to get to know my uncle instead of avoiding him and see what a good man he really is."

"Your father's friend, Jacob Tucker, told us briefly about what happened to your uncle, and I understand his reason for seeming so reserved. No one would be the same after such a horrible experience. After all I went through it took me a while to recover and your uncle went through far worse than that."

Lydie shuddered. "I never even let myself think about it. Sometimes just seeing some of his scars makes me feel ill."

Skye nodded in agreement, and her thoughts turned suddenly to Will. Her whole body felt cold just thinking of what could be happening to him. She didn't realize that she had tears in her eyes until Lydie asked, "Are you all right?"

Skye nodded quickly and swallowed. "I'm just worried about Will. I don't know how I could bear it if something happened to him."

Two tears escaped her eyes and rolled down her cheeks. Before she could wipe them away, Lydie drew her into a hug.

"I'm sure he'll be all right," she comforted. Stepping back, she took Skye's hands and said, "Let's pray for him."

Chapter Sixteen

Morning at the James estate was beautiful. Skye knew when she woke up that she would have to take a walk around the gardens. It would help clear her head after a troubled sleep.

Just after breakfast was eaten, Lydie, Molly, and Emma agreed to do a little work on their studies so they wouldn't get behind when they were so close to being done, and Skye took Ashley along on her walk. Ashley seemed quite proud when Skye asked her to show her around *her* garden. Skye thoroughly enjoyed listening to her point out all the flowers they came across.

When they came to a butterfly, Ashley pointed to it excitedly, and Skye knelt down next to her.

"Do you want to hold the butterfly, Ashley?" Skye asked.

Ashley nodded.

"Okay, give me your hand."

Skye took Ashley's hand and slowly moved it under the butterfly. To Ashley's delight, it didn't fly away, but perched on her fingertips for several moments. When it did fly, Skye said, "Say 'goodbye, butterfly'."

Ashley repeated her nearly perfectly and Skye grinned.

"Good job," she praised.

Ashley giggled with pleasure, and Skye looked up to a sudden voice.

"You do amazingly well with children." It was Stephan.

Skye smiled. "Thank you. I worked at the orphanage caring for the children before my father came back so I guess I've had a lot of practice. I really enjoy it though."

"Well, I'd say that is something to be proud of. I know a lot of people who don't enjoy them," Stephan remarked.

"I know some too. I always feel sorry for them because all they think about is all the work children are and miss out on the joy."

"I agree." Stephan paused. "So, did Chris go out last night to ask about Hendricks?"

Skye nodded. "My father and Caleb went with him. Your uncle, Edward, wanted to go, but since so many people know him, Chris thought it might be better if he didn't."

"Did they find out anything?"

"No." Skye shook her head sadly.

Stephan looked disappointed as well. "I was hoping they would hear something right away."

"So was I," Skye replied. "They went out again early this morning to see some people. They're still gone."

"What about Edward? Did he go in to work?"

"Yes, but I do not think he is going to stay all day."

"I wouldn't either." Stephan frowned a little as he looked at her. "Are you feeling well, Miss McHenry? You look tired."

Skye shrugged. "I didn't really sleep well, that's all. It's hard knowing just how horrible the men are who have Will."

"Yes, I'm sure it is, but try not to worry too much. If it is ransom that they're after, I would expect them to think they'd get more if Will was well-treated," Stephan reasoned.

Skye nodded slowly. "I hope you're right." She wanted to be optimistic, but she remembered that Chris had been treated horribly despite Hendricks wanting a ransom for him.

There was a silence and then Stephan spoke, sounding a bit hesitant. "Miss McHenry, would you mind if I asked you, well, more of a personal question that has had me curious?"

"No, I don't mind," Skye replied wondering what he was going to ask.

"Well, after I mentioned the other night that you'd make someone a lucky man, you said then that you were thinking about Will. If I may put it bluntly, are you two . . . in love?"

Skye smiled and blushed a little. "Yes, Mr. Daley, we are."

Stephan nodded. "I can see then how it would make this whole situation much more difficult for you."

"Yes, it is very difficult," Skye told him. Finally, changing the subject to something less depressing she asked, "What about you, Mr. Daley? Do you have someone?"

Stephan smiled and shook his head. "Not yet, but I do look forward to having my own family."

"Well, I hope you find someone who is exactly what you're hoping for and that you have a wonderful family some day," Skye said returning his smile.

"Thank you, Miss McHenry."

"Please, call me Skye."

"All right, if you will call me Stephan. And by the way, I think you have a very lovely name. Very unique."

Skye smiled. "Thank you. It was my grandmother's name, and I'm very happy to share it."

"It suits you perfectly." Stephan told her with smile. He then glanced around. "Well, I suppose I'll go back into town and see if there's anything I could help Edward with. That's the reason I came, to see if he was going to be working and also to see if Chris found out anything. You can tell Rebecca and the girls I said good morning."

"I'll do that," Skye promised.

He looked down at Ashley and told her goodbye. Looking back to Skye, he said, "Good day, Skye."

"Good day, Stephan."

Will grasped the ratlines firmly and began his climb up the mainmast. His ascent was quick and with ease. He found himself remembering for a few moments his first experience in sailing on the ship that had taken him and Matthew to Tortuga to find John. It almost made him laugh to remember how little he'd known and how he'd felt as though he'd never be able to climb the rigging as fast and easily as other sailors. Now, he barely gave any thought to it.

When Will reached the mainsail, he carefully made his way along the footropes that hung below the main yard. Before beginning to work on some of the rigging he looked out at the shimmering Atlantic Ocean. The fresh breeze ruffled his loose hair and tugged on his clothes. Up here, he could hardly hear the men working on deck. Everything seemed almost peaceful, and Will was glad for the brief time away from everyone.

Very quickly, the longed for peace was broken dramatically when Will looked down and spotted Slade making his way up the ratlines. Will immediately saw evil intent in Slade's eyes and knew he wasn't coming up for any other purpose than to hurt him. Looking around for an escape, Will saw that the only direction to go was up, but he didn't want to be any higher than he was already. He looked again at Slade and saw that it would only be another moment before he reached his position. *Protect me, God. Help me out of this.*

Slade reached the main yard and worked his way towards Will, smirking as he did so. His movements were slow and deliberate like a predator stalking its prey. Will watched him with a steady gaze.

"What do you want, Slade?" he asked when Slade stopped only a foot or two away. "I know you didn't come up here to help me."

"No, I didn't."

Will tightened his grip on the ropes around the main yard just as Slade struck out and kicked his legs hard. Will was just barely able to stay on the footrope. His mind worked desperately to find an escape. Slade tried again, kicking Will in the side this time. It nearly took Will's breath away and one of his feet slipped, the suddenness of it nearly causing him to lose his grip on the ropes. As he quickly regained his footing, he glanced over his shoulder and made a split-second life and death decision. Directly behind him, a couple of feet away, was one of the supporting shrouds of the mast. If he jumped, he might just be able to reach it. Either that or Slade was going to knock him off. Both options could result in death, but he had a far better chance by jumping.

Will took a deep breath and just as Slade was going to strike him again, he turned, letting go of the main yard and pushing off the footrope. Reaching out, he barely caught the other rope, the momentum from the jump sending him hurtling down the near vertical line. Will tried to slow himself with his feet, but he had to let go for the rope was burning his hands. He hit the deck hard, his legs buckling underneath him. Everyone turned in confusion.

Painfully, Will pushed back to his feet, looking up at the mast. Even from where he stood, he could see Slade's rage at being foiled again. The man immediately began to descend.

"Will!"

Will turned and saw Worthy hurrying towards him. Several of the others were gathering as well.

"What happened?" Worthy asked.

"Slade tried to kill me," Will answered, causing all of the men to look at each other. "He tried to knock me off the main yard."

Worthy looked angry, and Will noticed many of the other men did as well.

"Captain!" Worthy called loudly towards the quarter-deck.

Hale heard him and made his way over to them just as Slade was nearing the deck.

Worthy quickly got the first words out. "Captain, Mr. Krahn just tried to kill Mr. James."

"I did not!" Slade exploded. "He tried to kill me!"

"No, I did not," Will defended himself firmly.

"Everyone knows what a liar you are, Slade," Worthy said angrily. "And we all know how many men you've killed for no reason." He turned to Hale. "Captain, he's broken so many of the articles he should have been shot a long time ago."

"Yer the one that oughta be shot!" Slade bellowed at Worthy. "You've never belonged here."

Chaos ensued quickly as Slade and Worthy continued to argue, and it could easily have turned into a fight, but Hale's voice quieted them.

"That is enough!"

All eyes turned to him.

"Obviously, these two men have a problem with each other." Hale nodded at Will and Slade. "And the articles clearly state that any arguments will be settled on land with either pistols or cutlasses. That is exactly how this one will be settled, first bit of land we come to."

"But Mr. James has never done anything to Mr. Krahn. He—"

"Those are the articles, Mr. Worthy, and we will follow them." Hale looked at Slade. "Are you in agreement with this, Mr. Krahn?"

Slade smirked viciously at Will.

"Aye, Captain," he replied.

Hale looked at Will. "What about you, Mr. James?"

"What I say won't make a difference one way or another, will it?"

Hale glanced at Slade, almost as if consulting him, and then shook his head. "No, Mr. James, it won't." His voice was quieter, clearly influenced by Slade.

"Then I need not say anything," Will replied solemnly.

Hale looked at him for a moment and then glanced at the rest of the men. "We'll set course for the nearest land."

He returned to the helm. For a few moments, everyone stood and watched him go. Some men sided with Slade, others weren't sure what to think, but most, Will sensed, were angry like Worthy that Hale was letting Slade get away with all that he had done. No one had much hope that Will would pull out a victory. He could see that they were preparing for his defeat.

Will wasn't sure what to think. He didn't know whether the duel would be an opportunity to change his position or if he was faced with certain defeat as the crew expected. Whatever the answer, his life was entirely in God's hands.

The pain that had been absent during the ordeal returned suddenly, and Will winced as he looked down at his rope-burned hands. Some skin had rubbed away, leaving them very raw and painful. He felt a hand on his shoulder and turned to Worthy.

"We should take care of that, Will."

Will followed Worthy to his cabin.

"Sit down," Worthy instructed. "I'll get some water."

Will took a seat at the table, and it wasn't long before Worthy set a bowl of water in front of him. Slowly, he dipped his hands in and though it was more painful at first, the cool water helped. He looked up at Worthy. His friend appeared angry and discouraged.

213

"How far is the nearest land?" Will asked finally.

Worthy sighed heavily. "There's a small island near here. We'll reach it by morning."

Will nodded slowly, and Worthy sighed again as he stood.

"I'll see what I can find for bandages," he said.

Left alone in the cabin, Will quietly whispered a thanks to God that he was still alive and asked Him for His help the next day. Will's prayers ceased when he heard shuffling in the hall a few moments later. Les walked into the cabin holding a small wooden bowl. When he set it on the table, Will saw it contained a creamy mixture of herbs and other ingredients he wasn't sure of.

"I made this up. Have Worthy put it on yer hands," he mumbled. "It'll help."

"Thank you," Will said gratefully. "I will."

Les looked like he was going to leave the cabin, but leaned closer to Will instead and said in a lowered but surprisingly clear voice, "Listen lad, if it's swords yer usin' to fight Slade, watch yer feet. He'll try ta trip ya and getcha on the ground where you'll lose yer defense."

Will was very surprised that Les, who always seemed like a loner, cared to give him advice. Quickly, Will thanked him again. Les nodded and patted him once on the shoulder before moving back out the door.

Once darkness fell outside, everyone gathered in the drawing room after the evening meal. Skye and the girls sat playing with Ashley on the floor, Edward and Stephan were at a desk discussing business, and Rebecca sat on the sofa with some of her embroidery. All of it was to keep busy as they waited anxiously for Chris to return with Daniel and Caleb with any news. The three had been gone for most of

214

the day, and when they'd returned for dinner, Chris said that he thought they were getting close to finding some information.

Everyone expected them to be gone late into the night, but they were surprised when they heard the front door open about an hour later. They all stopped what they were doing and hurried to the foyer.

"Anything?" Edward asked.

Chris nodded. "Someone saw Hendricks down near South Carolina a week and a half ago. We're going to see a man in the morning who may know more. Either way, Captain McHenry and I decided that we're going to sail tomorrow. We can probably pick up more information south."

"I am going with you," Edward said. "I'll take care of things at work in the morning so I can leave."

$$\sim\!\!\iota\!\!\sim\!\!\iota\!\!\sim$$

As the afternoon had progressed, Les hadn't been the only one to give Will advice or wish him luck. Nearly half the crew had something to say to him. It encouraged him to know that so many were behind him.

Just before going to the forecastle for the night, Will met with Worthy in his cabin.

"I talked to Slade," Worthy told him. "He's so confident he'll win that he's agreed to let you choose the weapons. It may not be that much of an advantage, but it is something."

Will nodded and considered his choices. Worthy spoke again.

"Pistols would give you an even chance being Slade is bigger and no one thinks you can best him with a sword. Actually, because he's bigger, you might have a slight advantage with pistols because he'd be harder to miss."

"That's true," Will replied slowly, "but I feel that it would be better to choose swords. Slade is not going to miss if I choose pistols. I may not miss either, but then we'll both be dead. I think I can beat him with a sword."

Worthy sighed, knowing that neither option was good. "I hope you're right."

"God will be with me no matter what happens," Will told him. "He already knows the outcome, and I accept whatever it is."

After a few more words, Worthy wished him luck, and Will continued on to the forecastle. Everyone looked at him when he walked inside. Slade grinned at him from his hammock.

"You prepared to die, James?" he taunted cruelly.

Will looked at him and calmly answered, "I've always been prepared to die, but that doesn't mean I will."

Slade scoffed. "You don't have a chance."

The whole house was abuzz with commotion the next morning. Skye could barely wait for her father and Chris to come back so they could set sail. Caleb had gone to the *Grace* to help load supplies, and Skye had decided to stay at the house, but she wondered if perhaps she should have gone just to keep busy.

An hour after her father had left, Skye started for her room to pack her things. She stopped when someone called to her from the drawing room. Entering, she saw Rose as well as Stephan who had spent the night and had been doing some paperwork for Edward all morning. Rose hurried over to her.

"Isaac just gave me this. He told me that someone left it for you."

Skye was confused as Rose handed her a small note. Who would know her here and leave her a message? Her name was clearly written on the front, but there was no other information. Slowly, she unfolded it and read.

Miss McHenry,

The person who knows the information you need and is responsible for what happened to Mr. James' son is someone you know. Tell no one but your father, Edward James, Chris James, or Mr. Jordan.

A Friend

Skye could only stare at the words. What was she to make of it? Who would know and tell her this? Even more confusing and even frightening, who did she know that could be responsible for what happened to Will, and how well did she know them? Was it someone here in Port Henry or back in Kingston? Her head spun with these questions.

"What's wrong, Skye? What does it say?" Stephan asked as he came from across the room.

Skye refolded the note, perhaps a little more quickly than she meant to, and looked up at Rose and Stephan. They looked worried. Skye licked her lips in hesitation. The note clearly said to tell no one but the four people mentioned.

"I . . . I think I would prefer to discuss it with my father if you don't mind," Skye told them.

"You're sure? It doesn't put you in any danger does it because you look pretty shaken," Stephan observed.

Skye shook her head. "No, I'll be fine. It's just something I have to talk to my father about."

"All right, if you're sure." Stephan didn't sound completely convinced.

Skye nodded and forced a smile. "Thank you for bringing this to me, Rose."

She turned and hurried again to her room. Once she had closed the door, she leaned back against it and read the note again. If only there was more information that she could use to make sense of it, but her mind was full of questions that were unanswered. Skye felt she had to tell someone, but her father and Chris were gone, Edward was in town, and Caleb was at the ship. She had to go to one of them. *I'll go to Caleb,* she thought.

Immediately, Skye grabbed her duffel and stuffed all her belongings into it. She then changed out of her dress and into her sailing clothes. Trying to calm her nervousness, she searched the house for Rebecca. When she found her, she said, "I am going to take my things to the ship. May I take Charlie?"

Rebecca nodded. "Of course, unless you'd rather have Isaac take you in a carriage."

Skye knew it would be quicker to just take Charlie so she shook her head. "No, that is all right. I will bring him back later when I come to say goodbye. If my father returns before I do, tell him where I've gone."

Rebecca nodded. "I will."

Skye hurried out to the stable, looking around for Isaac to help her with Charlie. She also wanted to ask him about who had left the letter. Oddly, she couldn't find him anywhere and decided she could wait to ask the questions until after she told Caleb.

Putting down her duffel, Skye went to Charlie's stall and led him out. After she had tied him up, she hurried to the tack room. Just as she was about to go through the door, someone stepped in front of her. She gasped loudly, but then sighed with relief when she saw who it was.

"Stephan, I didn't expect to see you out here." Skye took a deep breath to slow her heart.

"Well, I was just going to take something to Edward." He frowned. "Skye, are you sure everything's all right? You're obviously scared of something."

"Yes, I'm fine," she insisted.

"Where are you going?"

"I am going to take my things to the ship."

"Are you sure you should go alone? I'll go with you," Stephan offered.

"No, that's all right, really. I can take care of myself."

She moved to walk past him, but he caught her by the arm.

"I do believe that, Skye, but I can't let you go."

Skye frowned at him. "Why not?"

"Because you are going to talk to Mr. Jordan about the note, and I can't let you do that."

Skye stared at him wide-eyed. "What do you mean?" *How could he possibly know what the note said?*

Stephan didn't answer but stared at her with an odd look. Skye's whole body felt suddenly cold as she realized something terrible and pulled away from him.

"It's you, isn't it?" she asked. "You're the one the note referred to. That's why you don't want me to go to Caleb."

"Listen to me, Skye." Stephan started towards her.

Skye didn't give him a chance to continue speaking. She turned and started running out of the stable, barely able to comprehend what she had just learned. But just as she reached the door, a strong pair of hands grabbed her and pulled her back inside. Her scream for help was instantly stifled as one of the hands covered her mouth. She struggled desperately to get away, but when a sharp blade was placed at her throat, she stilled instantly.

"Make another sound and you die," a strange voice warned.

The man took his hand from her mouth and pushed her back over to Stephan.

"How could you?" She glared at him, astounded by his betrayal. "How could you lie and pretend that you actually care about Will?"

"Skye—" he began.

"Miss McHenry," Skye shot back. "And I don't want to hear you try to explain. You lied to everyone when really you are responsible for the kidnapping of the man I love. He's your kin. How could you?!"

Chapter Seventeen

In mere minutes, the *Seabird* would drop anchor in front of a small, green island. Mere minutes before Will would face Slade on the very beach he was staring at from the bow of the ship. He had done a good job of staying calm about it, though deep inside he was a bit afraid of what would happen. Anyone would be. He was very grateful that Worthy and the others had told him that they'd do his work for him that morning so that he could just prepare for the fight. Will did that by sitting and reading his Bible, drawing strength from the words.

"Take a good look, James . . ."

Will sighed at Slade's words and heard the man walking up behind him.

". . . 'cause once you leave this ship, you ain't comin' back alive."

Will glanced at him briefly, but said nothing, wishing the man would go away. To his relief, Worthy joined them a moment later.

"Slade, I want to speak to Will alone."

"Yeah, you'd better get in yer last goodbye," Slade sneered as he stepped past him.

Once alone, Will and Worthy faced each other.

"How are your hands?" Worthy began.

"The salve Les made seemed to have helped quite a bit," Will said. He glanced at the bandages. Time would tell whether or not the burns would be a problem during the fight.

Worthy nodded. "Good."

There was a short silence.

"Worthy."

"Yes."

"Will you do something for me if . . . things don't go well today?"

"Anything," Worthy answered.

From his waistcoat pocket, Will pulled two folded pieces of paper. He handed them to Worthy. "Please, try to get these letters sent to Kingston."

"To the young woman you love?" Worthy guessed.

Will nodded and made certain he couldn't be overheard. "Yes. She is Skylar McHenry, Captain Daniel McHenry's daughter. Please see that they get to her if you can."

"The daughter of Daniel McHenry?" Worthy looked quite surprised. "I had no idea."

Will smiled wistfully. "Yes."

"Well, I'd tell you what a lucky man you are, but these are hardly the circumstances in which to do that."

"That's all right," Will told him. "I am lucky. God has blessed me greatly."

"If you get through today, I promise that I will do all I can to get you off this ship and back to Miss McHenry even if it means taking you to her myself."

Will smiled again. "Thank you. She'd be very pleased to meet you." He nodded to the second letter. "That one is for my father, and she'll be able to get it to him. I only just found out he is alive, the day Dreger brought me here. I've never met him, and I still hope that I will, but if I don't, I want him to know how much I wanted to."

"The letters will get to her," Worthy assured him. "You have my word."

"Thank you," Will said once more.

Any further words that might have been spoken were cut short by the loud splash of the anchor hitting the sea.

"I guess it's time to go ashore," Worthy said, his voice reluctant, revealing his sadness over what was about to take place.

Will nodded.

All of the long boats were quickly lowered. No one wanted to stay with the ship. Worthy had told Will that this was only the second time a man forced onto the *Seabird* had lived long enough to end up dueling Slade. That time, the duel had been fought with pistols, but the poor man, barely older than Will, hadn't had a chance since he'd never used a weapon in his life. Will, on the other hand, had experience. Though he'd only ever seen real battle once, he'd practiced countless hours and been taught well. Slade was not going to take him down without a hard fight—Will was determined of that.

The beach drew closer as the boat that Will was in skimmed over the clear blue water. Before long, sand scraped the bottom and everyone got out, pulling it ashore. When Will's feet touched land, he gloried in the feeling of being free from the prison-like *Seabird*. Staring at the trees that rimmed the open beach, he longed to escape, but beyond those trees was only another beach. The crew would either hunt him down or leave him to die of thirst and starvation. Oddly, returning to the *Seabird* was his only hope of ever truly escaping, and he would have to fight to get back there.

Will turned his head then to look at Slade. The man had been gloating for hours now, not showing one tiny glimmer of doubt. Will's hope was that Slade's overconfidence would be his downfall.

The boats were left in a row on the sand as everyone gathered in a large group. In the middle of it, Will and Slade faced each other. Captain Hale stood between them. First, he looked at Slade.

"Mr. Krahn, I have been told that you have let Mr. James choose the weapons."

Slade nodded with a smirk.

Meanwhile, Worthy leaned closer to Will from where he stood beside him and whispered, "You're sure you still want to use swords?"

"Yes," Will answered. At the same time, Hale looked at him.

"And you, Mr. James, what have you chosen?"

"Swords," Will told him confidently.

Slade looked very surprised and laughed. "Yer crazy!"

Will gave him no response. Worthy stepped past him and up to Hale.

"I've got the swords here, Captain," he said.

In Worthy's hands were two swords, both identical. He held them out, one to Will and one to Slade. Will grasped the hilt and weighed the weapon in his hand. It was slightly heavier than he was used to, but it seemed well-balanced.

Every man backed away, but Worthy lingered for a moment. He put his hand on Will's shoulder.

"Good luck, Will," he told him earnestly.

Will nodded and their eyes locked in one final moment.

As Worthy walked away there was nothing delaying the fight now. Will rested his eyes on Slade and, seeing evilness in his face, Will prayed. *God, I can't do this without You. Help me react quickly and not make mistakes. Please, guide me through this.*

Barely could the prayer be finished before Slade lunged at Will, sword raised. Their blades came together with an echoing ring of metal. Slade came at Will again. Blow after blow, Will parried or dodged with relative ease as the two circled around the beach. Slade's attacks were very quick leaving Will virtually no time to counterattack, but he used less energy by focusing only on protecting himself. He knew that Slade would soon begin to tire and slow down, and when he did, Will would be ready to try to gain some ground.

When several minutes had passed, Slade was getting frustrated, and Will could see it because the man's moves were getting more and more sloppy. With each attack, Will looked for an opportunity to retaliate. Finally, it came, and Slade was visibly surprised when Will's sword nicked his shoulder, putting a rip in his sleeve and a small cut in his skin. Slade's eyes burned with rage, and he attacked fiercely again.

Will had confidence that he could continue to defend himself until his next chance to attack, but then Slade smashed his sword into Will's with all his strength. At the same time he took a step closer. The warning Les had given Will the day before flashed suddenly in his mind. He tried quickly to step back, but he felt one of his feet kicked out from underneath him. His balance was lost, and he began falling back. Will expected to hit the ground and feel the blade of Slade's sword in the next moment, but he found his footing again and, after taking a step, his balance returned. Though shaken, he was ready for Slade again.

This plan had never failed Slade in the past, and now he fought like a mad man. It was hard to predict where his blade would fall next, but Will remained successful. The fight seemed to last for hours, though only a half had passed. Both men grew weary, but Will could see that Slade's energy was declining much faster. His breathing was heavy and the front of his shirt was soaked with sweat. Soon, Will was attacking just as often as Slade.

Then, to most everyone's surprise as well as relief, came the final move. Will managed to bring his sword down on the top of Slade's hand, slicing it deeply. Slade hissed in pain, and Will struck again at his blade. The sword sailed into the air and dropped into the sand with a thud. No one moved, their eyes glued to the two exhausted combatants.

Will dragged in deep breaths of air and stared at Slade, his sword inches from his enemy's face. Slade had caused him so much grief, so much turmoil, in the last week. With one simple move it all could be ended, avenged. Struggling to get hold of his emotions, Will shook his head, dismissing those thoughts. Wearily, he let his sword arm drop limply to his side. Slade looked at him, both stunned and angered.

"You'd better kill me, James," he muttered darkly, "'cause if you don't, I swear I'm gonna kill you."

"God will decide that," Will told him, "but if you want to try to kill a man after he spares your life, that's your choice."

He turned his back on Slade and walked towards the others. Nearing them, Will let his sword fall. Every blow he'd received and given had shot pain through his injured sword hand and up into his arm. Now they tingled with numbness and fatigue.

Worthy stepped out of the group, breaking the line of staring, speechless men, and came to meet Will. However, it was not words of relief or congratulations he had to say.

"Will, you should have killed him," Worthy said, troubled. "He's going to go right back to trying to kill you again."

"I know, but he was defenseless. I could not just kill him outright."

Worthy shook his head in disbelief. "Think of what he's tried to do to you! What he is going to do!"

Will looked him in the eyes. "It doesn't matter. I disarmed him. He had no weapon and no way to hurt me."

"He would have killed you had your places been reversed."

"Yes, but if I had killed him now, while he was unarmed, I would be just the same as him."

Whether Worthy understood or not was unreadable on his face. Finally, he sighed.

"At least you are all right."

Will nodded and the two of them headed for the boats. Hale quickly got over his surprise and ordered everyone else to the boats as well.

Skye winced when the ropes around her wrists were yanked tighter than necessary. She glared at Stephan, but could say nothing because of the gag in her mouth. He stared back having not said a word to her since she'd told him he must call her Miss McHenry.

Stephan looked around worriedly.

"Are you done yet?" he asked impatiently.

The man who stood behind Skye tied one more knot in the ropes and nodded. "Done."

"Good, let's get out of here before we get caught."

The man took Skye roughly by the arm, and Stephan led them out of the stable. They made their way very cautiously into the forest which bordered the property. They had gone quite a ways before a clearing came into view where several men were waiting. Skye noticed that one of the men was Isaac. He was tied up, and it became clear to Skye that he must have written her the note.

As they stepped into the clearing, the man facing Isaac turned. When she saw that it was Dreger, Skye sucked in her breath. The horror of coming face to face with him again, without the protection of her father, was eclipsed only by the hope that Will was here somewhere.

"Well, Stephan, you sure made a mess of things," Dreger spat scornfully, "if even *he* figured out it was you." He jerked his head toward Isaac.

"But I've taken care of it," Stephan retorted. "No one else knows, and if Hendricks takes care of Miss McHenry until everything is the way we want it then it will all be fine."

"Yeah, but the fact is you still made a mistake. The captain ain't happy about it and warns that it better not happen again."

"It won't."

"You can tell 'im that yerself. He wants to see you."

"I have to get back to the house or everyone's going to know what I've done."

"Come back later," Dreger told him in a voice that made Stephan realize he really didn't have a choice in the matter.

"Fine," Stephan replied uncomfortably. He looked at Isaac. "Now what about him?"

"He won't say anythin' unless, of course, he wants somethin' to happen to that sister of his or the rest of his servant friends . . ." Dreger looked at Isaac and finished, "will you?"

Isaac looked nervously from him to Skye, deeply conflicted. She could only imagine how he felt. Noticing his reaction, Dreger asked, "Miss McHenry, you wouldn't want him to go sayin' anythin' about you and condemn his family and friends, would you?"

Skye glanced at Dreger and looked back at Isaac. He was the only one who knew about Stephan and the only one who could tell her father what happened to her, but she knew she couldn't ask him to say anything if it meant risking the lives of Rose and the others. She shook her head.

Dreger grinned in satisfaction. "I thought not." He turned to Isaac. "Now, yer gonna go back to that stable, and remember, one word or one more note to anyone about any of this and they're all dead. And make sure no one suspects that you have any idea what happened. Do you understand?"

Isaac nodded in defeat and glanced sadly in Skye's direction.

"Cut 'im loose," Dreger told one of the men.

Isaac's hands were freed, and he started away from them, but paused near Skye.

"I'm sorry, Miss McHenry. I only wanted to help."

Skye nodded quickly as Dreger pushed Isaac forward. "Go," he said angrily.

Isaac quickly disappeared into the trees, and Skye was left alone with her captors.

"I should go too," Stephan said. He looked seriously at Dreger. "I do not want her to get hurt in any way. Remind the captain of that."

Dreger scoffed at his concern. "Why not?"

"Just remind him," Stephan repeated.

"I will, but if I happen to forget, you can remind 'im yerself, and I can't promise anythin' in the meantime if she causes trouble."

Stephan nodded. "I'll be there tonight." He looked at Skye. "Just do whatever they ask and you'll be fine."

Skye stared at him with no expression at all leaving him unnerved which caused his gaze to falter. He glanced once more at Dreger and followed after Isaac.

"Well, Miss McHenry, it'll be a pleasure to be in yer company again," Dreger said with a mocking grin. "The captain too looks forward to meeting you."

Skye looked at him loathingly, but he quickly took out a long cloth and blindfolded her. She prayed desperately for God to protect her. The one tiny glimmer of hope she had was knowing that perhaps she'd get to see Will. Little did she know how wrong their assumption was that Will had been taken to Hendricks' ship.

229

Celebration was the only word to describe the atmosphere on the deck of the *Seabird*. Everyone congratulated Will on his victory and talked about the fight. Everyone that was, except for Slade and his friends who had gone below to take care of his hand and Captain Hale who disappeared into his cabin. The men insisted that Will rest, and he gladly complied. The duel had left his body drained of most of its energy. When all the excitement died down, he sat near the bow and thanked God for all He had done to help him.

Below deck, Worthy made his way along to the captain's cabin, having just received word that Hale wanted to talk to him. Hale's voice beckoned him in after he had knocked, and Worthy entered the cabin.

"What is it, Captain?" Worthy asked.

"Mr. Worthy, I've made a decision that you are not gonna be happy with, but I think it is in the best interest of this ship and her crew," Hale said quickly as if he'd been rehearsing it.

Worthy frowned knowing that Hale rarely made any kind of decisions without the influence of someone else, most usually Slade.

"What kind of decision?" he asked suspiciously.

"When we return to port, you, Mr. Worthy, will no longer be quartermaster and are to leave this ship."

Worthy was stunned. "Why?"

"Because I've come to realize that a lot of the difficulty we have between the men never was much of a problem until you came aboard."

"And just who will take my place?"

Hale hesitated.

"It's Slade, isn't it?" Worthy demanded.

"Yes," Hale answered reluctantly.

Worthy was horrified. "It's him, not me who's responsible for the problems we have. He can't be quartermaster!"

"Why not? He's been here longer than a lot of the men, includin' you."

"Slade is a cruel, horrible man with no regard for anyone but himself. You are going to have a lot more trouble if you give him that kind of power. The men won't stand for it."

"Well, that won't be yer problem will it? You won't be here."

"Just answer this one thing. This is Slade's idea, isn't it?"

"I'm not going to discuss it."

Worthy shook his head and could no longer keep in check what he'd been feeling for years. "You allow him to get away with anything. He might as well be the captain of this ship." He stared hard at Hale. "Are you so afraid he'll lead a mutiny? Honestly, with what you've just told me, I'm very close to leading one myself!"

Hale didn't reply, and Worthy shook his head again in disbelief. "You won't even stand up to me! Fine, I will actually be very glad to leave this ship, and it won't surprise me if others follow. When I do go, Will is coming with me."

"No," Hale said quickly.

"One day on this ship with Slade as quartermaster and he'll be dead anyway. He's coming with me."

"I am being paid to keep him here, and if you try to take him, Worthy, you won't leave this ship alive," Hale warned.

Worthy could feel his anger rising. "I know you couldn't kill me and as far as Slade goes, Will defeated him, so what makes you think I couldn't too?"

"You can't defeat my entire crew."

"I wouldn't have to. Those men are my friends. Trust me, once you give Slade my position, you will lose any small amount of control that you have, if you have any at all."

Worthy turned without another word and stormed out of the cabin. In the hall, he met Les.

"Les, would you tell Will that I would like to see him in my cabin."

Les nodded, but he could hear how tight Worth's voice was. "Is somethin' wrong?" he asked with a frown.

Worthy clenched his fists angrily. "Our *captain* may just as well have gone and sold the ship to the devil."

"What do ya mean?" Les asked.

"I've just been fired as quartermaster and next port we make Slade will take my place."

Les was dumbstruck. "He's doin' that?"

Worthy nodded. "He just informed me of it."

"He can't go and do somethin' like that without talkin' to the rest of us."

"Well, he already has, and Slade's going to make sure he sticks to it. Personally, I will be happy to leave this ship, and I suggest any man who doesn't want to be ruled over by Slade leave as well. However, I'm not so sure I'm going to leave it alive."

"Why not?"

"I will not leave without Will. He stays here and he dies, first day out of port. You know it and I know it."

Les nodded. "Well, I'm not gonna leave without both of ya. I know a lotta the men won't either."

"Thanks Les, I will be very glad of your help. Maybe together we can pull something off," Worthy said hopefully. "Just don't let anyone know we've talked about it unless you trust them to keep it a secret."

"I won't."

Worthy nodded. "I'm going to my cabin."

"All right, I'll tell Will."

Worthy made his way down the hall to his cabin, his mind working the whole way on how they might all leave the ship without having to fight their way off. He came to his door and pushed it open. What he saw when he walked

232

in made his anger boil back up. Slade was sitting at his table, flipping through some of his books with a smirk.

"What are you doing in my cabin?" Worthy demanded furiously.

"It'll be mine soon," Slade replied. "I'm sure you've spoken to the captain."

"I have, but this is still my cabin so get out!" Worthy roared.

Slade got up slowly and made his way towards the door in no particular hurry. He was about to walk out when Worthy grabbed him by the front of his waistcoat and glared at him with a look that could freeze an ocean.

"You set foot in this cabin one more time before we make port, and I'll kill you myself," Worthy threatened.

Slade only smirked again and pulled away from Worthy, leaving the cabin without a word.

Chapter Eighteen

By the time Skye was finally allowed to pause, her legs were aching and perspiration had plastered her clothes to her body. She had been dragged blindly through the forest at a pace that was very difficult to manage without sight. The forest ground, littered with leaves, sticks, and rocks had suddenly changed to sand, and she could once again hear the ocean directly in front of her.

Dreger's rough hand brushed against Skye's face as he pulled off her blindfold. She squinted her eyes against the bright sunlight and focused on what lay before her, a small cove. She wasn't at all surprised to see a ship anchored in the middle of it.

"There she is, Miss McHenry, Captain Hendricks' ship, the *Nightshade*."

Dreger took the gag from Skye's mouth as well, but she had nothing to say to him. He pushed her forward, towards a waiting boat, and ordered her into it. With the rowing of the oars, they crossed the distance between land and ship. Skye stared up at the *Nightshade*. The hull was painted black and the name was crisply painted in white letters. It was not hard to see the ship was highly prized and very well-kept.

When the boat came to a stop, Skye was helped aboard. Most of the crew was on deck either sitting or standing around with not much else to do. Skye scanned them hopefully, looking for Will, though she knew how unlikely it would be to see him on deck. As she was guided to one of the hatchways, she looked to the quarterdeck. There was a man standing there amongst a few others. He was a tall, brown haired man, older, seasoned. Just by the way he stood, watching her intently, Skye had no doubt that he was Hendricks. But he didn't get to watch her for long because Dreger quickly led her below deck, down to the ship's cells.

As Skye laid eyes on the iron bars, she quickly scanned each of several cells, hoping. Her heart sank when she found that all were empty, and she feared where else Will might be.

With little consideration, Dreger cut Skye free and shoved her into an open cell. She turned back to face him.

"I want to talk to the captain," she said fearlessly.

"The captain will see you when 'e wants to see you."

"What did you do with Will?"

Dreger laughed harshly. "You really want to know?"

Skye braced herself. "Yes."

Dreger took a step closer and lowered his voice. "Well... you can ask the captain." He threw back his head and laughed again.

Skye glared at him. "Is Will alive?"

Dreger shrugged. "Like I said, ask the captain."

He turned his back and walked away. Skye stared after him feeling very unsure. She had no way of knowing if Will was alive or dead. It frightened her to not have seen any sign of him. And always at the edges of her mind were the horrors Chris had suffered on this very ship. Shuddering at the thought, tears came to her eyes as she fully took in her situation. Now both she and Will needed to be found. What would her father and Edward do now? It would now be twice as difficult to find Will because they had to find her too. *Oh, if only I'd stayed at the house and waited for Father to come back!* Skye shook her head miserably. *Why didn't I just stay?*

Twin tears trickled down her face as Skye slumped down on the bench behind her. Burying her face in her hands, she cried out to God to help her not to question herself now that nothing could be done. She also prayed for her safety, for Will's safety, and that they'd both be found. Knowing how worried her father would be, Skye prayed for God to help him too.

It seemed Skye waited for hours down in the darkness. To keep her mind busy and away from terrifying thoughts, she continued to pray and recite Bible verses. Quite some time later, she felt a mixed feeling of relief and dread when she heard someone coming down. Skye both wanted and didn't want to speak with Hendricks, but she knew she didn't have a choice. Dreger appeared with the keys to her cell.

"Come on, the captain will see ya now."

He let her out and hurried her along until they reached the captain's cabin, after which he opened the door and pushed her inside. The man Skye had seen on the quarter-deck earlier sat at a table. He stood as they entered.

"Ah, Miss McHenry, what a pleasure it is to finally make your acquaintance," Hendricks greeted her smoothly.

"Captain Hendricks," Skye murmured in distaste.

"I take it you've heard a bit about me."

"Enough." Her displeasure was evident.

Hendricks smiled, amused. "I can see now why Mr. Daley fancies you."

Skye was momentarily taken aback. Having been pre-occupied with finding Will, she realized now that Stephan had indeed exceeded his role as a gentleman. Looking back on all the flattering compliments he'd made in her presence repulsed her.

"Well, he can certainly forget any reciprocal feelings," Skye replied coldly. "He knows I love someone else and nothing could ever possibly change that. Furthermore, he betrayed his entire family and is the reason I'm here. He can't possibly expect me to overlook that."

"I suspect then that he's going to be in for a disappointment," Hendricks remarked dryly.

"He would be a fool to expect anything from me," Skye retorted. "Now, I want to know where William James is." She said it forcefully, leaving no doubt as to how serious she was.

"I see. Well, unfortunately, Miss McHenry," Hendricks began slowly, taking far more time than he needed to, "he is not here. He and Mr. Dreger parted company back in Lucea."

Skye was crestfallen by the news and very shocked. "Lucea?" They had been chasing after Dreger and Hendricks for days, and now she realized how pointless it had been.

Hendricks nodded.

"Is he alive?" Skye needed an answer.

"Well, Miss McHenry, he was alive when Mr. Dreger left him, but I can't say for certain now, considering where he is."

"And where is that?"

"A ship where he will be kept from causing trouble, but that is all I will say."

"But what is it about this ship that makes you talk as though he could likely be dead?"

"Are you sure you want to know?" Hendricks questioned.

"Of course I want to know." Her voice wavered a little. "I love him."

"Well then, in answer to your question, he is not the first to have been placed on that ship. All the others have died within a few days."

Skye swallowed hard. "How?"

"Let's just say that they were not well received."

Skye felt her heart breaking. "I won't believe that he has been killed," she declared bravely.

Hendricks shrugged. "Believe what you want, Miss McHenry," he said, caring little. "I'm only giving you what information I know."

"Tell me this, is Will a prisoner on the ship or a slave?"

"I wouldn't necessarily say a prisoner or a slave. If he cooperates and works hard he'll be treated as part of the crew, by some anyway," he added cryptically.

Skye stared at the floor, trying not to give way to sorrow. A knock at the door startled her, and she looked up. The door opened halfway, and a pirate looked in.

"Dinner'll be ready soon, Captain."

Hendricks nodded and looked at Dreger who had been standing there throughout the exchange.

"Take Miss McHenry to her cabin so she can freshen up after that long walk and the wait down in the cell." He looked at Skye. "I apologize for both."

Skye received the apology skeptically, but made no attempt to comment. Dreger told her to follow him, and he sounded impatient, so she didn't protest. Back down the hall they went until they came to a cabin door. Dreger pushed it open and looked at her expectantly. Having little choice, Skye stepped inside, and Dreger closed the door behind her. The lock clicked, and he walked away. She was trapped, but at least the cabin was better than a cell.

Taking stock of the cabin, Skye noticed sunlight pouring through a small porthole. It was too small, unfortunately, to use for escape, but at least there was light. There was a bed against one wall and a dresser on the opposite. At the foot of the bed sat a trunk. On the bed Skye noticed her duffel, which she remembered Stephan had picked up on their way out of the stable. She was glad at least of that.

Atop the dresser, she saw a large glass pitcher and basin and some folded towels. Walking over to it, Skye looked at her reflection in the mirror hanging above. Her face was smudged with tears and dirt, but she hoped that Hendricks hadn't realized that she'd been crying. Skye pushed up her sleeves and poured water from the pitcher into the basin. She dipped her hands into it and brought the water to her face. For a few moments she stood, bent over the basin with the water dripping from her skin until she picked up a towel and wiped it away.

Turning away from the dresser, Skye laid eyes on the trunk. Already she suspected what was inside it, but she opened it anyway. It was piled to the top with dresses. She closed the lid soundly with a scowl and had no intention of ever wearing any of them.

With a sigh, Skye sat down on the bed next to her duffel. Her hand rested on her pocket and, after a moment, she reached inside to pull out Will's portrait. Gently she ran her fingers over the glass and stared at his face, shaking her head.

"You can't be dead. I won't believe it. I need you," Skye whispered sadly. "Somehow, I'm going to find you. I hope you know I'm trying." She quickly rubbed away tears. "I trust You, God, with all my heart and will accept whatever happens, but please, don't take Will from my life. I don't think I could bear it."

Skye heard the lock again a short time later, and the door opened. She stood up as Dreger stepped into the cabin.

"The captain wants you to join 'im for dinner," he said.

"I'd prefer to eat alone."

"You have two choices, Miss McHenry. Either you go under you own power or under mine."

Skye clenched her teeth. "Fine."

Again, Dreger led her to Hendricks' cabin. He let her inside, but she found that Hendricks was not there.

"The captain'll be back in a coupla minutes," Dreger informed her.

The cabin door closed, and she was alone. Venturing farther inside, she glanced at the table set for two laid out with a full silver service, but it was the desk which caught her eye for there was much piled upon it. Listening carefully with a look over her shoulder, Skye walked to the desk. She would be careful not to touch anything, suspecting there had been motive behind leaving her alone in the captain's cabin.

She quickly scanned various documents and maps which were strewn across the surface of the desk. One she found especially interesting. It was a map of Virginia and the Carolinas. In addition to the neatly printed city names there were also many names added which were not so neat. Skye had never heard the names before and decided they must be those of safe pirate havens.

Out of the corner of her eye, Skye noticed a letter sticking out of a large leather bag. Peering closer, she read the beginning of a name which caused her heart to leap. Forgetting her caution, Skye pulled the letter from the bag. The name was indeed William. She immediately remembered the letters that Edward had written to Will and that Dreger had taken them from the island. Unable to help herself, Skye turned the letter over and, finding the seal already broken, unfolded it. She read the first few lines and then refolded the letter, feeling very emotional again. She lifted the flap of the bag it had come from and was amazed by what she saw. The entire bag was full of letters. There had to be close to hundreds. Flipping through some of them, she found that each one had Will's name on it. There was nearly twenty years' worth of letters in that bag. Edward had put so much love and thought into each one, and it broke her heart to think Will might never get to read them.

"Sure shows dedication, doesn't it?"

Skye jumped and looked up to see Hendricks standing in the doorway. She tried to hide her surprise at being caught.

"Yes, and it shows an amazing amount of love," Skye replied.

"Too bad it was all a waste of time."

"It's the thought that really matters," she murmured softly, "but why do you think it's such a waste of time?"

Hendricks shrugged. "He's never going to read them."

"You don't know that," Skye countered.

"Miss McHenry," he drawled patronizingly, "how exactly do you think he ever will? I could easily just take them and drop them into the ocean."

"Have you read through them all yet?" Skye asked.

Hendricks frowned. "No."

"Then you won't drop them into the ocean."

He gave her a quibbling shrug. "Why not?"

"Because you're trying to find something, and I know what it is."

Hendricks stared at Skye, but she couldn't tell what he was thinking.

"So, you know about the Monarrez Treasure?" he said finally.

Skye nodded.

"I see. How much do you know about it?"

"That depends on how much there is to know."

Skye knew what she was doing was dangerous. She could see that she was irritating him, but she didn't want to tell him much. He stared at her for a long moment before a smile erased all signs of irritation. Stepping to the table, he pulled out a chair.

"Won't you sit down?"

Warily, Skye sat and Hendricks took a seat across from her.

"I was glad to hear that you decided to join me," he said after a moment.

"Did I have a choice?" Skye questioned.

"I'm glad that you decided to join me *willingly*," Hendricks corrected himself. "Now, I hope you found your cabin satisfactory."

"Cabin or cell, I'm still a prisoner."

Ignoring her comment, Hendricks asked, "And did you find the trunk of clothes I had put in there for you?"

"Yes," Skye muttered.

"I would have expected that you would have changed," he chided.

"I never wear a dress on a ship, Captain."

"Well then, I suppose I'll have to see if perhaps some other clothes can be found."

"You could also see that I'm given the courtesy of having people knock before they enter as has not been the case," Skye said irritably.

"I will do that, Miss McHenry. Though, it may comfort you to know that Dreger and I are the only ones with a key to your cabin."

"And why would it comfort me to know that two cruel pirates can enter my cabin whenever they wish," Skye demanded, eyes glittering bright and hard as diamonds.

Hendricks narrowed his own eyes. "You may be pleased with your clever responses, Miss McHenry, but I tire of them," he said softly. "You do not want to try my patience. I'm perfectly willing to go along with Stephan and see that you're not harmed while you're here, but if you cause me trouble, I will just as quickly remove the source of my troubles."

For a long moment the two of them stared intensely at one another. The silence was broken when the door opened and food was brought inside by two pirates. They set the large trays of food on the table and walked away. Hendricks quickly began filling his plate.

Skye was silent as she served herself. She was not hungry, but she knew she might regret it later if she did not eat. She looked uncertainly down at the silverware, frustrated with the fact that she always had so much difficulty remembering which piece to begin with. She could feel that Hendricks was watching her. Finally, she picked up the first fork and brushed the others off to the side.

"I take it, Miss McHenry, that you have not had the proper dining lessons, which seems a strange thing to me," Hendricks said.

Skye looked up at him. "I have, Captain Hendricks, but I am a prisoner on a pirate ship. I hardly see this as a prime opportunity to display proper etiquette."

She was pleased and relieved when Hendricks seemed unable to come up with a good reply. Instead he said, "So tell me about you and Mr. James. You said that you loved him. Are your feelings returned?"

"Yes, they are."

"You are betrothed?"

"No."

"Not betrothed?" Hendricks sounded surprised. "You two are so close and yet he has not asked you to marry him?" There was a sly look in his eyes.

"No," Skye responded, watching him closely.

"It would seem that if he loved you so much he would have. Perhaps it's not quite as you think," Hendricks suggested.

"You have no idea what you're talking about," Skye told him coldly.

"I'm sorry, I didn't mean to upset you," Hendricks fussed soothingly. "I was only—"

"I know what you're doing," Skye cut him off. "You're trying to make me doubt someone I love in a way I believe you could never possibly understand. You don't know Will, and you don't know me, and just because he hasn't asked me to marry him doesn't mean we haven't talked about it."

243

"No, I don't know him," Hendricks acknowledged. "But perhaps I'll get the opportunity to meet him sometime, that is if he's still alive," he added sardonically.

"Well, I hope he never has that misfortune," Skye shot back crisply.

Hendricks' eyes filled with anger. "I've warned you once about trying my patience. I don't know how many warnings you need, but don't count on many more."

He turned his attention back to his food. Skye was silent for a long moment but decided to chance asking some of her own questions, though she did take care to speak more cautiously.

"Captain Hendricks, what is it you want? If all you want is the treasure why are you keeping Will captive?"

Hendricks glanced at her. "The treasure is only part of it."

"What else do you want then?"

"The less you know, the better, for your sake at least, but maybe you might be able to help me."

Skye found it ridiculous that he would think she would help him, but she kept silent. Hendricks stood and retrieved an old tattered piece of leather from the drawer of his desk. When he laid it on the table next to her, Skye saw that it was a map of sorts with an island in the middle. She was unable to tell just how big it was since she didn't know what scale is was drawn to and no other land was shown. There was no name on the island or anywhere else on the map, but strangely, the island had two perfect ovals drawn next to each other at its center. At the top edge of the map was a sentence written in Spanish. Hendricks noticed her looking at it.

"It says—"

"Hidden in metal, revealed by glass," Skye interrupted.

"You can read Spanish." Hendricks nearly sounded impressed. "You are quite full of surprises."

"I'm just well educated," Skye told him, preoccupied.

"Then maybe you have some ideas as to what it's supposed to mean," Hendricks said. "I've been searching for the answer for years. Whatever island this map leads to must be where the treasure is."

"Where did you get the map?"

"From a man who had no further use of it," Hendricks said casually.

Skye remembered what Edward had said about his friend. "From a man named Ben?"

"What difference does it make?"

"You killed him."

"I've killed a lot of people, but right now we're talking about the map," Hendricks reminded her.

Skye glanced again at the map, carefully committing it to memory. "I don't know what it means."

"You're sure?"

"Yes."

Hendricks looked at her suspiciously. "But you wouldn't tell me if you did know, would you?"

"No, I wouldn't," Skye told him bluntly.

Hendricks stared at her closely for another moment.

"It's a good thing then that I know you're not lying."

As the meal progressed, Hendricks continued to ask Skye more questions. Most were about her father or the time she'd spent as Kelley's prisoner. Why any of it concerned or interested him, she didn't know, but she kept her answers short and void of detail. She was relieved when finally Hendricks had finished eating, and she was taken back to her cabin.

Skye spent the remainder of the afternoon deep in thought or reading her Bible. She hadn't learned as much from Hendricks as she wished she could have, but her mind kept going back to the map. If only she could make sense of the clues. She might be able to use it to make a deal with Hendricks, but she only found herself more confused over it.

As the sun began to sink outside the ship, Skye found some candles in the dresser and lit them quickly. Several minutes later, she heard footsteps outside her door and a knock.

"It's Stephan. May I come in?"

Skye ground her teeth together as she stared at the door. Stephan was the very last person she wanted to see.

"Will it do any good to say no?" she called.

Just as she expected, the lock clicked, and Skye scrambled up from the bed as the door swung open. Stephan stepped in, and Skye crossed her arms.

"Skye, just hear me out," he began.

"I told you to call me Miss McHenry," Skye replied, her voice tight.

Stephan sighed. "All right, Miss McHenry," he said dramatically. "What I wanted to say is as soon as this is all over you will be set free, and Captain Hendricks has assured me that you will be treated well if you cooperate."

Skye shook her head. "I do not believe that, Mr. Daley. How could I be set free when I know what you've done?"

"Well, I was hoping we could come to some sort of agreement," Stephan told her.

"The only kind of agreement I'll ever make is one that involves everyone, including Will, returning home unharmed and never being bothered by you or anyone else again," Skye declared vehemently.

"If you insist on being that way," Stephan said regrettably, "then I guess things are going to be more difficult."

Skye wondered exactly what that meant, but refused to be intimidated. "How can you do this? You've betrayed your entire family. What could possibly be worth doing that? I think I deserve to know exactly why I'm a prisoner here and why Will is one too."

Stephan looked unsure. "It's all rather complicated to explain."

"Try."

Stephan opened his mouth, but the words were difficult for him to find. "If my uncle were to . . . die, I wouldn't be the least bit surprised if he left everything to Will even though he's never seen him since he was a baby. I don't see how that's right when I've been at his side all these years. I have helped him a great deal and do not deserve to be cast aside."

Skye frowned as she put pieces together in her mind. If Will were not in the equation, everything Edward owned would likely go to Stephan, his closest male heir. "So you disposed of Will so that Edward would leave everything to you." Still there was something she didn't understand. "But your uncle is young yet, why do this now?" Just as soon as the question had left her mouth, she realized the horrible answer. They were going to have Edward killed.

Stephan saw the light dawn in her eyes, and said quickly, "I've told you too much already."

Skye was nearly speechless. "How could you?" She paused as everything was becoming clearer. "And the Monarrez Treasure, you're only trying to find that because that is how you're paying Hendricks for helping you."

"Something like that," Stephan acknowledged.

"I don't know how you could possibly do something so horrible!"

"We do what we have to do," he said darkly, "and you'll get used to it. In time, you and I, we'll forget all about this. I'll have my rightful place, unchallenged, and quite ironically, you'll have what you would have either way. Except it will be with me instead of Will."

Skye shook her head, dazedly. "You and I? I think there's something we need to get clear right now, Mr. Daley. I want you to know that I could never have feelings for you, especially not now."

"Why not?" he asked, shocked, and then needled scornfully, "Don't tell me you're going to continue loving someone you'll never see again?"

"I will always love Will. *Always*. It doesn't matter if I ever see him again or not. And you don't know that I won't," Skye shot back.

"Fine, Miss McHenry, but you just may find that it causes you problems." He sounded frustrated.

"Is that a threat?"

"It's whatever you want to think it is."

Stephan turned for the door, but paused. Looking back, he took pleasure in saying, "By the way, your father is near frantic with worry. It's a shame you never got to say goodbye." His voice was like ice.

He slammed the door as he left, leaving Skye staring at the spot where he'd been. Her heart ached for her father, but more than that, fear crept in as well. What exactly had Stephan meant about not saying goodbye? Was he suggesting that something was going to happen to her father as well? It made Skye sick to think it, and she immediately knelt down to pray.

Chapter Nineteen

Balanced atop the bowsprit, Skye watched the water race past the *Nightshade*. Hendricks had set sail right after Stephan had left two nights ago. Once out at sea, Hendricks had let Skye wander the ship at will, for the most part. She had spent most of the previous day in her cabin, feeling uncomfortable to leave it, but she quickly grew tired of the small, confined space and stayed on deck instead. All the men kept their distance, but she still watched them closely.

Mid afternoon was upon them when Skye heard one of the lookouts shout that a sail had been spotted. Skye scanned the horizon and shortly spotted a small white dot which grew rapidly larger. She left the bowsprit just as Hendricks came up to the forecastle deck. A few feet away, he stood with a spyglass. Dreger was just behind him.

After waiting a bit, Dreger asked, "What do you see, Captain?"

Hendricks lowered the glass and spoke quietly so that Skye could not hear him.

"I think it's the *Seabird*."

"What do you want to do?" Dreger asked.

Hendricks glanced at Skye. "Take her below . . . down to one of the cells."

Dreger nodded and went to do his captain's bidding. "Come with me," he told Skye gruffly.

249

Skye followed him, wondering what was going on. They had gone only a couple of yards when Hendricks called Dreger back. Skye remained where she was and watched them speak quietly. She got a very bad feeling when Dreger nodded with an unsettling smile. He returned to her quickly and guided her below to the cells. Dreger pushed her inside of one, but just before he released the hold on her arm, he suddenly reached into one of her pockets and, to her horror, pulled out Will's portrait.

"What are you doing?" Skye demanded.

Dreger simply shoved her farther into the cell and slammed the door closed, locking it quickly. All Skye could do was watch helplessly as he walked away.

⁂

"It's the *Nightshade*, Captain Hendricks' ship," Worthy said.

Will sent him a quick look. "Hendricks? The man who wants me here?"

Worthy nodded. "He's probably checking to see if you're still alive and to pay Hale for taking you."

The two of them watched as the *Nightshade* drew steadily closer. Before long it came up alongside the *Seabird*. Quickly, the two ships were lashed together and the gangplanks were laid across. Men crossed over from the *Nightshade*.

"That's him there," Worthy said, gesturing to Hendricks who was just boarding.

They watched Hale go quickly to meet him.

"Captain Hendricks," he said.

"Captain Hale, how fortunate to have run into you. Now we can finish our deal." Hendricks held up a bag full of coins and tossed it to Hale. Then he asked, "So, is he still alive?"

Hale nodded. "Yes, he is."

"Really?" Hendricks sounded surprised. "Where is he?"

Hale looked around and called Will's name. Will glanced at Worthy, and the two of them left the forecastle deck. Will walked up next to Hale and looked at Hendricks.

"Well, he's quite alive," Hendricks commented. "A surprise, I must say."

Hale made a face showing that he agreed.

Hendricks turned his gaze back to Will. "Mr. James, finally we meet."

Will decided not to reply.

"How are you getting along?" Hendricks asked him pleasantly.

"Every day I'm faced with death and deeply miss the people I love," Will told him.

It amused Hendricks to hear this frank comment, so reminiscent of the comments his prisoner was fond of making. "You speak of Miss Skylar McHenry?"

For a moment, Will was afraid to even think of how Hendricks might know about her, but he calmed himself realizing that Dreger must have told Hendricks about Skye.

"She was a very lovely young woman," Hendricks continued, his amusement growing.

Will's fear returned in an instant. "You've never seen her."

"Oh, but I have."

"When?" Will demanded, though his voice nearly faltered.

"Just yesterday," Hendricks replied. "I enjoyed the privilege of having her on my ship though I must admit she did not come willingly."

"Where is she?" Will's voice raised, his heart pounding.

"I hate to be the bearer of bad news," Hendricks began slowly with a convincing remorse, "but in trying to locate you, she learned too much and the risk was too great to keep her around any longer."

Will quickly shook his head, fighting the emotions which threatened to overwhelm him. "No, I don't believe you."

"Funny, Miss McHenry said the same thing when I told her that you were most likely dead," Hendricks said. "I guess I was mistaken concerning you, but since I killed her myself I can't really make the same mistake concerning her."

He pulled something out of his pocket, and Will's heart nearly stopped. Hendricks tossed the object to him, and the portrait fell into Will's hands.

"I suspect she'd want you to have that. A brave young woman, I'll give her that. Kept saying how God would bring you two together again, but I guess she was wrong . . ."

Any words that followed became a buzzing blur as Will's entire body was paralyzed by a sorrow no words could ever describe. His heart raced, and he could barely breathe. *It can't be,* he told himself over and over. His mind shouted at him to do something, but he could not tear his eyes from the portrait, which was no longer simply the gift he'd given to the woman he loved so much but proof of her death.

Will barely felt the hand laid on his shoulder, but it brought him out of his daze. He pulled away from Worthy and walked numbly to one of the hatchways, the only place to go to get away from everyone. He half stumbled down the stairs and came to a stop near the side of the ship.

"No," he gasped, but nothing could reverse what had just happened. The portrait and Hendricks' words, they all told him the horrible truth. Skye was gone. Will leaned heavily against the wall, and his entire body began to shake. Every tear that he had held back through this nightmare he'd been living flooded his eyes and fell in streams down his face. He fell to his knees.

"Why God?" he cried. "Why?" Will's shoulders shuddered heavily with sobs. "I don't understand. Please show me Your reason for this."

Never before had he felt such sorrow or despair. How could he live without her? Without her smile, her kindness, her love?

"Help me, God," he pleaded miserably.

Skye paced back and forth across the cell and sighed. She could barely make out a slight hum of voices, but nothing more. She knew that they had met with the other ship, but who were they and why? Twenty minutes or so later, there was some commotion. Another few minutes passed before finally Dreger appeared and let her out. He brought her back up to her cabin where Hendricks was waiting.

"What is going on?" Skye wanted to know. "I want the portrait back."

"I'm sorry, Miss McHenry, but I no longer have it."

"What have you done with it?" Skye demanded, her ire piqued.

Hendricks raised his brows at her temerity. "Well, now it's in the hands of the person I imagine gave it to you."

Skye was stunned. "Will is on that ship?"

"As a matter of fact, he is."

Skye couldn't help the brief smile that touched her face as a swirl of emotions flooded her body. To know that she had been so close to Will, to know that he was alive! But as Hendricks and Dreger watched her, a coldness crept in. Hendricks looked much too pleased with himself.

"What have you done?" There was no boldness in her now.

"I thought he might wish to know that you were here. So I gave him the portrait we took from you."

It didn't really surprise Skye that they would want to taunt Will with the information that she was aboard the *Nightshade*, but . . . "Why would you give him . . ." The words caught in her throat as it all made sense. "Please, tell me you didn't."

"Didn't what?"

"Tell him that I am dead. Please, tell me you did not tell him that!"

Hendricks smirked. "I cannot."

Skye burst into tears. "No," she cried. "Why would you do something so cruel? Do you have any idea how he must feel?"

"Well, by the look on his face, there was no need to use my imagination."

With those words, he and Dreger turned to leave the cabin. Once the door had closed behind them, all Skye could do was drop to her knees and cry.

"Please, God, be with Will. Help him and comfort him."

For a long time she sobbed loudly, not caring who might hear, her heart broken for Will.

⁓⁓⁓

When Will had been down below for what seemed hours, Worthy went to check on him.

"Will, why don't you come with me and get some air." Worthy spoke quietly and gently helped Will up from where he was slumped against the ship's side. Slowly, he led Will up into the fresh air. The sun had melted into the horizon, and the ship was quickly growing dark. They stopped at the side, and Will leaned against the railing. Looking out at the ocean, tears fell again.

"I don't know what I'll do without her," he said bleakly, his throat raw.

Worthy placed his hand on Will's shoulder. "I know this will be of no comfort, but I know exactly what you are feeling. I too lost the woman I loved. I wish I could tell you of a way to dull the pain, but I don't believe there is one."

"God . . . God is the only one who can."

Worthy was greatly surprised by Will's words. How could Will possibly still turn to God when He had allowed this tragedy to happen? Worthy could not understand, but he kept his thoughts to himself, not wanting to upset Will any more than he already was.

Will stayed on deck until well after dark. Just after the rest of the crew had eaten their supper, Les had come to him, saying that if he needed a place to be alone, not many ever went to the galley, especially not at night.

Will pushed away from the rail and made his way down into the silent ship and through to the galley. Lighting a candle, he took a seat at the table, resting his elbows on the tabletop and his head in his hands. For a long time he had tried not to think about anything at all because after the initial shock, during which there had been a cascade of memories, there had come the awful wondering. What had Skye been through? How had she been killed? Will could hardly bear those thoughts, and he prayed for relief.

When one of the floor planks creaked Will looked up to see Worthy again.

"Do you want to be alone?" he asked.

Will shook his head. Company might be just what he needed.

Worthy stepped in and took a seat next to Will.

"Here." He set a bottle of rum on the table.

Will glanced at it and quickly shook his head again. He couldn't let grief turn him from his principles. "No."

"Well, it's here if you change your mind," Worthy said.

There was a long moment of silence.

"Will . . ." Worthy began slowly. "Les and I were talking, and we agreed that when we get off this ship, we'll do what we can to help you track Hendricks down."

Worthy's words caused Will to admit to himself where his thoughts had wandered, and now he was very sorry. Somewhere deep inside, going after Hendricks was exactly what he wanted to do. He'd wanted it desperately. He had visualized avenging Skye's death several times over the hours, but now he was very ashamed.

"I'm not going after Hendricks," he said dully. "I'm going to find my family and try to start life over without Skye. Right now I cannot imagine it, but I will try because I know that is what she would want me to do." Seeing the look of surprise on Worthy's face, Will continued. "I admit that I did want to go after him, but vengeance belongs to God, not to me."

Worthy was stunned, but Will didn't notice for he was once again filled with regret over his feelings. *I'm sorry, God. Forgive me.*

"Excuse me, Worthy, there's something I need to do."

Quietly, Will went to the forecastle. All the men were sleeping soundly. He found his Bible without a sound and returned to the deck. He needed to read God's Word, especially now. The full moon and a couple of lanterns gave him just enough light to read by. He sat down against the rail and opened his Bible to Psalms, the book he always read for comfort. Some of what he read brought him to tears again, but, though his pain hadn't dulled, he felt comforted. He felt that God was there and that He was reminding him that He would never leave him. He would help him through his sorrow.

Will flipped to one of Skye's favorite verses. Psalms 107:28-29, *Then they cried to the Lord in their trouble, And He brought them out of their distresses. He caused the storm to be still, So that the waves of the sea were hushed.* He knew that God would help him through this storm and calm it at His appointed time. He had every other that Will had ever faced.

"Thank You," Will prayed. "Thank You for Your love and for being with me through everything."

An hour passed as Will read. Worthy's watch came, and he joined Will on deck. For a while he only stood quietly nearby, but then Will spoke to him.

"I know you're wondering how I can still trust God after what has happened."

Worthy was a little surprised and felt bad that Will knew what he was thinking.

"To be honest, I guess I am."

Will looked at him. "Sometimes it can be difficult, but if I turn my back on God now when I need Him the most who will I turn to for comfort? Right now, He is all I have and even though I don't understand this, I need Him desperately. I know He cares about my pain and has a reason for allowing this to happen."

Worthy sighed wearily and sat down next to Will. "I used to believe that God cared, but then . . ."

"What happened?" Will asked.

"I was in love with a woman named Jennifer. I loved her more than anything in this world. I was just going to ask her to marry me when something terrible happened. One night she was on her way home when two drunken men came storming out of a tavern. One pulled out a gun and the other shot to defend himself. Jennifer happened to be in the wrong place at the wrong time. The bullet killed her instead. The man who shot her was actually a man I had trained with. He got off with a light sentence, and I was furious. I wanted to kill him, but someone beat me to it. I don't know who it was or why, but I was blamed for the murder and that is when I ran away. I just don't know why God would do that."

Will sighed heavily. "It is not for us to understand everything, Worthy. I don't know if I will ever understand this, until I get to Heaven." After a painful pause, he shook his head. "I can't even believe yet that she's really gone. Like you, I was planning to ask her to marry me. I even bought a house for her as a surprise. Now I'll never get to tell her."

Worthy watched the tears roll slowly down his friend's face. He had never seen anyone so heartbroken, and it saddened him very deeply.

"I'm so sorry, Will."

Chapter Twenty

Overcome by what had transpired, both Will and Skye spent the next day in solitude and prayer. It proved to be the longest day of Will's life. He was grateful to most of the crew who offered to take over his work for him, especially since he had not slept at all the night before. This night, he lay for hours awake in his hammock, staring at the ceiling. Memories came to him of being on the *Grace* with everyone he loved. He'd been so happy, so content. Now, a huge part of his joy was gone, and he didn't know if it could ever return.

It was hardly dawn the next morning, when the noise of the crew beginning their day woke Will from the very little sleep he had gotten. Will kept his eyes closed and tried to shut out the noise, but then he heard Worthy's voice.

"Will."

Turning his head, Will looked at his friend. "Yes?"

"Will, I really didn't want to wake you, but Hale insists that you get back to work today. I tried to get you more time, but he won't listen."

Will got out of his hammock with a sigh. His body protested with lack of rest as he groggily slipped on his waistcoat. On deck, the sky was cloudless and a tiny sliver of sun sparkled just above the water. Yet, the state of Will's mind did not allow him to notice its beauty as he would have otherwise. He set about his work without much

259

thought for it had become something done by rote. He didn't even notice when some of the men would pause to watch him and murmur to themselves about how really tragic it was. Most had come to really like Will, and they could see that he was very different. Now a part of him seemed to have died along with the woman he loved. He barely spoke to anyone, and no one expected a smile for a very long time.

Worthy, Les, and Robbie went out of their way to make sure that Will was never bothered by anyone who was not sympathetic to his plight, especially Slade. Luckily, they didn't have to try very hard. Slade seemed content just to watch Will suffer without trying to make it worse. He knew he'd get to do whatever he wished as soon as they got rid of Worthy.

The sun climbed slowly as the day passed by a grieving Will, unnoticed. Midday, the sky began to darken with clouds that would drop rain before nightfall. Fog was just beginning to blanket the water when a shout came from one of the masts.

"Sail ho!"

Everyone looked up and saw one of the men pointing west. They all hurried to the side of the ship to see. Hale quickly joined them with a spyglass. The ship was already close, having not been spotted right away because of the fog. Will watched it, wondering what new turn of events it might bring.

"She's a merchant ship," Hale announced. "Likely load-ed with goods for England."

"Let's take 'er," Slade replied eagerly.

Hale glanced at Worthy. The quartermaster decided what ships to attack, but Worthy had been in no mood to assume his responsibilities since Hale had given him the news that he would be replaced. Hale looked again at Slade and then around at the rest of the crew.

"We've been out at sea for weeks now and this is the first merchant vessel we've seen. I say we take 'er," Hale stated his opinion.

Most everyone shouted loudly and that settled it even without Worthy's input. Hale began giving hasty orders to ready the cannons and bring out the weapons. The *Seabird* was quickly steered towards the other ship.

"Mr. Worthy," Hale said. "It is still yer job to lead the boardin' party."

"Yes, Captain," Worthy replied with little enthusiasm.

Hale then turned to Will who was standing nearby.

"Mr. James, you will board with 'em and don't even think about turnin' against my crew. I'm givin' 'em orders to kill you if you do," Hale warned.

"I won't do that."

"Good."

"No, you don't understand," Will told him purposefully. "I won't attack that ship."

Hale narrowed his eyes. "Are you refusin' to do as yer told?"

"I may have been forced into this crew, but that doesn't make me a pirate or a murderer. I will not attack innocent people," Will said firmly, temporarily putting aside his grief.

"You do know you'll be sorry for this," Hale told him.

"The only thing I'd be sorry for would be attacking that ship."

Hale glared at him. "Mr. Worthy, take Mr. James down to one of the cells. We'll deal with 'im later."

"But Captain—"

"Do it," Hale ordered angrily, "or I'll find someone else who will."

Reluctantly, Worthy led Will below.

"This is not good, Will," he said. "Slade's going to make sure Hale punishes you this time. He'll probably have you killed or wishing that he had."

"I'm not going to turn to piracy to save myself," Will declared. "I could never do that."

He stepped into one of the cells, and Worthy handed him the lantern.

"I don't know what to say, Will." Worthy shook his head. "I understand how you feel, but I wish there was something else you could do."

"I know." Will paused. "Be careful, Worthy. Whatever happens to me after today, I still want to know you're here."

Worthy nodded. "I will." They heard some shouting on deck. "I have to get up there."

Will found himself alone in the cell just as he'd been his first day on the ship. And, just as that first day, he was wondering what was going to happen to him. Worthy was right. Hale would probably have him killed this time.

Will sat down on the bench that still stood where he'd put it next to the door. Listening, he heard more shouting, and then the *Seabird's* cannons fired in warning. A few minutes later, the two ships came together. There was the commotion of the crew boarding, and Will thought of the poor people on the ship.

"Keep them safe, God," he prayed. "Don't let anyone get hurt."

There was more shouting and then pistol shots. Will prayed that they had only been in warning as well. The commotion died down a little, and he expected that the merchants had surrendered and Hale's crew was looting the ship. Yet, after several minutes, a loud sound startled Will. It was another cannon blast, but not from the *Seabird* or the merchant ship. There was another ship out there, but whose side was it on?

Will got quickly to his feet as there was a shot fired even closer. Loud shouts came from above him. They sounded panicked. A cannon blast erupted closer yet, and the whole ship shuddered. Will grabbed at the cell bars to keep his balance as the deck above him splintered loudly.

The *Seabird* was under attack.

Some return shots were fired, but whoever was attacking fired much faster, and with every blast the ship shook violently. There was a deafening crack as Will heard one of the masts crash to the deck. He barely realized what had happened when the side of the ship seemed to explode not far from him. Water gushed in through a gaping hole in the hull and rapidly began flooding the hold.

It seemed no time at all before the water reached Will's ankles. If he didn't get out of the cell before the hold filled, he would be drowned. He tried throwing himself against the door, hoping the rusted lock or hinges might break, but though he tried several times, they did not budge. By this time the water was sloshing around his knees as the *Seabird* sank farther into the ocean. Desperately, Will tried all of the bars to see if any were loose, but all were rusted tightly together. Water soon lapped at Will's chest, and he struggled not to panic as it crept steadily up to his neck. It was not long before he was pulling himself up the bars to keep his head above water. Another few feet was all he had left. He had almost given up hope when he heard a splash. Looking towards the hatchway, Will spotted Worthy just emerging from the water.

Worthy swam quickly over to the post where the cell keys always hung. Taking a deep breath, he dove under the water to find them. Will waited anxiously, praying that the keys would still be there, but he was afraid that the water had washed them off the hook.

It seemed like a very long time, but finally Worthy surfaced. Will let out a sigh of relief when he saw that Worthy had the keys. He swam over to the cell and went under again to unlock it. Close to a minute passed, and he came up for air.

"It won't unlock," he gasped, gravely.

"Please, Lord, make it work," Will prayed.

The water was rising faster, and he and Worthy had only another foot and a half before the water would reach the ceiling. Once again, Worthy disappeared into the dark water, and Will kept praying. Worthy seemed to be under much longer this time, and Will began to worry. Finally, he came up.

"Go! It's open."

Will wasted no time. He immediately pulled himself down to the door and out of the cell, emerging beside Worthy. The water was so high now that their heads nearly touched the ceiling. As fast as they could, they swam towards the hatchway. Just before they reached it, the water completely swallowed them up. Reaching the hatchway first, Will quickly pulled Worthy up with him.

"What happened?" Will shouted as they ran through the nearly destroyed cabins to reach the upper deck before it was too late.

"A British warship came upon us. We were trapped," Worthy panted.

The water rushed swiftly around them as they reached one of the stairs, swirling at their feet as they climbed. They had barely reached the debris littered deck before water washed over it, causing Will and Worthy to lose their footing. Both grabbed whatever they could find to stay afloat as the ship disappeared from beneath them.

Will looked around amid the debris and the smoke of burning wreckage floating where the *Seabird* had been. Not far off sat the merchant ship and a British warship. The men on the warship were pulling crewman from the *Seabird* out of the water. Will looked at Worthy knowing that getting rescued also meant death for his friend.

"It's our only chance," Worthy said, knowing what Will was thinking.

They both abandoned the wreckage they were clinging to and swam towards the ship. They were brought aboard and put with the group of crewmen. Will found only about half the crew was present, and he couldn't see anyone else in the water. Slade, Les, and Robbie were among those on deck, but Will saw that Hale was missing.

"That looks like all of them, Captain," a soldier said.

The ship's captain nodded. "Take them below. We'll bring them to Lieutenant Graham at Fort Camden."

"Aye, sir."

Will wanted to tell the captain that he was not a pirate, but he got the feeling the captain was not a man who would care to listen, so he decided to bide his time. He and the rest of the men were escorted below deck and put into two cells. Feeling somber, they said little. For hours they sat there, pirates turned prisoners, but it gave Worthy time to tell Will all that had happened. It was just after they had boarded the merchant ship that the warship had appeared, trapping them. They'd tried to fight back, but it had been hopeless. Will was just glad to hear that no one on the merchant ship had been harmed.

The ship came to a stop late in the afternoon. A large company of soldiers gathered at the cells and everyone's hands were chained. They were led off the ship and down the docks. Sprawling before them was a prosperous North Carolina city. Off to their left stood a large fort. They were brought there and placed into one big cell while the soldiers went off to find the commander of the fort.

Worthy turned to Will intently. "When he gets here, tell him who you are and why you're here. I'm sure they'll set you free."

Will took that advice, but it made him sad. All afternoon he'd been thinking about what would happen to Worthy and the others.

"What's wrong?" Worthy asked.

"I feel terrible saving myself when you can do nothing," Will explained. "I've already lost someone close to me. I hate having to lose you too."

Worthy smiled wryly. "Will, it's my own fault I'm here. I knew someday I'd get caught. But you were forced into this and now it looks like God has given you a way out. Don't feel bad for taking what He's giving you."

Will nodded, surprised but heartened to hear Worthy talk about God like this. A moment later the soldiers returned with Lieutenant Graham. The man, about the same age as Worthy, looked them all over. Worthy stepped forward.

"Lieutenant, this man is not a pirate." Worthy gestured to Will. "He was forced onto our ship by our captain. He had nothing to do with the attack today. I rescued him from a cell just before the ship sank."

Lieutenant Graham stepped closer and looked Will over.

"Is this true?"

"Yes, sir."

The words barely left Will's mouth before Slade cut in.

"They're lyin'. They're only sayin' it 'cause our captain ain't here to say otherwise."

Worthy glared over his shoulder. "Shut up, Slade." He looked back at Lieutenant Graham. "He's the one who's lying."

Lieutenant Graham glanced at Worthy, but continued looking at Will. "What's your name?"

"William James." Will pulled off the locket around his neck, hoping maybe it would be enough proof. "This has my name on it, and the names of my parents."

Lieutenant Graham didn't even get a chance to look at it before Slade spoke again.

"He got that off a man 'e killed. It's all a lie."

"No, it's not," Will insisted calmly.

Lieutenant Graham looked back and forth between the two of them, gauging.

"Do you have any family who can prove who you are? Or Friends?" he asked Will.

Will hesitated. "My mother was just killed, and I have never known my father. I just recently found out he is alive. I was told he owns a trading company in Virginia. Besides them, Captain Daniel McHenry is my friend, but I don't know where he is right now. I know he is trying to find me and has probably gone to my father."

Slade scoffed. "He ain't never even seen Daniel Mc-Henry. Don't tell me you're going to believe a story like that? I heard them plannin' the whole thing on the way here."

Worthy tried to say otherwise, but Slade shouted back at him and for a brief time there was only chaos until Lieutenant Graham got them to be quiet. Worthy looked at him, frustrated.

"Lieutenant, may I please say something?"

Lieutenant Graham nodded.

"Lieutenant, six years ago I was an officer in the navy. The woman I loved was killed by accident, and the man who killed her was then murdered. Because I was falsely accused of killing him, I ran away. I became a pirate, and ever since then I have been the quartermaster on the pirate ship attacked today. Over the years, I've seen many young men forced into service on that ship and each one has been murdered by Slade for reasons I can't understand. Will truly was forced onto our ship and has been lucky enough to survive. You can be sure anything Slade says about him is a lie."

Lieutenant Graham looked at him thoughtfully and turned to Will. "You said that you never met your father, but you do know that he owns a trading company in Virginia?"

"Yes, that is what I was told by a close friend of his," Will answered.

"Do you know where in Virginia?"

"No, I didn't get a chance to find out."

"How is it that you never met him?"

"My mother left him when I was a baby and took me with her. She then left me in an orphanage. I only just found out about both of them a couple of weeks ago."

Lieutenant Graham mulled that over for a few moments. Finally, he said, "I do know of a James in Port Henry, Virginia who owns a trading company. If he is truly your father, he'll be able to confirm what you have said. I will send a message to him and have him come here."

"Thank you, Lieutenant," Will replied gratefully. "That is all I ask."

Lieutenant Graham nodded and walked away.

Worthy turned to Will. "I think it would take about a half a day for one rider to get from here to Port Henry. If he sends someone right away and your father can come, he should be here sometime tomorrow afternoon."

Chapter Twenty-one

Skye's fingers ran idly up and down the small cross tied around her neck, the metal warm from her touch. The necklace was the only other thing she had from Will, and she was glad that Hendricks hadn't known about it otherwise he probably would have taken it too.

The hardness of the mast pressed into Skye's back as she sat leaning against it. She had been on deck for over an hour. There was nowhere else for her to go, and she felt very downcast. She grieved for Will and missed him terribly. She also missed her father and prayed earnestly for both.

Skye whiled away another half hour, thinking and praying. She had grown used to the men passing and talking nearby, but when she happened to hear Hendricks and Dreger, their conversation gained her full attention.

"We'll make port sometime tonight," Hendricks said.

"I'll let the men know," Dreger replied.

As Skye watched them walk past, her mind immediately began working on a plan. She had not yet looked for a way to escape because they were at sea, but if they were going to reach land it gave her a small chance. No doubt Hendricks would lock her in her cabin while they were there. She needed to find some way to get out without anyone knowing and then sneak off the ship. Skye looked around with new eyes, wishing she had some sort of weapon. Her eyes came to rest on a belaying pin. They were laying all over below deck. Hendricks had made sure that Skye couldn't get at any weapons, but he'd forgotten the most obvious.

Maybe, if she could get someone to bring her something, Skye could knock them out and tie them up. There was plenty of rope that she could hide in her cabin. If she succeeded, she would not only be free, but she would also gain a sword and maybe a pistol.

Anxious to prepare, Skye got up and slowly made her way below, being careful not to arouse suspicion. She found everything she needed in one of the supply cabins. Picking up a belaying pin, she also found several pairs of manacles. They'd be far easier to use than ropes.

Skye made her way back to her cabin with extreme caution, praying the whole way not to be found out. Safely inside, she let out a sigh of relief as she closed the door behind her. Quickly, she looked around for a place to hide the belaying pin and manacles. *Perfect*, she thought when she saw the trunk that was still in her cabin. She opened the lid and hid the items underneath the dresses that were still there.

Skye shut the lid, but stayed kneeling by the trunk. If her plan went wrong, she knew it would be disastrous for her.

"God, I only have one shot at this. Please, help me succeed."

Night at the fort had been very long and unpleasant. The cell was cold, damp, and crowded, and Will could barely sleep. When he was awake, he prayed that his father would come and have him freed. He also prayed that God would spare Worthy and save the other men he'd come to be friends with too.

The daylight hours passed just as slowly as Will waited anxiously. However, he was unaware of all that had been taking place in Port Henry. He couldn't know that Edward and Chris had left with Daniel and Caleb days ago as soon as they'd realized Skye had been kidnapped. The letter that Lieutenant Graham had sent ended up in the hands of the very last person it should have. Stephan.

Upon receiving the letter, Stephan had started for Fort Camden immediately. He'd had no choice. Hendricks couldn't help him with this. Stephan had wanted nothing to do with any of the kidnappings and killings that he knew were going to take place, but things were not going as smoothly as planned. And now he must be much more involved than he'd ever cared to be. Will could not leave that fort alive. If he did, it would jeopardize everything.

Grudgingly, Stephan climbed the stairs of the fort late in the afternoon. He was taken inside by one of the guards to Lieutenant Graham's office.

"Lieutenant Graham, I'm here in response to this letter." Stephan held up the letter that Graham had written. "My name is Stephan Daley. I am the nephew of Edward James. My uncle is away on very urgent business, and his family has asked me to take care of this on his behalf."

Lieutenant Graham nodded. "Mr. Daley, I have a man here, just taken from the wreck of a pirate ship, who claims to be your uncle's son. Does your uncle have a son by the name of William?"

"He did, yes," Stephan began the story he'd rehearsed throughout his journey, "but William disappeared about four years ago."

"This man said that he's never met his father," Graham told him.

"Then that cannot be him. William lived at home with his family until he took a voyage on one of his father's ships.

The ship was attacked by pirates, and we all assumed that he had been killed."

"Did this belong to him?" Graham held up Will's open locket.

Stephan paused carefully for a moment, but as soon as he saw the names inside, he quickly nodded. "Yes, that belonged to Will. Whoever you got that from must have taken it from him."

Graham remembered that Slade had said the same thing. He had been inclined to believe Will, but now it seemed likely he was lying. Graham didn't know why that should bother him so.

"All right, Mr. Daley, why don't you come with me to confirm that he is not your cousin."

Stephan followed Graham through the fort. Though he didn't show it, he was very reluctant. He did not want to see Will, and he wished that Graham would have taken him at his word.

When they reached the cell where all the pirates were being held, Stephan knew instantly which man was Will. There was no doubt. Will frowned when he saw him, sensing something was not right.

"This is Edward James' nephew," Graham said to Will. "He has told me that Mr. James' son was attacked by pirates four years ago. I have reason to believe that you were one of them."

Will was stunned. "What? That's impossible. I am not a pirate. I am Edward James' son, and he has not seen me since my mother left him."

Stephan looked at Graham, affecting surprise. "My uncle's wife never left him. She died when William was three."

Graham looked at Will who shook his head indignantly. "She did not. I just saw my mother, Marie, and watched helplessly as she was murdered by a man named Dreger. I also just spoke with a friend of my father's in Lucea named Jacob Tucker. He will vouch for who I am and tell you that I've never seen my father."

Stephan quickly countered what Will was saying. "My uncle has no friends in Lucea and none anywhere named Jacob Tucker."

How could this man possibly know for certain every single acquaintance known by his father, Will thought indignantly, but Graham spoke before he could.

"Mr. Daley recognized the locket you gave me as one belonging to his cousin. This leaves only one possibility. I can only surmise that you are one of the pirates who killed him, and that you took it from him just as your crewmate suggested last night."

"No," Will insisted desperately. "That locket was given to me on my fourth birthday by one of the women who cared for me in the St. Thomas orphanage in Jamaica."

"Are you saying that Mr. Daley is lying?" Graham asked.

Will glanced at Stephan who stared at him coldly.

"Yes, I am," Will answered, feeling the hostility from this stranger who claimed to be his cousin.

"Why would he lie?"

"I don't know, but I believe he must have a connection to those who forced me from my home and left me in the hands of pirates."

Stephan looked at Graham, obviously annoyed. "Lieutenant, I take offense at that and have no reason whatsoever to lie. Don't you think, if this man were my cousin, that I'd be overjoyed to see him and bring him home? Nothing would make my uncle happier. I truly believe that this man is one of the pirates, or likely *the* pirate, who killed my cousin, and I am expecting you to see that he doesn't get away with it. My cousin's death was a horrible tragedy in my family, and it would be a very great relief for all of us to know that his murderer was brought to justice."

Graham nodded. "Of course. Thank you for taking the time to come here so quickly."

"No, thank you for taking care of this," Stephan replied magnanimously.

The two of them turned to leave. Will called after Graham, but it was no use. He stared after them, unable to believe what had just happened. There were very few feelings worse than the helplessness of knowing your innocence, but not being able to prove it. He turned slowly to look at Worthy who was equally stunned.

"Will, I . . ." He didn't know what to say.

There was a despairing look in Will's eyes. "I'm not going to get out of here, am I?"

Those who cared for Will were silent for a very long time. When Graham returned later in the day, Will knew he had only one more chance.

"Lieutenant, please. I am William James. In Kingston I am a blacksmith and sometimes sail for Daniel McHenry. For months I have planned to propose to his daughter, Skylar. I just purchased a house from a man named Ryan Collins of Kingston. Find my friend and employer, Matthew McHenry, or Jacob Tucker in Lucea, Caleb Jordan first mate of the *Grace*. Get word to any one of them, all of them. Everything I have told you about my parents is true. What more can I say to convince you of my innocence?"

Graham appeared genuinely troubled but held up his hand for Will to stop. "I truly do feel sorry for you because I do think there is good in you, but you are all pirates," he said, appealing to them, though why he felt the need he could not understand. "Therefore you are in no position to expect your word to be trusted, especially when all the evidence is against you."

"Lieutenant, what evidence?" Worthy demanded. "You have one man saying one thing and one saying another. How can you really be sure which one is telling the truth?"

"Because one was caught with pirates," he said simply. "And the only stories that match are his . . ." Graham pointed to Slade, "and Mr. Daley's. I have no reason to doubt Mr. Daley and every reason to believe that this man is guilty."

Worthy sighed heavily. "But they're both lying."

"It seems highly unlikely that two lies could match so well," Graham said. "Now. I've come to say that all of you are scheduled to be hanged at dawn tomorrow."

"Without a trial?" Worthy asked with a frown.

"We've had far too much trouble with pirates around here so when we catch them in the act of attacking our ships there is no need for a trial."

"But Lieutenant, what if it turns out that Will is telling the truth?"

"If you were an officer, you know that you have to do what you feel is best. That is what I'm doing."

"There it is, Miss McHenry. Hendricksville." Hendricks grinned proudly at the approaching port. "The people there were kind enough to name it after me."

Skye stared at the town lights glittering in the darkness of night. Her mind was only on one thing, her escape. She was glad for the lateness of the hour. It would be much easier to escape at night.

As the city drew closer, Hendricks turned to Dreger. "Take her below."

Dreger nodded and swiftly took Skye down to her cabin, locking her inside. Once the ship had reached port and was moored to the dock, Hendricks told Dreger, "Stay here with the ship for now. I'll take most of the men ashore."

"Aye, Captain," Dreger replied.

As Hendricks led his band of rowdy men into the ramshackle town, they came to their favorite tavern and entered eagerly. The main room was large and full of pirates drinking and swapping stories. Hendricks worked his way up to the bar where the barkeeper, a man Hendricks knew well, hurried over to him.

"Captain, ya gotta man waitin' for ya in the first room," he said quickly. "Says 'e's got news for ya."

"Did he give you his name?" Hendricks questioned.

"Just the last. Daley."

Hendricks nodded his thanks and entered a dark hall off the main room where a couple of private rooms were located. Coming to the first one, he pushed the door open easily because the latch was broken. At a small table sat Stephan. Hendricks closed the door behind himself though it stayed open a crack, and he took a seat at the table across from Stephan.

"Well, what's going on?" Hendricks asked.

"The *Seabird* got caught attacking a merchant ship. Half of the crew was killed and the other half was taken prisoner." Stephan waited for Hendricks' reaction.

"Is the boy dead?"

Stephan shook his head, and Hendricks looked worried. "If he tells them who he is, they'll set him free."

"He already has told them, but fortunately the lieutenant there was cautious enough to write a letter to my uncle."

"Well, you're just going to have to go and see to it that this lieutenant doesn't believe him."

"I already have. The lieutenant now has no doubt that he's a pirate."

Hendricks raised his eyebrows, pleasantly surprised. "Well. I didn't think you had it in you, especially since you insisted that you didn't want him killed in the first place."

"Yeah, well things have changed since then, and I didn't see any other way."

Hendricks smirked. "Things have changed, huh? Like the fact our Miss McHenry would rather have him than you?"

Stephan's temper flared momentarily. "It doesn't matter. The only thing that does is that William James will be taken care of once and for all and we can go on with our plans."

Hendricks chuckled. "So, they're going to hang him for piracy. When?"

"It's scheduled for dawn tomorrow."

"Where?"

"Fort Camden. That's where they were taken."

Hendricks nodded with satisfaction. "Good. Now why don't you tell me exactly what happened, from the beginning. I'm rather curious as to how you pulled it off."

As they continued to speak, Stephan going into detail about what had taken place at the fort, neither man noticed the dark figure standing just outside the partially open door, able to hear every word. Hearing all he needed to hear, Captain John Morgan began to creep away silently. However, he cringed when one of the floor planks creaked suddenly causing Stephan and Hendricks to fall silent. He heard Hendricks' chair scrape the floor. *Help me, God*, John prayed frantically, his mind racing. Only one thing came to him. It seemed ridiculous, but he had no time to think of something better.

The door burst open and instantly Hendricks had John pinned against the wall by the collar of his shirt. He called John names that made John want to stick his fingers in his ears, but he had to keep his act together.

"What are you doing spying on us?" Hendricks bellowed, jerking John sharply.

John screwed up his face and tried hard to focus on Hendricks. Of course it was all an act.

"I . . . uh . . . want a . . . uh . . . shrink . . ." Trying to sound as intoxicated as possible, John prayed the fact there was absolutely no alcohol on his breath at all would go unnoticed by the enraged pirate captain.

"What?" Hendricks yelled.

"I want a *drink*." This time John made himself sound annoyingly forceful, accentuating the last word with a drunken nod, hoping he could irritate Hendricks enough to forget the fact he'd been spying on them.

Hendricks was greatly provoked, and John hoped that was a good thing. A brief silence followed in which Hendricks became convinced that John was completely inebriated. Finally, Hendricks yanked him away from the wall and pushed him forward, towards the main room. Once in the doorway, Hendricks released him and shoved him hard. It was no act when John stumbled and fell.

Knowing Hendricks was still watching, John made a show of trying to get back on his feet. He cringed again when someone cried out his name in alarm. In mere seconds, Kate and a few of the other crewmen were at his side. He glanced at Kate and whispered, "We need to get to the ships. Play along." He reverted quickly to his slurred speech. "I want a drink!"

Though shocked, Kate did as she was told. "No, I think you've had quite enough already."

The room erupted with loud, rough guffaws. Amid the noise, they helped him up, which wasn't easy for he was doing a very good job of acting.

"I want a drink!" John said again in a whiny voice.

"No, you want some fresh air," Kate replied. If she wouldn't have been so confused she would have had a hard time not laughing. John was putting on such a good act that anyone would have had a hard time believing that's all it was.

Once outside the tavern, they headed in the direction of the docks. They had not gone far when John whispered, "Is there anyone followin' us?"

Kate glanced over her shoulder. "No."

"Good." John stood up straight and shrugged Riley off who had been pretending to help him walk. Quickly, he took the lead towards the ship.

"John, what's goin' on?" Kate asked. Seeing him snap right back to his normal self was quite amusing, but all amusement quickly fled with his next words.

"Will's in trouble."

"Will James?" Kate asked, praying that maybe it was not their Will.

John nodded tersely, and Kate immediately felt her stomach tie in a knot. "What kinda trouble?"

"We need to get to Fort Camden before dawn and figure out how to get 'im out of there or he'll be hanged for piracy."

Kate was stunned. "Piracy?"

"I overheard Hendricks talkin' to someone named Stephan at the tavern. Whoever this Stephan is lied to the lieutenant at the fort and made 'im believe that Will's a pirate."

"How are we gonna get 'im out?" Kate asked.

John shook his head. "I don't know, but I'm hopin' Levi can help us figure out a plan, and then it's all up to God."

Very shortly, the docks came into view and they hurried aboard the *Finder,* John's ship.

"Levi!" John called.

In a few moments, a middle aged man appeared from below, followed by the rest of John's crew.

"Yes, Captain?"

"Once again we are in need of yer former military skills, and this time it's urgent," he stressed. "I'm sure you've heard me speak of William James before."

Levi nodded.

"He's involved in a terrible mistake, and we have to get 'im out of Fort Camden before dawn."

"Before dawn?" Levi repeated in surprise.

"Yes, or he'll be hanged unjustly for piracy."

Levi thought this over and sighed heavily. It would not be an easy problem to solve, even for him.

"Well, forcing our way in is out of the question," he said. "Fort Camden is a very well established fort. But, even if we can get in some other way, I'm not sure how we'd get out again, let alone bring someone out with us."

"I was hopin' we could just go in there and tell the one in charge that Will isn't guilty of what they're hangin' 'im for. The problem with that is we can't go in as pirates."

"No, we can't . . ." Levi smiled, "but we could go in as soldiers. We still haven't returned those uniforms."

John grinned. "Genius."

"And maybe we can disguise the *Half Moon* as a British ship being she's the fastest of the two as well as smaller and easier to disguise." Levi looked at Kate for her approval.

She nodded. "I was thinkin' the same thing."

John looked at the rest of his crew. "I want everyone to get all the military uniforms and supplies over to the *Half Moon* as fast as ya can."

The men were quick to obey their captain. Kate hurried over to her ship to inform her crew of what they were going to do and to oversee the loading of supplies. Levi and John made sure that everything they needed was taken aboard. Miraculously, fifteen minutes saw everything accomplished. As soon as his men had returned to the *Finder*, John said, "All right men, me and Levi are goin' with Kate. You can follow behind us and wait for us outside of Fort Camden."

280

"Aye, Captain," the men answered enthusiastically.

John and Levi hurried back to the *Half Moon* and quickly set sail. It would take a couple of hours at least to reach Fort Camden, and it was imperative they get there as soon as possible.

Chapter Twenty-two

Skye waited in her cabin for almost an hour until the ship was silent. She knew that most of the men had left and that was a great advantage to her. Trying to calm the nervousness building up inside, Skye prayed for God to help her. She stepped to the door, knocked loudly, and waited a few moments. When she heard nothing, she tried again. This time she heard someone coming.

"What do you want?" Dreger demanded in irritation.

"Will you please bring me some water?" Skye said through the door.

There was a silence, and then she heard him walk away. Skye wasn't sure if he would come back, but she quickly prepared for action. Picking up the belaying pin, she held it behind her back, and in another minute, she heard Dreger returning. Her heart raced. *Please, God, help me.* She'd never attempted anything like this alone before.

The key turned in the lock, and the door swung open. Dreger stepped in with a bucket, muttering under his breath. Everything fell into place perfectly as he took a step past her to the dresser. His back was turned to her as he bent to set the bucket down. For a split second, Skye froze, but finally she acted. She hit Dreger hard with the belaying pin, and he collapsed with a loud thud. Skye held her breath for a moment, fearing he'd get back up, but he didn't move. She listened for anyone who might have heard, but all was silent.

Skye immediately closed her cabin door and dashed over to the trunk to take out the manacles. With as much speed and quietness as possible, she chained his arms behind him, something that was extremely difficult with his size. She chained his ankles next and then connected a chain from them to his wrists to keep him from being able to get up if he woke. Grabbing strips of cloth she had torn from one of the dresses, Skye gagged him.

Finally, she was finished. Skye pulled on her coat and stuck her Bible and her mother's portrait into one of the inside pockets. Going back to Dreger, she unbuckled his sword belt and buckled it over her own shoulder. She tucked his pistol in her belt and picked up the key to her cabin. The very last thing she did was pull out a bundle from under her bed which was wrapped in her pillowcase to stifle the metal clanking inside.

Skye stepped out of her cabin and locked the door behind her. With as much stealth as she could manage, she started for Hendricks' cabin having decided earlier that she could not just leave the ship. She needed to know what ship Will was on, and she'd have to find out from Hendricks. When she came to his cabin, Skye let herself inside. It was dark, but moonlight shone through the cabin windows just enough that she could see her way around.

Scanning the room, Skye found her attention drawn to a large wardrobe which stood behind the table. That would be the best place to hide when Hendricks came back. She placed the bundle in the wardrobe and then sat at the table facing the door to wait.

The *Half Moon* bustled with activity as Kate's crew worked to disguise the ship. Meanwhile, John and Kate, with Levi who had selected a few men to help, went below to go through the navy uniforms and make further plans for rescuing Will.

"Captain, you can be Lieutenant John Morgan," Levi said. "Hopefully we haven't been around here long enough for people to recognize your name." He dug through the chest of uniforms and pulled out everything needed to impersonate a lieutenant. "This should do for you."

John eyed the clothes with uncertainty but took them anyway. Levi quickly supplied everyone else with red soldiers' uniforms.

With every minute that passed, Skye grew more and more anxious. She knew that Dreger could wake at any time and even though he was chained up he might be able to make enough noise to alert someone.

A good hour passed while Skye sat at the table waiting. Finally, she heard someone coming up the gangplank and moved quickly into the wardrobe. Closing the doors so that she had a tiny crack to see out of, she pulled out Dreger's pistol and waited. Footsteps neared the cabin and the door opened. Hendricks stepped in and set a lantern on the table. Skye's heart skipped a beat when he turned back to the door. She was afraid that he was going to find Dreger, but he only pushed it shut which worked perfectly in her favor.

When Hendricks walked to the table and stood right across from Skye, she knew it was time to come out. She pushed open the wardrobe doors and pulled back the hammer on the pistol at the same time. Hendricks stepped back in surprise.

"Do not make a sound," Skye warned.

Hendricks was stunned. "How did you get out of your cabin?"

"Sit down." Skye motioned to one of the chairs without answering.

Slowly, Hendricks obeyed. Without taking her eyes from him, Skye picked up the bundle and set it on the table. With one hand, she opened it to reveal several additional pairs of manacles.

"Chain your ankles," Skye ordered.

He did as he was told and then Skye had him chain his hands behind the back of the chair. Once he had done that, Skye took two more manacles and chained the ones on his hands and ankles to one of the back rungs between the chair legs.

"You do know that by doing this, you're signing your death warrant, don't you?" Hendricks asked darkly.

Skye did not answer and stepped in front of him again. "What ship is Will on?"

Hendricks chuckled low and menacingly. "So that's why you're still here and not safely away already."

"Just answer my question," Skye demanded, raising the pistol to his chest.

"You won't use that gun," Hendricks said confidently, "because if you do, all my crew will come running and you'll never get away."

"But I would still get you," Skye warned, hoping to concern him enough to answer her. "Now, what ship is Will on?"

Hendricks paused and an evil smile crept across his face. "The *Seabird*."

"He's on the *Seabird*?"

He shrugged maddeningly. "Maybe, but good luck locating it at the bottom of the ocean."

Skye frowned. "What?"

"I just found out tonight that the *Seabird* was caught attacking a merchant ship. It was sunk."

"Do you really expect me to believe you? You lied to Will, telling him that I was dead. You're probably doing the same thing to me." Though Skye realized she was saying it more to herself than Hendricks.

"Oh, I didn't say he was dead. I only told you where you could find the *Seabird*."

"If the ship sank and Will's not dead, where is he?" Skye demanded, beginning to get frustrated.

Hendricks purposely let a long moment pass before he finally answered, looking inordinately pleased with himself. "He was taken prisoner with the rest of the surviving men."

Skye frowned deeply. "Why does that please you? If Will tells them who he is, they'll let him go."

"Steps have already been taken to see that they won't."

"What kind of steps? What are they going to do with him?"

"They're going to hang him for piracy," Hendricks informed her, baring his teeth in a despicable grin.

Skye's blood ran cold. "When?"

"Dawn."

"Where?"

"You'll never get there in time if that's what you're thinking."

"Tell me where he is," Skye ordered in desperation, her pistol hand trembling in frustration. When that caught his attention, she added threateningly, "Do you really want to know how far I'll go to find out?"

"All right, Miss McHenry, but you do realize that I'm going to know exactly where you are. You're precious William is in Fort Camden."

Skye quickly grabbed the map she'd seen on Hendricks' desk. She found Hendricksville and, after a moment, her eyes came to Fort Camden. It was far to the southwest, but

286

she knew that she would do everything she could to get there before dawn.

"I will come after you," Hendricks said, bringing her attention back to him.

Skye stepped back to the table and pulled a gag out of the bundle. Quickly, she gagged Hendricks and said determinedly, "That doesn't mean I won't try."

As she turned to leave, Skye caught sight of the bag full of Will's letters. She could not leave them behind. Slipping the leather strap over her shoulder, she remembered one more thing that might give her something to bargain with if she got caught. Skye heard Hendricks turn to see what she was doing as she pulled out one of his desk drawers. Inside lay the old map with the clues. She took it out and stuffed it into her pocket. Hendricks did not look pleased by this at all.

Finished here, Skye moved past the table to the door. Opening it slightly, she peered out. There was no one in sight. Glancing over her shoulder, Hendricks gave her a glare which sent chills through her body. With that last look, Skye slipped silently out the door and made her way cautiously to the upper deck. All was quiet except for the lapping of water against the ship and the shore. With a deep breath, she left the shadows of the hatchway and quickly crossed the deck to one of the gangplanks. With every second, she expected a shout to signal that she'd been found out, but all was still. Her speed increasing, Skye stole away down the gangplank and hurried up the dock.

When Skye reached shore, she felt relief, but it did not last long. She had only gone a few yards when she heard shouting and looked back to see lanterns being carried frantically around the *Nightshade*. They knew that she was gone. No longer in need of secrecy, Skye turned and ran as fast as she could into Hendricksville. She could hear the footsteps of the men pounding up the dock behind her as she ran into the shadows of the buildings.

Down a dark alley and around another corner, Skye paused. The men were not far away, but she couldn't just keep running aimlessly to avoid being caught. There was no time for her to waste. She had to go southwest and that was the opposite direction she was running.

With extreme caution, Skye made her way through the town, keeping to the darkest streets. A few times she had to hide quickly from Hendricks' searching men, but she finally made it to the edge of town and paused in the dark shadow of a building. Many yards of wide open space lay between her and the forest she had to reach. Her eyes searched the darkness for men, and though she saw no one, there were shouts not far behind. She had no choice but to go.

Hesitating only a moment more, Skye started running. She wasn't sure what she noticed first, the loud bang echoing in the clearing or the intense pain that suddenly burned in her arm. Stumbling, she grabbed at the pain, but kept running. There was someone behind her, she could hear them. Crashing into the forest, Skye searched desperately for a place to hide. The blackness of a huge tree stood not far ahead, and she dashed over to it.

Crouching down behind it, she took her hand away from her arm aware her palm was wet with her own blood as she reached down to grab her pistol. Pulling back the hammer, she stayed perfectly still, pressed against the tree trunk, barely daring to breathe.

Whoever was behind her reached the forest only a moment later. The underbrush cracked loudly and the person slowed, making their way more stealthily as Skye heard them getting closer and closer. They stopped only feet from the tree, and Skye's heart pounded so loudly she was afraid they might hear it. She could barely keep from jumping when Dreger's voice broke the silence.

"I know yer here somewhere," he said in a low, frightening voice.

Skye clutched her pistol tightly.

"I know too that yer wounded," Dreger continued. "If you come out now, you can return to Hendricks unharmed, and he'll forget what you've done."

Skye didn't believe a word of it.

"You'll never reach Fort Camden before dawn, but when you do get there, we will be waitin'," Dreger warned. "I can promise you that."

Skye sat stone still, waiting him out.

"Yer a fool, girl!" Dreger spat, losing patience.

He turned and made his way back out of the forest. Still, Skye did not move, afraid that he was waiting just outside the trees for her to try and get away. By the time she thought it was finally safe to move, her whole body was stiff and tense. She stood slowly, shakily, noticing the feeling of blood trickling down her arm. When she looked at it, she could see only a rip and a dark spot of blood on the upper part of her left sleeve. If Dreger would have shot a few inches to the right, she would have been killed.

Cautiously, Skye stuck her pistol back into her belt and clasped her hand over her arm. Praying that Dreger was not merely waiting for her to move, she moved away from the tree, cringing with every snap of a stick or rustle of leaves. Once she had gone quite a distance, Skye knew that Dreger could not be following so she increased her pace. She had lost so much time, and Will's life depended on her reaching him before dawn.

All the men from the *Seabird*, locked in a cell deep within Fort Camden, were quiet and solemn as the night passed. Sitting against the back of the cell, Will rolled his head along the wall to look at Worthy when that man sighed heavily. "I can't believe you weren't set free, Will."

"I guess it's just my time," Will said, reconciled with his fate.

Les, who had overheard him, said, "You don't sound worried about dyin'."

Will looked at him. "I don't want to die, but I'm not worried to because I know where I'm going and that I'll live with God forever. I'll also get to see Skye again and hopefully my mother too."

"How do ya know?" Les asked.

"Because I believe in Jesus as my Savior and have received His gift of salvation. It's free to anyone who will believe and accept it," Will answered.

"But I've been a pirate all my life and have done some terrible things. How could God wanna save someone like me?" Les asked in dismay.

"God loves everyone," Will expressed with great feeling. "Jesus died for all of us, Les, not just the ones you would consider good. Everyone has sinned. I sinned when I wanted to take revenge on Hendricks for killing Skye. There is not one of us who hasn't. It's not how good or bad we are that determines if we'll go to Heaven. It's only by faith in Him."

Les opened his mouth to speak, but Slade cut him off.

"Shut up. I don't wanna hear this," he grumbled.

But Les didn't care. "How do you receive His gift?"

"By believing. Believing that He died to save you and that you can do nothing on your own to save yourself. He fully and completely paid the penalty for sin," Will answered. "That is all you have to do."

Slade glared at them. "I told ya to be quiet."

Ignoring him, Les nodded slowly, but confidently. "I believe it."

Will saw a couple of the other men nodding and heard some murmurs. He was amazed and rejoiced at how God was using him even in this cell where each one of them awaited their deaths.

But the joy of the moment was cut disappointingly short when Slade spat furiously, "That's it!"

Quickly, Will stood as Slade started towards him. There was nowhere to go so Will stood his ground firmly. Slade did not stop, and Will took a deep breath, anticipating that he probably wouldn't even make it until dawn. Slade grabbed Will and slammed him into the wall, but Will's impact was lessened when Worthy tried to stop Slade. Worthy attempted to pull Slade away, but the men who still sided with Slade quickly came to his aid.

Everyone joined the fight then, some on Will's side, some on Slade's. It was all a blur of commotion. Will tried to pull away from Slade who kept him pinned against the wall, while at the same time, Worthy grabbed Slade again. Slade began to lose his grip, but there was a sudden flash of metal, and Will felt a sharp blade cut through his waistcoat and into his left side. Before he could react, Slade hit him hard and he fell, clutching his midsection tightly. Worthy yanked Slade away and smashed his arm against the cell bars. The bloodied knife that had been hidden in his boot flew out of Slade's hand and into the next cell. Spinning around, Slade punched Worthy, nearly sending him to his knees.

Presently, there was a shout, and the cell door opened. Lieutenant Graham walked in with several soldiers who quickly broke up the fight.

Ignoring everyone, Worthy pulled away from one of Slade's friends and hurried to Will's side. Will groaned as Worthy helped him to his knees, finding blood staining the ripped edges of Will's waistcoat.

"Lieutenant." Les was the first to speak. "Please, take them somewhere else," he said motioning to Will and Worthy. "They're gonna get killed in here."

"Yeah you better taken 'em," Slade spat furiously as he tried to pull away from two soldiers. "I don't wanna see or hear 'em again unless it's at the end of a rope."

Graham looked to Worthy. "Can he walk?"

At Worthy's inquiry Will nodded slowly. Carefully, Worthy helped him up, and they walked slowly towards Graham. Along the way, Les put his hand on Will's shoulder.

"Thanks Will," he said quietly, knowing they would likely not get to speak with each other again.

"You're welcome, Les," Will said, grimacing at the pain. "Thank you for all you've done for me."

Les only smiled.

Will and Worthy followed slowly after Graham to a different part of the fort away from the others. When they reached a smaller cell, Worthy helped Will sit down against the wall. He pulled aside Will's waistcoat and lifted his shirt to see the wound. There was a cut, several inches long near his ribs. Worthy didn't think it was particularly serious, but the bleeding needed to be stopped, and if they weren't going to die in a few hours anyway, it would need to have been taken care of by a doctor.

"How is he?" Graham asked from the door.

Worthy glanced at him. "If he were free he'd need a doctor's care, but since we only have a few hours I ask only for bandages to stop the bleeding."

Graham nodded. "I'll get them."

He and his soldiers walked away. Worthy took the edge of Will's waistcoat and pressed down on the wound gently but firmly. Will winced and looked at him with only one thing on his mind.

"How many do you think responded?" he asked.

"I think many of them did, at least half. Robbie seemed to." Worthy paused and smiled. "I did."

Will was overjoyed. He returned Worthy's smile. "I'm very glad to hear that."

"I've been a fool," Worthy told him. "I should never have turned my back on God in the first place." His expression became sad. "Will there's something I feel very bad about."

"What?" Will asked.

"The day that you found out about Miss McHenry and told me everything you did about God, hearing it and seeing how you never lost faith in Him is what made me realize I'd been wrong. I feel bad that her death is what God used to show me that."

Will breathed deeply and fought against the sorrow that was starting to resurface.

"Don't feel bad," he said quietly. "I'm sure she knows that and is very happy that you were saved as a result of her death."

"Still, I wish it wouldn't have had to be that way," Worthy said sadly. "I don't think I am worth the cost of her life."

"That's not true," Will told him. "Skye would be the first to tell you that getting to live isn't worth someone else going to hell."

A few moments later Graham returned with the bandages. Worthy took them from him gratefully and proceeded to bandage Will's wound. For several minutes, Graham stood at the door watching them. Will glanced at him a few times. It was hard to tell what he was thinking, but Will suspected that Graham was still troubled over the whole issue of his identity. Will could see that he was only trying to do what was right, and he did not resent him for that.

Perhaps an hour had gone by. Already, Skye's legs ached and begged for rest, but she pushed on, running almost blindly through the forest, pausing only to use the stars as navigation. When she came to a grassy clearing, her foot suddenly caught on a hidden branch and she fell forward. Putting her arms out to catch herself, intense pain spread through her injured arm. She cried out and grabbed it as she sat up. Wincing, she squeezed her eyes shut tight. Tears flooded behind her eyelids, though it was not really from the pain. She was beginning to realize just how impossible it might be to reach Fort Camden before dawn.

"Please, help me get there in time," she prayed, her voice quiet and desperate.

When Skye opened her eyes, she looked down at her left hand. The back of it was dark with the blood that had run all the way down her arm. She had to do something to stop the bleeding as she should have done long before now.

Though difficult, Skye pulled out the bottom of her shirt and, being she had no knife, held the sword between her knees using the blade to start cutting a strip of cloth. She tried to work quickly, but it was not easy when she could barely use her arm without causing herself a great deal of pain. Once she had a long strip lying in her lap, she carefully eased her arm out of her coat. Her shirt sleeve was red all the way to her wrist. She carefully pulled back the torn pieces of fabric to better see her wound. In the moonlight she could tell that it was deep, but not as serious as she had feared. She was thankful that the bullet had missed her bone. Picking up the fabric strip and wrapping it around her arm, Skye used her right hand and teeth to tie it tightly so the bleeding would stop. Slipping her arm back into her coat, she stood, desperate to be moving on. Skye looked up at the brightly sparkling stars and started again in the direction of Fort Camden.

Chapter Twenty-three

"Think she'll pass as a navy ship?" John questioned Levi as he inspected the progress on the *Half Moon*. They had replaced a couple of the older sails with new ones, given some of the worn spots on the hull a new coat of paint, and hung a big British flag from the mizzenmast.

Levi nodded. "I think so. After all, no one's going to see her in daylight and everyone will probably be sleeping anyway."

John agreed. They turned to Kate as she walked down from the quarterdeck.

"Riley says we'll reach Fort Camden in less than an hour," she told them.

"We'd best get ready to go ashore then," Levi said. He looked at John. "I'll go below and help the men dress properly. After that I'll help you if you need it, Captain."

John nodded and Levi walked away. Kate looked at John with a smile.

"Well, Lieutenant John Morgan, are you gonna get yer uniform on?"

"Yeah," John replied with little enthusiasm.

He started for Kate's cabin where he had stowed the uniform. Kate stared after him with a bewildered look, wondering about his attitude. When he disappeared below, Kate shrugged to herself and returned to the helm with Riley.

Some twenty minutes later, Kate wandered down to her cabin. John had not come out yet, and she could not imagine it taking quite this long for him to dress. Stepping to the door, she listened and thought she heard some low grumbling. With a frown, she finally knocked, knowing time was running short.

"John, are you dressed yet?" Kate asked.

Something that sounded like a very mumbled *yes* came from inside. Kate's frown deepened, and she pushed the door open.

"John, are you all . . ." Her words fell short. John was fully clothed in the lieutenant's uniform, staring at himself in a mirror. Turning towards her, he looked like he could be sick. Seeing the look on his face combined with his slightly wrinkled and not yet straightened clothes as well as his disheveled, uncombed hair sent Kate to the verge of laughter, but she restrained herself. Slowly, she began, "You look like . . . a naval officer . . . sort of. We'll just have to fix a few things . . . like, well, yer hair."

Kate had never seen John look so miserable.

"I look ridiculous!" he burst out. "What man in 'is right mind would ever wanna dress like this? If it were not one of my best friends in that fort, I'd have to have God Himself tell me to go in there lookin' like this!"

Kate bit her lip in a desperate attempt to keep from laughing.

"Oh go ahead and laugh," John muttered miserably.

Kate quickly composed herself and shook her head. "John, it's really not as bad as you think. Levi used to dress like this all the time. Do you really think he was crazy and looked ridiculous?"

"No," John mumbled grudgingly. "But I *do* look ridiculous."

Kate shook her head again. "You're just not used to lookin' like this. Besides, there are still some things we hafta fix yet that I'm sure will change the whole look."

Kate walked over to him and began straightening out his waistcoat and jacket. John stood limply with a pouting look on his face. Finally it came to the point that Kate had to laugh.

"What's so funny now?" John asked in dismay.

"Just the thought of how this must look. I feel like a mother helpin' her pouting child to dress."

This time John laughed too. When Kate was finished, she stepped back and looked him over giving him a nod of approval.

"That's better, now we just have to fix yer hair," she said.

John groaned loudly. "Do we have to?"

"Ya see, now you're startin' to sound like a child. Of course we have to. You can't go in like you are now."

John sighed heavily in defeat, and Kate handed him a brush. She almost laughed again when he stared at it suspiciously.

"John, it's not gonna bite you," Kate told him with an impish grin.

John made a face and took it from her.

"Good, now start brushin'," Kate instructed, sounding more like a captain giving orders, and John felt he had no choice but to comply. He started running the brush through his hair. Every couple of seconds he would come to a snarl and yelp until Kate finally said, "Oh, don't be such a baby."

"I'm not, this isn't pleasant," John retorted.

"If you would brush everyday like I do, it wouldn't be this bad."

John rolled his eyes. "I don't like brushin' it," he said a bit shortly.

Kate only smiled and replied good-naturedly, "Well then, you can't complain."

John sighed again and continued brushing. Fifteen minutes later, he could finally run the brush through without it snagging.

"See, that wasn't so bad," Kate said with a smile. "I was afraid it would take a good half an hour for you to finish."

John literally glared at his smoothed, dark hair. "Now I look even more ridiculous."

"We can fix that." Kate picked up a dark ribbon from her desk. She pulled John's hair back and tied it with the ribbon. It made all the difference. Kate smiled. "There, now you're a handsome naval officer."

A smile came to John's face as well. "Ya think so?"

Kate nodded and would have said more, but Levi looked into the cabin from the door.

"You ready, Captain, or rather, Lieutenant?" he asked.

John nodded. "Yeah, I'm ready."

Levi walked in all the way, dressed as a soldier, to check whether everything about John's uniform was as it should be. Finally, he held up a black tricorn.

"Put this on," Levi instructed.

John took it from him and set the hat on his head.

"Perfect," Levi said. "No one would ever know that you're really a pirate captain."

John grinned in satisfaction as he and Kate followed Levi out of the cabin. On deck stood seven of Kate's crewmen dressed as soldiers. John was quite impressed with all of their transformations, including his own. He thanked God that they still had the uniforms in the first place.

"There's a reason for everythin'," John murmured to himself, quoting the words he'd heard so many times from Matthew and had once scoffed at.

Kate stepped forward and looked at each of her men.

"You all look great," she said. "Now, we'll be reachin' Fort Camden very soon, and I think we oughta pray that all goes well."

Everyone agreed, and Kate looked at John. "Do you want to say the prayer?"

John hesitated because he didn't think he was very good at praying out loud, but he nodded. They all bowed their heads as he began.

"Dear God, thank You for puttin' me right outside that tavern room just in time to hear about Will. It's obvious that I was meant to hear it. And thank You for providin' us with the uniforms so that we can get inside the fort. We ask that You continue to help us rescue Will. Let the soldiers at the fort believe what we say so that Will is released and we can all get away safely."

At the end, *amen* was murmured by everyone across the ship.

Moving to stand close to John, Kate smiled warmly. "That was nice," she said quietly.

John smiled in return, reddening ever so slightly. "Thanks."

In another few minutes, a couple of tiny specks of light were seen in the distance. The hour was early, just past three o'clock. They had reached Fort Camden with a couple of hours to spare. Kate took over at the wheel and steered the ship into port. They saw not a soul stirring in the sleeping city. Kate's men quickly moored the ship, and John and Levi gathered near the gangplank with their men.

"We'll have the ship ready to leave quickly if we have to," Kate told John.

"Good," he said. "Hopefully this won't take too long if all goes well. If you see soldiers comin' that ain't us, I suggest that you go, and quickly."

Kate shook her head. "I'll wait for you as long as I have to."

"Just so long as you don't get caught," John stressed.

Kate nodded. "We'll all be prayin' for you."

John smiled in answer to that and led Levi and the men down to the dock and into the dark city streets towards the fort. Along the way, Levi gave him last-minute advice.

"Just always act like you're in charge and that you know what you're doing. All you have to do is continue to be a captain, but remember that you're a lieutenant."

"I can do that," John said confidently.

"One more thing. Try to speak like a well educated English gentleman."

Though John knew these particular instructions would be more difficult to follow, he nodded.

It took only a couple of minutes before they reached the courtyard of the fort and walked to the front door. After another silent prayer, John knocked forcefully like he meant business. A moment later, a soldier opened the door.

"Yes?" the young man asked, looking at each of them questioningly.

"I am Lieutenant John Morgan. I must see the commanding officer of this fort immediately."

"Sir, Lieutenant Graham is asleep. Can it wait until morning?"

"No, it cannot. A man's life is at stake."

The soldier was hesitant but let them inside.

"I will go wake the lieutenant," he said.

John nodded and the soldier hurried away. *So far, so good*, John thought. *At least we're inside*. It was close to ten minutes before the soldier returned with a sleepy looking Lieutenant Graham who was just pulling on his uniform jacket. Obviously, he'd had very little time to dress.

"What can I do for you, Lieutenant Morgan?" he asked.

"Lieutenant, I have heard that you have a man prisoner here by the name of William James," John said crisply.

"That is who he says he is, but I have evidence that he is lying."

"That evidence, Lieutenant, is false. I know William James. Furthermore, I am aware that you were told he is a pirate and other such nonsense, but none of it is true."

"How do you know that?"

"Because he is a friend of mine. Will doesn't have a pirate bone in his whole body. Also, if you must know, I overheard a man speaking to the pirate captain, Hendricks. He said that he had come here to Fort Camden to make certain you would believe Mr. James is a pirate thereby reinforcing your intent to hang him for piracy."

"Hendricks?" Graham was stunned. "Where was he?"

"A pirate port a few hours northeast of here, around the coast. They call it Hendricksville. I was doing some spying there and thankfully overheard them." John was relieved not to have to lie since spying on Hendricks was exactly what he'd been doing.

"The man who told him these things, what was his name?" Graham asked.

"Hendricks called him Stephan. He was younger, about twenty-five, and had light colored hair and eyes," John supplied quite readily. He noticed Graham's expression clouding and continued. "Now, Lieutenant, are all these questions necessary? I have business to attend to but came here to get Mr. James before he was hanged."

Graham looked apologetic. "I am truly sorry. I just wanted to find out how I made such a terrible mistake. Here, come with me."

Graham led them farther into the fort. Along the way, he spoke.

"I'm afraid that Mr. James is injured. Some of the men he was with attacked him."

"How badly?" John asked, feeling instantly sick with worry.

"I don't believe it is very serious, but he will need a doctor's attention."

John nodded, somewhat relieved. "We have one aboard our ship who can take care of him."

When John first saw Will, he frowned deeply in surprise and great concern. He could see the blood on Will's waistcoat and the darkness of a bruise on one side of his face from where Slade had hit him. More than that though, there was something different about him that John could see. He was definitely not the same Will that John had known two years ago. *What has he been through?*

Both Will and Worthy looked up at the sound of men approaching. It seemed that perhaps their end was coming sooner than they had expected. But Will could barely believe his eyes.

"Will," John said with obvious and genuine concern.

Will replied hesitantly, realizing that John was pretending to be an officer.

"Don't worry, Will, we've come to get you out of here," John said, putting Will at ease.

Graham made short work of opening the cell door. John hurried inside where both he and Worthy helped Will to stand up. Will walked out supported by John's arm, but when Graham was busy relocking the door, Will motioned toward Worthy and whispered to John, "Help him."

John hesitated for a moment, trying to put together a plan.

"Lieutenant Graham," he began.

Graham turned to him. "Yes?"

"Who is this man?" John nodded at Worthy.

"He is one of the pirates captured. He has admitted to me that he was a naval officer who deserted after being accused of murder."

John looked at Worthy. "What is your name?"

Worthy glanced at Will. He had seen him whisper to John so he knew that something was afoot.

"Michael Worthington."

John looked to Graham. "Have you heard of him before?"

Graham shook his head. "I don't believe I have."

"Well, if he is a naval officer he should be punished accordingly. Perhaps one of my commanding officers has heard of him. I could take him along with me." John cringed inside, wondering if Graham would believe any of it or if he'd just blown their cover. He was very surprised when Graham nodded.

"I'll get a pair of manacles," he said.

John suspected that Graham was feeling guilty about Will and was trying to make up for it by agreeing to whatever they asked. He felt bad about taking advantage of him, but John wasn't sure what else to do.

Graham hurried away, and John heard Will sigh in relief.

John looked at him, frowning. "Are you okay, Will?"

Will nodded slowly. "I'm all right."

John wasn't so sure, but he didn't have time to question him further. Graham returned and unlocked the cell again. He handed the manacles to two of the men that John instructed to see to Worthy. While they were in the cell, Graham turned to Will.

"Here, I know now that this really is yours."

He pressed something into Will's hand, and Will looked down to see that it was his locket. He thanked Graham and slipped the chain over his head. John also thanked Graham.

"Thank you, Lieutenant. I apologize for the time, but we wanted to get to him before it was too late."

"Of course. I'm glad you did." Facing Will again, Graham said remorsefully, "I'm sorry I did not believe you."

"It's all right," Will said. "I do understand." He was not upset at all because he knew there'd been a reason for his having been kept there. If he had been freed, Worthy and the others would not have been saved.

They left then, John and Levi helping Will and two of the other men escorting Worthy. Once outside the fort John breathed a sigh of relief. They had done it. *Thank you, God.*

As quickly as was possible, they returned to the *Half Moon*. When Kate saw them coming, she gave orders to prepare to cast off as soon as everyone was aboard. John, Will, and the others made their way swiftly down the dock and up onto the ship. Kate hurried to meet them, and when she saw that Will was injured, she said his name worriedly.

"Where's Bradley?" John asked.

"I'll get him," Kate answered. "Take Will to my cabin."

John nodded and once inside Kate's cabin, he told Will to sit down on Kate's bed. He then helped Will to start taking off his waistcoat and shirt. Behind John, Levi asked, "Captain, what about Mr. Worthington?"

"Unchain him, Levi," John said over his shoulder. He knew Worthy must be a good friend of Will's.

Levi turned to leave the cabin. At the same time, Kate came in followed by Bradley, the old ship's doctor.

"Let's have a look," he said stopping next to Will.

Bradley slowly pulled back the bandages and took a good look at Will's wound.

"How did this happen?"

"A man came at me with a knife," Will answered.

"Was the blade rusty?"

Will shook his head. "I don't know."

Worthy, who had come to the door with Levi, walked closer. "It may have been, a little."

Bradley glanced at him and nodded.

"Is he gonna be all right, Doc?" John asked with concern.

"If I clean the wound real good, stitch it up, and we do everything to avoid infection, he should be just fine," Bradley answered.

Everyone looked relieved.

"I'll go get everything I need. Does someone want to give me a hand?"

"I will," Levi offered.

Bradley nodded. "Thank you."

The two of them left the cabin, and John looked at Will questioningly.

"How on earth did you end up so far from home and in a fort scheduled to be hanged for piracy?"

Will sighed heavily. "It's a very long story, and I don't even understand half of it."

He glanced at Kate as his mind turned to Skye. The two of them had been such good friends. He didn't know how to tell her what had happened so he waited.

Bradley and Levi returned a couple of minutes later and set the medical supplies on the table. Most pirates weren't lucky enough to have medicine and other things needed for injury or sickness, but John and Kate paid and traded a great deal to make sure they had a large supply.

Pulling a chair up alongside the bed, Bradley began cleaning the wound, trying to spare Will as much pain as possible. Then came the unpleasant, but necessary task of stitching it. When he was finished, Bradley applied ointment and bandaged Will back up with fresh, clean bandages. Lastly, he took the time to check for any more injuries Will might have received but found nothing that wouldn't heal itself over time.

"There," Bradley said. "Now, I think you should get some rest. You look like you've had quite a lack of it."

Will nodded and Bradley stood to gather up his supplies. Looking at John and Kate, who had been hovering around anxiously, Will said in a low voice, "I have to talk to you."

By his tone and the sorrowful look in his eyes, they knew how grave and horrible it must be. John nodded to him, his heart pounding with somber anticipation.

Once Bradley had everything picked up, he left the cabin. Worthy and Levi prepared to go too, realizing that Will wanted to talk to John and Kate alone.

"I'll see you later, Will," Worthy said. "Be sure to get some rest."

Will nodded. "I will."

Worthy stepped to the door and heard Kate tell Levi to have Riley show them where to sleep. When both men had gone, Kate closed the cabin door behind them, and she and John turned their full attention to Will.

"What do you have to say?" John asked slowly, not sure he was entirely prepared for it.

Will was hesitant. "I don't know any easy way to tell you this . . . but a couple of days ago, I spoke with a pirate named Hendricks . . ."

He paused and John nodded. "We know 'im."

Will continued though it was visibly very difficult for him. "He told me that . . . Skye was trying to find me and . . . he caught her and he . . ."

John and Kate looked as if they'd both been shot.

"He . . ." John could barely say it. ". . . killed her?"

Will could not speak. With tears in his eyes, he nodded. Kate's eyes flooded with tears that stung her nose and trickled down her face. John's eyes glistened with tears as well.

"I'm so sorry, Will," he said finally, his voice breaking. He could hardly imagine how Will felt.

All Will could do was nod as he wiped away his tears.

John stayed with Will for a few minutes more, but Kate had to tearfully excuse herself. Not much more was said, and Will finally lay down to rest. John let himself quietly out of the cabin. Looking around deck, he spotted Kate standing at the rail not far away. Even in the darkness, he could tell that she was crying, and he walked over to her.

"Kate," John murmured, gently putting his hand on her shoulder. "Are you all right?" He could feel her trembling.

Kate shook her head. "No. She was one of the best friends I've ever had. I can't believe she's . . . gone." She paused forlornly. "And poor Will! I know what it's like to lose someone you love. I can't imagine anything worse."

Kate turned towards him, her face full of sorrow. John gently pulled her closer, and she hugged him tightly. Feeling her sobs as she cried into his shoulder, tears slid down his face too. He wept for Skye, for Will and Kate, and for all of the people who had loved Skye so dearly. John hated losing someone and it was difficult to see people he cared about so full of pain and sorrow.

Chapter Twenty-four

The stars gradually disappeared as the sky brightened, and the forest became more than just black shadows. Running had long since become an unconscious reflex. Skye couldn't even feel her legs anymore. She was afraid that she might collapse and not be able to get back up, but she pushed herself on. The thought of Will kept her going. She didn't know how far she had traveled or how far she had yet to go, but she prayed that any moment she would come out of the forest and find Fort Camden. Dawn was coming very quickly.

Another several minutes later, the forest did open up, but not to a city, a road. For the first time in what must have been hours, Skye came to a stop. Panting, she looked down the dirt road. Would it lead to Fort Camden or would it be a mistake to follow it? Had she even been going in the right direction in the first place?

Skye heard some wood creaking, approaching from the other direction. Through the quickly growing light, she saw a wagon coming up the road towards her. She didn't hesitate to run and meet it. The old man driving the wagon pulled his horse to a stop when Skye came up alongside him. He squinted at her in the dim light and then looked very surprised to realize that it was a woman.

"Can I help ya, miss?" he asked uncertainly.

"Which way is Fort Camden?" she gasped.

"This road'll take ya right to it." The man pointed down the road.

"How far is it?"

"Three or four miles."

Skye's heart sank. How could she get there in time when dawn was nearly upon them?

"Do ya need a ride?" the man asked.

"Only if you can get me there faster than I can run."

"I don't know if my old mare can go that fast pullin' a cart."

Skye had already turned to go. "Then I have to go myself. Thank you anyway."

She ran down the road as fast as she could. The only thing on her mind was Will, and she prayed constantly that she would reach the fort in time to save him. Three and a half miles later, Skye reached the edge of Fort Camden and saw the fort near the shoreline, but by now, the sun was sparkling high in the treetops. Skye felt her heart sinking, and she barely paused before running towards the fort.

When she reached the courtyard, Skye was stopped by two soldiers.

"I need to see the man in charge of this fort," she gasped urgently, out of breath.

"What's wrong, miss?" one soldier asked.

Skye didn't have time to notice the looks of confusion they wore over how she was dressed and the blood that stained her sleeve.

"A man who was going to be hanged here at dawn is innocent. I must see your commander!"

The soldiers hesitated and looked at each other, and Skye suspected they wondered if she was crazy.

"Please. I escaped from pirates, was shot, and ran almost all night to get here. Please let me in!" Skye was desperate.

"I'll go see the lieutenant," the first soldier stuttered, glancing at his partner who only shrugged.

He turned and hurried into the fort. When he was gone, Skye looked at the second soldier.

"There are a group of pirates held prisoner here, right?" she asked.

The soldier nodded. "Yes."

"Has your lieutenant hanged them yet?"

He nodded again.

Skye's heart skipped a beat and then pounded painfully. "All of them?"

"Yes, miss, about a half an hour ago."

Skye took a step back, grief-stricken. She was too late. Finally, her legs gave out, and she fell to her knees. Tears spilled from her eyes as she sobbed sorrowfully. The soldier quickly came to her and asked if she was all right, but she barely noticed him. A moment later, his partner returned with Lieutenant Graham who hurried to Skye and helped her up.

"What's wrong?" he asked.

Tearfully, she raised her face. "One of the men hanged here this morning was innocent. He had nothing to do with the pirates."

"What was his name?" Graham asked quickly.

"William James," Skye answered mournfully.

Graham was quick to ease her pain. "He wasn't hanged!"

"What?" Skye didn't know if she could believe it.

"Mr. James was not hanged. He was scheduled to be, but during the night I was informed of his innocence."

Skye closed her eyes in immense relief. "Thank You, God!" She opened her eyes then, joyful beyond description. "Where is he? I must see him."

"He is not here," Graham told her. "The lieutenant who came and told me he was innocent took Mr. James with him."

Skye couldn't imagine who the lieutenant could be, and it frightened her to think that maybe Hendricks had something to do with it. What if he now had Will?

"What was his name?" Skye asked, sounding desperate once more.

"Lieutenant John Morgan," Graham answered. "He said he was a friend of Mr. James."

For a moment, Skye could only stare, stunned. "John Morgan?" she finally managed.

"Yes, do you know him too?"

Feeling ridiculously overjoyed, Skye nodded and was relieved all over again. "Yes, he's a friend of mine as well. Tell me, when did he come for Will, and how did he know he was here?"

"Lieutenant Morgan arrived here around three o'clock this morning," Graham explained. "He said that he overheard a conversation between a man, the one who told me that Mr. James was guilty, and the pirate, Hendricks, while the lieutenant was spying in a pirate port called Hendricksville."

Skye made a sound, half laugh, half sigh, shaking her head when she realized that she'd probably just missed John. It's quite possible he'd still been in Hendricksville when she'd left. She might even have run right passed his ship.

"Is something wrong?" Graham asked.

"No," Skye answered. "It's just that I was in Hendricksville at the same time. For the past few days, I've been held captive by Hendricks and escaped last night. I didn't even realize that John was there."

"What is your name?"

"Skylar McHenry."

Graham looked a little surprised, yet not. "Mr. James mentioned you. I'm afraid I didn't believe him until Lieutenant Morgan came."

Skye nodded, understanding how these things happen, and then Graham frowned, noticing her bloodied jacket.

"Are you injured, Miss McHenry?"

"Yes. I was shot while escaping."

"Please, come with me, and I will get a doctor and anything else you need," Graham offered, sounding very concerned.

As she followed him inside, Skye quizzed him further. "Lieutenant, who was the man who told you that Will was guilty."

"He told me his name was Stephan Daley," Graham answered.

Skye was not surprised, and after her unpleasant dealings with Stephan it made her sick to know that he had almost succeeded in getting rid of Will forever.

"Do you know him?" Graham asked, seeing her sour face.

"Unfortunately, yes, more so than I'd like."

"Perhaps then, you can tell me why he lied to me," Graham said, needing badly to salve his conscience over this matter.

"I don't know everything, but he is after Will's inheritance. If Stephan can get rid of Will, and if Edward James were to die prematurely, Stephan would be free to claim the inheritance."

"So Stephan Daley really is Edward James' nephew as he said?"

"Yes, it's probably one of the only things he told you that is true."

Graham nodded and Skye continued. "Stephan has hired men like Hendricks to carry out his plan. He had me kidnapped by Hendricks' men because I found out that he was the one behind the plan to kidnap Will."

Graham shook his head. "I had no idea this was such a complicated plot."

"Nor did I."

"Is there anything I can do to help?" Graham asked.

"Well, as long as Will is safe for now, I need to get back to Port Henry to tell his family what has happened. At the moment, they trust Stephan, and I have to warn them. I also need to leave as soon as possible because Hendricks knows I am here. He said he would come for me."

"Don't worry," Graham reassured her, "I'll make sure that you get safely back to Port Henry."

"Thank you so much." Skye was very relieved by this. She hadn't thought of Hendricks since arriving at the fort, too worried for Will, but now she wondered just where he was.

By now, they had reached the hospital area of the fort. Graham went to get the doctor, and Skye sat down on one of the beds. Wincing, she removed her coat. Her arm and shirt sleeve were dark with dried blood.

Skye looked up as Graham returned with the doctor. He was a kind old man with a quiet and gentle voice.

"Well, it looks as if you've been through quite an ordeal," he commented after looking her over.

Graham himself was surprised and concerned by the amount of blood on her shirt. The doctor cut her sleeve open carefully and unwound the cloth she'd tied around it. Skye cringed when she saw her wound in the light, though it looked worse than it actually was. The bullet had left a deep gash across her upper arm. Like Will, she would need stitches. After examining it, the doctor got to work cleaning away the blood. The stitches came next, and as he was finishing up, Graham spoke to Skye.

"Would you like me to find you a new pair of clothes, Miss McHenry?"

"I would be very grateful if you would, but please, not a dress. I'd far rather travel as I am until I know I'm safe," Skye explained.

313

Graham nodded and went off to find Skye some clothes. In another minute, the doctor finished with the stitches. He began bandaging her arm and instructed, "Keep the wound clean and have the bandages changed at least once a day. Make sure also to have a doctor check it once in a while for signs of infection and to take the stitches out."

"I will."

"Good." The doctor started picking up. "You're very lucky, Miss McHenry. That injury could easily have been much worse. You may not have made it here alive."

"I know," Skye said. "I thank God that it was not any worse."

The doctor smiled. "He always takes good care of His children."

Skye returned his smile, feeling great happiness to meet and be near someone again who shared her faith.

A couple of minutes later, Graham returned with a woman who looked about his own age.

"Miss McHenry, this is my wife. I thought you might need some assistance."

She smiled in appreciation. "Thank you."

Graham handed her a pair of clothes and led both women to a private room where Skye could change.

"I have a carriage waiting as soon as you are ready, Miss McHenry," Graham said just before he left the room.

Skye thanked him again and when the door closed, she began to undress with help from Mrs. Graham. The woman was very kind and pleasant to talk to. Skye was very glad for her help.

When Skye was fully dressed, she and Mrs. Graham left the room and went to Graham's office. He stood up when they entered.

"Miss McHenry, before we go, do you think you could show me on a map where Hendricksville is?" Graham directed her to a map that was laid out on his desk. "I've been searching for Hendricks for quite some time, and it would be very helpful to know the location of one of his hideouts."

Quite easily, Skye pointed to the exact spot where the pirate port had been on Hendricks' map. "It's right there."

Graham quickly marked it down and then noticed how far it was from Fort Camden.

"You ran all that way last night?" he asked in disbelief.

Skye raised her brows admitting what a feat it had been and said simply, "I had to get here."

Graham remembered then what Will had told him about wanting to marry Skye. He didn't say anything, of course, but he was becoming increasingly relieved that Will had been rescued before Graham had made the worst mistake of his life.

"Well, Miss McHenry, if you are ready, we can go."

"Yes, I am ready."

Skye turned to thank Mrs. Graham and say goodbye. She then followed Graham outside where he helped her into a waiting carriage.

"I will escort you most if not all the way to Port Henry," Graham informed her. "And if you do not object, I will join you inside until we're well away from the city."

"I do not mind at all," Skye told him.

Graham climbed in and took a seat across from her. The carriage jolted forward a moment later, and they were on their way to Port Henry.

With a sigh, Will rolled onto his back and opened his eyes. He glanced around the cabin. Through the windows above the bed, he could tell it was bright and sunny. Voices could be heard, friendly voices, that made him feel safe, finally. He pushed back the covers and sat up. It was the first morning in weeks that he did not have to wonder how he would survive the day.

Standing, Will saw a folded pile of clean clothes sitting on the table. Obviously they'd been left there for him. He changed into them and sighed deeply as he remembered that Skye's portrait had still been in Worthy's cabin. Even if it had been in his pocket, the water would have ruined it. Either way, it was gone, just like Skye. He'd lost everything he'd had with him. Both portraits, his Bible, and the two letters from his father.

Will walked slowly across the cabin and opened the door. Climbing up through the hatchway leading to the upper deck, he was greeted by warm sunshine and was not surprised at all to see the sun already at its peak. Taking a few more steps, he looked around at the unfamiliar surroundings. He'd never been on the *Half Moon* before, but he saw several men from Kate's crew that he recognized.

"Will."

Looking to his right, Will saw John coming down from the quarterdeck.

"How do you feel this mornin'?" John asked. "Or I should probably say afternoon."

Will hesitated. He really couldn't say that he felt well emotionally, but health wise he did.

"I'm all right."

Just then his stomach growled, and he realized how hungry he was. John smiled.

"Come with me," he said. "Bailey has been keepin' dinner for you. We figured you'd be up soon."

Will followed John below deck to the galley where Kate's cook set a plate of food on the table.

"Have all you want," Bailey told him kindly.

"Thank you," Will said.

He sat down to eat, and John took a seat across from him. After Will had taken a few bites, John said, "Yer friend,

316

Worthy, told me what happened, at least on the *Seabird*. He wasn't sure about anythin' before that. I'm very sorry for it, and I can't understand why all of this has been done to you, Will."

Will shook his head. "Neither can I. I wish I could."

"Well, Worthy told us about yer father, and we've been sailin' towards Port Henry. We should reach there later on tonight. Maybe then you can figure it out."

"Thank you, John."

John nodded. "I also thought I'd stick around, secretly ya know, to help out if you need it. Maybe, bein' a pirate, I can find out some things for you."

"I'd be very grateful for that, John."

"This is what friends are for," John replied with a smile. "Besides, you might not know yet," John squared his shoulders with the importance of what he had to tell, "but we're brothers now too."

The barest bit of a spark lit Will's eyes. "Yes, we've known about you and Kate for a long time actually. We heard people talking about your change of habit about a month after we all returned to Kingston, and we suspected that you had trusted Christ."

John smiled wryly. "I guess when two pirates suddenly start helpin' people the news travels fast."

"It makes me very happy, John," Will said, remembering Skye's joy with the news as well.

Hendricks slammed his fist furiously on the desk. "So she's gone?"

"A carriage left the fort early this mornin'," Dreger informed him. "She must've been on it."

Hendricks lashed out and knocked several items off his desk, sending them crashing to the floor. "How did we lose both of them? And who's the devil that got the boy out?"

"Some lieutenant that knew 'im s'posedly, but I didn't think 'e knew anyone here."

"Neither did I! Did you get his name?"

"Took a while, but yeah. His name was John Morgan. Maybe he's some lieutenant the boy knew down in the Caribbean."

Hendricks suddenly spun round to face him, his expression livid.

"Oh, he's from the Caribbean all right!" he bellowed. "But he isn't a lieutenant, he's a pirate captain! And I'm willing to bet anything," he ground out, "that he was the drunk I caught listening to Stephan and me at the tavern. That's how he knew about the hanging." Hendricks slammed his fist down again. "I should have killed him!"

"What do you want to do now, Captain?" Dreger asked.

"The boy could be anywhere so we can't go after him, but the girl will be heading back to Port Henry to tell everyone what she knows. Luckily, Mrs. James and her daughters are the only ones at the house, and I've warned Stephan not to go back. I want to set course for Port Henry, and when we get there tonight, you and the men are going to pay a visit to the James family. You will take Mrs. James and her daughters captive. That way we'll have control again."

"What about Miss McHenry?"

"Find the map she took, and then I want you to kill her. Kill her dead this time!"

Dreger was a little surprised. "Kill her?"

"Yes. She is of no use to me. She knows too much and can handle herself too well. As we have both unfortunately found out," Hendricks added furiously.

"What about Stephan? He won't be happy about it."

"Right now, I don't care. I'm furious with his ineptness too, but he hired me to take care of everything and that's exactly what I'm doing. Besides, he knows as well as I do that he doesn't stand a chance with the girl. Now, I'm sure you don't have any objections about killing her."

Dreger sneered, rubbing a sore spot on the back of his head where Skye had hit him. "None at all."

"So, why did you and Kate leave the Caribbean?" Will asked as he took a second helping of food. It felt like forever since he'd eaten.

"We had a few close calls and decided to come here for awhile where no one knows us," John explained. "We never planned to stay as long as we have, but what we've been doin' is goin' so well that we think God wants us to stay and keep on."

"What are you doing?" Will asked curiously.

"We've been buyin' slaves and freein' 'em."

"Really?"

John nodded. "There's a man we met who bought some slaves, freed 'em, and helped 'em set up a village on an island northeast of Port Henry. He wanted to bring more there, but 'e didn't have the money or the ships. Me an' Kate have both."

"How many have you freed?"

"Last count was about a hundred and fifty. That was a couple of months ago so it's more than that now."

"John, that's amazing."

John smiled. "We're just doin' God's work. Every slave we bring to the island is told about Him. Some, of course, never do accept Him, but many more have."

"I wish Matthew could hear all of this," Will said, thinking fondly of his friend, missing him.

319

John laughed. "He would see quite a difference, wouldn't he?"

A smile finally came to Will's face. "Yes, he would."

"I wish 'e could be here too," John said wistfully. "I really wanted to tell 'im myself that I finally turned to God, but that was impossible."

"Trust me, he was very happy when he found out. We all were."

There was a short moment of silence until Will looked up at John questioningly.

"John, how did you find out I was in Fort Camden and going to be hanged?"

"I was in a tavern meetin' with a friend, and God put me in the right place at the right time. I was just comin' out of one of the private rooms and overheard Hendricks and someone else talkin' in another. I heard everything I needed to."

Will breathed a sigh of relief. "I'm glad you did."

"So am I," John said with great seriousness.

Will turned back to his food. In between bites, he asked, "I was wondering, this man talking with Hendricks, do you know who he is?"

"His name was Stephan, that's all I know. Seemed to be well acquainted with Hendricks, but definitely not the pirate type."

"He's the same man who convinced Graham that I was a pirate. He said that he is my father's nephew."

John made a face. "That would make him your cousin, Will. Why would he want you dead?"

"I don't know." They traded a long look. "He could have been lying."

"Yes, he didn't really look like he could be your cousin, but I s'pose we can't really go on that," John said.

Will sighed heavily. "I just wish I knew why this was happening. Kept from everyone all this time, I know *nothing*."

⁓⁓⁓

A short time after dinner, John decided that it was time to return to the *Finder* which was following a short distance behind. Kate brought the *Half Moon* to a halt and the *Finder* came to a slow stop next to it.

"I'll take you home with the *Finder*," John told Will. "Kate's gonna go on to that island I told you about to give 'em the supplies we got."

Will and Worthy followed John and Levi over to one of the gangplanks which bridged the gap between the *Half Moon* and the much bigger *Finder*. Kate met them there and looked at Will with sadness in her eyes.

"Will, I want to tell you again how sorry I am about what happened. I know what it's like to lose someone you love so much. I hope that your family can help ease your pain."

"Thank you, Kate." Will's eyes glistened as he fought a rush of emotion. "I am sorry too that you lost such a good friend. Skye spoke of you often."

"Everyone who knew her lost something very special," Kate said with feeling.

Will and John agreed, and then it was time to conclude their farewells.

"Goodbye, Will. I really hope to see you again," Kate said. "Maybe after I deliver the supplies I could find John in Port Henry. If not, I'm glad I at least got to see you now."

"So am I, Kate. Thank you for what you and John did to rescue me. Words cannot express my gratitude."

"Oh Will, how could we have done anything less?"

"Goodbye, Kate," he said.

Turning, Will made his way up the gangplank. Halfway across, Kate called to him, "I'll be prayin' for you, Will."

Will turned to her for a moment and replied with the utmost sincerity, "Thank you."

On the *Half Moon*, Worthy and Levi said their goodbyes to Kate before following after Will. When only John and Kate were left standing there, Kate looked at John with serious eyes.

"Be careful, John. Don't get caught. We can't lose you too."

John gave her a small smile. "Don't worry. Nothin' will happen to me that's not meant to happen."

A smile grew on Kate's face. "I'll see you soon then."

They held each other's smile for another moment before John turned and crossed over to his ship. He paused to wave at Kate from the railing and then took his place at the *Finder's* helm.

A little more than an hour later, John's eyes trained on Will who had been standing alone at the ship's bow for quite some time. Unsure whether to leave him be or not, John finally called Levi up to the helm.

"Take the wheel for me please, Levi."

"Aye, Captain."

After Levi took his place, John slowly descended the stairs, still watching Will. At the bottom he took a detour into his cabin to get something before again directing his steps towards the bow. Will was unaware of John's presence until he spoke.

"How are you doin'?"

Will turned to him and shrugged. "All right, I guess."

"Looks to me like you could use this." John placed a Bible in Will's hands, and Will smiled.

"Thank you," he said. "I was just thinking of asking you for one."

"I'm glad I decided to come over here then."

He and Will both fell silent for a moment as they gazed at the sea.

"You know," John remarked thoughtfully, "this reminds me of the day that Kate's crew rescued me and Kate, and Matthew and Skye from that island."

Will looked at him. "How so?"

"Just after we'd eaten, Skye was standin' up at the bow of the *Half Moon* just like you've been. I went up and talked to her a little and told her not to worry 'cause we were gonna rescue you. Kate came then with a Bible she'd had stashed somewhere below. She told Skye that whenever she needed to be alone she could use her cabin."

Will knew without John having to say it that he was telling him the same thing.

"Thank you, John."

Chapter Twenty-five

Are you sure you would not rather have me come all the way to Port Henry with you?" Graham asked Skye when they had stopped briefly about an hour from their destination.

Skye nodded. "Yes, I'll be fine."

"All right, Miss McHenry. I hope the rest of your trip goes well. If you ever need help, just send word," Graham told her.

"Thank you. I will," Skye said with a smile.

Skye watched Graham mount his horse, wish her a good day, and then ride off. She was glad to be away from Fort Camden. Their journey had been pleasant and without incident. In another hour she would be able to warn Rebecca and the girls about Stephan. She hoped that her father would be there, but she knew he would probably be looking for her.

The driver told Skye that he was ready to be on their way, and when she had climbed back into the carriage, they continued on. The last hour seemed to be the longest. Without Graham to talk to, Skye pondered over Hendricks' map. The clues were no less confusing so, eventually, she gave up.

The sun had sunk low when finally they made it to Port Henry. Skye gave directions to the James' estate, and they made their way through the city and into the country. A little less than a mile from the house, Skye asked the driver to stop. She got out of the carriage taking all of her things with her.

"I'll walk from here," she said.

"Are you sure, miss?" the driver asked.

Afraid that Stephan might be there, she wanted to arrive at the house unnoticed. Who knew what he might try if he saw her coming?

"Yes, quite sure, thank you."

The driver turned the carriage around and drove away. When he was gone, Skye started walking, keeping her hand on her pistol just in case. It wasn't long before she was standing at the edge of the estate. Seeing no one, she cautiously approached the side of the house, avoiding the front door and trying to stay out of sight as much as possible. Finally, she reached a side door that led into the kitchen and knocked quietly. A moment later, it was opened by Samuel.

"Miss McHenry!" he exclaimed in shock.

Skye looked around him to see if there was anyone else in the kitchen. Only Rose was there, and she looked as surprised as Samuel did.

Skye stepped inside. "Is Stephan here?"

"No, he's not," Rose answered.

"What happened to you?" Samuel asked.

"It's a long story for later," Skye told him. "Is my father here?"

Samuel shook his head ruefully. "They're all out looking for you."

"I need to see Rebecca then. Do you know where she is?"

"I think she's in the study," Rose answered looking quite shaken.

"Thank you," Skye said, reaching out to touch Rose's arm, to reassure her, "but make sure you don't let anyone else know I'm here."

Skye hurried out of the kitchen and through the house. When she reached the study, she saw that Rebecca and the girls were all there. Looking up from their individual pursuits, they were all quite shocked to see her standing in the doorway.

"Skye!" they exclaimed. This already dearly loved young woman was the very last person they expected to see, and she was very quickly surrounded by them.

"Skye what happened?" Rebecca asked. "We've been so worried! Your father has been looking all over for you."

"I was kidnapped."

"By who?" Emma wanted to know, her eyes huge.

Skye hesitated. After all, Stephan was their cousin so she didn't know what to say. She looked at Rebecca seriously.

"I must talk to you." She felt bad excluding the girls, especially Lydie, but she felt that it was best.

Rebecca nodded, looking concerned, but sent her daughters an encouraging look. "Girls, will you let me talk to Skye alone, please."

Lydie nodded quickly and told Molly and Emma to come with her. She picked Ashley up and the four of them walked out of the room. None of them wanted to go, but they were too worried to protest. Once the door had closed behind them, Skye turned to Rebecca.

"What is it, Skye?" Rebecca asked with motherly concern which made it even harder for Skye to tell her what she knew.

"I found out who is to blame for all of this. Rebecca . . . it's Stephan."

Rebecca was stunned. "Stephan?"

Skye nodded. "He is responsible for what happened to both Will and me, and he's planning even worse than that."

"How can this be? Are you sure it's Stephan?"

"Yes, without a doubt. He was there when I was kidnapped, and I've seen and talked to him since. That is how I know what he's up to."

"What *is* he up to? Why would he do this?" Rebecca couldn't understand it.

"He's after everything. The house, your husband's company, and his money. That's why Stephan tried to get rid of Will, so that Will would not be able to claim his inheritance."

"But unless something unforeseen would happen that time would not come for many years. Why would Stephan be concerned with that now?"

"Because he has something unforeseen planned," Skye told her regretfully. "In order for Stephan to claim the inheritance, Edward would have to be out of the picture too."

Rebecca gasped. "He wants to kill Edward?"

"He's hired someone to do it," Skye said, divulging the awful truth. "Hendricks."

Shaking her head, Rebecca looked overwhelmed. "How can he do this? How could he possibly betray Edward this way?"

"I don't know," Skye answered quietly. "Rebecca, has Stephan been here recently?"

"No," Rebecca answered, looking up from her preoccupation with these new and horrible thoughts. "He said that he had some business to take care of and would be gone a day or two. He left late the day before yesterday."

"So he has not come back yet?"

Rebecca shook her head.

"The reason he left is terrible, but thankfully his plans went wrong, and I do have some good news."

"What is it?" Rebecca wanted to know, needing to hear something good.

"Will is safe." Skye's face blossomed into a smile she could not hold back. "I have not seen him, but I know he's with some friends of ours."

"Oh, Skye, that is good news. The best." Rebecca was very relieved, but then looked troubled again. "How do I tell the girls about Stephan?"

Skye shook her head. "I don't know. That's why I wanted to speak with you alone."

Rebecca looked suddenly worried. "Skye, what if he comes back here?"

"I don't really think he will because I suspect that he was probably warned that I escaped, but if he does, with a little help from Samuel and Isaac, I can take care of it."

Rebecca nodded and looked towards the door. "I should tell them now. They need to know."

She called her daughters back into the room. They looked very concerned after being excluded.

"What's wrong, Mama?" Emma asked.

"Skye found out who is responsible for kidnapping her and Will, but it is something that will not be easy for you to understand. I don't even understand it."

"Who is it?" Lydie wanted to know, feeling a dreadful sensation in her stomach.

"Stephan."

Emma's mouth popped open. "Stephan kidnapped Skye and Will?"

"Why?" Lydie asked in disbelief.

It was not easy for her, but Rebecca explained as best she could what Stephan intended.

"But why did he kidnap you, Skye?" Emma questioned when her mother had finished.

"Because I was starting to find out that he was the one behind it all."

Lydie was quickly beginning to realize more. "But Father would have to die too for Stephan to claim the inheritance. Not just Will."

Rebecca looked at her gravely. "Yes, he would."

All three girls looked horrified.

"He's going to kill Papa?" Emma asked with tears in her eyes.

"Not if we warn him first," Rebecca answered, with a steely resolve.

"But Papa's gone."

"I'm sure he will be back soon to see if we've heard from Skye."

"I hope so," Emma fretted worriedly.

"In the meantime, we'll all pray that he does," Rebecca told her.

Emma nodded readily.

"Skye does have good news," Rebecca said after a moment.

They looked at Skye with eager faces.

"I found out today that Will is safe. He's with our friend, John."

"John Morgan?" Emma asked.

"Yes," Skye answered, smiling at Emma's quickness.

"How did he find him?"

"I think I should tell you everything from the beginning."

Later that night, Skye sat in the drawing room staring at the map again. She really wanted to figure it out because it would give them a big advantage against Stephan and Hendricks. When she heard someone enter the room, she looked up to see Emma in her nightgown, ready for bed. She walked up next to Skye.

"Have you figured it out yet?" Emma asked.

Skye shook her head. "No."

"What do you think those circles are supposed to be?" Emma pointed on the map.

"I don't know."

"What does the clue say again?"

"*Hidden in metal, revealed by glass,*" Skye answered.

Emma frowned in thought. "How can something be hidden in metal and revealed by glass?"

Skye shook her head again. "I wish I knew."

"What do you think you're trying to find that is hidden?"

"Well, it could be anything, but the island does not have a name so maybe that's it."

"How can you hide a name in metal?" Emma wondered.

"I don't know, but if you think of anything, let me know."

Emma smiled. "I will."

A moment later, Rebecca walked into the room.

"Emma, it's time for bed."

"Okay, Mama." Emma looked at Skye. "Goodnight, Skye. I'm glad you're back."

Skye smiled. "So am I. Goodnight, Emma."

Emma said goodnight to her mother too and hurried off to her room.

"Are you going to stay up?" Rebecca asked Skye.

"I think I will for a little while."

"Unless you want company, I think I'll go to bed," Rebecca said.

Skye nodded with a gentle smile knowing that Rebecca had received quite a shock today. "Go ahead."

Saying goodnight, Rebecca left the room, and Skye turned her attention back to the map.

The room was dark when Skye opened her eyes. She was still in the chair having fallen asleep a short time after Rebecca had gone to bed. The candle had gone out, and Skye was not sure of the time. She glanced around the shadowed room feeling strangely uneasy and suspected that was what had woken her. She stood up, but before she could make another move, something flashed in front of her face and was immediately pulled tight against her throat barely allowing her to take in air. As she tried desperately to get her fingers beneath the leather cord around her neck, she was pulled roughly away from the chair. In her ear she heard an all too familiar voice.

"You didn't think just because you got away from Fort Camden we wouldn't come for you, did you?"

Keeping the cord tight around her neck, Dreger reached down and picked up the map that had fallen from Skye's lap. She prayed frantically for help.

"Please, Dreger," she gasped. "Take . . . the map . . . go." She didn't have much hope he would listen, but she had to try.

Dreger chuckled evilly. "You've angered the captain and me and you won't be gettin' away with it." He pulled the cord tighter making it a terrible struggle just to breathe. "Now, since the captain doesn't have a hostage and you are too much trouble, Mr. James is gonna come home to an empty house."

Oh, what have I done? Skye thought. *I've put Rebecca and the girls in danger.* She pulled on the cord as hard as she could and was just able to gasp, "Don't, please . . . take me... I won't . . . escape again."

"It's far too late for that."

With those words, Dreger pulled the cord even tighter, completely cutting off her air. Skye's struggles were hopeless. Her body grew weak from lack of oxygen, and her vision darkened.

<hr/>

"Accordin' to the directions Levi was given, the house should be just on the other side of this point," John announced.

Standing beside him, Will watched anxiously as the *Finder* sailed slowly around the point. It had taken a little longer than they had anticipated to reach Port Henry and get directions to the James' estate, but now, finally, Will was about to reach his family's home.

John turned to Will with a smile. "Lookin' forward to meetin' yer family?"

Will nodded. "Yes . . . it's a little unnerving though."

John put his hand on Will's shoulder. "Anyone would feel that way."

Just as John finished speaking, Worthy came running up from the ship's bow.

"Captain Morgan, I think you should stop the ship. There's another ship anchored near the house."

John and Will could just barely make out the silhouette of a ship in the dark. Immediately, John spun the wheel and gave his men orders to bring the ship around. Once the *Finder* had come to a standstill, John picked up a spyglass. Raising it, he took a look at the ship which could just be seen in the darkness. After a moment, he lowered it.

"I'm not sure I like what I see. It could just be one of your father's ships, but the flag on it looks a little too dark to be a British flag," John told Will.

"May I see?" Worthy said.

John handed him the spyglass, and Worthy took a good look.

"She's not a British ship," he told them, grimly. "She's Hendricks'."

"Hendricks!" Will exclaimed. He looked at John in alarm. "If he's after my family, we have to stop him."

John spun around to face Levi. "Lower two of the boats now!"

Levi hurried to see that it was done and the others followed just behind him.

"As many as can fit in the boats, get yer weapons and be ready to go as soon as those boats are in the water," John called to his crew. "Hendricks is here, and we need to stop him." He hurried to his cabin and came back with his sword and one each for Will and Worthy.

As the first boat was lowered, John and Levi led the way followed by Will and Worthy and several other men. In a few moments, the other boat was full and the two boats were rowed with all speed towards the shore. Once land was reached, they pulled the boats onto the sand, and John quickly gave his men orders.

"I want to try to sneak up to the house without Hendricks' men knowin', so I want everyone to be quiet. When we get inside we have to find Will's family quickly and bring 'em back here."

"Aye, Captain," the men said quietly.

Without another word, John turned and the whole group made their way through the woods towards the house. Within minutes, it came into sight and, keeping to the shadows, they made their way to the front. When Will saw the front door standing open, his heart filled with fear for his family, and he murmured, "They're already inside."

John said what they were all thinking. "Hopefully they have not left."

They had seen the *Nightshade* still anchored, and he prayed that Hendricks didn't have Will's family on board already. He motioned for his men to follow, and they cautiously approached the door. All was dark and quiet inside. They entered the foyer and paused when they came to the stairs. They could hear footsteps upstairs, but just barely and it seemed that there was more than one person.

"They're up there," John whispered, motioning up the stairs.

Everyone started up, but Will stopped when he thought he heard a voice from somewhere down the hall. Feeling a sudden urge to find out where it was coming from, he whispered to John, "Keep going."

Confused, but having no time to ask questions, John and his men continued while Will went back down the stairs and crept down the hall. A few feet from an open doorway, Will heard the voice again and though he couldn't make out any words, he recognized the voice. Dreger. When he reached the door, he cautiously peered inside. The sight that met his gaze caused his heart to skip a beat and his jaw to drop in astonishment. For a moment, he had to wonder if it was real. Dreger stood in the middle of the room and standing in front of him was Skye, alive, but obviously in peril. She was struggling mightily, and Will realized in a flash that Dreger was strangling her.

His astonishment vanished, and Will reacted instantly. Pulling out his sword, he rushed at Dreger. The evil man was so fixated on killing Skye that he didn't even hear Will until it was too late. Will brought his sword hilt hard against the man's head, and Dreger fell away from him. However, Will had no further thought for Dreger as Skye fell to her knees, gasping and choking.

Will dropped his sword and reached down to take Skye by the arms, lifting her with great care and concern. "Skye?"

At the sound of his dear voice, she lifted her face and whimpered his name through a cough. Tears of reaction and joy leaked out as she fell into his arms at the very moment he dragged her into them, hugging her so tightly she didn't think she'd be able to breathe.

"Will. I need air," she whispered, nearly laughing. The joy was so great.

"I'm sorry," he said, gentling his hold. "I thought you were dead." *Thank You, God! Thank You a thousand times!* His broken heart filled to bursting with joy.

"I know, they told me," Skye replied. "I'm so sorry."

And as much as she hated to, she pulled gently away, the horror returning.

"Will, your family, Dreger probably wasn't alone."

"Don't worry, I didn't come alone either. Come with me."

He waited as Skye grabbed the map from where Dreger had dropped it and the bag of letters that sat near her chair. After retrieving his sword, Will took Skye by the hand, and they left the room without a sound.

"Everyone was upstairs, sleeping," Skye whispered as they started towards the staircase.

Will nodded, glad that John and the others had gone up there. When they reached the top, they didn't need to go any farther. Rebecca and the girls appeared escorted by John and his men.

"John!" Skye said with gladness when she saw him.

John was truly stunned, and Skye knew Will must have told him she was dead. But there was no time to tend to his shock. They had to hurry. "We took care of Hendricks' men," he said. "Is this everyone?"

"Yes," Skye told him glancing over Rebecca and each of her daughters.

"All right, we need to get outta here. We've left a few of em' behind," John said with a toss of his head, "but

Hendricks will probably send more men before long. We'll take you all somewhere safe to hide."

Everyone hurried back downstairs, the girls stealing peeks at Will as they hurried along. At the door, Rebecca paused and turned to John.

"I have to warn our servants," she said.

"Where are they?"

"In the servants quarters, outside."

John took them all outside, and Rebecca led the way to one of the large outbuildings. She went quickly up to the door and knocked. A few moments later, Samuel opened the door.

"What's wrong, Mrs. James?" he asked worriedly. He was quickly joined by the others inside.

"You must all get away from here. Quickly," Rebecca urged.

"What happened?" Samuel asked.

"Pirates broke into the house and more will come soon. Go to my sister's house. Tell them what happened, but make sure to tell them that we are safe."

Samuel nodded. "I will."

"Good, now hurry. Don't take time for anything, just go!"

Rebecca turned away from the door, and John led them all into the forest. It was hard to make their way in the darkness, but finally they reached the beach and climbed into the boats. The men rowed them quickly towards the ship, and it was not long before everyone was aboard. John immediately gave orders to set sail, afraid that Hendricks might spot them. In record time, the *Finder* was heading out to open sea, and everyone relaxed as they left the *Nightshade* far behind.

As soon as all the commotion died down, Will turned to Skye. Her hand was still in his, having barely let go since they'd left the house, and now they hugged tightly once more.

"I've prayed for this every day since you were taken," Skye murmured.

"Thank God for answering our prayers," Will breathed thankfully. "I missed you so much, and then, when I thought you were gone . . . I honestly don't know how I could ever tell Him just how thankful I am."

When they finally parted, which was almost painful to do after all they had been through, Skye smiled up at Will.

"Are you ready to finally meet your family?"

A smile spread across Will's face too. "Yes, I am."

They turned and Will finally took in the full sight of Rebecca and the girls standing a few feet away, at long last free to focus his attention solely on the family he'd waited so long to meet. They all smiled as Skye led Will towards them, eager to welcome him into their family. Despite how wonderful this moment was, Skye knew it also had to be a little awkward for Will to finally meet the family he'd never known, and she gladly stepped up to introduce them.

"Will, this is Rebecca, your father's wife, and their daughters, Lydie, Molly, Emma, and Ashley."

Rebecca was the first to speak with a gentle and loving smile that reassured Will. "Will, it's so good to finally meet you. I can't wait for . . ." her voice faltered as she looked at this wonderful young man who looked so much like her husband. As her throat cleared, and her smile shone through teary eyes, she finished, "I can't wait for Edward to meet you."

"I wait for that as well, Rebecca. Thank you for such a warm welcome to your family."

"*Your* family," she stressed.

The girls each said their greetings too. As expected there was some shyness between all of them at first, but Emma warmed up to Will very quickly.

"I've always wanted a brother," she told him with a grin. "When Papa told me about you, I hoped you'd come home someday. Papa sure hoped you would too."

Will smiled, enchanted by her. "I've always dreamed of having a family. God has given us all what we've longed for."

"Yes, He has," Emma replied happily.

A moment later, John joined them, though a little hesitantly.

"Excuse me, if I'm interruptin'," he began.

They told him that of course he wasn't, and he looked to Rebecca. "Mrs. James, whenever you and yer daughters would like to rest, yer welcome to my cabin. I've had my men make room for beds, and I had a trunk of clothes brought up. There should be everything you need inside."

Rebecca smiled at him. "Thank you very much, Mr. . . . ."

"Morgan, ma'am."

Emma gasped. "Are you Captain John Morgan!"

John looked down at her. "Yes, I am."

"Skye told us all about you," Emma said excitedly.

John glanced at Skye and looked back at Emma with a smile. "Did she?"

"Oh yes, all about how you helped rescue Skye and Will from pirates. She told me that you stopped the pirate captain yourself."

"Well, God had more to do with it than I did, and Skye and Will were the real heroes, not me."

"We still couldn't have done everything without your help," Skye reminded him.

John shrugged modestly and after that the conversations resumed between Will and his family for quite some time. Finally, Rebecca put her hand on Emma's shoulder as she asked a question that would have started another long discussion. "Emma, it's the middle of the night, and I think

338

that any more questions should be saved for tomorrow. We should all get some rest."

"Do we have to?" Emma asked in disappointment.

"Yes. It is very late and we need to get some sleep."

Emma sighed. "All right."

"I will show you the cabin," Skye offered.

"Thank you," Rebecca said.

Skye turned briefly to Will to tell him she'd be back and then led the way across the deck to John's cabin. Will watched them go.

"Looks like you have a very nice family, Will," John said coming up behind him.

Will smiled and nodded. "I still can't believe it, even now having seen them. It's amazing and wonderful to truly have a family."

John agreed. "I wouldn't have admitted feelin' this way a coupla years ago, but I wish I had a family."

Will looked at him wonderingly. "Have you ever had a family, John?"

John shook his head slowly. "Not really. I can barely remember my mother 'cause she died when I was real small and my father, well, not really anything I'd care to remember. Always drunk, stealin', and had a hand in a few murders I suspect. Just disappeared one day when I was about ten. Never heard from him again. About the only thing I remember real clearly is him braggin' about how he was the son of the famous pirate, Henry Morgan. I've never known whether it's true or not. For all I know he coulda made up the story and the name Morgan, but it's the only name I've got."

"You didn't have any siblings or other family members?"

"None that I know of." John paused and then smiled. "Oh well, I'm in God's family now. That's what matters to me most."

Inside the cabin, Skye helped Rebecca and the girls prepare some beds on the floor where the older girls would be sleeping. As she helped Skye spread a blanket, Emma asked, "Skye, is this ship the *Finder*?"

Skye nodded. "Yes, it is."

"Wow. This is where you were held prisoner?"

Skye nodded again. "This is the very cabin where I first spoke to Kelley."

"I can't wait to see the ship in the morning," Emma said. "Could you show me the cell that you were locked in?"

Lydie frowned at her. "Why do you want to see the cell? They had such horrible times down there."

Emma shrugged. "I guess I'm just sort of curious."

Skye smiled at her. "Of course I'll show you. I kind of want to see it myself after all this time. Like Lydie said, we had some horrible times down there, but it was all part of God's plan. Also, down in those cells is where Will first told me that he loved me so not all the memories are bad."

"Yes, that's right," Lydie said, remembering that part in Skye's story. She and Molly both smiled dreamily.

Rebecca looked at them with a smile as well. "I never heard that part of the story."

Lydie fixed her gaze on her little sister. "I think Emma left it out of her version."

"I didn't leave it out on purpose," Emma quickly defended herself. "I just forgot."

"But it was one of the best parts. How could you forget it?" Lydie questioned.

"She was too interested in all the action parts to appreciate the special relationship between Skye and Will," Molly suggested.

"I do too appreciate it," Emma retorted. "I think they are perfect together, and I'm happy they love each other."

Everyone smiled.

"Well, Emma, it looks like there's hope for you after all," Lydie teased.

Laughing, they started getting into the finished beds. Skye, however, got up.

"I'm going to talk to Will for a while."

Rebecca nodded with a knowing smile. "You do that."

"I wish I could talk to Will some more," Emma said.

"There will be plenty of time tomorrow," Rebecca replied. "Besides, don't you think Skye and Will need some time to talk alone?"

"Yes, Mama," Emma answered meekly.

Skye wished them all good night and quietly left the cabin. Outside, she found Will waiting for her. They smiled warmly at each other. After such a painful separation and the sorrow heinous lies had caused, being together again was like a wonderful dream.

"I have so many things I want to ask and tell you, and I'm sure it's the same for you," Skye said.

Will nodded. "Yes, it is, but I might just stand here and drink in the sight of you without a single word," he declared which made them both laugh. "But I do want you to meet someone."

"All right," Skye replied with interest.

They took each other's hand, and Will led her across the deck to where a man was standing. He turned to face them with a kind smile.

"Skye, this is Worthy," Will began. "He saved my life many times."

Skye smiled, tears springing to her eyes as they did so easily these days. "I'm very glad to meet you, Mr. Worthy, and I will never be able to thank you enough."

"It's a great pleasure to meet you, Miss McHenry. You are every bit as lovely and amazing as Will described you. I am overjoyed to be able to see you two together again."

"Thank you, Mr. Worthy. I'm so glad to know that Will has had such a good friend to help him."

"You are quite welcome, but I can assure you that Will has helped me just as much if not more than I've been able to help him. If it were not for him I may have forever turned my back on God."

Skye was very happy and smiled. "I'm very glad. God uses some of the worst times to do great things."

"He certainly does," Worthy agreed. "Now, I'm sure you have much to talk about so I will leave you both alone." He bid them goodnight and walked away.

Skye and Will sat down next to each other on two barrels near one of the masts and talked for a long time, sharing their stories. Skye was able to tell him all about his family and of Stephan's plans. Finally, Will could understand the reason for all that had happened. He could not only see Stephan and Hendricks' plans, but also God's. Many men had become saved because of what Will had gone through, and he was very thankful to be used in such a big way.

Chapter Twenty-six

Waking with a comfortable feeling of peace, Skye yawned and looked around the cabin from her bed on the floor. Looking at the girls who were sleeping beside her, she saw that Emma was not in bed. Skye sat up and smiled when she saw Emma standing on her tiptoes at the cabin door, peering through the window at the ship's decks. She could only imagine how badly Emma wanted to go out and look around. Getting up, Skye walked quietly over to her.

"Good morning, Emma," she whispered.

Emma was a little startled but turned to Skye with a grin. "Good morning, Skye."

Skye smiled. "Do you want to go out?"

"Can we?" Emma asked, her excitement raising her voice.

Skye glanced at the others, but none of them woke. She looked back at Emma.

"Yes, but why don't you get dressed first."

"Okay."

Emma hurried over to the trunk and opened it. Digging through the clothes, she found some that fit and started dressing. Meanwhile, Skye tucked her shirt back into her breeches and put on her waistcoat and boots. As she was finishing, she heard Ashley's sweet voice. The little girl was sitting up next to Rebecca who was still asleep in John's bed.

343

Very quietly, Skye walked over to them and picked Ashley up. She wanted to let Rebecca and Lydie and Molly sleep. Picking up a blanket in case it was cool out, Skye wrapped it around Ashley, and the three of them left the cabin. She smiled watching Emma take everything in.

"She's so big," Emma breathed, her eyes large with amazement. "Most of Papa's ships are a lot smaller than this."

"Yes, she is a big ship," Skye agreed, though a bit preoccupied as memories clouded her mind. She saw the mast where she'd been tied up for almost three days without food or water, remembering how she'd battled the discomfort of those long hours. Her eyes touched briefly on the exact spot where Kelley's whip had connected with her body leaving a scar she would carry with her always, and less painful but no less memorable, the place where she and Kate had worked side by side scraping the salt off the main deck under Kelley's close scrutiny. Each place caused her memories to come vividly alive.

Skye heard someone say, "Good mornin'." She and Emma looked up to see John on the quarterdeck.

Skye smiled brightly. "Good morning, John."

To Emma's delight, they started for the stairs leading up to the quarterdeck.

"Did you all sleep well?" John asked when they neared the wheel.

"Yes, very well," Skye said contentedly.

"Everyone else still asleep?"

Skye nodded. "What about Will? Is he still sleeping?"

"I haven't seen 'im yet, so he must be. Doesn't surprise me after everything he's been through."

Skye shook her head. "I still feel horrible that you all thought I was dead."

"At least it was not true," John said pragmatically.

There was a brief pause before Emma asked, "Captain Morgan, where are you taking us?"

"To an island where you will be safe."

"And, when we get there, you will get to meet Kate," Skye added. "She sailed on to the island while John brought Will home."

Emma smiled. "Really?"

Skye nodded. In another moment, Emma's expression clouded, and she asked, "What about Papa and Chris, and your papa? Now there's no one to warn them."

John was the one who answered. "As soon as you are all safe, I intend to find 'em and help 'em put a stop to all this." Noticing that she still looked worried, he changed the subject. "I don't think you ever did tell me yer name."

Emma's cheery smile quickly returned. "No, I didn't. It's Emma."

"Emma," John repeated with a nod. "Now that's a real pretty name. Perfect for a real pretty young lady like you."

Emma flushed with pleasure. "Thank you."

John smiled looking at Ashley then. "And what is yer name, little one?"

Ashley smiled shyly and hid her face against Skye.

"That's Ashley," Emma said. "She's always shy around strangers, but she'll get used to you."

John nodded and Emma asked him a question. "Captain Morgan, is it hard to sail a ship?"

"Sometimes," John answered. "Like during bad weather, but when you know yer ship and what she can take it's easier."

"I want to sail my own ship someday," Emma said. "Then I can be like Skye and won't have to wear dresses."

John and Skye smiled at the statement.

"So, you'll be Captain Emma James?" John said trying the title on for size.

"Yup," Emma answered proudly. "And I'll have the fastest ship in America."

"Sounds like you've got it all planned out."

"Yes, and Papa said he'd have a ship built just for me." Emma made a face. "But I have to wait until I'm twenty. Ten whole years. I wish I could grow up faster."

"You don't want to grow up too fast," John cautioned.

Emma thought about it for a moment. "I guess you're right."

John looked past them with a smile. "Good mornin', Will."

Skye and Emma turned. Will had just reached the quarterdeck. He smiled and said good morning to them, his eyes resting on the wonderful woman he thought he'd never see again.

"Have you three been up long?" he asked her.

"No, only a few minutes. I should check soon to see if Rebecca and the girls are awake so that Ashley can get dressed."

Noticing how lovely she looked holding his new little sister, Will said, "I thought I heard them talking as I passed the cabin."

"Well, I suppose I should take Ashley to them now then." She looked at Emma. "Are you going to stay here?"

"I would," Emma replied, "but I want to ask Mama if I can wear clothes like you while I'm on the ship."

Already she had started for the stairs.

"Oh dear," Skye said, watching her go. "It looks like I've started something."

"I wouldn't blame yourself," John said. "She strikes me as one who's already asked this question before."

Skye smiled. "More than likely."

She turned and hurried after Emma. As soon as she was gone, John turned to Will with a very familiar glint in his eyes.

"Since Skye's death turned out to be a vicious lie, I'm free to say that I would have expected her to be wearin' a ring by now. Engagement or even wedding."

"Well, if this whole attack on us had happened even one week later, she probably would have been," Will said, with a trace of frustration.

"So you do intend to marry her?"

"Oh, yes. I've been planning to propose for months. I'm sure I would have by now if none of this would have happened. I've even bought us a house."

"Really?" John's interest was piqued. "Does she know about it?"

"Not yet. I'm saving it as a surprise until after I ask her. I kind of wanted to make sure she says yes first."

John grinned. "I don't think you have to worry about that."

"I hope not," Will said with a smile. "Speaking of getting married, has anything changed for you, John? You did say that you wished you had a family."

"Unfortunately, no. I've never worked up enough courage to talk to Kate."

"So, you really do love her."

"I'd be a fool to deny it."

"Does she have any idea that you feel this way?"

John shrugged. "I doubt it. And she probably wouldn't share the same feelings anyway."

"I wouldn't say that," Will encouraged him. "Until that day you heard me tell Skye that I loved her, we had never mentioned it before, yet we both felt the same."

"I think you two are a little different."

"Not really," Will said, noticing John's rather glum response.

"Well, maybe sometime I will talk to her," John decided, shrugging again.

"Don't forget what you told me. You never know when a time might come you realize you've lost your chance."

"Oh, I haven't forgotten."

"Thanks Mama!" Emma exclaimed excitedly.

"But remember, Emma, I said only while we're on the ship," Rebecca stressed.

"Yes Mama," Emma replied dutifully though she had already turned anxious eyes to Skye. "Can we go ask Captain Morgan for the clothes now?"

Skye nodded. "All right, come on."

Emma nearly skipped out of the cabin after Skye. Climbing the first few steps to the quarterdeck, Skye looked at John.

"Do you have a pair of boy's clothes?" she asked. "Rebecca gave Emma permission to wear them while she's on the ship, and she wants to enjoy every minute of it that she possibly can."

John smiled. "You see Levi over there?" He pointed to a man standing not too far away. "Ask 'im to show you where we keep the extra clothes."

"All right," Skye said with a nod.

She and Emma walked over to the man John had pointed to.

"Levi?"

"Yes, Miss McHenry?" He straightened up from his work with a smile.

"Captain Morgan said to ask you were the extra clothes are kept."

"Come right with me," Levi instructed.

He took them down into the ship where a few trunks were sitting.

"Here they are," he said. "Do you need anything else?"

"No, thank you," she said smiling.

Kneeling down beside one of the trunks, Skye lifted the lid, and Emma helped her go through it. In a few minutes, they had found a pair of breeches and a shirt that would fit Emma. They closed the trunks and wasted no time going back up to John's cabin where Skye helped Emma to dress. Once she had on the new clothes, she stood in front of the mirror with a beaming grin.

"If we pulled my hair back I might really look like a boy," she said, perfectly pleased with herself.

"Well, you may be dressed like a boy, but don't forget that you are a girl and to act like one," Rebecca told her.

"I won't," Emma promised.

When they all turned to leave the cabin, Skye spoke to Rebecca on the way out.

"I hope I didn't cause trouble with Emma, wanting to dress like me."

"Oh no, not at all. This is not the first time she has asked. I don't mind really if she does dress this way when she has reason, like you have," Rebecca pointed out. "She just has to remember that she can't always do it."

Skye smiled with understanding and a bit of relief that she had not influenced Emma.

Will met them outside, and after they had all traded morning greetings, he told them that John had said that breakfast would be ready soon.

"Good, I'm hungry," Emma piped up.

A moment later, Ashley suddenly said, "Will," though her l's sounded more like w's.

Everyone was completely charmed by the way Ashley smiled at Will.

"Yes, Ashley, that's your brother, Will," Rebecca said.

Ashley reached out for him, and with a smile, Will took her in his arms. She continued to look at him wonderingly.

"I've never seen her take to someone so quickly," Rebecca remarked.

"I think she knows he's part of our family," Lydie said.

"Little children are very smart," Skye observed. "A lot smarter than some people realize."

"Yes, they are," Rebecca agreed.

Everyone smiled and laughed when Ashley gleefully said Will's name again and clapped her hands with a happy giggle.

"Ashley, do you love Will?" Emma asked her giggling sister.

"Yes!" Ashley exclaimed grinning.

"Why don't you give him a hug?" Rebecca urged her with a smile.

Ashley didn't hesitate to throw her small arms around Will's neck and hug him tightly. Will gently hugged her back feeling very happy and comfortable with her when some might not have.

"Ah, that is so sweet." Lydie voiced what they were all thinking.

John walked up to them grinning as he watched Will with Ashley.

"I think a sight like that would make almost any man wish for a family and some kids," he remarked. Will looked up at Skye, and she flushed becomingly.

Noticing this sweet exchange, Rebecca asked of John, "Do you have any family Captain Morgan?"

John shook his head. "Sadly I don't, but I wish I did."

"Maybe you will yet. Have you prayed for one?"

"Yes, I have, although even though I'm doin' God's work I'm still always on the run, and that's not a life I'd want for my family."

"I'm sure someday, if God plans for you to have a family, He'll provide a way for you to stop running."

John smiled. "I hope that's exactly what He has planned."

They weren't able to discuss it further as one of the men announced that breakfast was being served below. Instead of dining in his cabin, John led the way below deck and ate with Will and his family where they could continue to visit and get to know each other better.

Soon after the meal was over, Skye, with help from Will and John, fulfilled Emma's request for a tour around the ship. Worthy joined them too and was just as interested as the girls. Seeing it all firsthand brought Skye's stories alive for Rebecca and her daughters. They were the most fascinated by the cells where Skye had spent so much of her time captive on the *Finder*.

Stepping into the cell she and Kate had been locked in, Skye quietly took in every detail of it. Meanwhile, Will stepped into the one next to it, also studying the familiar surroundings. He walked slowly over to the bars that separated him from the cell Skye was in, just as he had that fateful day two years earlier when they had thought they might never see each other again.

Skye turned and noticed Will standing there. Instantly, the memories and emotions of that day came flooding back to her. She walked over to him, put her hands on the bars, and just stared up into his brown eyes, experiencing almost the same feelings she had just before they had been separated.

"I love you, Skye," Will whispered very quietly, placing his hands tenderly over hers on the bars.

She smiled softly, her eyes glistening with tears. Unlike last time, there was no cruel interruption. "And I love you, Will."

They gazed at each other for a moment more, and then Skye remembered they were not alone. She looked out of the cell and saw everyone watching them. Blushing a little, Skye said, "This is exactly where Will first told me he loved me."

Everyone smiled at that and quite happily they continued on their tour full of chatter and questions.

Later that afternoon, Skye smiled as she watched Will and his sisters a little farther down the deck. Ashley was in Will's arms again, and the older girls were standing around him. Skye could hear their laughter mingling with their joyful voices. It was obvious how much they already adored him. Skye couldn't put into words how happy she was to see Will with his family.

"Thank You, God, for giving this to him," she prayed quietly.

Skye's smile deepened when she heard Ashley's giggle mingle with Will's laugh. Before that day, Skye hadn't ever really seen him interact with such a young child. He did so well, and it looked so right. Skye found herself imagining him with his own children and family. She blushed a little to realize she'd been imagining herself as the mother of that family, and what a wonderful image it was.

"He's very good with children, isn't 'e?"

Turning, Skye saw John standing just behind her.

"You've read my thoughts perfectly," she told him with a smile.

"Were there any other thoughts besides that?" John asked in his usual roguish way.

"What ever makes you say that?" Skye questioned, trying hard to sound as if she didn't know what he meant, but her smile couldn't be hidden.

"Well, there was just a certain look on your face that was kinda hard to miss," John teased. "Kinda like you might have been . . . imaginin' yer future life perhaps?"

Skye laughed lightly. "You know, John, you sure pick up on a lot more than some might give you credit for."

John grinned. "So does that mean you admit it then?"

Skye blushed again. "I guess it does."

"Well, there's certainly nothin' wrong with that," he said kindly.

Skye smiled, her cheeks still a little flushed.

"Now," John continued after a moment. "If yer not busy I've been wantin' to show you somethin'. Why don't you go on over by Will 'cause I want to show them too, and I'll be right back with it."

"All right."

Skye headed over to Will while John disappeared into his cabin.

"John has something to show us," Skye said once she had reached Will and the girls.

"Do you know what it is?" Emma asked curiously.

"No, I don't. But he went to his cabin to get it."

A short minute later, John came towards them with a folded black cloth.

"This here," he said proudly, "is the new flag that me an' Kate use. We didn't care much for the skull anymore."

John took hold of two of the corners and shook the flag out for them to see. It caused smiles all around. In the middle of the black flag was a pure white cross and below it was the Bible reference, Deuteronomy 31:6.

"That is a wonderful idea, John," Skye praised.

"You'd be surprised how well it works too," he said animatedly. "Back in the Caribbean after we started usin' it for a while, we had a lotta pirates surrender without a fight when they saw the flag. It also worked to show we were friendly when we returned goods."

"I agree with Skye," Will said. "It is a really good idea, John."

"What does the verse say?" Emma wanted to know.

"Be strong and courageous, do not be afraid or tremble at them, for the Lord your God is the one who goes with you. He will not fail you or forsake you," John recited.

"That's a good verse," Emma said.

"Yes, especially for that," Lydie added to which everyone agreed.

"Well, thank you all for showin' such high approval," John said beginning to refold the flag, "but I can't take all the credit. It was mostly Kate's idea."

"I want a flag like that on my ship," Emma told him.

John looked at her thoughtfully for a moment.

"You know," he began, "this flag is an extra that has just been layin' around. I don't really need it. Could you take it for me? I'm sure you'd put it to much better use."

Emma's face lit up with excitement and surprise. "Can I?"

John held the flag out to her. "Yes."

Emma reached for it with a wide grin. "Thank you, Captain Morgan!"

John stopped just short of handing it over. "But you have to start callin' me John."

"Okay, John," she said laughing, wrapping the flag in her arms.

"Now, why don't you put that flag someplace safe and then come up to the wheel. I could use a little help steerin'."

Emma could barely contain her excitement as she ran off to put the flag away.

"She is never going to forget this," Lydie said to Molly as they shared a smile.

"You're very good with children too, John," Skye observed quietly, just between the two of them.

John shrugged. "I wouldn't know. I haven't had much experience with any."

"It seems to come naturally to you."

354

"Thank you," John said. It was charming how pleased he was with her assessment.

He turned to head up to the quarterdeck. They all knew it would take little time for Emma to find a safe place for the flag.

The remaining afternoon hours seemed to pass quickly. The sun was nearing the horizon when Will saw Skye heading to the ship's bow. It was a very welcome sight to see again. He turned his gaze from her to look at Rebecca with whom he'd been talking.

"If you'll excuse me for a little while, Rebecca, I am going to talk to Skye. Watching the sunsets is something she's always done with her father, and when he can't, I like to."

Rebecca smiled. "Go right ahead, Will. I would hate for us to keep you from spending time with her."

"Don't worry about that. I know that it brings her joy to see me spending time with all of you."

Gently, Will lifted Ashley from his lap and gave her to Rebecca. Crossing the deck, he glanced back to the stern where Emma and her sisters were standing around John. He had given them all a turn at the wheel and was once again helping Emma.

Skye's smile drew Will closer when she heard him coming.

"I hope you didn't stop talking to Rebecca and come up here just on my account," Skye said.

"I came up here because I love you," Will declared earnestly, "and we really have not had that much time to talk since last night."

Skye's eyes smiled into his and Will continued, "I now count every moment together as a blessing. I don't even want to remember what it was like thinking I'd have to live without you."

Skye was touched deeply by his words. "Oh, Will, I love you so much." She stared at him for a long moment. "I didn't mention this last night. It was only for a few minutes, but I thought you were dead too."

Will was surprised. "You did?"

"Yes. Before I got to speak to Lieutenant Graham, one of the guards told me that everyone had been hanged. I thought I was too late. It was horrible." Skye shook her head, grimacing painfully at the memory.

Will put his arm around her comfortingly, and she leaned her head against his shoulder for a moment.

"I'm so glad you're finally safe, Will," Skye said looking up into his face. "I never want to lose you again."

"Neither do I," Will replied with feeling, recalling all too well the memory of losing her.

"I pray every day that God will keep us safe and together."

"I do too."

Their eyes locked in a loving gaze, and with Will's full attention on her, Skye had something else she wanted to say.

"It's been a wonderful thing to watch you today with your family. It must be a marvelous thing to finally meet and know them."

"Yes, it is. A bit strange yet, but wonderful."

"I know what you mean. It was a little strange for me too when my father came back. The feeling must be so much greater for you though. Twenty-two years is a long time to live without even knowing you had a family and then to suddenly find yourself in their midst."

"A very long time," Will agreed. He stared out over the ocean and then said with feeling, "I can't wait to meet my father."

Skye smiled softly. "You're going to love him, Will. He's a wonderful man, just like you."

Will was captivated by her soft smile, warmed by her love and respect. "Thank you, Skye."

No more words were necessary for a long time as they simply enjoyed each other's company. The painted sky the two of them so greatly enjoyed had not yet dimmed when land suddenly appeared in the distance. They heard John call out that they'd reached the island, and they knew it would not be long before they could enjoy the feeling of complete safety again.

Chapter Twenty-seven

Will stood with Skye and his family at the ship's bow while John brought the *Finder* into the island's small but beautiful harbor. The water shimmered, reflecting dark, red-orange from the sky and casting the rich hue onto the few buildings standing along the beach. Behind the buildings was a dark green forest with a clear path disappearing into the trees. Two docks stretched out perpendicular to the island, and Skye smiled when she saw the *Half Moon* moored next to one of them.

The beach quickly came alive with men, all of African descent, who hurried to help moor the *Finder*. Once the ship was secure, John's men lowered the gangplank and John led the way with everyone following behind. Near the end of the dock he stopped, met by a big, friendly man who grinned at John and gave him a bone-crushing hug.

"It's great to have you back, John," he said in a rich, deep voice.

John smiled. "It's always great to be here, Silas. I thought I'd be comin' back empty handed this time, but after a near disastrous event, I've brought along a few friends to put in your safe keepin'."

John turned and introduced everyone to his friend. When he introduced Skye, the man looked surprised.

"I thought . . ."

John quickly explained before he could finish. "I know. Hendricks lied, and here she is, thank God." Finally, he turned back to the others and said, "Everyone, I would like you to meet Silas Jeswick. He more or less owns this island and takes care of everyone here."

"It's a pleasure to meet all of you," Silas told them to which he was kindly thanked for his hospitality.

After this introduction, John asked, "Silas, where's Kate?"

"I sent one of the boys back to the village to let everyone know you were here so she's probably on her way."

John quickly turned to Skye and said, "Wait for me on the beach. I'll be right back." There was a grin creeping across his face, and his eyes sparkled so she knew he was up to something. John hurried off the dock, up the path, and into the forest.

Everyone waited on the beach for him to return, and it wasn't long before John emerged leading Kate along behind him because her eyes were closed. Skye was filled with joy to see her friend again and hurried to meet them. John brought Kate to a stop in front of her.

"John, what is goin' on?" Kate asked quizzically having been told she was about to receive the best surprise she could possibly imagine. "Can I open my eyes yet?"

John grinned. "All right, open 'em."

Kate's eyes opened and astonishment wiped her face of all expression.

"Skye!" she exclaimed in utter disbelief. And then she began to cry.

They came together and hugged tightly.

"I thought you were dead!" Kate said tearfully when she stepped back to take a good look at Skye.

"Hendricks lied in order to hurt Will. That's all," Skye told her, simply, gently.

Kate was overjoyed, but Skye noticed some concern.

"By the look of yer neck, I'd say he tried to kill you," Kate said, observing the bruises and redness around Skye's throat.

"Yes, one of his men tried to strangle me. Thankfully, Will got there just in time."

"When did this happen?"

"Last night, at the James estate. Hendricks' men broke in, intending to kill me because of what I know, and they planned to take Will's family prisoner. Will and John, and the crew, fortunately arrived about the same time."

"That's why you've all come," Kate realized.

John nodded. "I knew Hendricks would never find 'em here."

Kate beamed a smile at him. "I'm so glad you did."

Introductions quickly followed. Kate was very pleased to meet Will's family, and they were delighted to meet her, especially Emma. Finally, having met both John and Kate and not only seeing the *Finder* but getting to sail on her had made Skye's stories complete for Emma.

Once everyone was acquainted, John and Silas led the whole group away from the beach and up the path. Several hundred yards into the forest, they came to a village. It was small with a few houses and larger buildings, as well as a few in the process of being built. All were very simple and made of wood, and the feel of the village was very welcoming. Fire pits crackled with flames and men, women, and children gathered near them, conversing and laughing contentedly. All but a few were the former slaves that John and Kate had helped to liberate.

"Everyone, come and welcome our guests," Silas called in a loud voice.

As the people quickly came to meet them, there was yet another round of introductions. However, there were far too many people from the village for Silas to introduce them all.

Everyone was incredibly friendly and made them feel very welcome.

Silas turned back to John while the others were saying hello. "Have you all had your supper yet?"

"Yes, on the ship."

"Surely you wouldn't mind a little something more," Silas said with a grin. "We have plenty left over."

"Well now, if you're tryin' to tell me that it's some of your famous venison stew, I don't think I'd be able to resist," John grinned back.

Silas chuckled. "I wouldn't exactly call it famous, but that is exactly what I'm trying to tell you. Somehow you always show up right when I make it."

John's grin grew as Silas led them towards one of the fires. Along the way, John said to Skye and Will, "Wait 'til you try this stew. You're never gonna want to eat anythin' else ever again."

When they came to the fire, they all took seats on the logs that were used as benches. Silas, along with his wife and two daughters who were about Emma's age, dished up bowls of stew for everyone. Soft, warm rolls were also passed out. One bite of the stew proved John right. The stew and the rolls were delicious. Though neither had been hungry, both Will and Skye soon emptied their bowls and even had a little more.

By the time they had finished, the sun had gone down and the stars were twinkling above them. Emma looked sleepy and tried to hide a yawn, but it did not go unnoticed.

"Looks like some of you could use some rest," Silas said. He looked at his wife. "Shauna, you can show Mrs. James and her daughters, and Miss McHenry, where they can sleep, and I'll take care of John and his friends."

Eager to make them welcome, Shauna nodded to her husband and with a smile aimed at Rebecca and the girls, she invited, "Come with me."

The six of them followed her to a large house just across from where they'd been sitting. Kate too, followed along. Inside, the house was all open. Many beds were placed in neat rows and a few trunks and other furniture stood against the walls. Shauna explained that all of the unmarried women and girls shared the house while they waited for more to be built. Even though it was a little crowded no one ever complained because they were so grateful to be free.

"You and your daughters can share these two beds," Shauna said to Rebecca, gesturing to two beds near the end of the room.

"Thank you, Mrs. Jeswick," Rebecca said gratefully.

Shauna smiled. "You're welcome."

Before she could search for a bed for Skye, Kate said, "My bed is big enough for both of us."

"Perfect," Shauna said, "thank you, Kate." She turned again to Skye and Rebecca. "There are nightgowns and clothes for tomorrow in the trunks. Help yourselves. They are there for anyone to use."

"Once again, thank you," Rebecca said, ever mindful that she and the girls could be aboard Hendricks' ship right now.

Skye thanked her as well, and Shauna simply said she was glad to have them before leaving the house to get her own children off to bed. After goodnights, Rebecca and the girls prepared for sleep while Kate brought Skye across the room to their bed.

"Are you going to sleep now?" Skye asked Kate.

"I think I'll stay up for a while."

Skye smiled. "I was hoping you would say that. I hardly feel sleepy."

Kate quickly shared her smile. "Good. There's far too much I'd like to talk to you about for me to be able to sleep. Let's go back out to the fire and talk there."

Happily, the two of them left the house. They were pleasantly surprised to find that John and Will were still by the fire when they got there.

"It appears we're not the only ones who decided to enjoy a beautiful night like this," John commented to Will as Skye and Kate neared.

"Skye and I have too much to talk about to just go off to bed," Kate responded.

John smiled. "I wasn't expectin' you would."

Automatically, Skye took a seat next to Will. Kate dropped down next to John just as easily. Following a moment of peaceful silence, John looked around with a satisfied smile and said, "A lot like old times, isn't it? The only difference is Matthew ain't here."

"He would love to be," Skye said as they all agreed with John. She shook her head. "Poor Matthew. He must be worried sick."

"How long has it been now since you left home?" Kate asked.

"A few weeks. I'm not sure exactly. Father did send Matthew a letter soon after we reached Port Henry, but who knows if he's even gotten it yet. This is all just such a big mess."

"Yes, and I certainly don't mean to sound impatient, but I'm quite anxious to hear more of your side of it," Kate said.

Skye understood and recounted everything once more for Kate. Afterwards, Kate had some questions and then they all spoke of life before the whole ordeal. For a long time, they talked and laughed, recalling old memories. During that period of time, all worries were temporarily forgotten.

As it got later, the air grew cooler and a shiver ran through Skye's body. She rubbed her arms to warm them up. Noticing this right away, Will took off his coat and draped it around Skye's shoulders. They shared a smile.

Seeing this, John realized Kate must be getting chilly too and removed his own coat to drape it around Kate's shoulders. She looked at him with a bit of surprise and smiled warmly. "Thank you, John."

"You're welcome," he murmured with a bashful smile.

Their talk continued for another half hour as the village slept peacefully. The fire started burning low and with a contented sigh, John voiced everyone's thoughts.

"I think it's about time we got to bed. I intend to get an early start in the mornin'."

Skye slipped off Will's coat, as they each rose from their seats, and handed it back to him.

"Good night, Will," she said, smiling sweetly.

"Good night, Skye."

Before they parted, he placed a soft kiss on her cheek. Skye smiled tenderly and held his gaze for a moment before following Kate away from the fire. Will and John lingered behind for a few moments, watching them go, before heading to the house where the men slept. Along the way, John looked at Will resolutely.

"I've made up my mind, Will. I'm gonna talk to her," he said with determination. "Watchin' you and Skye together makes me wonder too much about me and Kate."

Will smiled, understanding John perfectly.

"You will always wish you had if you don't." Will spoke from past experience. "No matter what her response is, at least you will know her feelings, and she will know yours."

"Yer right, but I gotta admit the thought still scares me to death."

The look on his face made Will chuckle. "Don't worry. If you really love her, it will be fine."

John looked at him with all seriousness. "I do. I want a family, Will, and Kate is the only woman I've ever loved."

With a smile, Will put his hand on John's shoulder. "You've come a long way since the first conversation we had about this."

"Yes, but it's certainly taken long enough to get here," John replied dryly. "It's time I finally came out with it."

"I'll pray for you," Will told him.

John looked relieved. "Thanks. I'll probably need a bit of help."

With those final words, they quietly entered the house where the men were sleeping soundly. Will walked soundlessly to his bed and began taking off his boots and waistcoat. He knelt beside the bed then and prayed silently, thanking God for His love and care and for how He had used him so greatly in spite of the hardships. After praying for God's continued protection over himself and all those close to him, he prayed for God to help John find his father and Skye's. Finally, Will prayed that He would help John when he decided to speak to Kate.

Once Will had finished, he got into bed. The soft mattress felt wonderful after sleeping in a hammock for so long. Closing his eyes, Will quickly drifted off into a peaceful sleep.

* * *

"So, the Carolinas is probably where I'll find 'em?" John asked Rebecca.

"Yes, that is where they said they were going, and if they have not returned home yet, I would expect them to be there."

"All right then," John said with a decisive nod. "God willing, I'll find them in a couple of days." He turned his eyes to Will and Skye. "And if I don't, I'll come back here and get you just like I promised."

"Thank you, John," Will spoke for both himself and Skye.

"Best save yer thanks until after I find 'em," John cautioned.

From the ship, they heard Levi call out that they were ready to set sail.

"Well, I'll see you two in a few days, hopefully sooner," John told them. He said goodbye to Rebecca and the girls and finally worked his way down to Kate.

"Remember," Kate reminded him seriously, "if you're not back in a week and a half, I'm comin' to look for you."

John smiled handsomely, a smile which grew slowly into a broad grin. "The tone of yer voice tells me that if I am gone any longer, I'd better have a good reason."

Kate raised her brows in a no-nonsense look. "A very good one."

After a brief and tentative pause, John told her, "Listen, when I get back, remind me that I've gotta talk to you about somethin', and don't let me say it's nothin' when the time comes."

Kate looked confused but didn't question him. "All right, I'll remind you."

John smiled again, taking the memory of her sweet face with him. "Good."

He turned away and walked down the dock to his waiting ship.

"I wonder what that was about," Kate said as she watched him disappear on board.

She glanced at Skye who shrugged with no knowledge of John's feelings. Though Will knew exactly what John meant, he said not a word and kept his eyes on the ship as it left the bay.

Once the *Finder* had almost disappeared from sight, everyone followed Silas back to the village. Along the way, he beckoned Will closer.

"John told me that you are a blacksmith."

Will was quick to acknowledge that truth. "Yes, I am."

"Don't hesitate to say no, but I was wondering if sometime before you leave you might want to do a few things for us. We've got a new shed and forge, but no one who can use it yet. Anything you could do would be very greatly appreciated."

Will smiled with pleasure. "I'd be glad to do what I can."

"Thank you." Silas was very pleased. "Whenever you feel like starting, I'll show you the shed and what needs to be done."

"I can start now," Will offered.

"You're sure?"

"Yes."

Will paused to let Skye know where he was going and followed Silas to the small, but neatly organized blacksmith shed. Silas explained most of what needed to be done and helped Will fire up the forge.

"Now, I don't want you to work too hard or too long otherwise I'll feel like we're taking advantage of you," Silas said just before he left. "Take breaks and spend time with your family."

Will nodded. "I will, don't worry."

After Silas had left the shed, Will began heating the metal he would be using. He greatly enjoyed doing some work again after so long a time. It made life seem a little more normal. An hour was very quick to pass. Will hardly realized it until Worthy walked into the shed.

"Now I get to witness your work," he said with a smile. "Unless you prefer not to have company."

"No, please stay. Actually, I'm not used to working alone," Will told him. "Usually Matthew is working nearby."

Worthy grabbed a stool from the corner and set it close to Will so he could watch him. A moment later, Will looked up with a question.

"Have you thought yet about what you're going to do now that you won't sail on the *Seabird*?"

"Yes, I have given it some thought, but I'm not sure yet. I'm finished with being a pirate, but like I've told you, the sea is all I know. Honestly, I've considered turning myself in," Worthy admitted.

Pausing, Will looked at him again. "If that is what you believe you should do, I don't want to try to stop you, but have you thought about sailing with John or Kate?"

"It would be an honor to sail with them, but I expected that they had all the men they needed."

"I'm sure one of them would let you join the crew," Will spoke confidently. "Just ask them."

"All right, I will. I would love to be a part of what they're doing here."

Will smiled. "Then I'm sure they would be very glad of your help."

"I hope so. I just want to be useful."

Worthy kept Will company for another hour and then went to help work on one of the new houses that was being built. It was getting close to noon when Will had another visitor. This time it was Emma.

"Hi, Will," she greeted him happily.

"Hello, Emma," Will said, pausing to give her a smile.

Emma tilted her head a little to the side as she studied what he was doing.

"Do you mind if I watch you?" she asked after a moment.

"No, I don't mind at all."

Emma smiled and crawled up onto the stool that Worthy had left.

"Where did you learn how to do that?" she wanted to know.

"Skye's uncle taught me. I work for him."

"Do you like it?"

"Yes, very much."

They were silent for a couple of minutes until Will asked, "What were you doing?"

"I was playing with Tasha and Susanna Jeswick, but then Mrs. Jeswick needed them to help her. They're really fun. I'll be sad when we have to leave, and I won't get to see them anymore."

"Maybe if we talk to John we can find a way for you to send them letters," Will suggested.

Emma smiled. "Think we could?"

Will nodded. "I think so."

After another bit of time, Will's thoughts turned to something he had been thinking about earlier.

"Emma, do you know what day it is?" he asked.

Emma shook her head. "No, but I think it's May now."

"Could you do something for me?"

Emma perked up at the prospect of helping him. "Sure."

"Can you find Kate for me without Skye knowing? I want her to help me with a surprise for Skye."

Emma grinned. "I can do that."

She hopped off the stool and dashed out of the shed. Will continued working anxiously while he waited. Finally, Emma returned with Kate.

"What did you want help with, Will?" Kate asked.

"Well, first I need to know what day it is."

"It's May 3rd."

Will was visibly relieved. "Good."

"Why?"

"Tomorrow is Skye's birthday, and all morning I've been wondering if I missed it. I would like it if we could do something special for her."

Kate was instantly excited about this. "Definitely. I will talk to Silas. He'll be more than happy to help. Everyone else will too."

"Can I help?" Emma asked eagerly.

Will smiled. "Yes, and let's make it a surprise."

Kate and Emma nodded.

"This is going to be so fun!" Emma said excitedly. "Can I tell Lydie and Molly?"

"Just as long as Skye doesn't find out."

"I'll make sure she doesn't," Emma assured him.

"Speakin' of Skye, she's comin'," Kate warned swiftly.

A moment later, Skye stepped into the shed.

"There you are," she said to Emma. "Lydie and Molly were looking for you."

"Tasha and Susanna couldn't play anymore so I came to watch Will," Emma explained. "I'll go see what they want."

Emma ran quickly out of the shed to find her older sisters and tell them the news about Skye's surprise party. Kate too prepared to leave and talk to Silas. On the way out she said, "You're doing a great job, Will. Silas is very happy that you can do this for everyone."

"You're all very welcome, Kate, thank you. I'm glad I can help."

Kate disappeared out the door leaving them alone. Skye looked over Will's work and smiled.

"Have you gotten a lot done?" she asked.

Will shrugged. "As much as I could."

"Are you almost done?"

"No. There's quite a bit to do yet."

"Well, Silas told me to have you stop and come to dinner," she said relaying the message. "He doesn't want you to work too hard."

"I don't think he realizes how much I enjoy working," Will said, "but I am hungry and dinner sounds good."

He took off the heavy apron he was wearing and followed Skye out of the hot shed into the refreshing breeze which was cooling the island.

That afternoon, Will did not return to the shed. Silas and Kate encouraged him to spend time down at the beach with Skye and the girls which gave the rest of them the perfect opportunity to prepare for Skye's birthday. Though he regretted not getting more done for Silas, Will was eager to spend the beautiful afternoon with Skye and his sisters.

They made their way slowly along the beach for hours collecting driftwood that Emma and Ashley used to make castles later when they decided to sit and talk for a while. They shared childhood stories, and Emma succeeded in making them laugh many times, which delighted her. By the time evening was upon them, they were all more wet than dry as a result of a brief water fight which had ensued earlier. Happily they began their walk back to the village, with Emma leading the way. Ashley, who had fallen asleep some time ago, slept peacefully in Skye's arms, and Will walked beside them carrying some driftwood and rocks Emma had wanted to keep.

Halfway through the village, they saw Rebecca coming towards them. Emma raced over to tell her all about their afternoon, but Rebecca was the first to speak.

"How did you get all wet?" she asked her daughter.

Emma giggled. "We had a water fight."

"Oh really." There was a smile on Rebecca's face. "Who started that?"

"Well . . ."

"She did," Lydie spoke up before Emma could finish. "First she started splashing me and Molly, then she splashed Skye and Ashley—"

371

"Yeah, and Will splashed me when I wasn't looking," Emma said. She glanced at Will with narrowed eyes, but couldn't keep a straight face and giggled again.

"Did he?" Rebecca looked at Will, eyes sparkling with love for her new stepson.

Will shrugged and smiled. "Skye and Ashley needed some defense."

"That's true," Emma admitted. "But I did get you back, didn't I, Will?"

"Oh yes," Will said expressively.

Rebecca chuckled. "It sounds like you all had a very good afternoon."

"We sure did," Emma sighed happily.

By this time, Ashley was just starting to stir. Rebecca smiled at her little girl and took her from Skye.

"I should get her changed into some dry clothes. Supper will be ready shortly," Rebecca said. "You girls should change too."

"I think that's what I am going to do," Will said. He turned to Emma and gave her back her driftwood.

"Thank you for carrying it for me, Will."

Will gave her a smile. "You're welcome."

They parted then and the girls hurried off. Will, however, did not head directly for the men's house. He wanted to find Kate first and see how Skye's birthday preparations were coming.

"Should I go see if she is awake yet?" Emma asked hopefully.

Will looked down at her and smiled to himself. Obviously, his little sister was trying to imitate him. She was leaning back against the outside of the house with her arms crossed exactly like he was.

372

"No, I think she'll be up soon."

He heard her sigh. It had been ten minutes since they'd first come to wait for Skye to wake up. Everyone had gotten up early so they could be in the meeting hall when Will brought Skye there for her surprise breakfast. Will knew what an early riser Skye was, and he didn't expect they'd have to wait very much longer. However, Emma could barely contain her excitement as it was.

When they finally heard the door opening, Emma nearly jumped for joy. Skye walked out and looked around, clearly confused that there was no one in sight.

"Good morning," Will said cheerfully.

"Good morning," Skye replied. "Where is everyone?"

"The meeting hall," Will answered simply.

"Why?"

"It's a surprise."

"A surprise?" Skye repeated, raising her eyebrows. She had no idea what was going on.

"Yup," Emma replied with a grin.

Smiling, Will extended his arm to her. Though still thoroughly confused, Skye took his arm, and Emma led the way to the meeting hall. When they reached the door, Will told Skye to close her eyes before he led her inside. Once they were through the door, he stopped.

"All right, you can open them," he instructed.

The instant Skye opened her eyes, everyone cheered, "Happy birthday!"

Skye was stunned. She turned to Will, speechless.

"Happy birthday, Skye," Will said, delighted by her reaction.

Kate stepped forward to wish her a happy birthday as well and gave Skye a hug.

"How did you all do this?" Skye asked finally. "*I* didn't even realize it was my birthday."

"Will told me yesterday, and we all worked together to make today special for you," Kate answered, happy that they had been able to.

Skye scanned the room, her eyes sparkling with happiness. "Thank you all so much. This is a wonderful surprise."

"We are all happy to make your birthday special," Silas told her. "It is a wonderful thing to celebrate the day the Lord brought you into this world."

Skye smiled and was led to a seat at one side of many long tables set for everyone. Will and Kate sat down on either side of her. A wonderful breakfast was served, and Silas prayed right before they ate. Everyone happily ate their fill, and when they had finished, Shauna brought out the cake that she had made the day before.

For the rest of the morning, Skye was kept happily entertained by all the children who had many ideas for fun games to play and other activities to do in celebration. She gladly joined in with all of them and found herself having more fun than she'd had in a long time. It was greatly rewarding to Will to watch her enjoy herself and hear her laughter.

Later that afternoon, Skye finally excused herself from a game that Emma and the Jeswick girls were teaching her and walked over to Will who wasn't far away.

With a sweet and happy smile she asked, "Do you want to go for a quick walk down to the beach?"

Will nodded eagerly. "I'd love to."

As they started walking towards the beach, Skye shared what was on her mind.

"I wanted to take time to really thank you. With everything that has happened, I never thought my birthday would turn out like this, and it wouldn't have if it wasn't for you. I am really enjoying this day."

"I'm glad. I only wish I had a gift for you," Will said with regret.

"I need no gifts, Will. Just being able to celebrate with you, your family, Kate, and everyone else is gift enough."

Will understood that perfectly but finally made up his mind on something he'd been giving quite a bit of thought. "Actually, Skye, I do have a gift for you, but it's back in Kingston. I bought it for you just before we left."

"You did?"

Will nodded, his eyes twinkling down into hers. "Yes, and I can assure you that you will love it."

"I can't wait to find out what it is."

Will smiled to himself, enjoying the thought of what she would think when she knew. "It's been difficult not to tell you about it. I'm a little surprised I've been able to keep it a secret for so long."

Skye couldn't quite help wondering what it was, and her smile grew, enchanting him. "Now you've got me really curious, but I won't ask any questions and you can keep it a surprise."

Presently, the two of them came to the beach and paused at the water's edge. Skye rested her eyes on the horizon and spoke her thoughts aloud. "I wonder if John has found them yet."

The same thought had also jumped to the front of Will's mind.

"He may have," Will said after a moment. "I'm sure he's reached the Carolinas by now."

"I hope he has so that they know we're safe," Skye said, praying it was so.

Will agreed with prayers of his own.

Nightfall arrived after a very pleasant afternoon, and many people from the village gathered on the beach where a large fire was built. The evening was warm and beautiful with stars shining brightly overhead. It was just the kind of night that Skye enjoyed immensely.

Blankets and benches were put around the fire and everyone sat as Silas started telling stories at the insistence of his daughters and many of the other children. Skye and Will found that Silas was an excellent storyteller. Some were true stories and some were made up. The best were the Bible stories he was able to make come alive in everyone's imagination.

The hour grew late quicker than they would have liked and most families with young children returned to the village for the night. Soon, only about half of the people remained. Though Rebecca took Ashley back, Lydie, Molly, and Emma stayed, along with Kate, Worthy, and the village's young people.

Watching Skye as she spoke to Kate, Will thought it the perfect time for something special he had planned. When Skye was not looking, Will nodded to Silas who smiled and nodded back. Silas reached into his coat for something, and Will turned back to Skye.

"I may not have a gift for you, but I do have a promise to keep," he said her cryptically.

For a moment, Skye couldn't remember what he meant, but then soft music came from the wooden flute that Silas was playing, and she remembered what she had told her grandfather after their dance lessons. Will stood with a smile and extended his hand towards her.

"Would you like to dance? On a beach, under the stars, with no worries?" he added.

A radiant grin spread across Skye's face. "I would love nothing more."

She put her hand in his and stood up. Will led her a couple of feet from the fire. Slowly, they started dancing to the beautiful melody that Silas was playing. Very soon they were joined by other couples.

Silas played for a long time, and it was a night that both Skye and Will wished would last forever. Sometime past midnight, they finally let the fire burn out and walked in a sleepy but happy group, quietly back to the village. Escorting Skye and his sisters back to the women's house, Will paused at the porch while Skye had a few last words for him before parting for the night.

"I don't know how to thank you, Will. This has been the most wonderful day."

Smiling, Will squeezed her hand gently. "I'm glad. I hope you enjoyed tonight as much as you dreamed you would . . . and as much as I did."

Skye nodded, the moonlight illuminating her smile. "Yes, I did."

"We will do it again."

Skye's smile grew wider. "I look forward to it."

Finally, Will bid her a sweet goodnight which she returned as he backed away from the porch and turned towards the men's house.

Chapter Twenty-eight

The next afternoon was a quiet one after how late the previous night had been and most everyone could be seen sitting randomly around the village. Many of the women sat in groups sewing and mending clothes while the children played quiet games under the shade of the trees. Will was busy at work in the blacksmith shed trying to get as much as he could done for Silas. However, the rhythmic beating of his hammer ceased suddenly when Skye came running into the shed. She was a little out of breath, but a smile was on her face.

"One of the boys just came from the beach. John is back," she told him excitedly, "and the *Grace* is with him."

Will immediately took off his apron and followed Skye outside. The two of them met Kate and Rebecca and the girls as they all hurried to the beach. They were overjoyed to see the *Grace* anchored in the bay with the *Finder*. Will smiled as Skye hurried ahead of them when they reached the docks. The very first person she came to was Caleb.

"Caleb!" she exclaimed, rushing into his arms to give him a big hug.

"Skye, it's so good to see that you are safe."

Letting go, Skye looked around for Daniel. Will too looked for his father, but neither Daniel nor anyone fitting the description Skye had given Will of Edward could be seen. They were nowhere on the docks, and the ship looked empty. Skye and Will quickly looked back to Caleb.

"Where's Father?" Skye searched his face for an answer, but there was only a look of remorse. Skye's face fell. "Oh no, now what's happened? Is he all right?"

"For now," Caleb answered slowly.

"For now?" Skye repeated in confusion.

"Hendricks has him."

"And my father?" Will asked, stepping forward.

Caleb nodded solemnly. "He's got him too."

Will looked back at Rebecca and the girls. The horror and fear for both Daniel and Edward was clear on their faces.

"What can we do?" Skye asked Caleb desperately.

Obviously troubled, Caleb answered, "I don't know, but we'll think of something."

For the moment, he turned his attention back to Will. "Before I get into further explanations about what has happened, there's someone you should meet." Caleb turned a little. "Will, this is your uncle, Chris."

Chris stepped out from behind Caleb. Will could see that his expression was of mixed emotions; grief over what had happened, but happiness to, at long last, meet his nephew.

"Will, I can't tell you what a joy it is to finally meet you," he said, extending his hand.

Trying to overcome his own disappointment and worry about his father, Will took Chris' hand and shook it firmly. "I share the same joy," he said, his eyes taking in the face of his uncle, making him wonder what it would be like to finally see the face of his father, something he prayed desperately would still happen.

"I look forward to getting to know you," Chris told him, feeling the emotion of meeting this fine man his brother's son had grown into.

"As I do you," Will replied earnestly.

Glancing past Will, Chris noticed how distraught Rebecca and the girls were. Poor Emma couldn't hold back the tears in her eyes. Trying to give them some hope, Chris said, "We're going to find a way to rescue them."

Though the words were only for comfort and there was no assurance they would be fulfilled, Will and his family would strive to believe them.

The rest of the crew came forward to greet Will and Skye though everyone was somber. Finally, they all walked back to the village where they gathered in the meeting hall to talk. Rebecca asked Lydie to watch the girls and joined everyone inside.

"What happened?" Skye wanted to know. "How did they get captured?"

Caleb sighed heavily. "We had split up into groups to check out the taverns in this one town where we'd heard Hendricks was. Chris was with Daniel and Edward when they were captured, but Hendricks let him go to come back and tell us he had them, and to give us a message," he said ominously.

"What kind of message?" Will asked.

Caleb sighed again. "The thing is, Hendricks has no intention of ever freeing Edward, which as we all know does not surprise us, but he wants to use Daniel to bargain with."

"Bargain for what?" Skye asked uncertainly.

Caleb reluctantly pulled a piece of paper from his pocket. "Hendricks ordered me to give you this though I wish I didn't have to."

Taking the paper, Skye unfolded it with mounting dread. She read aloud. "Miss McHenry, if you ever want to see your father again, you will do exactly as I tell you. I know how much you love him, and make no mistake, if I don't get exactly what I want, I will kill him. If you want to know how it will be done, just ask Chris James." Skye had to pause for her vision to clear as two tears spilled from her eyes. "I want you to bring me . . ." Her words caught again, this time in stunned horror as everyone wondered what was coming next. She kept reading, but her voice wavered. "...bring me William James and your father's ship. You have a week and a half. No more."

No one could speak for a long moment. Finally, Skye managed it, her tears now falling steadily.

"How can he do this?" she asked with deep sorrow. "How can he expect me to choose like this?" Kelley had made her choose between Will and her promise to her father. This was much worse, because she had to choose between Will and her father. "Does he really expect me to do this?"

"Skye, before you think much about it, go somewhere and read this." Caleb handed her another paper. "It's from your father. Hendricks let me see him before we left."

Skye grasped the letter tightly and left the hall to read it somewhere in private. Meanwhile, Caleb turned to Will.

"There are two letters for you also. One is from Daniel, and the other is from your father."

Will took the letters and decided to go somewhere else as well. He found the men's house empty, so he sat down on his bed to read them. First, he read his father's. In the letter Edward told Will how much he loved him and how much joy it gave him just to know Will was alive and well. Overcome by the emotion and sorrow of reading the letter, Will had to pause for several minutes before opening Daniel's letter.

Will,

I am writing to ask you to take care of Skye. I know how difficult this will be for both of you, but I know that together you can get through it. I know how much you love her, and I expect that you have plans to ask me someday for her hand in marriage. I

give it to you gladly, without hesitation. You've always been so
wonderful to my daughter, and I am very glad to leave her in your
care. God will be with you both.

Daniel

Will could only stare at the letter for a long time. He had just received something he'd wanted for so long, but it had come at such a high price he could not celebrate it. All he could think about was how Skye felt. He couldn't imagine anyone having to make the kind of choice that Hendricks was forcing her to make.

Closing his eyes, Will began to pray, pouring out his sorrow and begging God to step in and make everything right. After praying for some time, Will finally pushed himself to his feet. He stepped out of the house and started through the village in search of Skye. He hadn't gone far before he met Worthy.

"I heard what happened," Worthy told him. "I'm so sorry about your father and Captain McHenry, and I can't believe what Hendricks is asking Miss McHenry to do."

Will shook his head at the thought and sighed. "Have you seen her? I need to talk to her."

"Yes, I saw her going into the woods towards the beach some time ago," Worthy said. "I have not seen her come back yet."

"Thank you."

He walked to the forest edge and made his way through it slowly, looking around for Skye. He didn't find her until he reached the beach, quite a ways from the docks. She was sitting on a rock, facing the ocean with the breeze fluttering the letter in her hands. Approaching her slowly, Will gently spoke her name. She turned to him, and he saw her face wet with tears. Will didn't think he'd ever seen her eyes so full of sorrow.

"Will." Skye's voice was so fragile, so helpless. It broke Will's heart to see her like this. He closed the last bit of distance between them. Skye stood and immediately went into his arms, desperately needing comfort. She buried her face in his chest and tried not to cry, but Will could feel her silent sobbing. After a few moments, he spoke to her with a quiet determinedness.

"Skye, I know how important your father is to you. I will go to Hendricks." He longed to marry her and spend the rest of his life with her, but he loved her so much that he would give up even that to make her happy.

"No!" Skye cried. She pulled away just enough to look him in the face. "No," she said again. "I will not let you do that . . ." Skye paused and the sorrow in her eyes increased. "I don't know how I could condemn my father either, but the only way I can do this is to keep telling myself that I'm obeying him. In his letter he told me not to follow Hendricks' instructions. He forbid me to." She had to pause again. "The hardest part is remembering what Hendricks said about killing him. I don't know exactly what happened to Chris, but I know it was horrible, and I can't bear the thought of it happening to Father or you either. And on top of that, I feel so bad because I'm not the only one losing my father, you and your sisters are too, and Rebecca's losing her husband. That is another reason you can't go, they can't lose you too."

Fresh, hot tears ran down Skye's face. And then she grew angry. "How can Hendricks cause so much pain and sorrow without a thought?" Her anger then melted again into sadness. "When will this all end?"

Will cupped Skye's face gently in his hands and looked her in the eyes.

"It will, Skye, it will. And there is still hope of rescuing them. You're not choosing one way or the other yet, and I promise you, I will do everything I can to bring your father back."

Comforted by his words, Skye hugged him tightly again. She wiped away the last remnants of her tears, and the two of them returned to the village. On the way back to the meeting hall, they passed the women's house, and Will paused when he thought he heard something.

"What is it, Will?"

Will shook his head, unsure, and they walked around the corner. They found Lydie and Molly and Emma sitting on a bench against the side of the house. There were tears in all their eyes. Emma and Molly's fell freely, and though Lydie was trying to be strong for her sisters, there were traces of tears on her face too.

Sitting down between Emma and Molly, Will put his arms around them, and Skye took a seat next to Lydie.

"We've been praying," Lydie murmured, her voice squeaking a little.

"Good," Skye replied, placing her hand over Lydie's hands which were folded in her lap.

Emma looked up at Will with sad eyes. "Will, are you going to leave?"

Skye answered before Will could. "No, Emma, he's not. He's going to stay here and help find a way to rescue my father and yours."

"Do you think you can?" Emma said.

"I don't know," Will answered truthfully. "Just keep praying. God is the only one with the answer."

"I will," Emma promised in a small voice.

Will and Skye sat with them for a few minutes more. They didn't say much, but the girls seemed to be comforted just by their presence. Finally, they got up and returned to the meeting hall. Inside, Caleb stood to meet them and gently put his hand on Skye's shoulder.

"Are you all right?" he asked.

Skye nodded and murmured, "Yes."

Everyone seemed to be watching her, wondering what her response would be to Hendricks' message. Looking at each of them, she said, "I'm not going to give in to Hendricks' demands, no matter what happens. We have to find some other way to rescue my father and Mr. James. That's what my father wants . . ." she looked at Will, "and what I want."

Everyone nodded, and Skye and Will sat down.

"We've been talking about how we could do that," Chris told them. "The problem is, Hendricks more or less owns the town so has everyone on his side. Even along with everyone who would agree to help us, we'd be vastly outnumbered, and we couldn't go to the authorities because Hendricks would just kill Edward and Daniel if he suspected we had."

"If only we had something else to bargain with to get both of them back," Skye said wishfully. "As much as I love the *Grace*, I'd gladly give her to him and everything else I had if it were enough."

Chris shook his head. "I'm afraid anything we could bring together wouldn't satisfy him. Edward could barely raise enough money for my ransom, and I wasn't even worth anything. He won't settle for anything less than a fortune."

Skye fought the urge to panic. "Even if we could think of enough to satisfy him, we'd never be able to get it in time."

As night fell, the sky clouded and heavy rain poured down on the island accompanied by low, rumbling thunder. Many sat around in the meeting hall with somber, blank expressions. When it grew later, they slowly began leaving through the rain to go off to bed. Rebecca and the girls were among the first to go, and Skye followed a short time later. Knowing he could accomplish nothing by staying where he was, Will decided to try to sleep as well and first walked Skye to the women's house. On the porch, they paused just outside the door.

"Good night, Will," Skye murmured. She tried to smile, but it would not come.

"Good night, sweetheart." Skye put her arms around him and they hugged for a long, quiet moment. "I hope you will be able to sleep," he said.

"You too," Skye replied, though both knew how futile their statements were.

She turned and walked quietly inside. Will waited until the door had closed behind her before he turned away and trudged through the downpour to the other house.

After a long, heartfelt prayer, he got into bed and made a desperate attempt to sleep, but it just would not come. For hours he tossed and turned, never even coming close to sleep. Finally, it became unbearable, and he sat up. When he glanced around the house, it appeared that everyone was asleep, but he had to doubt that some really were. Unable to just sit there, Will got out of bed and quietly made his way to the door, careful not to rouse anyone.

Outside, the rain-freshened air felt good, but it was not enough to make him feel any better. For a few minutes Will stood at the edge of the porch and stared into the darkness where the rain was still falling, though not as heavily now. With a sigh, he took a seat on the bench behind him.

Not long after that, he heard the door creak and looked up to see Chris just stepping out of the house.

Seeing Will sitting there, Chris asked, "Did you want to be alone?"

"No," Will said quietly. Truth was, he was just wishing for someone to talk to. "I just can't sleep."

"Neither can I," Chris said, sitting down near Will. For a moment, there was silence. "We haven't gotten to talk much yet."

Will looked at Chris and shook his head. "No, we haven't."

Though neither was sure where to begin, Chris said finally, "I still remember very clearly the day you were born." There was a bit of smile on his face. "That was a wonderful day for everyone. One of the happiest of your father's life."

Though it brought a smile to Will's face too, he wondered how long that happiness had lasted. "Exactly how long after that did my mother leave?"

"Eleven months. You were just about a year old."

"Did my father suspect that she was going to leave?"

Chris nodded. "We all did. Did your mother tell you about Brandon?" At Will's nod he continued. "Edward and I knew that he was meeting with your mother. I even went to talk to him once." Chris shook his head for it clearly had not gone well.

"What happened?"

"He threw me out with the threat that if I ever came back I'd regret it. I wasn't afraid of him, but Edward never let me go back. I guess if I had, likely I would have gotten hurt or even killed. I was just barely eighteen at the time."

"My mother told me that my father and Brandon were friends at one time."

"Yes, Edward and Marie, Brandon and I, we were all friends in school, but then Brandon just changed. I think it was when Edward and Marie started courting."

"Jealousy," Will murmured.

Chris nodded.

"What did my father do after she left?"

"He didn't do or say much of anything to anyone. Most of the time he spent praying. I was still living with our parents, but I moved in with him. Eventually though, he told me I didn't have to stay. He knew how I'd always wanted to be a sailor, and he wanted me to follow that dream.

"That brought me here, to America. Now I regret that I didn't stay closer to home because your father had some really hard times. He couldn't find a job and our father died. Then, on top of all that, I got caught by Hendricks." He paused for a long moment, and Will could only imagine what kinds of horrible memories Chris had. Will was silent, waiting for him to continue if he would. "It was just after Edward paid for my ransom and I was recovering that I finally trusted Christ."

"You hadn't before that?" Will questioned, surprised.

"No. Your father did as a child and I wish I had, but I didn't. I believed in God, but for some reason I just thought I was fine because I never lied, stole, drank, or spent any time with any women, and I thought that was enough. But being near to death made me uncertain of what would happen if I died. I knew I wasn't ready."

"How old were you then?"

"Twenty-two."

As the rain continued to fall, Will and Chris continued their conversation. Will enjoyed talking to his uncle. Though he'd known him for less than a day, Will felt more comfortable talking to him than a lot of people he'd known his whole life. Chris cared deeply for him, and Will could feel that.

They didn't keep track of time, but when the rain ceased to fall some hours later, their talking ceased with it. Both were tired.

"Do you think you can sleep now?" Chris asked.

Will nodded. Now he could. "Yes."

They got up and went back inside. With a quiet sigh, Will lay down. His exhausted body welcomed the bed's comfort. He pulled the quilt over himself and closed his eyes.

～ৎ ৎ～

Rain returned with daybreak. Will could hear it when he got up. The villagers gathered drearily in the meeting hall to have their breakfast there. Smiles and laughter were absent. Even those unaffected by what had happened were feeling bad for Will and Skye and the others. Everyone tried to help, many had good suggestions, but it was no use. In every plan they found some flaw. The people even offered to give what little of value they had, but the amount would never satisfy Hendricks.

The day drug on like a bad dream. Discouraged, everyone went their own way after dinner. Wanting to at least do something helpful with his time, Will went to work in the shed. With the warm glow of the forge and the splash of raindrops outside, it would have been a very cozy place to spend the day, but Will's spirit matched the gloomy weather. His mind was not on what he was doing, and his hands seemed to work of their own accord.

Will's thoughts were on his father. First he'd been told that he was dead, then he'd found out he was really alive, and now he was going to die. And there was nothing Will could do to stop it. The longer he thought about it the worse he felt. He was frustrated, and he hated feeling helpless. His throat constricted with tears and his vision blurred. In that moment, his hammer missed its mark, and the side of his hand hit the red-hot metal instead. Will yanked his hand back and dropped the hammer. There was a long red burn across the edge of his palm. He gritted his teeth in pain and was frustrated over his thoughts. He could not work like this.

Taking off his apron, Will hung it up and slipped on his coat. Though it was still raining, he stepped outside. Against the shed there stood a barrel overflowing with rain water. Will dipped his hand into it, relieving the burn. When finally he pulled it out, he sat down on a bench. Leaning his head back against the shed, Will closed his eyes as the rain hit his face.

"God, only You can give us hope. Please, show us what to do . . . please," Will entreated desperately.

For several minutes, Will remained seated and examined his feelings. He realized how foolish was his frustration with his own helplessness. Of course he was helpless—God was the one in full control. Finally, Will let go of everything and decided in his heart that no matter what happened it was for the best. God would either provide them with a way to rescue Edward and Daniel or He would not. And if He did not, He would instead help everyone deal with the loss.

Standing finally, Will walked back into the shed. Glancing over his work, the list Silas had written of what needed to be done caught his eye. Something about it made him think of the map Skye had taken from Hendricks.

"If only we had that treasure," Will murmured to himself. "Hendricks would take that."

Feeling renewed, he walked over to the bench where the list lay and turned it over. Picking up the quill that was also laying there, he dipped it in ink and drew the map as best he could from memory. After all the hours Skye had already spent trying to figure it out, added to all the time he had spent, it seemed pointless to persist, but he wanted to try once more.

"God, if this could be a way to save them, show me," he prayed.

For a long time, Will stared at the drawing. Very little came to him for they had already tried so many possibilities.

He was close to giving up and letting it be, when without conscious thought, he began to fiddle with his cross necklace as he had a habit of doing when he was thinking idly. His hand brushed against the locket he wore, and right at that moment, he realized God had given him the answer. *Can it really be?*

Reaching behind his neck, Will unclasped the locket, and let it slide off the chain. He opened it up and laid it in his palm. Opened flat, it looked as if it would fit perfectly into the ovals on the map.

"Thank you, God!" Will exclaimed as he left the shed and dashed over to the women's house where he expected Skye to be.

At the door, he knocked loudly and called her name. He could barely wait for her to come to the door. Finally, it opened, and Skye stepped out.

"What is it, Will?" she asked in confusion.

"Where is the map you took from Hendricks?"

"In my coat, why?"

"I think I figured it out."

Looking stunned, Skye hurried back into the house to get the map. She brought it out to Will, and he spread it quickly out on the porch railing. He then opened the locket and laid it on the map. A perfect match. Skye looked at Will with her mouth open.

"How did you know it was your locket?" she asked.

"I didn't. I asked God to show me the answer if it could help us save your father and mine, and He did," Will answered. "Skye, if we can find the treasure, we can trade it for both of them."

Joy came to Skye's face for the first time in nearly two days.

"Tell Kate, and Rebecca and the girls," Will said. "I'll go find everyone else. They're probably in the men's house. We'll join you at the meeting hall."

Skye nodded, and Will hurried over to the other house. Just as he expected, almost everyone was there.

"I have an idea," he said, taking them all by surprise. "Come with me."

They followed him to the meeting hall, barely able to keep from asking questions along the way. The women and girls were all waiting for them. Will turned to a table and laid the map out, looking round at everyone.

"This is the map that Skye took from Hendricks when she escaped. Supposedly it leads to the Monarrez Treasure. There are no names on the map, only clues that no one has been able to figure out, but God has given me the answer." Will put the locket down on the map. "This is what you need."

"That's the locket your father gave you," Chris said in surprise.

Will looked at him. "Yes! Where did he get it?"

"From our friend, Ben," Chris answered. "Ben always thought it might have something to do with the treasure, but he gave up on it and told Edward to give it to you."

"I think Hendricks got the map from Ben," Skye told Chris. "That's probably why he was killed."

Chris nodded. "This map must have been what he found that he was so anxious to show us. He probably figured out that the locket was needed too."

"So what does the map say?" John asked.

"Hidden in metal, revealed by glass," Skye answered.

"What does that mean?"

Skye shook her head, but Will answered, "I think I figured that out too. The designs on the locket are not just designs, they're letters, but they are backwards. You need a mirror to read them. They're hidden in metal and revealed by glass."

Everyone looked at him in astonishment and sudden realization.

"You're a genius," John stated matter-of-factly.

Laughter came from everyone, from his words and from relief. Their hope for rescuing Daniel and Edward had been restored.

"We need a mirror," Will said.

"I'll get one," Kate volunteered.

She quickly left the hall. Meanwhile, everyone else tried to read what the locket said, but they were only able to decipher a couple of letters since they were purposely distorted to blend in with the designs. When Kate returned, she handed Will the mirror, and they crowded around as he held the locket up to it. After a moment, he gave them both to Skye.

"It's all in Spanish," he told her, "you'll have to read it."

Taking the mirror and locket, she started reading slowly.

"*Isla de Ríos. Gran río. Estrella constante. El punto. Sol cueva,*" she read. "The first part seems to be the island's name. It's Island of Rivers."

"There's an island south of the Carolinas that I've heard called Isla de Ríos," Chris said. "It must be the island. What is the rest of it?"

Skye frowned. "I'm not sure. It says, *Great river. Constant star. The point. Sun cave.*"

"Sounds like more clues," John observed.

"Or directions," Chris remarked. Looking back to the map, he said, "Great river must mean this one here. It's the largest one on the island."

Everyone agreed.

"Now, what does constant star mean?" John wondered.

This took a little more thought, but soon Skye had an idea.

"The north star?"

"Yes," Chris agreed. "That must be it, which probably means we have to follow the river north, and if we do that it leads to the point of the island just like the third part of the directions."

"Now all that's left is *sun cave*," Skye said.

"Well, constant star was a direction, and maybe sun is too. The sun rises in the east and there's probably a cave on the eastern side of the point," Will reasoned.

Chris nodded with a look of amazement. "We have it. We know where the Monarrez Treasure is."

"The question now is what do we do with it?" Caleb asked. "We have to make sure Edward and Daniel are safe before giving Hendricks anything."

"We should go and get the treasure ourselves and then make the trade," Chris said.

No one noticed the sly look on John's face until he spoke. "Ya know, this also presents us with the perfect opportunity to stop Hendricks for good."

"How?" Caleb asked.

"Well, if we got the treasure and hid it somewhere else, with a little help from, let's say, Lieutenant Graham, we could set up a nice little trap for Hendricks."

"What kind of trap?"

"I've got this place in mind, a small cove that's big enough for a coupla ships, but the mouth of it is only big enough for one. If we could lure Hendricks inside and had soldiers hidin' in the forest and eventually a ship or two waitin' for 'im at the mouth of the cove, he'd have nowhere to go."

"Sounds like a good plan," Caleb said, nodding.

Chris agreed.

"How soon can we leave?" Skye asked anxiously.

"I say we get ready now and leave first thing in the mornin'," John suggested.

Caleb seconded that. "It will give us enough time to get the treasure and set the trap and still have a day or two to spare."

394

For a moment, no one else spoke, but suddenly smiles broke out simultaneously on everyone's face. Relief shown in their eyes.

"We need to pray," Caleb said.

Everyone bowed their heads and joined hands. They praised God for His amazing power and the plan He had for their lives. With all their hearts they thanked Him for showing them how to rescue Daniel and Edward. After each one said amen, they rose and left the hall. Outside they found that the rain had ceased again, this time for good, and the sun was peeking out from behind the breaking clouds. It was as if they could feel God's love in its warmth.

As they turned in the direction of the beach, Caleb pulled Skye aside with something he'd been waiting to tell her until things were not so difficult.

"Because there didn't seem to be much hope we'd rescue your father, he wanted me to tell you that the *Grace* is yours. You are the new captain."

"Me?" Skye was surprised.

Caleb nodded.

"But you've always been the first mate and Father's best friend. You should be captain," Skye told him quickly. "Besides, we are going to rescue them."

"Yes, but the *Grace* still needs a captain in the meantime. I have no desire to be captain, Skye. Your father and I agreed a long time ago that the *Grace* would be yours."

Skye thought about it for a long moment, conflicted.

When she didn't speak, Caleb said, "Should I inform the men?"

"Yes, but this is *only* temporary," Skye emphasized.

Caleb smiled. "Yes, Captain."

As soon as the news spread that they had a plan, many offered to help them get ready so they could leave quickly in the morning. The *Grace*, the *Finder*, and the *Half Moon* were all loaded with fresh supplies. No one knew just how big the treasure might be, and they thought that sailing together would be safer once they went to meet Hendricks.

Skye found herself slipping into her new role as captain with ease. It was in her blood. She supervised some of the loading and then went to her father's cabin to see that everything was in order there. Like her father, she liked things neat and organized. Emma, who was hovering around but still making certain to keep out of anyone's way, followed Skye everywhere she went.

"It must be wonderful to be captain of a ship," she said, bubbling with excitement over Skye's new position. "Even if it is only for a few days."

Skye smiled with understanding. "Well, maybe it would be under different circumstances, Emma, but I've hardly had time to give it much thought other than to notice how strange it seems. I hope only that I can do as good a job as my father."

"Oh, I'm sure you will," Emma said with much enthusiasm. "You know so much about the ship and the ocean."

"That is true."

Skye looked up from the desk and saw Will standing in the doorway. With a smile, he stepped inside the cabin.

"I know you'll do your father very proud," he told her confidently.

Skye smiled. "Thank you, both."

"You're welcome," Emma replied cheerfully. After a moment, her mood changed a little and she said longingly, "I wish I could come with you. It's no fun being young and not getting to do anything exciting."

Will smiled gently at her. "Don't worry, you won't be young forever."

Emma nodded but asked with a sudden grin, "Are you *sure* I can't come?"

"I'm afraid not," Will told her. "We aren't certain what will happen when we meet Hendricks, and it will make us all feel better knowing you're safe here."

"Well, I guess if it helps, I don't mind staying," Emma decided, though they could tell that she was still disappointed.

"I'll tell you exactly what happens when we get back," Will promised her.

"Thank you, Will." Emma grinned again in satisfaction and wandered off to see if she could help anyone.

Skye got up to put some things away and glanced at Will. "Have you finished reading your father's letters yet?"

Will shook his head. "No. I've only gotten through about half of them. I plan to finish while we're sailing." He paused. "Thank you again for safeguarding them. Reading them has meant a lot to me."

"I'm so glad I remembered them. Hendricks would just have thrown them away, and with pleasure. It would have been such a terrible waste."

"Yes, it would have," Will said with feeling. He would have hated to lose them.

"What kinds of things did he write about?" Skye asked curiously.

"Everything," Will answered with an animated smile. "Some of the letters are several pages long. In each letter he wrote about everything that happened since the last. One of the last ones I read, he wrote about rescuing Chris from Hendricks." Will's smile faded, and he shook his head. "It sounded like it was really hard."

"It must have been awful," Skye murmured. "Poor Chris, and your father."

Will agreed, and it was very quiet for a moment until they heard a knock. Skye looked up to see Caleb in the doorway.

"Yes?" she asked.

"Everything is loaded," Caleb informed her. "John and Kate are about done too."

"Good," Skye said. "Now at least we won't have to work in the dark or take time to finish in the morning."

Before leaving the ship to return to the village, Caleb asked Will to come with him down to the forecastle. When they got there, Will found that there wasn't anything Caleb wanted help with as he'd expected. The first mate had something he wanted to give him.

"Daniel told me what he wrote in his letter to you, and he wanted me to give you this." Caleb took a tiny leather pouch from his pocket and gave it to Will. Opening it, Will pulled out what was inside—a ring decorated with silver and set with a small glittering sapphire. He had never seen a ring more beautiful.

"That is the engagement ring that Daniel gave to Grace," Caleb explained. "He thought it would be very special for Skye to have it now."

"It's beautiful. More beautiful than anything I could have gotten her, and it will mean a lot to her," Will agreed. He slipped it back into the pouch. "Keep it for now," he told Caleb. "I know Captain McHenry has already consented to my wish to marry Skye, but I want to speak with him in person."

Caleb looked pleased. "That decision shows a lot of patience and respect, Will. Daniel is very blessed for God to have provided you as a husband for his daughter."

"Thank you." Will was so gratified that was all he was able to say, and it showed on his face.

Chapter Twenty-nine

T hree days of constant sailing lay behind them when Isla de Ríos appeared on the horizon as a dark spot which grew quickly into land. Looking from a spyglass, they could see that the island was rocky and forested. The closer they got, the more they realized that finding a place to anchor was not going to be an easy task for the island was surrounded by shallow water from which sharp rocks protruded and lay hidden beneath its glassy surface, easily capable of gashing a hole in the hulls of the ships. However, as a result of Skye's careful navigation, they found an area of deeper water on the eastern side of the island where all three ships dropped anchor.

Preparing to go ashore, Skye asked Jesse and Corey to bring them some lanterns and rope, and Nick and Pete helped lower one of the boats. Once the supplies were loaded, Skye and Will, along with Caleb and Chris and Worthy got into the boat and rowed it ashore. On the beach, they met John and Kate with a few of their men.

"Well, here we are," John said, taking in the view of the forest in front of them. "Where do we go from here?"

They looked to Chris who was the keeper of the map.

"The river should be straight west from here. I think we should find it and follow it to the point," he said. "We could travel along the beach, but I thought it looked too rocky and uneven."

"I thought so too," Skye agreed. "Finding the river is probably best."

Since they were all in agreement, they gathered up the lanterns and ropes and left the beach. Vegetation was thick once they entered the forest, but they pushed through the thick undergrowth determinedly. Not even a half hour later, they came to a stop, panting and hot since the weather was warmer than they were used to. The island was a lot farther south, and even though it was more like home, Will and Skye had gotten used to a cooler climate. Hoping to have had the worst behind them, they were disappointed to see what yet lay ahead of them. Endless pools of green, slime-coated water created a swamp that stretched in all directions. Their only choice was to go through it or go back.

John shook his head. "Right now I'm wonderin' if the beach would've been a better idea."

Chris looked around. "We could go back, but we're probably closer to the river."

John shrugged. "If everyone else wants to brave the swamp I'll be right there with you." He grinned optimistically. "Look at it this way, we'll have some more fond memories to look back on."

Everyone chuckled. Their spirits lifted, they trudged into the swamp. In most places the water came to their knees, but sometimes it was a little deeper. At first they tried to find places where there was soggy land to walk on, but it was like trying to walk through a maze and they soon gave up, not wanting to get off course. No one said anything as they concentrated on trying not to lose their balance in the sometimes over-ankle deep mud that lay beneath the water. They weren't sure how long they had been passing through the swamp when suddenly they heard a noise that was a cross between a surprised cry and a yelp and then a loud splash. Everyone turned in time to see John clambering up out of the water dripping from head to toe and sputtering loudly. Bright green algae clung to his hair and clothes. Confusion showed on everyone's face as they stared at him. John pointed several times at the water alongside of him before finally speaking.

"Do not step there," he sputtered.

"What happened?" Kate asked, frowning deeply in confusion.

"It's a hole," John answered. "A very *deep* hole."

At first, no one spoke, but suddenly Kate burst out laughing and everyone else couldn't help but join her. John looked like he might be upset by it, but he started laughing too.

"I told ya we'd have some more fond memories."

That made everyone laugh even harder.

"You know, John," Kate said. "I think God might be usin' you to keep us all in good spirits."

John smiled. "He can use me however He wants."

With one last laugh, they continued, however, they were now much more careful about where they stepped. Finally, an hour after they had left the beach, they reached the end of the swamp and heard water running up ahead. Hurrying on through the last bit of forest, they came to the river. Turning north, they followed it upstream. Traveling was much easier for the riverbank was clear of trees. Now, the worst really was behind them.

A mile or two from where they had left the swamp, the forest came to an end and they walked out onto a bare, rocky point which was at least a hundred feet above the sea. Gulls screeched in alarm, disturbed from their nests, as everyone walked to the eastern edge of the point. The cliff side was near vertical making it impossible to tell if there was a cave, but Chris did point out what looked like an old, steep path leading down from the point.

"That must be where we need to go," he said. "There's nothing up here."

John looked at it and shook his head. "Could that path be any narrower?"

"Does it scare you, John?" Kate asked teasingly.

"Yes, I'm scared," John answered flat out, surprising everyone. "I'm afraid of heights."

Kate looked especially surprised. "You're afraid of heights?"

"Yes."

"Is that why you never help up in the rigging?"

John nodded.

"I never knew that," Kate said.

John shrugged. "I never mentioned it before."

"Well, you don't have to go down," Kate told him.

"And not get to see the treasure when you find it? I'm not that scared . . . I don't think."

Slowly, one at a time, they carefully followed the narrow path. John took a little longer than everyone else, but no one blamed him.

"Just don't look down," Kate said as she came behind him.

"Oh, it's too late for that."

"Well, I'd tell you to close your eyes, but that wouldn't work."

"Nope, not unless I wanted to step right off the edge." John's voice still held humor.

Finally, they reached the rocks at the base of the point. After working their way around and over the slippery, wet rocks for several yards, they found it, the entrance of a dark cave. They looked at each other with shades of anxiousness. What exactly would be inside? There was always the chance that the treasure had already been found, but they prayed it hadn't.

Quickly, they lit the lanterns and entered the damp, inky darkness of the cave. At first they had to slosh along in ankle deep water though after the swamp, they didn't even notice it. There were sharp, narrow bends along the way where the cave walls were coated with a thick layer of slime, but eventually the cave became more elevated, and they found themselves walking on dry sand. After another few yards they came to the end of the cave, the lantern light illuminating a wide area. For a long moment all they could do was stare at the many dark chests stacked neatly along the cave wall.

"How many do you think there are?" Skye asked with hushed astonishment.

Chris quickly counted them. "Twenty-eight."

"Do you think they're all full of gold?" John asked in wonder.

"There's only one way to find out," Caleb said. He bent down and picked up a large rock. Turning, he gave it to Chris. "You spent a lot of time looking for this. You should be the first to open one."

Chris went to one of the chests. After smashing the lock a few times, it fell open. As everyone crowded around, he lifted the lid. Sparkling gold met their anxious eyes. The chest was filled to the brim. John whistled and shook his head as he glanced at the other chests.

"I never thought I'd see another treasure that could compare to the McHenry's. Hendricks would never refuse this."

Chris looked around. "Now we need to figure out how to get them to the ships. One thing is certain, we can't bring it the way we came."

John laughed dryly. "We'd sink so far into that swamp carryin' this gold that we'd never get out, that is if we made it back up the path alive."

"Any way we do it is going to be a lot of work, but you're right, going back would be too dangerous. The beach doesn't offer us much hope either. I think the best and probably only way to do it is to bring the ships as close as

403

we can and use the boats," Caleb said. "With everyone helping, we should be able to get it all before nightfall."

John sighed. "But that still means we have to go back and get the ships."

"I say we try the beach this time," Chris suggested.

John agreed quickly. "Good idea."

With nothing more to be done in the cave, they began the climb back up the path. When they reached the top of the point, they didn't go south but instead turned east again and traveled along the edge of the island. The way was indeed rough, but by the time they got back to the beach where they had left the boats two hours earlier, everyone agreed that it had been better than traversing the swamp again.

"Well, this'll certainly be a story to tell the grandkids," John stated as he flopped down on a rock to take a little rest.

Kate looked at him with a curious look in her eyes. "Grandkids?"

John suddenly realized his simple comments might need a more complicated explanation. He glanced at Will who looked highly interested in what he was going to say. Looking back to Kate, John shrugged.

"I might have some, someday," he said, knowing it was a lame answer. "You never know."

Kate nodded but didn't say anything so he had no way of knowing what she was thinking, if anything at all.

Without further conversation, everyone got into their boats and rowed back to their ships.

Navigating around the point and finding the closet place to anchor took some time. It was too dangerous to get as close as they would have liked, but they got as close as they could. This time, several boats were lowered from each ship. They had already decided to divide the treasure between the three to distribute the weight and keep their speed. Cautiously, avoiding the rocks along the way, they reached the mouth of the cave once more.

"That Monarrez sure went to a lotta trouble to hide this treasure," John commented. "I could think of a lot easier places to hide it. Must've been a smart man to have thought of all this right before he died. But if he was dyin', what did he want to hide it for anyway?"

Chris shrugged. "The story Edward and I heard was that he meant to leave it for a woman he was betrothed to, which would explain why he left clues on a locket. He probably also wanted to make sure it stayed in Spanish hands. I'm sure they know more about it than we do."

"Yeah, that makes sense," John said. "It'd be interestin' to find out."

Kate looked at him teasingly. "You thinkin' of going to the Spanish and asking 'em?"

John laughed. "Nope. I don't think they'd be overly kind if they knew we'd found the treasure. I imagine they've spent some time lookin' for it too."

"Yes, they have," Chris said.

They picked up the poles they'd brought with and carried them into the cave. The chests were made to be carried with poles and that made them much easier to transport.

Since they really couldn't help carry the chests, Skye and Kate helped in different ways. Skye kept track of how many went to each ship, and Kate went up on top of the point to keep a look out for any other ships.

One by one the chests were carried out and carefully maneuvered over the rocks. Skye was concerned that someone might slip and fall and get hurt, but there were thankfully no mishaps. A couple of hours later, the last chest finally left the cave where it had been hidden for over a hundred years. There was a round of contented sighs as they watched the last chest being rowed towards the ship.

"It's amazing how God provides, isn't it?" John said.

"Yes, it is," Will spoke for everyone. Only days ago they'd had no hope.

"Now all that's left is to set the trap and get Hendricks to take the bait," John said after a moment.

"How far are we from the cove?" Skye asked.

"Well, if we set sail right away we oughta get there sometime in the mornin'."

"And Fort Camden is only another couple of hours from there?" Caleb asked.

John nodded.

"Good." Caleb looked towards the sun. "We still have another hour of daylight left so we should be getting on our way."

The six of them stepped into the last boat and headed for open water. After letting John and Kate off at their ships, Will and Skye, and Chris and Caleb rowed over to the *Grace*. The boat was hauled up, and after they had set sail, Corey made supper. Everyone, especially those who had taken part in the trek across the island, was very hungry.

～～～

The midmorning sun was bright as they approached the cove that John had described to them. They could now see for themselves what a perfect place it was to trap Hendricks. Because only two ships could fit, the *Half Moon* stayed at the cove's entrance while the *Finder* and the *Grace* sailed into it. After anchoring where it was still deep enough, some of them went ashore to look around. A small clearing drew their attention.

"This looks like a good place to put the treasure," John said. "Hendricks will see it right away, and it will keep him distracted while the soldiers come behind."

"Good idea," Caleb agreed.

"One other thing we need to think about," Chris warned, "is, knowing Hendricks, he might not give us Edward and Daniel without seeing the treasure first. We can try to avoid it, but we may be forced to bring him here before he makes the trade."

"I thought of that too," Caleb said. "Once we get all the treasure here, I say we open all the locks so that Hendricks can easily have someone check them if that's what he wants."

Chris nodded.

Instead of unloading both ships at once, everyone worked to unload the *Grace*. They decided that they'd save a lot of time if Skye and her crew left for Fort Camden as soon as the ship was unloaded. John and Kate could finish unloading their ships after Skye was gone and then meet them elsewhere.

With only nine chests aboard, unloading went quickly. All but one chest sat on shore when the *Grace* prepared to leave.

"We'll meet you tonight then," John checked with Skye as she and the others stepped into their boat.

"Yes. I don't expect us to have any trouble at Fort Camden. I'm sure that Lieutenant Graham will be glad to help us."

"I 'spose you could always offer 'im the treasure if 'e didn't want to help," John speculated.

Skye laughed. "I don't think he's the kind of man who would accept a bribe, but I'll keep that in mind."

Grinning, John helped them push off from shore. Once on board the *Grace*, Skye carefully navigated the ship out of the cove. On the way out, she waved goodbye to Kate who stood on the quarterdeck of the *Half Moon* and then concentrated on getting every bit of speed out of the *Grace* that she could. They wanted to meet with Lieutenant

Graham as soon as possible because they still hoped to meet with Hendricks later that night if all went well.

With Skye's expert knowledge of the ship, they made great time and were able to reach Fort Camden in just under four hours. They moored the ship to the dock closest to the fort, but kept it ready to leave as soon as they had spoken to Graham. While the crew stayed aboard, Will and Skye, and Chris and Caleb, took leave of the ship and headed determinedly towards the fort.

"Now let's pray that Lieutenant Graham is here and hasn't gone anywhere," Skye said as they entered the courtyard of the fort. "Otherwise we'll have to find someone else to help us who may not be so easy to convince."

Reaching the doors of the fort, they came to a stop before the guards.

"We need to speak with Lieutenant Graham about something of great importance," Caleb told them.

Will added, "Tell him that William James and Skylar McHenry are here to see him."

One of the guards nodded and turned to deliver the message. It wasn't more than a couple of minutes before he returned and brought them inside to Graham's office.

"Mr. James, Miss McHenry," he greeted them with much enthusiasm. "It does me good to see you together."

"We are very pleased to see you again," Will told him sincerely.

"I hope your situation has improved since our last meeting," Graham expressed his concern.

"In some ways, yes, it has," Will replied. He thought it a good time to introduce Chris and Caleb.

After extending to them his greeting as well, Graham asked, "What brings you back to Fort Camden?"

"We are in need of your help, if you can give it," Will answered.

"I'm at you're disposal," Graham said. "I'm sure I can do or provide anything you need."

"Well, what we want will be beneficial to you as well," Will told him. "We have a plan to capture Hendricks."

Graham looked greatly interested. "What kind of plan?"

Will proceeded to give Graham a brief explanation of their situation, but the plan he explained more deeply.

"It's a good plan," Graham told them after Will had finished. "I don't think there's really anything I could add to it."

"You will help us then?" Will asked.

"Yes," Graham answered readily. "Not only do I owe it to you but taking down Hendricks will be a great service to the people who live around here."

Will took out the map that John had drawn with very specific details concerning where the cove was and some notes about where Graham might want to place his ships and men. He laid it out in front of Graham. "We thought it would be a good idea to place your ships to the north so Hendricks won't see them when he arrives. You could have someone on shore to signal you when Hendricks is in the cove. Also, we thought it would be good to have men near the treasure to catch anyone who might leave the ship before your ships arrive. I'm sure you can understand our desire for you to make sure none of his men escape."

"Do not worry," Graham assured them. "I will see to it personally that we get every single one."

"One more thing we need to consider," Will said. "The likely possibility that Hendricks might make us show him the treasure before releasing my father and Captain McHenry."

Graham nodded. "My men won't do anything until we know you're all safe and have left the cove."

"Thank you," Will replied. "We appreciate this more than we can say. Is there anything else you need to know or something you have thought of that we haven't?"

Graham shook his head. "The only other thing I need to know is when Hendricks will be there. Other than that, I think we've covered it all."

"We plan to meet with him tonight. If he starts for the treasure right away, he'll be there sometime tomorrow morning, but if he doesn't start until morning, it will be late afternoon."

"I'll get my men together right away. We'll be in position by tonight."

"We should be on our way then," Will said to Skye, "so we aren't late to meet him."

"Yes," Graham agreed. "Good luck."

"Thank you."

Very pleased with their meeting, they hurried back to the *Grace* and cast off immediately. The pirate town where Hendricks was staying lay another few hours to the south. They thanked God for the strong, fresh wind which gave the ship a great deal of speed. It was just getting dark when they met John and Kate a little over an hour from the city. They paused only briefly to tell them of Graham's full cooperation before sailing on together.

A fiery sunset lit part of their way, and then the sun sank into the sea. The moon rose above them and gave them some light until finally they slipped into the pirate port. Town seemed like too grand a word for it. Though it seemed to be a large place, hideout was a more appropriate word. A few rickety docks jutted out into the water and buildings that looked like they'd been put together with driftwood and pieces of old ships lined the shore with a haunting air. Just looking at them gave Skye goose bumps.

Tentatively, they steered the ships up to the docks. The small harbor was quiet, but voices and shouting drifted from the taverns farther inland. Keeping a close watch for trouble, they moored the ships and met on the dock.

"Who's gonna talk to Hendricks?" John asked. "I don't think it would be a good idea for us all to go. It would look too threatening and someone would likely get killed."

Everyone agreed.

"I'll go," Will said suddenly. "Hendricks will be expecting me."

"I'll go with you and show you where he is," Chris quickly volunteered.

Will nodded and they looked at the others for their reactions.

"Sounds all right to me," John more or less spoke for everyone.

"Be careful, Will," Skye said with concern. "This place gives me such a bad feeling."

"I'll be careful," he assured her. "Everything will be fine."

Skye nodded, and Will turned to follow Chris into the town. The streets were dark with no lamps lit, but Will could still see garbage lying everywhere. Even if he couldn't have, the smell would have told him it was there anyway. The buildings loomed menacingly, looking more like oddly shaped shadows than solid structures. Finally they came to what appeared to be the largest of the buildings. Light shown from cracks in the door and voices were loud from inside.

"This is where Hendricks said he'd be," Chris told Will, having to raise his voice above the noise.

Hating to have to enter yet another tavern, especially here, Will nodded and pushed the door open resolutely. A scene of loud, boisterous behavior met them as they scanned the room. Will was repulsed. The floor of the tavern held just about as much garbage as the streets and between that and the smell of rum and ale, it was a struggle not to become sick. After a long look, Chris shook his head. "I don't see Hendricks."

"Where do you think he is?" Will asked. *What if he gave up on us?*

"There's only one quick way to find out," Chris knew.

He and Will worked their way to the middle of the crowded room and stopped. Leaning close to Will, Chris warned, "Beware, this could get a little rough."

After a moment, he spoke loudly, making sure he could be heard by everyone except those who were the most drunk. "We're here to see Captain Hendricks."

Quietness swept through the room with surprising speed. Everyone turned to stare at them. Will barely had a chance to feel uncomfortable before pistols clicked loudly behind them.

"Drop the swords," a man growled.

Without hesitation, Will and Chris removed their sword belts and dropped them. Two men quickly scooped them up.

"Move."

A pistol barrel was driven hard into Will's back, and he stepped forward. He and Chris were guided to the back of the tavern and up a very narrow staircase. Rats scurried away from them along the way. At the top of the stairs was a long hallway and some doors. One of the men knocked on the first door.

"Yes?" Hendricks called from inside.

"The boy's here."

"Bring him in," Hendricks instructed eagerly.

The door opened, and Will and Chris were pushed inside. Will quickly scanned the small room, hoping to see his father and Daniel, but it was only Hendricks, sitting at the far side of a crooked table, leering at them. He looked slowly back and forth between Will and Chris. Will could almost feel how tense Chris was, and he remembered again

412

what had happened to his uncle under the pirate captain's command.

"What? Did she decide to trade the two of you instead of her precious ship?" Hendricks said finally. "I'm rather surprised. I thought she loved you."

"She decided not to trade anyone," Will told him indignantly.

Hendricks smirked. "I bet you decided to save her the trouble and just come yourself."

"I would have, but we're not here in trade, we're here to offer you something else."

Hendricks shook his head dismissively. "I told Miss McHenry what I want, and if she doesn't come and tell me I can have you and her ship, I'm just going to kill you and your uncle and the deal is off."

He pointed a loaded pistol at Will, but Will didn't flinch.

"I think you'll want to hear what we have to say," he said confidently.

Hendricks scoffed. "There's nothing you could offer me that would make me reconsider the deal."

"We wouldn't have come if we weren't sure you'd want what we have to offer," Will argued.

Finally, Hendricks' curiosity seemed piqued.

"All right, but I'm only listening because I want to see what kind of pathetic, desperate plan you've come up with." He motioned to a chair across from him. "Sit down."

"Not until you and your men put your pistols away."

Narrowing his eyes, Hendricks reluctantly slipped his pistol into his belt. His men did the same, and Will slowly sat down.

"Now, what could you possibly offer me that would be worth as much as your life and a very valuable ship?"

413

Keeping his eyes on the man, Will reached into his pocket for the Monarrez map and laid it on the table. Before he could speak, Hendricks started laughing loudly.

"You think I'd trade for that?" he mocked. "I know everything on it by memory. It's worthless to me."

Will quickly cut in. "No. But I'm quite sure you'd trade for what the map leads to."

The laughter subsided immediately as Will's statement wiped Hendricks' face clean of all humor. "You figured it out?"

"Yes," Will answered, eyes steady on Hendricks' face.

Hendricks shifted uncomfortably in his chair. "And you know where the treasure is?"

Will nodded.

"How do I know that for sure?" Hendricks questioned suspiciously.

"Because I can show you the answers to the clues."

"Do it."

Will took the locket from his neck, opened it, and set it on the map. "That is what you needed. The designs are letters, only backwards. You need a mirror to read them. That's what *hidden in metal, revealed by glass* means. The locket tells the name of the island and holds directions to the treasure."

Hendricks stared at it intently for a moment and then started chuckling low and menacingly as he pulled out his pistol again.

"Thanks for the information, boy," He smirked triumphantly. "Too bad you just gave away all you had to bargain with."

Will showed no reaction but said simply, "The treasure isn't there anymore."

Hendricks' smirk vanished as quickly as it had appeared.

"What?" he demanded.

"Do you really think I'd give you the location without first making sure you'd make a deal with us?"

Hendricks was furious. "Where is it?"

"We moved it and hid it again. This time you will have no clues to find it," Will warned, "so unless you make a deal with us, no one will ever find it." Hoping to make Hendricks want it all the more, Will continued, bluffing just a little but fairly certain he was right. "My cousin was going to use the treasure to pay you for helping him. What do you think you'll get now? Nothing he could give you would ever be near what that treasure is worth. You're only choice is to trade with us unless you're loyal enough to Stephan to help him without pay."

"I don't care about Stephan," Hendricks spat. "I'd catch him for you myself in return for the treasure."

"All we want is for you to safely release my father and Captain McHenry."

"I'll release anyone you want me too," Hendricks declared greedily.

"Come to the docks," Will said. "You release them, and we'll give you the exact location of the treasure."

Hendricks nodded. "My men and I will meet you there."

"If anything goes wrong, you won't see a penny of that treasure," Will warned.

Hendricks shook his head. "I don't care what happens to any of you, which is lucky because it makes no difference to me if you all go free just so long as I get the treasure."

Glad of that, Will picked up the locket and the map and stepped over to Chris.

Before leaving, Chris looked at Hendricks. "We want our swords back."

"I'll give them to you back at the docks," Hendricks said.

415

"No. We're not about to go back through that room downstairs, let alone the streets, without them."

Hendricks stared at him for a long moment, smiling in a most unnerving way. Will glanced at Chris. His uncle stared right back at Hendricks, unflinching. Will had great respect for him knowing how hard it had to be to face someone who had treated you so cruelly, especially knowing they were at Hendricks' mercy.

Finally, Hendricks nodded to his men, and they handed Will and Chris their swords. Without looking back, they left the room and went back down the narrow staircase, keeping their hands on their sword hilts as all eyes watched them walk silently out the tavern door.

Walking quickly back along the dark, foul-smelling streets, Will looked at Chris.

"Do you think we can trust him to keep his end of the bargain?" Hendricks was the kind of man you could not read, and Will worried that he might be the one tricking them.

"He really can't afford not to," Chris replied. "He is ruled by his greed, and it won't allow him to jeopardize the treasure."

When at last they came within sight of the docks, everyone hurried to meet them. They were all nearly bursting with questions.

"How did it go?" Caleb asked on behalf of everyone.

"He accepted the trade," Will told them. "He's bringing my father and Captain McHenry here."

There was a unified sigh of relief from everyone.

"Did he give you any trouble?" John asked.

"At first he didn't want to even consider a different trade," Will answered, "but once he realized it was the treasure we were bargaining with, he agreed to everything."

"Good."

Knowing Hendricks would be along shortly, they turned anxious eyes towards town. Will focused his eyes into the darkness. What was it going to be like to see his father for the first time? And under such awful circumstances. He breathed deeply after a few moments, and then he felt Skye take his hand and hold it tightly. He looked at her and smiled. At that moment, Will heard John say, "Here 'e comes."

Looking anxiously ahead, Will and Skye saw Hendricks appearing from one of the streets with several of his men; however, Edward and Daniel were not with them. Will frowned when Hendricks came to a stop a couple of feet away.

"Where are they?" Will demanded.

"Very close, but before you see them, I want to know if you can show me something of the treasure. For all I know, you might not have the treasure at all."

Without answering, John motioned to two of his men on the dock. They picked up a large object and carried it towards them. It was the one chest they had left on the *Grace*. They set it down in front of Hendricks and lifted the lid revealing the shimmering gold inside. Hendricks' eyes popped.

"How much of this is there?"

"There are twenty-seven chests exactly like this one," Chris told him.

Hendricks beckoned to someone they couldn't see. From behind a building several yards away, two more of Hendricks men appeared guiding Edward and Daniel. Will felt his breath catch when he saw his father. Their eyes locked as Edward was led towards them. For this tiny space of time and despite the gravity of the situation, there was nothing but the fact they were seeing one another, finally.

"Will," Edward murmured once they stopped, a corner of his mouth lifting, his joy so great in spite of all that was happening around them.

Will could barely speak, but his eyes traveled over his father's face as he said one word. "Father."

Relieved to have his brother back again, Chris looked at Hendricks. "Let them go."

"Tell you what," Hendricks began. "I'll let you have one of them while you take me to the treasure. Once I see it, I'll give you the other one."

Chris shook his head. "No. We want both of them. The treasure means nothing to us so we have no reason to lie to you about it."

"I don't trust you any more than you would trust me," Hendricks snarled. "We're doing most of this your way, and it's time to do something my way." It was obvious he would accept nothing less than what he'd demanded. "And just so no one gets any ideas, we'll each go with one ship and an equal number of men. That's how it's going to be. Keep this in mind, I know that I could kill one of them, and you'd still trade the treasure for the other one so don't push me."

Chris glared at him, but it seemed they had no choice.

When no one spoke, Hendricks asked, "Which one do you want me to release?"

The choice was left up to Will and Skye as everyone looked at them. Will stared at his father wishing so much for him to be free, but another part of him knew how much Skye longed to have her father safe. He had just decided that his father would understand if he asked for Daniel to be released when Skye's voice penetrated his thoughts.

"Release Mr. James."

Both Will and Hendricks looked at her in surprise.

"Skye . . ." Will protested.

"It's all right, Will," Skye murmured. She looked amazingly sure of her decision.

Will could only look at her as Hendricks' men un-chained Edward's hands, and Hendricks told him to go. Edward glanced at Daniel who nodded in support of his daughter's decision. Walking straight to Will, Edward dragged his son into his arms. For a moment there was nothing else, just this, everything else just seemed to disappear.

"Will, I can't believe you're really right here," Edward said, his voice rough with emotion.

At first Will's throat constricted. Finally, he managed to say, "I've been waiting so long for this."

"So have I," Edward murmured. "So have I."

Their happy reunion was cut short as Hendricks' voice cut in.

"So where is the treasure?"

Chris took charge of the situation. "As long as you still have Daniel, we won't tell you exactly where it is. It's a few hours north of here. We'll show it to you."

Hendricks didn't seem especially pleased with that answer, but he made no trouble. The Monarrez Treasure was an obsessive incentive.

"When are we leaving?" he asked.

"Whenever you want to."

"How about now," Hendricks suggested impatiently.

Chris nodded. "We can do that."

"Since the McHenry's ship is the same size as mine, that is the one I'll go with," Hendricks decided.

"Is that all right, Skye?" Chris asked.

"Yes," Skye answered with a nod.

"How many men do you have in your crew?" Chris asked Hendricks.

"Fifty-three."

Chris nodded. "We'll match that number."

Satisfied, Hendricks told a couple of his men to go find the rest of the crew still back at the tavern and to meet him on the ship.

"Some of my men will be happy to fill your crew," John told Skye.

"Thank you, John," Skye said, but she was distracted.

As Hendricks and his men started to move towards the *Nightshade*, Skye stepped forward and stopped them.

"Captain Hendricks. May I please have a moment with my father?"

Hendricks looked at her, very tempted to say no after all the trouble she had caused him, but he nodded, not willing to do anything to risk the treasure.

"Very quickly," he muttered grudgingly.

Skye hurried to her father. He had a smile for her.

"I'm so thankful to see that you are safe," Daniel said. "Hendricks told me that you had been shot."

"I'm fine. My arm was only grazed."

"That relieves me." And then he said, "I'm glad you chose to release Edward."

Skye smiled and glanced at Will and his father. "It's so good to finally see them together."

Hendricks' voice broke in, saying their time was almost up. Looking at the crew, Daniel said, "It looks like you've done a good job as captain."

Skye smiled again, though it was with some sadness. "I'm trying, but we all miss you."

"It won't be much longer," Daniel told her comfortingly.

They could tell that Hendricks was getting impatient.

"I love you, Father," Skye said.

"I love you too, Skye."

Though he couldn't hug her back because of his chains, Skye hugged him tightly. As she did, she whispered in his ear, "We have a plan to capture Hendricks."

He nodded so slightly only she noticed, and Skye reluctantly stepped away from him. Still, she kept her eyes on him until Hendricks took him onto the *Nightshade*. Skye finally turned back to her crew, and they headed to the *Grace*. Pausing on the docks between it and the *Finder*, John said, "You need thirty-nine men." He lowered his voice a bit. "Levi and I can't go because Lieutenant Graham knows us. Worthy can't either, but except for a few of Kate's men who helped us rescue Will, anyone could go. It's actually a good thing that Hendricks only wants the *Grace* to go so Lieutenant Graham won't see us."

Skye nodded. "Yes, that is good." She looked around at everyone. "Who wants to go?"

Quickly, many of the men volunteered to go with her, as did Kate.

"We'll meet you north of the cove after everything is taken care of," John told them just before they boarded. "We'll make sure to sail well around Lieutenant Graham without bein' seen." He looked at Kate. "Be careful," he said. "I still have somethin' to say to you."

"I'll still make sure you do," Kate told him with a smile. "You nearly have me dyin' with curiosity."

"Well, I didn't mean for it to be like that," John apologized, suddenly self-conscious.

"It's all right," Kate told him, amused. "We'll talk soon enough."

Within the next few minutes, the *Grace* and the *Nightshade* were ready to go. The *Grace* took the lead, and they left the *Finder* and *Half Moon* behind. Skye didn't like having to leave without them, but she was glad for everyone she had with her. At least if the worst happened and Hendricks did decide to attack, they could put up a good fight.

421

Chapter Thirty

O nce the harbor lay behind them, Skye put Caleb in control of the wheel and left the quarterdeck in search of Will and Edward. They had helped cast off and were still helping the crew, but Skye knew how anxious they must be to talk. She wanted to give them that opportunity.

"I want you to use my father's cabin," Skye said to them, "to spend some time together. I don't think I'll sleep tonight, and if I decide to, I'll sleep in my cabin. That will give you a good place to talk where you won't be disturbed."

"Are you sure?" Will asked, liking this idea very much.

"Yes, I want you to."

"Thank you for this, Skye," he said, grateful for her thoughtfulness, "but let me know if you need me."

With that gentle push from Skye, Will and his father went directly down to the cabin. Lighting a couple of lamps, they sat down at the table. For a long moment, neither of them spoke, and then they both laughed softly.

"Where do we begin?" Edward wondered.

Will shook his head, at a loss as well, but happily so. "I don't know. There's so much."

"Yes, there is," Edward agreed. "It is amazing. After all the years I've been praying and waiting to see how God would answer, I can still barely believe you're right here with me."

"I know. I've gone my whole life without knowing I had a family. I never even knew your name until last month."

"That must have been hard for you," Edward said sadly. "I'm sorry your mother didn't leave you the whole locket so you would at least have known our names." He sighed realizing now, after all these years of hoping Will would find him, that without possessing both halves of the locket Will would never have had the means to even try. "There are a lot of things I'm sorry about, and I blame myself for them."

"Why?"

"Because this may never have happened if I hadn't done some of the things I did. I knew your mother was not a Christian, Will, but I married her anyway when I knew I shouldn't have. If I had been patient she might have become a believer and your life might have turned out differently. You've had to pay for my sin, and I'm sorry."

Will hated for his father to feel so bad, especially now so he said, "Though I've gone through some very difficult times, for the most part, I've had a very good life. I've experienced and witnessed some amazing things from God and have been blessed greatly."

"I am so thankful for that. It helps relieve some of the guilt I've felt all these years. I don't know if I can explain how horrible it has been thinking you might never know Christ, and it would be my fault." He brushed away a tear that had fallen down his cheek. Tears had pooled in Will's eyes too. Clearing his throat, Edward said, "Thank God for Skye, the answer to countless prayers."

Will smiled. "Yes. She has been, without a doubt, the greatest influence God has used in my life. If it weren't for her, I wouldn't be who I am today."

423

"She's quite an amazing young woman," Edward remarked.

"She is," Will agreed. "I love her so much. She's such a gift."

"I'm so happy that you have her," Edward said. "Daniel told me that he gave you permission to marry her in his letter. Does she know yet?"

"No," Will answered. "I never told her. After we got the letters we went through such a hard time, but even after we made plans to rescue you, I decided instead to wait to talk to Captain McHenry in person. I'd almost feel as though I was taking advantage of a bad situation if I didn't."

"That's a very good decision," Edward said. "I'm proud of you for it."

Feeling the warmth of his father's approval, Will said, "Thank you. I'm glad you approve."

"I approve of far more than just that," Edward said earnestly, the tone of his voice as proud as any father could be.

There was no end to all that Will and his father found to talk about. Hours passed with no notice at all as Will began first to tell his father about all that had happened after Dreger had taken him in Lucea. After that, they spoke of whatever came to mind. The hum of their voices brought a smile to anyone who was near the cabin.

When morning finally arrived, Will and Edward left the cabin for the first time all night. The ship's deck was busy with the full crew and many wished them good morning as they passed by. Will looked around for Skye and spotted her just coming up from below. Turning to his father, he said, "Excuse me for a minute."

Edward smiled. "Of course."

Will quickly crossed the deck and met Skye as she made her way towards the bow.

"Good morning, Skye," he said cheerfully.

Skye smiled up into his handsome face. "Good morning." She could see that, though he had been up all night, Will's joy hid any lack of sleep.

"Skye, I want to thank you again for choosing my father last night. I can't even explain what it was like being able to talk to him. I'm so sorry your father isn't here right now too."

"It's all right," Skye assured him. "He'll be with us in a couple of hours. And I am so happy for you and your father. In a way, I know exactly how you must be feeling."

Will smiled, knowing that she did, having thought her father dead for many years before they found each other again.

"Are you hungry?" Skye asked suddenly.

Will hadn't even thought about eating, but now he realized he was very hungry. "Yes, I am."

"Good, Corey just made breakfast. Everyone is just sort of helping themselves. If you want, I can have food brought to the cabin for you and your father."

"Only if you'll eat with us," Will said. "And Chris, and Kate and Caleb too, if they'd like."

"I'd love to," Skye said with a smile. "Kate and Caleb have already eaten, but I don't think Chris has. I'll go ask him, and then I'll tell Corey to bring the food."

Will walked back to his father as Skye went below again.

"Skye is going to have food brought to the cabin, and she and Chris are going to join us."

"Good," Edward smiled. "It will be nice to have them eat with us."

He and Will returned to the cabin and in a matter of minutes, Skye, and Chris and Corey, came carrying trays of food. Corey quickly set out the food and dishes for them at the table.

"Thank you, Corey," Skye said.

"You're welcome, Captain."

As he left the cabin and everyone sat down, Skye said, "I'm glad my father will be taking over again. I'm not sure I could ever get used to being called captain."

The three men smiled.

"How are you this morning, Skye?" Edward inquired.

"Good," Skye answered. "Of course, I'll be even better once this is over."

"Thank you so much for the difficult choice you made last night. I'm so grateful to you for giving me this time to spend with Will.

"It was what my father and I both wanted," Skye said. "Besides, Will almost got killed once protecting my father. The least I could do was free you and trust God to keep my father safe."

"Still, thank you," Edward said again.

Skye smiled gently. "You're welcome. It brings me much joy to see you together."

Just before they started dishing up the warm food, Skye asked Edward if he would like to pray. After a most heartfelt prayer, they filled their plates and ate hungrily.

"How were you treated by Hendricks?" Chris asked.

"A bit rough, needless to say, but nothing like what we could have been," Edward answered.

They were all relieved to hear it. Especially in light of the fact Hendricks still held Daniel prisoner.

"I'm sure Will has told you about Stephan," Chris assumed.

Edward nodded somberly. "Yes, he did. In one way I find it hard to believe, yet in another, I don't."

Chris sighed. "You know how things are between us, but I never would have suspected he'd do anything like this. We're his family. You've been like a father to him for so many years. And yet he was going to have you killed." Chris was sickened by the thought.

"Jealousy and greed are such terrible things," Edward said sadly. "I've always known that Stephan struggled in that area but not to this extent."

"What are you going to do once we get home?"

"It's going to be hard," Edward admitted. "We'll have to find him if he's not there. I just hate to think of one of our own in prison."

"I know," Chris agreed, "but he might try something else if he's not locked up, and I'm not just saying that because of the animosity between us."

Edward nodded, troubled. "I know."

Not long before they finished eating, there was a knock on the cabin door.

"Come in," Skye called.

The door opened, and Caleb stepped in.

"I wanted to let you know that we should reach the cove within an hour."

Skye nodded. "Thank you, Caleb."

He stepped back out, and Skye looked at Will.

"We've made good time. I hope Lieutenant Graham is ready for us."

"I'm sure he is. He said he'd be ready last evening."

Finishing what little of their breakfast was left, the four of them took places on deck. Skye returned to the wheel to take over the rest of the way, and Will and his father worked with the busy crew.

The miles passed swiftly, one after the other, as the shoreline slipped past. Finally, Skye spotted the cove up ahead. As they drew closer, they could see no hint of human presence. Graham had hidden his men and his ships well.

Within minutes, they came to the mouth of the cove, and the two ships slowed. The *Grace* led the way into the center of it and stopped. Skye made certain that everything was ready to make a quick escape without letting it be obvious that was what she was doing. The *Nightshade* stopped alongside of them, and Caleb joined Skye and Will, and Chris and Edward at the rail. Hendricks stood across from them.

"It's right there, Hendricks," Skye said pointing to the clearing where the chests were sitting. "All of it. Now let my father go."

Hendricks took a good look at the chests and finally nodded to Dreger who disappeared below for a long moment. Skye sighed in relief when he led her father up. He was brought over to Hendricks who unchained his hands. A plank was hastily laid across the railing by Skye's men, and Hendricks motioned to it.

"You're free to leave."

Before Hendricks had a chance to reconsider, Daniel hurried across. Skye was at the end to meet him. Immediately they embraced, but only for a moment. Skye knew that they had to get out of the cove so that Graham's ships could sail in. She turned to the men.

"All right, we're done here."

As agreed, Caleb quickly took the wheel and everyone worked together to sail away. Skye stayed with her father near the rail and kept a close watch on the *Nightshade* in case Hendricks decided to attack. However, it seemed that Hendricks had already forgotten them as no one even cared to watch the *Grace* leave. Still, Skye was immensely relieved when they reached the mouth of the cove and were out of range of the *Nightshade's* cannons. Just as they left the cove, they spotted Lieutenant Graham's two ships sailing towards them.

The *Grace* did not sail far. Instead they anchored where they could still see the mouth of the cove into which Graham's ships had just disappeared. Some shouting echoed from a distance and a few cannon shots rang out, but then there was only the sound of the waves lapping at the *Grace's* hull.

While waiting for the ships to reappear so they could learn the outcome of what had sounded like a very brief battle, Skye turned to Daniel with her full attention. How thankful she was now that they were all safe. Daniel's rescue seemed to finally mark the end of their long struggle. Skye smiled brightly as her father opened his arms to hug her again.

"We're safe," she said joyfully. "We're all safe."

"God has once again displayed His power and protection," Daniel said.

"Yes, He has." They reveled in that feeling for a long and glorious moment, and then Skye looked at her father seriously. "Before we get to anything else, I want to say that now that you're back, you are captain of the ship."

"You look like you've done a fine job," Daniel commended. "Are you sure you don't want to keep the position?"

"Absolutely. We're all used to you as captain. We're not ready for that kind of change. It just wouldn't be the same if the *Grace* wasn't captained by Daniel McHenry."

Daniel smiled. "Well then, I'll be glad to be captain again."

Hearing this, the crew along with Edward and Will came forward and welcomed him back. They were all so happy for his safe return. When Daniel saw Kate, he was especially delighted. "It's good to see you again, Captain Kate."

"You too, Captain McHenry," Kate said. "I'm very happy that you're safely back aboard yer ship."

A short time later, they all spotted ships leaving the cove. First came Lieutenant Graham's two ships and then the *Nightshade* followed. A proud British flag fluttered from her mizzenmast. Everyone aboard the *Grace* cheered and clapped with joy. It felt so good to finally have everything right again.

Once clear of the cove, the lead ship changed course and sailed towards them. After bringing the two ships together, Lieutenant Graham boarded the *Grace* with good news.

"We have Hendricks and his entire crew captive," he informed them. "He surrendered with only a minor struggle."

The joy was evident in everyone's smiles as Graham continued. "They will be taken back to Fort Camden where they will be dealt with."

"Thank you so much for helping us, Lieutenant Graham," Will said.

"You're more than welcome," Graham replied. "I really should be thanking all of you. You delivered Hendricks to us. Actually, there is a reward for his capture."

Will glanced at Skye before looking back to Graham and shaking his head.

"I think I can speak for everyone when I say keep the reward. We have all the reward we need."

Knowing of whom he spoke, Graham smiled and looked at Daniel and Edward, now rescued and safe at last. "You must be Mr. James and Captain McHenry. It's an honor to meet you both."

"We're very pleased to meet you, too, Lieutenant," Edward replied. "Thank you for your help."

Graham shook his head remorsefully. "I'm afraid I wasn't of much help to your son in the beginning."

"It was an honest mistake," Edward said. "No one blames you for it, least of all Will."

"I am glad," Graham said, genuinely relieved.

"Lieutenant Graham," Skye spoke after a moment.

"Yes, Miss McHenry?"

"We wanted to talk to you about the treasure and what should be done with it now."

Graham shrugged easily. "You are the ones who found it and went to the trouble of securing it so I don't see why you shouldn't keep it. I'm sure you'll find something to do with it."

Skye nodded readily. "It certainly will be put to good use."

"I'm sure it will," Graham replied with a smile.

Having nothing further to discuss, Graham prepared to leave the ship, however, he paused, looking back at them with a little grin.

"When you happen to see your friends again, *Captain* John Morgan and Mr. Worthington, tell them that I said hello."

Skye and Will looked at each other in surprise and a bit of uncertainty.

"You know about John?" Will said finally.

Graham nodded. "I realized that his name sounded familiar, and eventually I figured out why."

"We can explain," Will began.

Graham shook his head and smiled. "There's no need. As far as I'm concerned, they are not pirates. Any friends of yours must be good men."

"They are," Will said. "And neither of them will be doing any pirating except from other pirates."

Graham nodded. "I've heard that Morgan became a 'Daniel McHenry' as people say." He paused, glancing at Kate meaningfully as he spoke. "I also heard he sails with another ship captained by a woman, an ex-slave."

Kate spoke before anyone else could. "Aye, that's true, Lieutenant."

"Well, I wish them both the very best of luck," Graham said with a smile.

Kate smiled back. "They will be very pleased to hear that."

Graham nodded and looked back at Will. "Be sure to tell Captain Morgan that he made a very convincing Lieutenant."

Will grinned. "I will."

"Now, I'd best not keep my men waiting," Graham said. "Goodbye everyone."

"Lieutenant," Edward said, "if you're ever near Port Henry, we'd love for you to visit."

"And the same goes if you are ever down south near Kingston," Daniel added.

"I would enjoy that," Graham said. "Maybe someday I can do both."

With a last goodbye, Graham boarded his ship and sailed it slowly away to join the others. Everyone on the *Grace* stood together at the rail watching the three ships shrink into the southern horizon.

Kate broke the silence that had settled over them. "It's gonna be interestin' to see John's reaction when we tell 'im that Lieutenant Graham knows who we are."

"Yes, it will be," Skye agreed, the thought bringing a smile to her face and everyone else's.

Daniel looked at her. "So, what are our plans now?"

"We should find John. We are supposed to meet him north of here."

With Skye's blessing, Daniel took his rightful place at the *Grace's* helm and after giving a couple of orders they were sailing north. As they kept a look out for the *Finder* and the *Half Moon*, Will and Skye discussed the treasure with Edward and Chris.

"Skye and I think you and Chris should be the ones to decide what to do with it," Will told his father. "However, we thought that if you like the idea, we could give it to John and Kate, and Silas, to help bring more people to the island and buy more supplies."

Having been informed all about the island by Will and Chris, Edward nodded. "I think that is a perfect idea."

"I think so too," Chris said.

Will smiled. "God provided the treasure for us to use, and now He can use it."

A few miles up the coast they came to a rocky point. Hidden just on the other side were the *Finder* and the *Half Moon*. Everyone waved gladly as soon as they saw each other. Quickly, the ships were brought together, and they all gathered on the deck of the *Finder* because it was the largest.

John stepped forward with a grin. "Well, since Captain McHenry is here, I take it that all went well."

Will nodded. "Yes. Hendricks didn't give us any trouble, and Lieutenant Graham captured them easily."

"No trouble?"

Will shook his head. "They only put up a small fight."

"Did you talk to Lieutenant Graham?" John asked.

"Yes, we did," Will told him with a hint of amusement.

"What did 'e say?"

"Well, for one thing there was a reward for Hendricks' capture, but we didn't accept it."

John nodded approvingly.

"And . . ." Will paused as a grin came to his face, ". . . he told us to tell our friends, *Captain* John Morgan and Mr. Worthington hello."

John's eyes widened and his brows lifted. "He knows?"

"Yes," Will answered. "I'm quite certain he knew who Kate was too."

"What did 'e do?"

"Nothing. As far as he's concerned, you're not pirates."

John looked relieved. "Well, that's nice to know. You had me just a bit worried. So, did 'e take the treasure?"

"No," Will answered. "He said we should keep it, and we've already decided what we think would be the best thing to do with it."

"What's that?" John asked.

With a smile, Will answered. "We're going to give it to you and Kate, and Silas, to bring more people to the island and buy the supplies you need."

John and Kate were stunned.

"Are you sure?" John asked. "I mean, even just a part of it would be enough."

"We are very sure," Will replied. "God gave us the treasure and in this way we feel we're giving it back to Him."

John shook his head in disbelief. "I don't know what to say or how to thank you. We've been able to do quite a lot with what we get, but with the treasure we'll be able to do more than we ever imagined."

In very high spirits, all three ships returned to the cove where the treasure was awaiting them. Feeling jubilant and thankful, they loaded it one more time. Standing together on the beach afterwards, John looked at Will and the others from the *Grace*.

"I hate for this to be goodbye, but I was thinkin' that as long as we're all loaded up with supplies, it'd be the perfect opportunity to pick up some things before we return to the island. And I'm sure you'll be goin' back right away and will be gone by the time we return."

Will nodded, wishing they could go back together but knowing that John was right. "I'm sure everyone on the island would love to have you come back with some new things."

"They will have all of you to thank for it," John said.

"Well, it's partly our way of saying thank you to everyone for the help you've all given us," Will said. "I owe you my life, John."

John smiled and shrugged. "You would have done the same for me." There was a long pause, and John sighed. "I hate goodbyes."

Everyone agreed with him.

"At least it seems more likely now that we'll meet again," Skye said optimistically. "After all, I would love to visit the island again sometime, and you and Kate will be there often, right?"

John nodded.

"Then I'm sure this won't be our last goodbye."

Encouraged by those words, they each took turns saying goodbye to John and his crew. After her farewell, Skye walked over to Kate.

"Will you go with John," she asked, "or return to the island with us?"

"I think I'll go with John," Kate decided. "Together we could bring a lotta things back." And then she grinned. "Besides, if I don't find out soon what it is John wants to tell me, I don't know what I'll do."

Skye smiled, her eyes twinkling. "I don't blame you. I'd love to know too."

"It's too bad we can't keep in touch somehow," Kate said regretfully.

"Maybe we can," Skye said in such a way she attracted Kate's interest. "I was thinking of asking Mr. James if I can send letters to them which you can then pick up somehow. That way they can also send letters for you."

Kate smiled. "That's a wonderful idea, Skye. It would be so nice to be able to keep in touch and know what's goin' on with each other."

"It certainly would be," Skye agreed.

"I'm so glad we've gotten to see each other again."

"I am too. You and John were the last ones I ever expected would come to our rescue."

"I know, we never thought you would show up here." Knowing they couldn't keep talking for much longer, Kate said quickly, "I'm so thankful to have you as my friend, Skye. I've never had a friend like you."

Skye smiled and they hugged. "And I am thankful to have you as my friend too. I wish circumstances were different so we could see each other more often."

"It may never be that way here," Kate said, "but in Heaven we'll get to see each other whenever we want."

Skye smiled at that. "It will be wonderful."

As Skye and Kate finished their goodbye, there was someone in particular Will wanted to speak with. He worked his way through everyone until he came to Worthy.

"I guess this is goodbye for us too," Worthy said. "I spoke with Captain Morgan this morning, and he has added me to his crew, just as you said he would."

"Worthy, I'm so glad," Will said with a big smile. "I really didn't want you to turn yourself in."

"At least this way I can help people. I'm giving God full control of my life."

"I'm sure He will use you to help a lot of people," Will said.

"I pray that He does."

"I want to thank you once more for how you've helped me," Will said turning very serious. "My time on the *Seabird* would have been much more difficult if you had not been there. I don't think I could have survived."

"I'm glad for that, Will, because you've helped me in a far greater way."

Finally, the time came to leave, and Will and the others got into the boats.

"Tell Mrs. James and the girls, 'specially Emma, that we said goodbye," John said.

"We will," Edward promised. "And Captain Morgan, if you and Captain Kate are ever able, we'd love to have you for a visit. You'd be safe in our house."

John smiled. "We might just have to do that."

After one last round of quick goodbyes, the boats were pushed off and they rowed towards the *Grace*. Everyone waved as they sailed out of the cove until their friends on the beach were lost from sight. A quietness settled over the ship as it sailed through the open water alone. The horribleness of the last month was fading quickly. The ship itself seemed almost to breathe a sigh of relief.

For a long time, Will and Skye stood at the railing where they'd been waving goodbye. Neither spoke for both were tired after their sleepless night. Eventually, Will put his arm gently around Skye. Smiling, Skye leaned her head against him with a contented sigh.

"It feels like such a long time since we left Kingston, doesn't it?" Skye said finally.

"Yes, it does. A very long time."

Silence settled again, but after a time, Will heard Skye giggle slightly.

"What?" he asked.

"Oh, I was just thinking about John and Kate. I wonder what it is that John wants so badly to tell her."

Will smiled. "I know."

Skye turned her head to look up at him. "You do?"

Will nodded. "He talked to me about it."

"Can you tell me or is it private?"

"I don't think he'd mind if I told you," Will answered. "He is in love with Kate."

Skye looked surprised. "He is?"

"Yes."

"For how long?"

"A long time. Since before we even met them," Will said. "Matthew and I realized it that day we rescued you and Kate from that island after the storm."

"You've known about it for that long?"

"Yes. I would have told you, but I wasn't sure if I should because at that time John was still denying it."

"He's never told her all this time?"

"No. He's afraid that Kate won't feel the same way."

Skye smiled. "I don't think he had to worry that much."

"Does she love him?"

"I think she does," Skye answered. "She has never said so, but there are things she has said which have caused me to think so."

Smiling, Will nodded. "That's good."

"Yes, they are perfect for each other."

Just like we are, Will thought, and the two of them settled into another companionable silence.

A vivid, dazzling sunset lit the island's harbor when they arrived three days later just as it had the first time Will and Skye had come to the island. Having been spotted from a distance, the beach was already full of people when they docked. Rebecca and the girls were the very first ones to meet them as they walked down the dock. Edward hurried forward and hugged his family joyously. Will and Chris joined them, and Skye got to see Will with his whole family for the first time. It brought tears to her eyes.

"They are a beautiful family," Daniel said, coming alongside her.

"Yes, they are," Skye murmured.

Silas met them next, and Will and Skye were happy to introduce him to their fathers. When he inquired about John and Kate, they told him about the treasure. He could not have been more thankful for their generous gift. The news spread quickly, and everyone showed their gratitude.

As soon as they reached the village, Shauna and some of the other women heated up supper for them. Everyone crowded around them while they ate, and they told them all about the rescue and Hendricks' capture. Though there were a lot of questions waiting to be asked, Silas could see that

Will and the others were growing weary since two nights had not been enough to make up for lost sleep.

Soon after they had finished eating and the island had grown dark, Silas brought the questions to an end. Although they enjoyed speaking with everyone and answering their questions, Will and the others were happy to be shown where to sleep. Will and the crew slept in the men's house with Daniel and Chris, and Skye was glad to share beds with the girls while Edward and Rebecca were given a room of their own in a different house. But for a few last murmurs coming from the men's house and a couple of happy giggles from the girls in the women's house, everyone drifted off into very peaceful sleep.

The *Grace* stayed in the island's harbor for one final day which everyone spent to the fullest. The girls spent their time in the company of new friends they had made, and Will and the others spent time visiting and answering questions that remained. The portion of the treasure that was on the *Grace* was unloaded in the morning and taken to one of the storehouses, but not before everyone got a chance to see the wonder of it with their very own eyes. There was no end to the words of gratitude they offered.

That night, the people gave a small celebration to show their joy for the gift they had been given and thankfulness to God for His having protected everyone. It was a wonderful night that they would not soon forget.

Finally, it was time to say goodbye to everyone on the island. Most they said goodbye to up in the village, but some, like Silas and his family, followed them down to the beach.

"I could spend all day thanking you for what you've done for us," Silas said at the dock.

"The same is true of us," Will replied. "Your hospitality has meant a great deal."

"It's our pleasure to help anyone in need," Silas said. "We have loved having every one of you here."

"I wish I could have gotten more done for you to show you how grateful I am."

"What you got done is wonderful," Silas said. "And with the treasure we can finally hire a blacksmith though I must say that I will miss you working there. You do such excellent work."

Will smiled, touched. "Thank you, Silas."

Once everyone managed to say goodbye, they boarded the *Grace*. As it sailed away, Emma and a few others called goodbye to each other one last time before they were out on the open ocean heading towards Port Henry.

～～～

The moon and stars glittered on the surface of the water as the James' white house was spotted in the darkness. They anchored near shore and used boats to get to land. When Will and his family, and Skye and her father along with Caleb, made it ashore, a couple of the crewman returned the boats to the ship and prepared to sail it into the Port Henry harbor and moor it there. Everyone remaining on the beach trudged quietly towards the house anxious to reach the comfort of their beds. However, as they drew near, they were surprised to see that there was a light glowing inside. Edward held up a hand, and they all stopped.

"I bet Stephan's in there," Chris murmured. "He probably didn't expect us to come back."

He pulled out one of the pistols they'd brought as a safety precaution and snuck up to one of the drawing room windows. After a quick glance, he returned to the group.

"It's him. He's going through one of the desks. We can sneak inside and catch him by surprise."

Edward nodded and they cautiously made their way to the front door.

"Stay behind us," Edward told Rebecca and his daughters. They were glad that Ashley was fast asleep in Rebecca's arms and would not make any sound to alert Stephan.

Chris eased the door open careful not to make a sound, and they entered the foyer with extreme caution. As they made their way farther into the house, they could hear Stephan rummaging through the desk. When they reached the drawing room doorway, Chris motioned for everyone to stay. Under the close watch of Edward and Daniel, Chris stealthily made his way up behind Stephan, unnoticed. Keeping his pistol aimed at him, Chris stopped a couple of feet away.

"Looking for something, Stephan?"

Stephan spun around, almost knocking some piles off the desk. His eyes widened with shock and a bit of fear.

Seeing that Stephan had no weapon, everyone else joined Chris in the room.

"So, you're all alive?" Stephan said disappointedly.

Ignoring him, Chris took Stephan by the arm and forced him over to a chair.

"Sit down," he ordered. "I think we'd all like to have a few words with you."

Stephan slowly took a seat looking up at Chris with loathing.

"I bet this is giving you great pleasure isn't it, Uncle," he asked darkly.

Chris shook his head. "No, Stephan, it's not. It saddens me very deeply that you could turn on your family like this."

Stephan scoffed. "I hardly believe that."

"We may never have gotten along, Stephan, but you are my nephew, and I have always cared about you." Chris spoke from his heart. "You may believe it or not."

"I don't," Stephan sneered.

Chris only sighed regretfully.

While everyone's attention was on the two of them, the dark figure standing in the opposite doorway stepped into the room unnoticed.

They were alerted by the sound of a pistol being cocked and an unfamiliar voice. "Drop all of your weapons or someone will get hurt."

Everyone's eyes flew towards the voice of a man with a pistol aimed in their direction.

Chris took a step back, astonished and filled with disgust. "You!"

They looked from the man to Chris and then to Edward as he murmured, "Brandon."

Chapter Thirty-one

Their hearts sank. The relief and joy they felt from their victory over Hendricks evaporated in an instant.

"I said drop your weapons," Brandon repeated sharply. He narrowed his eyes and added menacingly, "Unless you want one of the little ones to pay." He waved his pistol in Emma and Ashley's direction.

Emma shrank back against her father, and Rebecca turned a little to shield Ashley, but they had no choice. They had to obey him. One by one, the pistols clattered on the floor as they were dropped.

"Gather them up, Stephan," Brandon ordered, "and bring them to me."

With a triumphant and self-satisfied grin Stephan quickly did as he was told, putting all of the pistols in a chair near Brandon.

"Now, I've got a little surprise for you," Brandon told them maliciously. Looking once again to Stephan, he said, "Why don't you get our guest."

Stephan picked up a pistol from the pile and left the room. There was only silence as they waited for him to return. No one knew what or who to expect, and they were too stunned and horrified to speak. In a moment, they heard Stephan coming back with someone else. When he shoved the other person through the door, Skye gasped.

"Matthew!"

"What are you doing here?" Daniel stammered.

Matthew sighed, glancing coldly at Brandon. "Shortly after I got your letter, I decided to come and see if I could help. When I got here, I asked around for you and then these two found me."

"How long have you been here?"

"Four days."

"You see," Brandon cut in. "This is what happens when people don't do as they're told. He was told to stay in Kingston and, Captain McHenry, you and your daughter were told to *go back*." He motioned to Stephan. "Tie them up."

Stephan went to get some rope from another room. One by one, he tied their hands tightly behind their backs. When he came to Emma, Edward stopped him.

"Leave her," he said. "She won't be any trouble."

Stephan glanced at Brandon who gave him a quick nod. Brandon then looked at Emma and Ashley. Rebecca had been forced to put down the child who was crying softly to be held again.

"You two, sit here." Brandon pointed to a chair.

Emma looked up at Edward for guidance. He nodded.

With a look of fierce determination coming to her face, Emma took Ashley by the hand.

"Come on, Ashley," she said, all the while glaring at Stephan and Brandon.

Emma guided Ashley over to the chair and helped her up onto it. She then took a seat beside her.

"Keep an eye on them, Stephan," Brandon said.

He strode over to the group and glanced at each one of them with a frightening and thorough scrutiny. His gaze paused on Edward.

"Well, you haven't changed much," Brandon observed with a cutting tone.

"Neither have you," Edward said accusingly.

444

Brandon gave a short and humorous laugh. "No, I can't say that I have. I'm—"

"You're still the same man who would run off with another man's wife and child," Chris broke in. "And now you've added murder to the list."

Brandon moved from Edward to within a few inches of Chris. His dark eyes burned with an intense hatred and an anger which clearly reflected what a dangerous and violent man he was.

"And you certainly haven't changed much," Brandon muttered tightly. "You still don't know when to keep quiet."

"I speak only the truth."

Brandon moved even closer and said very quietly, "Know that, when the time comes, it is going to give me great pleasure to kill you."

They glared at each other for a long moment until Brandon lost interest and sauntered over to Will. He looked at him closely with an unnerving glint in his eye.

"So, you're what became of the pathetic little baby your mother chose over me. You don't seem to have amounted to much, blacksmith," Brandon spat venomously. "I heard about you and Miss McHenry. Just what could you possibly have to offer her?"

Will felt no need to lower himself by answering this man, but Skye took great offense at his words.

"He offers me all I could ever want," she said in a strong and confident voice.

Brandon switched his attention to her and seemed amused when Will moved slightly to shield her with his body.

"Miss McHenry," he said with a grin that made her skin crawl. "Stephan has told me a lot about you."

Skye's eyes were as cold as her voice. "Has he?"

"Yes, quite a bit."

"Is that supposed to flatter me? Because it doesn't."

445

Brandon chuckled and turned to Stephan. "She's a spirited one, isn't she? Did you consider that when you were trying to win her over?"

Skye spoke quickly before Stephan could. "I show respect to good men," she retorted.

Brandon only chuckled again which infuriated Skye. Her glare was lost on him as he turned to point to the sofa.

"Sit down, all of you."

They had no choice but to obey and did so solemnly. From his seat, Will looked at his family sitting across from him and then at Skye and Daniel, and Matthew and Caleb, who were on either side of him. Every one of them was in jeopardy again, right when they had thought it was over. There had to be a way out of this. Will did not believe that God had brought them safely through all the many dangers that He had only to have them die now. As they sat there, Will begged Him to intervene and provide rescue.

Chris watched Brandon as he paced between the two sofas.

"This whole thing was your idea wasn't it, Brandon? You got Stephan and Hendricks to do your dirty work for you."

"Well, I couldn't very well be seen by you, now could I?" Brandon said cuttingly. "But yes, I have no problem taking credit for the whole scheme."

"Why? Why do this?"

"Why?" Brandon shrugged, but his eyes were hard. They switched to Edward. "To ruin his life. Again. Once and for all."

Though it was obvious and not surprising to them that Brandon still wanted to cause Edward pain, it was chilling to see it in action.

Feeling fidgety when their eyes turned to him, Stephan asked, "What are we going to do with them?"

446

"I've given a lot of thought to that," Brandon said with obvious pleasure. "We'll deal with Edward, his son, and Chris ourselves. As for the McHenrys and their friend, I was thinking of handing them over to the Spanish."

"The Spanish?"

"Yes," he said, turning to include them all. "We heard about Hendricks' capture. The only way you could have gotten him to cooperate with you is if you bargained with something of great value. I'm guessing that was the Monarrez Treasure, and I'm sure the Spanish will have a thing or two to say about that."

"You're going to give them Miss McHenry too?" Stephan asked, voice rather high-pitched and taken aback.

"Unless you can somehow convince her to keep quiet and stay with you."

"Forget it," Skye muttered.

"Well, there's your answer," Brandon said to a disappointed Stephan.

"What about my wife and daughters?" Edward asked.

"They will stay here," Brandon announced, chuckling at Edward's dark look. "Oh, don't worry, I'll take good care of them."

Edward shook his head. "You have to know I would never allow that."

"I don't see that you have much—"

A loud crash and the clattering of metal from somewhere in the house interrupted Brandon's threat. He spun around to look at Stephan.

"What was that?"

Stephan shook his head worriedly. Brandon frowned and looked suspiciously towards the dark hall.

"Are you sure there's no one else here?" he asked.

"I've been here for three days and you for two," Stephan said. "We haven't seen anyone."

The frown on Brandon's face only deepened.

447

"Stay here and watch them. I'm going to have a look around. If anyone causes trouble, shoot one of the girls," Brandon told him heartlessly.

After he had left the room, Edward looked at Stephan.

"You'd really shoot one of my girls?"

Pausing briefly, Stephan shook his head. "No, but I would shoot him." He switched the aim of his pistol to Will. "Make no mistake about that."

"I never imagined you could be a killer." Edward shook his head with sadness.

"I never intended to be. Anything I've done, I was forced to do."

"That's a very lame excuse, Stephan. You wouldn't have to do any of this," Edward argued.

"You don't understand my position," he snapped back.

"No, I don't," Edward agreed. "I don't see how you could do all this just to secure your inheritance. If you were that worried, why didn't you just come and talk to me about it?"

Before Stephan could answer, they heard Brandon call from another room.

"Stephan, come give me a hand with this."

Stephan frowned. "What about watching them?"

"They'll be fine for a minute."

Stephan encompassed them all with a menacing look. "Stay exactly where you are," he ordered, hurrying to help Brandon.

As soon as they were sure he was gone, Emma suddenly jumped out of her chair and dashed over to Edward.

"Let me see if I can untie you," she said.

Edward turned his bound hands to her. She wasted no time in trying to loosen the knots.

"Listen for them to come back," Edward said to the others, deathly afraid for his daughter's safety.

Emma worked as hard and as fast as she could.

"They're so tight," she said in frustration, but she kept on.

Just as she was beginning to make progress, they heard footsteps.

"They're coming back!" Skye whispered.

"Emma, go sit down," Edward said.

"But they're almost loose," Emma cried.

"Go!" Edward told her urgently.

This time Emma obeyed and hurried back to her chair. She sat down just in time. The footsteps reached the door and everyone looked up. Their mouths dropped open.

"You just can't stay out of trouble, can you?"

"John!" everyone exclaimed.

Immense relief swept through the room.

"Stephan and Brandon?" Edward asked.

"Tied up and unconscious," John said pleasantly. Kate walked in, saw them all tied up, and remedied that as quickly as she could with John's help. The joy of their rescue was doubled by John and Matthew's happy reunion. Both grinning widely, they embraced each other.

"It's so good to see you, John," Matthew said.

Still grinning, John replied, "I've been prayin' to see you again since we sailed away from Isla de Gracia."

Matthew chuckled happily. "So have I. It looks like God has answered many prayers tonight."

"John, what are you and Kate doing here?" Skye asked. "I would have thought you might be on your way back to the island by now."

"We are, actually, but we thought we'd drop by and see if you were all home safely." John shrugged. "We weren't plannin' to, but I guess God just guided us here."

"How did you know we were in trouble?" Edward said.

"Well, we figured Stephan was still on the loose so we were careful about comin' up to the house. When we saw just the one light we took a peek in the window," John explained. "Then we just sort of let ourselves in. I apologize for that, and we'll pay for anythin' that might've broke when we tipped over the shelf in the other room. We needed a way to get the two of them to come to us without bein' too suspicious."

Edward chuckled. "That's perfectly all right, Captain Morgan."

***

The curtains fluttered in the sun-warmed morning breeze drifting in through the open window. With a yawn, Will stretched and glanced around the room. It had been very late the night before and some tiredness still lingered, but he was ready for the new day. Today would finally mark the official end to the struggle they'd been through as soon as his father took Stephan and Brandon into Port Henry to turn them over to the authorities after having spent the night guarded down in the cellar.

As the last bit of sleep wore off, Will sat up in bed and reached for the Bible sitting on the nightstand. He missed his old Bible, but this one from his father would be equally cherished. Opening to Psalms, he read several passages that David had written in thanksgiving to God. The more Will read the more thankful and joyful he felt in his heart. He didn't know how he could ever thank God enough for what He had done.

After many verses and a long time spent in prayer, Will got out of bed and walked over to a new pair of clothes that lay in a chair across the room. While dressing, Will took in the room bathed now in daylight. It was a beautiful room— the nicest he'd ever stayed in. Edward had told him that this was the room he'd always meant to give him if he ever came home. It gave Will great joy to think of that.

450

He was very anxious to see the rest of the house and how his family lived. Emma had promised him, as well as John and Kate who had been persuaded to stay, a tour of the whole property.

Will stepped out of his room and into the large hall. He could see that the doors of the bedrooms where the other men had slept were open. As he passed Skye's closed bedroom door on his way downstairs, he heard Skye and Kate talking. Emma's laughter also came from inside. Will guessed that all the girls were in there, and he smiled to himself as he thought of the fun they must be having.

Downstairs, Will looked around for everyone else. When he came to the drawing room, he saw that the door to the terrace was open. He walked out to find John standing there admiring the view of the sea. John turned when he heard Will coming. Will was a little surprised yet not since he'd seen it once before. John was wearing a nice pair of clothes, likely borrowed from Edward, and his hair was pulled neatly back.

"Good morning," Will said with a smile.

"Good mornin'," John replied cheerfully. Sensing Will's surprise, he glanced down at his clothes. "It didn't seem very fittin' to be dressed like a pirate here," he explained. "Yer father kindly lent me some clothes."

Will grinned. "You look good."

"I never thought I'd like havin' to dress up like this, but it's not too bad," John said with a smile.

"No, it's not," Will said looking around. "Where is everyone?"

"Well, yer father and Captain McHenry took Stephan and Brandon into town pretty early. Yer uncle and Caleb went with 'em. Yer . . ." John paused. "Do you mind me callin' Mrs. James yer mother?"

Will smiled and shook his head. "No, I don't mind. She's my mother now too."

451

"Well, she's makin' breakfast."

"What about Matthew?"

"He and the girls must all still be asleep."

"The girls are awake. I heard them all talking in Skye's room when I came down. And I'm sure Matthew needs the rest. I can't imagine the four days he spent here were pleasant."

"No."

Will grinned again. "He'll be in for a shock when he comes down and sees you."

John laughed. "Do you think he'll recognize me?" he joked.

Will laughed too. After a moment, he asked, "So, John, did you talk to her?"

John grinned widely. "Uh-huh."

"And?" Will prompted when John didn't continue.

"We share the same feelings."

"Ah, that's great, John," Will said with a smile. "I'm very happy for you."

"In a way I wish I would've talked to 'er sooner," John said. "But it just seems right now."

"This is when you were meant to."

John nodded, his mind traveling back once again to the memories of his talk with Kate. He was slower to notice that someone else joined them on the terrace. Turning, he saw that it was Matthew, and both he and Will said, "Good morning."

"Good morning," Matthew said slowly as a very incredulous smile came to his face. He looked John up and down. "Who are you and what have you done with John Morgan?" he teased.

John and Will laughed.

"The look of a pirate didn't fit here," John said with a shrug.

"Well, I never thought I'd see the day," Matthew said. "You look really good."

"Thank you," John said, satisfied.

"You should see him dressed as a lieutenant," Will remarked.

"And just so you know," John added, "I hated it."

It was Matthew's turn to laugh. "I'd still like to see it."

A moment later, Rebecca came to the door of the terrace. She greeted them with a warm smile. "Good morning everyone. Breakfast is ready and on the table. I'll go get the girls so we can eat." Looking down at Ashley who was following her around, Rebecca asked Will, "Would you want to watch her until I get back?"

"I'd love to," Will answered with a smile.

"Ashley, go to Will."

Happily, Ashley walked right over to Will. Looking up at him, she raised her arms and said, "Hold."

Smiling, Will reached down and picked her up. She immediately settled comfortably in his arms.

"She's an adorable little girl," Matthew said.

Will nodded. "Yes, she is."

The four of them walked back into the house to wait for everyone in the dining room. They sat at the table and talked about this and that until the girls came in. Standing as they walked in through the door, the men all looked very surprised, especially John.

"Kate," was all he could manage to say at first. It was incredible. She was wearing a dress! Gown, petticoats and all!

Kate grinned as she approached the table.

"You're . . . you're . . . ." John could only stammer.

"Wearin' a dress?" Kate finished with a chuckle.

John nodded, dumbfounded.

"Yes, I am."

"I thought you didn't . . . ."

"I changed my mind."

"You look . . ."

"Yes?" Kate prompted.

John looked her in the eyes. "Absolutely beautiful."

For the first time, they saw Kate blush.

John pulled out a chair for her in a move surprisingly smooth, never once taking his eyes off her. Will and Skye exchanged smiles as they too sat down.

<hr />

The men returned from Port Henry a short time after the meal along with all the servants, now that it was safe for them to return. There was a very happy reunion, and they were overjoyed to meet Will. Shortly after that, Emma gave her promised tour, the end of which culminated in helping Isaac to find and catch all the horses he'd set free the night they left so they wouldn't starve.

After a very fun-filled afternoon, everyone was quite happy to relax together in the house. As supper was being prepared later in the evening, Will came to Daniel with one thing on his mind.

"Captain McHenry, may I speak with you?"

Daniel smiled knowingly. "Of course, Will. Would you like to talk on the terrace?"

Will nodded and they walked out of the house, pulling the door closed behind them so they could speak privately. They could still hear the hum of everyone's voices mingled with the sound of the waves. It was a beautiful, still evening, and Will couldn't think of a better time or place to be having this discussion with Daniel. Both of them walked out to the railing facing the ocean, and Daniel kept silent until Will spoke.

"I wanted to speak with you about your letter. In it you gave me permission to marry Skye because we all thought we might never see you again. I have not told Skye yet because if there was any chance at all that I could ask you in person, acting on your blessing that way didn't seem right to me."

Daniel smiled. "I respect that, Will."

"In that case then, I will speak as though there was no letter." Will became very serious. "I love Skye so much and have loved her my entire life. I will always take care of her, provide for her, protect her, and forever be faithful to her if you will permit me now to marry her."

Daniel nodded again. "I know you will. You are a remarkable young man and have proven that to me every day that I have known you. There is no one I would more willingly trust and allow to wed my daughter. You have my greatest blessing."

Will was filled with joy. "Thank you so much, Captain McHenry."

"You are most welcome, Will." Daniel reached into his pocket and pulled out the small leather pouch. "You will need this now."

Will smiled as Daniel handed it to him. Daniel put his hand on Will's shoulder. "I will be very proud to have you as my son-in-law."

"Thank you," Will said again with the utmost respect. "I will be sure to keep it that way."

With a final smile, Daniel turned and walked back into the house. Will opened up the leather pouch and pulled the ring out to look at it again. How beautiful it would look on Skye's hand.

Hearing someone approach, Will looked over his shoulder and saw his father.

"That's a beautiful ring," Edward said, coming to stand beside him.

"It was her mother's engagement ring."

"She is going to love it," Edward said. "When are you going to ask her?"

"Tonight," Will said decidedly. "I think I'll take her for a walk on the beach at sunset."

"That sounds like a wonderful idea."

Very shortly after that, supper was served. Although Will felt too anxious to eat much, he didn't let it show. Finally, when it had grown a bit later and everyone was still at the table talking, Will looked at Skye.

"Would you like to go for a walk?"

Skye smiled sweetly. "I'd love to."

The two of them excused themselves and left the room. Edward and Daniel smiled as they watched their son and daughter go. The sky was just beginning to change colors as Will and Skye walked hand in hand down to the beach.

"What a beautiful evening," Skye breathed.

"It's perfect," Will agreed.

They walked a little ways up the shore until the house was hidden behind the trees and they were completely alone. Will stopped and turned to face Skye.

"I have a reason for asking you to go for a walk." His heart pounded once hard and raced on. This was the moment. He wanted it more than anything but was still dismayed to find out how nervous it made him. "I have something I want to talk to you about, something I've wanted to say for a long time."

Will took her hands in his and watched her look up into his eyes, patiently waiting for whatever he was going to say. Oh, he loved this woman! And her beauty simply took his breath away.

Skye felt the tension flow from Will's strong hands and prayed for him, for whatever he was wrestling with. She loved him so much. He was such a good man, and after all he'd been through she wanted only peace for him.

"Skye, I can't even find the words to tell you how much I love you. We have been through so much together. You are the kindest, most beautiful and wonderful woman I have ever known. God has never blessed me more greatly than He did the day He brought you into my life."

"I love you too, Will, more than I can ever say."

"That's good," he smiled, laughing softly, nervous tension dissolving bit by bit. "I would like to say then, to ask," he amended, "Skylar McHenry, will you marry me?" Without taking his eyes from hers, he took the ring out of a small pocket in his waistcoat. "Will you be my wife and live with me forever?"

"Oh, Will." Tears of untold joy filled Skye's blue eyes. "Yes. Yes, I'll marry you."

Will gently slipped the ring onto her finger, both of them trying to see through the shine in their eyes.

"Oh, Will, it's my mother's ring," she breathed.

"Yes. Your father gave it to me."

"Oh, Will," she said again, laughing. It seemed all she could say. "I'm so happy."

He pulled her close, and Skye closed her eyes thanking God with all of her heart for a man so wonderful as this.

Holding Skye away from him only slightly, Will gazed into her eyes for a moment before kissing her, a kiss he'd waited for all the years he'd loved her.

Feeling slightly dizzy, Skye was glad for Will's strong arm at her back. "Skylar James," she murmured smiling, "I like it."

"So do I," Will said, with a smile to match hers. He kissed her once more before saying, "Do you remember that I told you I have a surprise waiting for you in Kingston?"

"Yes. Can you tell me now?" she asked impishly.

He nodded, watching her face with great delight. "I bought the Collins' house."

Skye was stunned, completely. "You did?"

Will nodded, thrilled with how excited she was. "It will be our home, Skye."

"Our home," she murmured, overcome with joy.

In the midst of one of the happiest moments of their life, Will and Skye marveled together over the amazing power and love of God. How wonderful He was to have brought them through one of the most challenging and trial-filled months they had ever lived to this cherished moment.

26184731R00271

Made in the USA
Lexington, KY
22 September 2013